Isabel

by

Hannah Bain

GROSSMITH BOOKS

GROSSMITH BOOKS

Published by Grossmith Books

86 Sarsfield Street, Auckland 1011, New Zealand

books@grossmith.co.nz

ISBN   978-0-473-11547-0

To Gretta, who said I'd write it,
and to Ana: my unwitting inspiration.

Part One

Chapter One

At the far end of what had been the refectory, obscured by a hessian partition from the curious eyes of Franco's wounded soldiers, an army doctor was finishing his examination of two prisoners. He turned his head as Isabel came into the alcove carrying a large jug of steaming water.

'Enemy soldiers,' she said, placing the pitcher on a small wooden table, 'are best left to rot where they have fallen.'

Roberto smiled, rather at the expression on her face than at her comment. Centuries of battles and their myths were buried in the stones of this paradox: a monastery castle, home of prayerful monks and princely battalions. He wondered how many, friend or foe, had died within reach of its stout walls.

'This one could have killed me,' he said. 'I look forward to asking him why he didn't.'

Familiar needles ran up Isabel's spine. On the battlefield,

Roberto and his medics were as vulnerable as the men they risked their lives to save. Today, as always, her relief was heart-felt when she heard he had arrived back at the monastery unhurt. Less pleasing were the two godless reds he had brought back up the hill for her to nurse.

Roberto made a note on one of the two charts. 'They're to be sent to Burgos for interrogation.'

She tutted her annoyance. 'I have better things to do with my time than mending Republicans. There are plenty of healthy ones in the barn to satisfy Federico.'

'You would do well to remember that the Commandant is one of the Generalísimo's most trusted officers,' he cautioned. 'It is my duty, and yours, to respect his wishes.' She bit her lip. Roberto was touchy on the subject of his cousin.

He instructed her on her patients' care and shrugged on his uniform jacket. She lifted aside the curtain as he turned to go.

'I'll take care of your rojos, if I must.'

The tiredness lifted from his eyes as he returned her smile.

'Goodnight, querida.'

'Goodnight, Roberto. Sleep well.'

She watched him make his way through the ward, saw him stop often to speak to the men in the long rows of hospital beds that had replaced the wooden boards and benches of the monks. Soft whimpers moved in the air, displacing centuries of prayer.

She moved back behind the curtain and let it fall. The idea of tending a Republican sympathiser, even one who had spared Roberto's life, brought with it no feelings of kindliness. Hating one's enemies was normal, she supposed, even for a nurse. It made war less complicated. Roberto, whose sense of honour was a more complex thing than her own, would see the matter quite differently. She doubted he hated the enemy at all and won-dered, in the face of all that he had witnessed, how that could possibly be. The longer she had known him the more confusions she had discovered in his view of things: his respect for her nursing skills for one, coupled with his displeasure at her taking up such work.

She poured water from the pitcher into a tin basin and pulled back one of the blankets. Except where it had been burned by the wind and sun, the soldier's skin was pale. A foreigner most likely. The dirt and blood matting his hair's natural redness to clay reminded her of the pots hanging against the white walls of her grandmother's house in Arcos: rough-surfaced terracotta filled with geraniums the colour of fresh blood.

When she had cleaned him, she turned to the boy in the second cot. Her care of him, tinged with resentment or not, would make little difference. His eyes opened, shocked and grey, staring through her as she bathed him as if searching for the source of his pain, or at least some explanation for it. She finished her task more gently, covered him, took up the bowl of filthy water and carried it through the darkening ward to the sluice beyond the cloister. She returned soon with a lighted kerosene lamp, set it on the night desk by the door and sat easing her feet from her shoes. If The Virgin was kind, she would ensure the hours to come proved less eventful than those already gone.

An orderly came with a mug of chicory. Isabel whispered her thanks and cupped her hands round the thick earthenware, glad of its warmth. She sipped the tasteless brew, eyes closed, thinking of the rich, dark chocolate she had drunk each evening from fine porcelain in Arcos and wondering at her naive decision to leave her Andalucían home to follow in Roberto's equally unlikely footsteps.

'There are other ways,' her grandmother had insisted, 'for a girl of gentle upbringing to show her loyalty to General Franco.'

She had retorted that her class was of no consequence, that the Army needed more nurses to care for the brave men fighting to free Spain from the Republicans; the Caudillo had raised his army in God's name and she would keep faith with her conscience no matter what anyone might say.

'And Doña Elvira?' her grandmother had queried.

'Even Doña Elvira,' she had replied, knowing full well how Roberto's mother would react to such extraordinary behaviour. The maid, Expira, who had served her grandmother for as long as anyone could remember, wept copious tears and wondered aloud where she and Doña Mercedes had gone wrong in their raising of the girl.

Her grandmother had relented. By the time the letter came from Doña Elvira, filled as expected with lines of disapproval and dismay, Isabel was already on her way to Burgos to begin her training. Her anticipation of further missives demanding her immediate return proved groundless: Roberto's mother had likely paused to wonder if such vehemence might not smack of disloyalty to the Caudillo.

Isabel was aware that the long-expected marriage between Roberto and herself was in some way clouded. She knew little of the matter other than that it had something to do with her grandmother's younger son, her uncle Eduardo who had moved away from Andalucía when she was a child. Why he should be a stain on the family when he had later died in Franco's service she had no idea.

From her grandmother's letters, Isabel learned that Doña Elvira had elected to make the best of what she deemed a most unfortunate situation by insisting that her future daughter-in-law stay well behind the Nationalist lines where Roberto and Federico could keep an eye on her. But her connections, powerful as they were, had not prevented Roberto from being sent to the Ebro, nor Isabel from being posted to the erstwhile monastery in the hills when her training was complete.

The days following her arrival were spent in drudgery, scrubbing already pristine staircases and the stone floors of the wards and cloisters. Grey ranks of iron beds were allocated blankets and pillows in readiness for the soldiers who would come. Expectant chatter among newly arrived nurses soon died under the stern eye of the nun who ruled over them, and when no wounded came to be tended with their gentle ministrations there was nothing for it but to scrub the floors again. The rhythmic swishing of soapy, hard-bristled brushes was less enthusiastic now as Isabel and other girls of good family paused more often, and with increasing dismay, to regard their reddening hands and broken nails. The more humble among them knew better than to laugh.

They were sitting at breakfast, the sun barely risen, early morning prayers spoken when the first gunfire echoed across the valley. Thirty pairs of eyes turned to Sister Magdalena, some shining with incipient heroism, others with fear. The nun prayed that none would buckle under what was to come. She instructed her charges to finish their meal in silence and, when the tables had been cleared, gathered them round her for more prayers. The planes of their German allies screamed overhead. Distant explosions came nearer.

That afternoon, a line of lorries with red-painted crosses groaned up the steeply twisting roadway. Orderlies ran to the monastery gates to bring in men on stretchers. Others handed crutches to the walking. Dazed soldiers appeared from the transports and were ushered like weary children urged on by white-aproned nannies to the wards. They were settled in cots, onto mattresses on the stone-flagged floor, and then onto the floor itself.

The noise and stench of blood and open wounds disgusted her. Isabel performed her tasks in horrified disbelief as men screamed obscenities, doctors shouted orders and nurses knelt with bandages or scurried for disinfectant and clean water. Some of the wounded were silent, stoic perhaps, or not so badly hurt;

others wept, begging someone, anyone, to take away the pain.

A passing nurse thrust a bowl into Isabel's hands and told her to bring more bandages. She looked down and saw her fingers clutching a tin basin filled with mangled flesh and hair. Her stomach heaved. She ran to the door, jostled by harried nurses. A voice shouted that more lorries had arrived. She must tell the orderlies there was no more room. She slammed the door behind her and leaned against it, eyes closed, waiting for her giddiness to pass. The thudding slam echoed through the cloister and faded to an imagined silence. She opened her eyes. Lines of men, soundless mouths wide open, lolled against walls that shifted as she watched. Tall stone columns bent like saplings. She heard laughter and reached out to an approaching shadow. A hand rose from its blackness and sent her reeling. The laughter, she realised, had been her own. Tears welled and trickled over the place where she had been slapped. Soldiers moaned around her as the cloister steadied. The basin, its contents spilled, was taken from her, her hands held under a tap, scrubbed and roughly dried.

'Pull yourself together!' Magdalena pulled open the door and pushed her back into the ward. A scene of disciplined action confronted her – no one had panicked but herself. Across the room, Roberto was on his knees beside a young soldier, reaching to close his eyes. She had failed him, failed them all.

In the months that followed, calm efficiency replaced innocence. She cleaned and dressed the most appalling wounds without flinching. She found unexpected words of comfort, wrote letters for the incapable or illiterate to wives, sweethearts and mothers, and promised to see them dispatched. She gave out bedpans to the living, cleaned them in the sluices, wrapped the dead in winding-sheets, and scrubbed the floors again. She, who had known a life of luxury and disregard for the peasants of Andalucía, began to wonder how men with stumps for legs would till their fields.

The dregs of chicory were cold. Isabel pushed the mug aside and bent to refasten her shoe-laces. She took up the lamp and began to make her way between the ranks of beds. Yellow lamplight followed her along the walls and, when she paused, fell on cadaverous faces, etching deeper hollows still. Whispered voices asked if it was true that there were communists behind the hessian curtain.

Later, Sister Magdalena came, as she did each night, to walk among them, stopping for a moment by each bed, offering comfort or a silent prayer. Isabel supposed she would retrace her steps when she reached the partition. Instead, the nun pushed aside the hanging and disappeared behind it. Her compassion, Isabel surmised, was about to fall on stony ground. A nun's prayers were of little use to the godless. The good Sister, apparently in agreement, reappeared almost at once but, instead of hurrying back past the rows of Nationalist soldiers, remained where she was, beckoned to Isabel and sent her running for the priest.

Three more men died that night, others muttered long after the boy's body had been taken away. Well one rojo less couldn't be a bad thing. But she remembered his grey eyes and how very young he had been.

Her remaining patients were all sleeping when dawn filtered through the clerestory windows. She took down the woollen shawl she had hung earlier behind the door, threw it across her shoulders and raised the latch.

The clean scrubbed cloister was empty of all but a few stone benches. The fountain in the centre of the patio was still, its playful effluence long since put to more pragmatic use. Her light shoes made soft patting sounds against the flagstones.

The sentry at the outer door offered a casual, smiling salute as she approached. Isabel grinned, put a finger to her lips and walked past him through the portico and across the open space that marked the summit of the ancient road. A dozen paces brought her to a jutting parapet, its low wall guarding her from a tumble into the valley far below. The early morning air was chill: it was less easy now to recall the heat of summer when the plains of the Ebro and the surrounding hills had been scorched by nature as well as by warring men.

The rising sun touched distant mountains. She breathed deeply, conjuring the purity of clean, fresh snow, imagining closing passes through which wrong-minded men were likely, even now, scurrying into France. Behind her, to the west and south, other mountains stood guardian over lands held safe by Franco. She imagined the broad handle of the Nationalist axe lying against Portugal, reaching from Cádiz to the Bay of Biscay; the axe-head lay over northern Spain, its sharp edge facing first one enemy province, then another. In time it would turn towards Madrid. Franco's army, meanwhile, had moved inexorably along the banks of the Ebro, separating the northern Republicans from their comrades to the south. The Catalonians, Isabel concluded, would have done better to have remained north of the river and admitted defeat. Instead, in July, they had had the gall to recross it. Now they were being beaten back again and would soon be trapped, not only by Franco, but by the northern mountains and the eastern sea. The sun rising from that sea was already washing the chill morning contours of the land with rays of red and gold: the colours of Spain, colours of blood and victory. Barcelona would fall, and then Valencia. The long awaited order would be given to take Madrid. The war would be won and she would marry Roberto. She hugged herself more tightly in her shawl thinking it would be less easy now, after all she had experienced, to slip into the formal, gracious way of life of the Álvarez family.

She turned from the parapet and began to retrace her steps. Sure as she was that the guard would not report her absence and that God would cast a benevolent eye on her brief respite from the ward, discovery by Sister Magdalena would be an entirely different matter.

She reached the patio in time to hear the approaching squeak of trolley wheels and their trundling clatter along the cloister. The orderly was bringing breakfast for the patients. She caught up with him at the refectory door.

'A bad night, Miss!' he said.

'Not one of the best, Pepe. Imagine it. I used to think I had done a noble thing by coming here, that I was brave and important.'

'And now, Miss?'

'Now I feel barely adequate, and very humble.'

'The soldiers say you're the best, Miss.'

She smiled and held the door wide for him to push the trolley through.

They moved among the patients, serving the simple meal of chick peas in a little olive oil, crushed to the consistency of cheese and flavoured with small pieces of salt fish.

When she had finished spooning the mixture into the mouths of those unable to feed themselves, Isabel served the last portion into a bowl and took it to the covered alcove at the far end of the ward. A soldier caught at her skirt as she passed.

'Not going to bother with the other one are you?'

She heard the harshness of his tone, saw the dull hatred in his eyes. Like his companions, he had known indescribable horrors in the battle to regain the river. Their wounds were obvious, less so the damage done to their minds. Beside him a boy thrashed against his narrow mattress, calling for his mother. She needed no reminding that the Republican soldier beyond the hessian wall did not deserve her pity.

Tom was awake, alert and listening to the voices on the other side of the partition when the curtain parted. A nurse came in. Food, he thought, noticing the bowl. He wondered when he had last eaten. He smiled a greeting, remembering the comfort of hands washing the dirt from him sometime in the night. Her expression did not change as she leaned to prop him, none too gently, against his pillow. Pain seared his shoulder. He moved his head to avoid the spoonful of mush she held out to him and asked where they had taken Danny.

'The rojo they brought in with you? The boy? He died last night.' Her dark eyes showed no emotion, no thought that Dan had been his friend. He had supposed himself well hardened by all he had witnessed since the madness began and was surprised to feel tears pricking at his eyes. He remembered waking in the night, seeing the nun, not realising, at first, the significance of her presence at Danny's bedside. He had watched her move to the partition and thought she had called for a nurse. He must have slept again because the next thing he remembered was a priest leaning over the lad, holding a crucifix to his lips and murmuring what he supposed were prayers. Then someone had shouted 'rojo' from the other side of the partition, and the priest had snatched the crucifix away. The look of disgust he offered to the dying boy and the expletive that accompanied it were anything but godly.

So much for Christian charity, Tom thought, remembering that he had tried to speak, and that the nun had turned towards him, a finger to her lips.

'He lied about his age,' he said now, angry with Dan for his deceit, angry with himself for going along with it.

'Then he was foolish.' The nurse turned from him to put the

bowl of uneaten food on the table. 'Sister Magdalena was with him at the end to pray for his soul. He died peacefully.'

Tom gauged the words pragmatic more than kind. Atheist Danny would have enjoyed the joke. He would have liked to tell her so, but said only, 'That was good of her.'

A jeer came from beyond the curtain followed by a sharp command, then silence. The hessian flap lifted. The doctor he had encountered on the battlefield stood framed in the space he had made.

'Another dawn! Others were not so fortunate.'

Tom had a clear view past the officer of several empty beds, probably not long vacated. 'Seems you and I made it out all right,' he said.

'You speak Spanish?'

'I lived with a family in Guernica before the war. They had a daughter. Your German friends bombed them and their town to smithereens.'

Sympathy flashed in the other man's eyes and was as quickly gone. 'Then I'm even more surprised you didn't shoot me yesterday. It seems foolish not to have done so – from your point of view. You had ample time to reach your own lines.'

'True,' Tom replied. 'On the other hand, young Dan wasn't in much shape to make a run for it, and taking a pot shot at you didn't seem a particularly bright idea at the time, what with you being a doctor. But then war does give people some funny ideas. Perhaps you hadn't noticed.'

'I have noticed,' Roberto responded dryly. 'I thank you for my life. I'm sorry we could not save your friend.' He unclipped Tom's chart from the bed. 'You know of course what will happen to you now?'

'I hate to think. Though I did have a small premonition last night with that nun hovering like the angel of death. And your young nurse has been glaring at me as if I'm some sort of toad.'

More soberly he added, 'So. What am I in for? Exactly?'

'There is talk of repatriating the International Brigades. But first you will be interrogated.'

'Of course. That should be a jolly experience. I've heard something of the procedures.'

'Much like your own, I imagine.' Roberto replaced the chart, paused for a moment as if he might say more, then turned on his heel, nodded to Isabel and left.

Tom stared at the ceiling, sighed and closed his eyes. Danny was dead. He would go and see the lad's mother when he got back. Tell her himself. If he got back. He supposed it must be true about the Brigades being disbanded. He had heard the rumours but it was a bit ironic having them confirmed by the enemy. This wasn't it, was it? The great fight against fascism come to this? God, he thought, the whole of Europe is in for it now. And then: I wonder if they've got the radio.

'I must change your dressing.'

He opened his eyes, surprised to find the nurse still there.

Her patient's accent as well as his conversation with Roberto confirmed what she had already suspected: that he was a foreigner. Isabel set about her tasks with seemingly detached efficiency while wondering why those who called themselves Internacionales would choose to risk their lives fighting someone else's war. It would make no difference in the end. He had mentioned a girl in Guernica who had died. Perhaps he had been in love with her. She would have enjoyed hearing Roberto tell him that the people of Guernica had brought it on themselves, that his sweetheart had died needlessly. It was common talk among the nurses that the petty disagreements of the Basques and Catalans had escalated until between them they had destroyed the city. Basques and Catalans! Why wouldn't they accept that there was only one Spain. One Catholic Spain. One people with one language and one religion. And then more communists had poured in from all over Europe and helped feed propaganda to the Spanish peasants who should have known better than to believe it, but didn't. Her patient, it seemed, had acted on a misguided grudge because he had been in love. What did the Germans, who were doing all they could to save Spain from her enemies, have to do with Guernica?

'Why didn't you leave when your novia died?' she asked him. 'This is not your war.'

'It's everyone's war. We're all fighting the fascists.'

She stiffened and he might have let it go at that. What was the point? Her views would be no less resolute than most other people's, no matter which side they were on. As resolute as his own most likely. Yet there was something about her that made him think she might understand. He would have liked to tell her about Maria, how much in love they had been, how full of hope: hope, not only for themselves, but for Spain's Republic. The people had made their choice – that much she surely knew, whatever other propaganda she chose to believe. Franco was the leader of a rebellion, out to overthrow a legitimate government. The people were being crushed – just as Maria had been crushed.

She began to unwrap the thick bandage covering his shoulder.

'I had to join the Brigades,' he said. 'Do what I could.'

Perhaps it was the pain, perhaps the image of Maria that made him stay her hand, perhaps only a need to explain. 'You think we're all Communists, don't you? Maybe most of us are, but it's not that simple. It's not just workers. It's everyone, all the way up to aristocrats. Educated people like writers and university professors, all fighting…'

She pushed his hand away. 'Aristocrats and professors do not become soldiers. Doctors, perhaps,' she added, as if she had only just thought of it. 'And nurses. But not soldiers.'

He yelped as she removed the dressing, angry with himself for letting her know she had hurt him, angry at her ignorance.

'Not on your side maybe,' he said. 'On ours they do. They've come from all over the world because they believe in what we're fighting for. They know that if fascism isn't done away with now, the whole world is going to go to hell. Men and women have come from Britain and Poland and America, even from Germany and Italy. Some have travelled from as far away as Australia because they believe in democracy, that what's happening here is wrong.'

'Communists and anarchists are not democrats,' she retorted. 'And Hitler and Mussolini are on our side. The Germans and Italians are not fighting for you. They are fighting for the Caudillo, for General Franco.'

'Tell that to the Garibaldis. They're Italian! They routed Mussolini's fascists at Brihuega!' Tom's capricious need for her to understand had become as unstoppable as the Ebro itself. 'The conscripted Italians sent over by Mussolini were defeated by their own countrymen who were here because they knew they had to come.' And now, he thought, clenching his teeth against his frustration as well as pain, not only are Spaniards fighting each other but Germans are fighting Germans and Italians are fighting Italians. And the world is about to go mad.

'Why did you let Roberto live?'

'I have no idea.'

He lay silent while she replaced the dressing, thinking of the months he had spent in the mountains with his comrades, the stifling heat, the lack of food and water, the bombardment that had gone on for four relentless months. He thought of the snow gathering on the high peaks above them, how it had cooled the air, and then, more vicious even than the sun, had sent its chill wind scooping down to freeze them half to death. He remembered the re-crossing of the Ebro, the unchanging order that there was to be no retreat; how he and Dan, guided by three Spaniards from a nearby village, had gone forward with the radio. They had come too close to the Nationalist line. Dan had been badly wounded: half his leg shot away. Tom, already bleeding from a wound in his thigh, was hit in the shoulder. But he had sent the required message back and the Republican attack had begun not long afterwards. Using his good arm, he had dragged Dan behind a patch of scrub where an overhanging rock would protect them from enemy fire and from their own guns. The semi-conscious boy had made no sound as Tom bound the remains of his leg to stop the bleeding. Their Spanish comrades lay unmoving, and unreachable, a dozen yards away, the radio beside them.

The battle raged for what seemed like hours but the sun had moved only a few degrees across the sky when the guns fell silent. Their own men had passed their hiding place, then fallen back – how far Tom didn't know. The Nationalist medicos were moving onto the field to retrieve their dead and wounded. He calculated the odds against escape and guessed he could make it alone, but not without confronting an approaching franquista soldier. He watched the man kick at the inert bodies of two of his Spanish comrades, fire a bullet into the third and drop to his haunches beside the radio.

Tom reached for his gun. The Spaniard, seemingly satisfied that the operator lay dead beside him, gave a cursory glance towards the rock and turned back to his prize.

Tom's relief at not having had to fire and so draw attention to their hiding place was short-lived. A rustle at his side informed him that Dan, who had lain still and apparently insensible till now, had regained consciousness. He turned, his hand raised to clap over the boy's mouth. But Dan was already pulling himself into the open, his teeth clenched on his knife, his useless leg dragging on the ground behind him. Seconds later the enemy soldier slumped forward with Dan sprawled on top of him. Neither had uttered a sound. But they had been seen. Tom aimed his rifle at an approaching officer: a doctor, he thought, remembering that the Spanish were in the habit of sending surgeons to the field in hope of saving those who would otherwise die before reaching hospital. The man looked straight at him but did not reach for his own firearm. Tom watched, astonished, as Dan was eased with gentle hands onto the blood-stained earth.

The nurse secured his bandage with a pin and turned away.

'I couldn't miss,' Tom said. 'He must have known that. But he ignored me. He wasn't there to kill anyone you see. He was out there in that carnage saving lives, saving Dan. Trying to. For weeks and months I'd seen nothing but men murdering each other, and for a split second I thought how pointless it all seemed. Kids like Danny. Day after day, scores of them being killed. Fit young men with their whole lives ahead of them maimed.' His voice jagged with the effort of explaining. 'But we had this dream, you see. About freedom. We thought if we could win this war, we could change the world. Show tyrants like Hitler and Mussolini that there's another way.'

He lay back exhausted, his eyes closed. 'Which doesn't answer your question. Or perhaps it does. Anyway, I didn't kill your doctor friend. And now I'm a prisoner and you – I suppose it was you, much against your better judgement, I imagine – washed off the dirt last night and patched me up so I wouldn't bleed to death.'

Chapter Two

The fighting moved further to the east. There were more empty beds in the ward now. More patients had died; others had been moved elsewhere. Tom's recovery had been slowed by the onset of fever and Roberto had ordered him kept in the alcove behind the hessian curtain.

Had anyone asked why she was drawn to him, Isabel would have been hard pressed to find an answer. He was often angry; his ideas were outrageous and completely alien to her own. Worse still, he did not believe in God. Perhaps it was the differences between them that attracted her but each night she stayed a little longer to talk to him. Sometimes he would talk only of his dreams for a better world, brushing aside her arguments and frequent interruptions informing him that he had been indoctrinated by communists. She asked him if he thought the war would end soon.

'When it does, the Republicans will lose,' he said. 'It would be foolish to think otherwise.'

'That,' she replied, 'is the most sensible thing you have said. It will be a wonderful day when General Franco takes Madrid.'

'It will be a tragedy.'

'How can you say that, after all I have told you? The Caudillo loves Spain as passionately as he loves God. He wants only what is good for us.'

'He wants power. He's a fanatic, just as Hitler and Mussolini are fanatics.' He waited for her contradiction but this time she was silent.

'Promise me one thing,' he said. 'That one day you will go to Guernica and ask the people who are left what happened there. Then you'll know I've told you the truth.'

She turned to go. He reached to stay her with his hand.

'I must go. I have work to do.' She loosed his fingers and slipped out through the curtain.

One night, she asked him about the colour of his hair.

'When you came here it made me think of a terracotta pot. Now it is clean it reminds me of the copper pans in my grandmother's kitchen.'

He laughed and said that red hair was not so unusual where he came from: the Scottish city of Aberdeen where he had been born and raised and whose northern coldness was redeemed only by the music of the bagpipes.

'Bagpipes? Like the gaita?'

'Bigger,' he assured her. 'What about you? I'd lay a bet you come from the south.'

'Andalucía,' she said. 'I live in Arcos with my grandmother.'

She told him that she had lost both parents when she was a child, her mother when she was eight and her father two years later. When he asked her about her home, she described the stately old Andalucían house with its flower-filled patios in the little hillside town of Arcos.

She told him of her many visits to Roberto's home in the larger town of Puente Nuevo; of summers spent at his family's country estate, the fighting bulls raised there for generations; of travelling in a bullock cart hung with floral garlands on the annual romería to El Rocío, the shrine of the Blanca Paloma there, and of the indescribable Andalucían hills which looked, she said, as if their pastel colours had been brushed on by the wings of a passing angel.

'I don't believe in your God,' he said, reaching for her hand. 'But I am beginning to believe in angels.'

Next morning, the orderly brought his breakfast. That evening he heard Isabel greet her patients as she came into the ward, but she did not come to him, and again it was an orderly who brought his food. He lay awake long after the ward lights had been extinguished, wondering what he had done to upset her. He slept fitfully and woke to see light shining from a lamp on the wooden table at his side. He turned his head towards the sound of water splashing into a tin basin, and the silhouette of Isabel against the light.

'The day nurse said you refused to be washed,' she said. 'Now Sister Magdalena tells me I must do it. As if I have not enough to do without having to clean Republicans in the middle of the night!' The clunk of the jug on the table top assured Tom he had not dreamed her. Instead of turning to him with a well-soaped cloth in her hand, she reached into the pocket of her apron. Her expression, barely discernible in the lamplight, but surely forbidding, changed, on closer inspection, to a teasing smile. A pack of cards appeared in her hand.

'I borrowed them from an orderly,' she whispered, perching on the bed beside him. 'Now there's no more fighting in the valley, the nights are as long and dull as the books in the monks' library. I've played patience for a whole hour and it has become even more boring than the books. Do you know any games?'

'Do you?' he countered, only half awake, confused by her avoidance of him and sudden reappearance. Was it his company she wanted? Or would anyone do to pass the time? As she reached behind him to prop up his pillow, he levered himself with his good arm to get a better look at her. She was a witch, he thought, the scent of good plain soap on her skin as alluring as exotic perfume. He stared hard at the cards as she dealt them out on the grey blanket, willing his mind to concentrate, not on the sorcery of her whispers, but on her careful instruction as to how the game was to be played.

'It's simple enough even for a misguided Scotsman,' she assured him, settling herself more comfortably. 'My grand-mother taught it to me when I was a child. Sister Magdalena would have a fit,' she added with a grin than almost undid his efforts. 'She says cards are instruments of the Devil and lead one to bad practices.'

She put her hand against his mouth to stop his laughter. He lifted his own to keep it there and kissed her palm. Instead of pulling away as he thought she would, she leaned to rest her own lips lightly, and for the briefest moment, on his forehead. A shudder rippled through him. Angel wings, he thought, incon-sequentially, as the cards slid one by one and then in a rush onto the floor.

'I'm to be married to Roberto,' she said. 'That's why I came tonight. To tell you.'

He stared at her, more shocked than if she had slapped him.

'It is not fair of me to let you think otherwise.'

'Married?'

'It was decided a long time ago.'

'Do you love him?'

'I am to marry him,' she repeated, scattering more cards as she rose from the bed and kneeling to collect those already fallen.

'That's not what I asked.'

'I have always loved him.' Her voice came muffled from be-neath the bed.

'What about me?' He sounded, he thought, like a petulant child. 'I love you, Isabel. You must know that.'

'It's not possible to love someone you have known for such a short time. With Roberto it is different. I have known him all my life.'

She reappeared from her foraging and sat on her heels pushing the last of the cards back into their box. He would have thought her entirely composed, cool even, were it not for the flush on her cheeks. She put the box in her pocket and stood.

'When you leave here you will be repatriated,' she said lifting her hand to the curtain flap. 'We will not meet again.'

'I love you.'

'Yes, I know.'

He watched her go, wondering why he had said it: that he loved her. She was just a girl, a nurse working with the enemy. He had had other girls, other nurses on his own side, and had told most of them the same thing. They had seemed to expect it, perhaps even believed it; had needed to hear those words as much as he had needed to say them. They had wanted to believe that love might exist where it did not, that there was another world beyond the killing. He told himself that his feelings for Isabel were no different, and if that were not true, then what he thought were feelings were hallucinations brought on by lack of sleep and pain. He lay awake long after she had gone and when he slept at last, he dreamed himself with her in the little Andalucían town she had described with such affection.

The following night she came again. There would be no harm, she said, in spending a little more time together now that he knew the truth. Besides, he would be leaving soon and she had nothing else to do. She had brought the cards again. Perhaps he would like to play?

The thing he wanted most in the world right now, he said, was to wring her neck – and was astonished to see tears flood her eyes. He pushed back his blanket, swung his legs to the floor, steadied himself against the wooden table and reached to take her in his arms.

'I have tried very hard,' she said when he released her, 'not to love you. I have tried very hard to stay away from you. I have told myself that a sane woman cannot love a communist. I have told myself every night for the last two weeks that you mean nothing to me. I have told myself that since everything that was normal in my life is no longer so, I have become deranged.' She looked up at him, eyes glistening. 'I have discovered that what I feel for you is entirely different from my feelings for Roberto. But it is important for you to understand that I love him, too – in another way.'

He felt tears in his own eyes. 'I'll come back for you,' he whispered. 'When this is all over I'll come back.'

The next evening when she came, she reached into her pocket for a photograph.

'My grandmother asked me to have it taken. I'll have another copy made.'

He glanced at the snapshot and then at her.

'Take it,' she insisted. 'Keep it so you won't forget me.' She rummaged in her pocket again and found a scrap of paper. 'This is my grandmother's address. You must learn it by heart. Write to me when you are back in Scotland. Roberto has told me again that the Brigades are to be repatriated and that you will be exchanged for one of our soldiers. Learn it,' she said again. 'You mustn't keep it. Sister Magdalena will have me punished if she finds out.'

'And the photograph?' he asked.

'Oh, there are lots of nurses. You can hardly tell us apart. It could be anyone.'

'Not anyone. You are unique.' He reached with his good arm and pulled her down onto the bed beside him.

When Isabel came into the ward next evening, she found Sister Magdalena seated at the desk. The nun nodded briefly in response to her greeting and directed her to begin her work. She moved through the ward attending to each man's needs, curbing her impatience and reaching the partition at last. She raised the flap, stared at the stripped and empty bed and retraced her steps. She stood waiting until the nun looked up, and asked, as casually as she could manage, what had happened to the rojo.

'The Englishman? He left this morning.'

Isabel breathed deeply and nodded, trusting her face to register an indifferent composure entirely opposite to her feelings. Tom, she guessed, was to be repatriated sooner than she had supposed. She was glad for him, and filled with hopeless certainty that he would forget her.

'Foolish child,' Magdalena said. 'For your own sake be thankful he has gone.'

Chapter Three

Isabel was wrong in thinking Tom's repatriation imminent. He had been taken to a barn behind the monastery where a dozen others waited in various states of misery and hope for transfer to Burgos. There were other Scots among the prisoners, Englishmen, a couple of Australians, but no Spaniards. Some had been held there for an hour or two before being taken elsewhere. Those who had witnessed their coming and swift going told of the rough treatment they had been given.

'God help the poor buggers,' someone murmured in the darkness, the accent introducing the expansive shadowed torso as Glaswegian.

The barn stank of excrement from leaking buckets, there were no windows and the door was solid. There was no light to read by and nothing to read anyway.

Some were optimistic about their fate in Burgos: with repatriation almost certain, conditions were unlikely to be worse than those they suffered here; with luck they would be a great deal better. Others argued in favour of escape. The Brigades had not yet been disbanded. They must get back to Barcelona. It wasn't over yet.

But eyes accustomed to the dark had already explored every inch of the place. Fingers had searched among the straw for whatever might be there to find; stronger arms had hefted forgotten bales of hay discovered in black recesses. They had found the shaft of an old plough and talked of a battering ram of men and rusting iron to break down the door. It was pointless of course: a way of keeping their minds alert, a game, something to pass the time. The sentries smoking the strong, black tobacco that seeped in tantalising whiffs through unseen cracks would be alerted long before the door was breached. In the unlikely event of overcoming them, there was still the open yard to cross and the high stone wall.

Perhaps, someone said, they could wrench off the rusting iron rings they had found attached to the wall and use them as weapons. The next night, two prisoners were seized, tied to the rings and whipped. Any attempt at freeing them, the guards told the others, would result in the rest of them being similarly secured. They flashed torches round the barn. Look, they said, there are plenty more rings for restraining communist beasts. Speculation circulated on the presence of a spy among them. How else would the guards have known? Jock McPherson, Glaswegian and self-elected peacemaker, told them not to be ridiculous.

A kind of respite came each morning. They were led outside, glad to see the dawn, grateful for lungsful of fresh air, and taken to the brooding winter fields sloping behind the monastery. Their task was to dig up stones and rocks and pile them into mounds. Cairns, Jock called them, and said they were building their own memorials in this benighted place. The big Scot worked alongside Tom most days, hefting the largest of the rocks, leaving smaller pieces for his injured companion.

On Sundays they weeded the cemetery and at midday were handed loaves of warm, fresh bread straight from the monastery oven. They tore at the crusts and stuffed chunks of the sweetest food they had eaten all week into their mouths. For nearly an hour they were allowed to hunker on the stony ground, shivering, staring out over the valley they had regained and held for so long and with such ultimate futility. Photographs, undevoured by hungry eyes in the night-dark barn, were taken from torn and dirty pockets as men talked of lost comrades and the hope of swift reunion with families, wives and sweethearts.

Tom took out his snapshot of Isabel. The man beside him leaned over for a closer look, whistled, took the photograph and passed it on. The next man winked and said what he would do with an enemy nurse given such luck. Tom lurched to his feet, fists at the ready. Jock pushed him down again saying there was nothing to be gained by fighting among themselves. Tom slouched against a tombstone, scowling, his brows drawing even closer when Jock's expression changed as he too claimed the picture. A guard approached and Isabel disappeared into the Scot's huge hand. He crouched down beside Tom.

'She's a bonnie lass,' he whispered. 'But it might be wise to lose this. I doubt the fascists will feel too kindly towards you if they get their hands on it.'

The guard passed. Jock slid the photograph into Tom's top pocket.

'I'm coming back for her,' he said. 'She's promised to wait for me.'

Jock looked at him askance but made no comment.

There were days when Roberto looked in on the prisoners. Not a bad sort of chap, they concluded, for a fascist. A bit on the hoity-toity side but decent enough and not above berating the guards for undue harshness. Tom's fluency in the language made him their natural spokesman. Most of the prisoners had picked up a few words of Spanish but the easy, rapid speech between the two was too fast for them to follow. It was clear Tom already knew the officer. The word 'spy' began to make the rounds again. How could they be sure he was relaying their complaints accurately, or that he was accurately translating the officer's remarks? The girl in the photograph was Spanish, wasn't she? Might be a good idea to shut him up. Jock took Tom aside and said he'd better open up a bit. They had a right to know how he came to be on friendly terms with a franquista.

That night, in the darkness of the barn, Tom told them how he had come face to face with Roberto on the battlefield. To Jock alone he told of Isabel's relationship with the doctor, that his own feelings for her made him an unworthy recipient of the officer's regard, and that he feared losing her to his unsuspecting rival.

'Ye'll not want me saying this, laddie,' said Jock. 'But the sooner you forget that wee nurse the better it'll be for all three of you.'

Chapter Four

The enemy had been flung back across the weary, bloody river and would not come again. The north-eastern front would soon stretch around Catalonia like a slingshot, one side anchored in the shallows of the Mediterranean, the other in the foothills of the Pyrenees. The hospital in the monastery was to close, the remaining patients transferred by train to Burgos. Isabel would travel with them, Roberto with the forward moving army. He asked Sister Magdalena if he might speak with Isabel alone before he left.

They stood together in the refectory. Dismantled iron bed-frames had been stacked against the wall, a pile of mattresses near the door. The hessian partition had been removed.

'Won't you at least consider returning to Arcos, querida?' he asked. 'It can be arranged quite simply.'

'I'm a nurse, Roberto. My work isn't finished.'

'Then let me use my influence to find you a position in Puente Nuevo. My mother would be delighted to have you stay with her.'

Doña Elvira would indeed be pleased to see her, Isabel supposed, if only to chastise her for running off in the first place. She would also be torn between the satisfaction of having the girl she expected her son to marry safely under her own roof, and the social dilemma of seeing that same woman continue her career as a nurse in the local hospital.

'You fuss too much, Roberto. I've no doubt your mother has already written to Federico telling him I am coming and that he must keep an eye on me. Besides,' she said, tipping her chin in a gesture she had perfected at around nine years old. 'I'm perfectly capable of looking after myself.'

'You will no doubt have your own way as always,' he said, unable to keep back a smile. She was nineteen, more than a decade younger than himself but no longer a child. She was a beautiful and capable woman. And wilful. In that she hadn't changed.

A fleet of army ambulances laboured up the hill, a dusting of snow on their roofs. They passed through the rusting iron gateway below the brow of the hill and halted outside the monastery. The drivers emerged from their cabs and stood in a huddled group, feet stamping as if to tread the biting cold back into the earth. A match flared. Wisps of smoke curled with frosted breath as a cigarette was passed from one man to the next. The last stubbed the butt under his heel as the great door swung open. Nurses came out with walking patients, orderlies with stretchers. Sister Magdalena directed the placing of their occupants into the transports. Several of the nurses disappeared under the canvas roofs with their charges and looked out again to call goodbyes to others not yet on their way to the front. The drivers cranked querulous engines and climbed into their cabs. Gears were engaged and rapid prayers sent up that their brakes would not fail on the descent.

To the exhausted, ill-fed men stumbling from the barn towards their own transport, the line of lorries looked much like a disjointed, hiccuping serpent as it crawled down the twisting, rutted roadway, appearing and disappearing round each bend.

At the foot of the hill, a wider road of equal disrepair led the convoy to a small town by the railway. There a hospital train waited to convey them on a longer, no less arduous journey through the valley to the western mountains.

A small troop of soldiers, detailed to guard them from hazards along the way, transferred the wounded men into the carriages. Isabel was settling the last of them when an open truck drove up and stopped beside the train. The grey-faced, silent men it carried wore threadbare jackets and the shabby, black felt caps of peasants. She gave them no more than a cursory glance as they shuffled past her carriage window followed by their guards. Tom, she imagined, feeling a sudden, familiar ache for him, would be in Scotland by now. She supposed it would become easier with time. What she felt for him was surely no more than an ephemeral thing, his feelings for her nothing more than a soldier's transient loving for a girl he meets along the way. It had been romantic, a little dangerous, and entirely unlike the tranquil, life-long affection between herself and Roberto. She returned her attention to the men stacked three tiers high on narrow bunks and when the train buckled, ready to begin its journey, directed her thoughts to her future life in Puente Nuevo and the more immediate prospect of Burgos. There, with the return of some of the comforts she had known, perhaps the forgetting could begin and her love for Roberto would return.

She was drowsing when they came to a shuddering halt. The accompanying solders leapt down from the roof of the train. A second explosion echoed not far ahead. Air, already sour, thickened inside the carriage. Gunfire spattered in the hills north of the track where remnants of the squabbling enemy persisted with their guerrilla war. The train lurched as if eager to go on. Iron screeched against iron and settled to an uneasy rest. Two hours passed before news came that the bridge ahead had been secured. The damage was slight and would not prevent their crossing. Couplings strained and creaked along with human nerves. The train began to move and rumbled on. Those closest to the windows dared not look down at the tumbling tributary beneath the bridge. All held their breaths as they crossed to safety on the other side.

Mountains, immense grey guardians, stood to the north. The valley was wide now, and flat. The river wound unseen between an honour-guard of dark green trees, washing the blood of battle and man's stupidity eastward to the sea. Soon there were orchards, their winter-bare branches of peach and almond waiting for the miracle of spring, for abundant blossom and the hope of peace.

The winter afternoon had darkened into night long before the train pulled into the siding. The prisoners travelling in a closed wagon – jammed up against crates of livestock from the monastery farm and wire-netted crates that tantalised with evidence of blankets – wondered if they had arrived in Burgos. The wagon door slid open. Guards jostled them to the ground with their rifles, lined them in double-file and ordered them to unload the wounded from the carriages. The nurses and their charges were to spend the night in a nearby barn.

Isabel followed the first half dozen stretchers. A prisoner stumbled. She called out sharply, berating him for his clumsiness, and told them all to take more care. The barn door opened spilling meagre light, showing the way across the frozen ground. Voices called a welcome; women came to usher them in from the cold. Inside, the air smelled sweet. Grain stored there in past years of abundance had left a lingering fragrance. Kerosene lamps dangling from wooden roof supports cast shadows on the walls. An iron stove in the centre of the room welcomed with its warmth, as did the women who had come from the nearby town to fill straw palliasses and prepare food for the men who had paid so dearly to defend their valley. Many prayed that by some miracle their husbands might emerge from the train, and one did recognise a cousin thought killed some months before. Another found a man who had lain beside her dying son.

A prisoner straightened awkwardly, as if putting down his stretcher had caused him pain. Isabel stepped aside as he passed her on his way back to the train. Blue eyes caught hers. A moment later he was gone. She stared after him into the darkness thinking she must have dreamed him. He returned not long afterwards with another stretcher but did not look her way. When he left, she slipped from the barn to follow him.

'I have to get something from the train,' she said to the guard at the door, and went quickly through the darkness after the prisoners' retreating shadows. She watched them hustled back into their wagon. Torchlight caught his face as he turned his head and looked back towards the barn.

'Silly of me,' she said to the guard when she returned. 'It was in my pocket all the time.'

Fifty men lay fed and warm under their blankets. The village women had returned to their homes. Sister Magdalena beckoned her nurses to a quiet corner of the barn for prayers. Isabel knelt among them, hoping for ease of confusion in the ritual, and finding none. When the prayers were done and all had been given Magdalena's blessing, she lay down on a pallet by the door trying to make sense of it, wondering how it was possible for him to have been on the train when she had thought him safely home. As the haze of sleep descended, the discordant snores and muttered dreams around her led to thoughts of a night of furtive loving behind the hessian curtain, of the naked body she had bathed and longed to touch again. When she slept at last, the rustling straw beneath her brought dreams of lying with him in a field of flowers and hay.

Chapter Five

Truckloads of prisoners were brought daily from the battle fields and villages to the freezing cold of Federico's mountain stronghold outside Burgos. Three times each day, three hundred men were taken from their cells and lined up in the castle courtyard to be counted. Some wore boots, some had bound their feet with rags, others stood in shoes worn thin and full of holes and wondered if, should they survive just one more day, their feet might not freeze into the icy slush from the previous night's snowfall.

The Commandant stood chatting with his officers while the count was made, then passed along the ranks of silent, shivering men, smiling, offering words of welcome to those not met before. He returned to stand before them, the inner walls of the sturdy fortress at his back, drew cold air into his lungs and expelled it steaming in the icy air.

'You will all be killed.' His words came as a scream. He cast his glance wide to include them all, smiled again and turned to strut into the castle and the comfort of his quarters.

After each dawn ritual, the men from the International Brigades, who were still waiting, praying even to forgotten gods for repatriation, were separated from their Spanish comrades and taken from the prison. They were given shovels and ordered to start digging. No one asked the reason for the steep-sided pits. All felt the horror of the task, although the weakest and sickest of them, bodies and minds unable to take more abuse, would have gladly lain down themselves and had their fellows cover them with dirt.

With the hard earth broken and the grave deemed deep and wide enough, their overseers returned the prisoners to the fortress. Carts had been loaded with bodies in their absence. More Spaniards would be shot at noon, their deaths an example to others who had chosen to uphold the Republic. In the Caudillo's mind, and therefore Federico's also, they were all Jews, Communists and Freemasons, and abhorrent to all right thinking Catholics.

The daily pattern concluded with the Commandant's sardonic smile and his wish that his guests enjoy a pleasant evening. The anticipated shots came not long afterwards. Thirty more Spaniards were absent at the dawn parade. Ninety men each day. Because they had voted for the Republic and fought for what they believed they had already won.

The Internacionales were not murdered, other than in circumstances deemed exceptional. With negotiations now under way for their repatriation such deaths might lead to awkward questions from governments who quietly regretted the embarrassment their citizens had caused.

Each night the prisoners fell silent as a dozen pairs of marching boots echoed through the labyrinthine passageways of the castle dungeons. The troop halted. Six names were called. Gates screamed against shrieking hinges as the guards came to take the chosen, and screamed shut again in protest as they left. The remaining prisoners were silent, fearing perhaps that their slightest sound might cause discovery of a name overlooked. The room where Federico conducted his interrogations stood two high floors above them. The walls and floors were thick. They would not hear their comrades' screams. Later, as the six shuffled one by one back to their cells, men talked loudly or stuffed their fingers in their ears to shut out the whimpering.

'Good luck, laddie,' Jock whispered when Tom's name was called soon after their arrival. 'I'd be obliged if ye'd plant a wee kick in the region of his sporran for me.'

The six were taken to a windowless ante room. Five were left there with a single guard, the first led away. Screams soon penetrated the wall. They wondered which would prove the worst, the beating or their own imaginations. In the midst of battle it was easier to be brave.

The door opened. Tom was hustled next into the high-ceilinged, wood-panelled, handsome room. Federico rose to welcome him, his mouth curved in its familiar smile.

Why, the Commandant asked pleasantly, would such a man as Tom, apparently honourable and of good heart, join the Brigades? Did he not love his king? When and where had he learned to speak such excellent Spanish? Who were his teachers? How many Spaniards had joined the forces of the foreigners now fleeing towards Barcelona? Why was he carrying a radio? Blows from the guards punctuated each question. Federico's smile widened.

'You are a spy. Why else were you and your young friend wearing our uniform?'

The thunder crashing inside Tom's head made it hard to think straight but he was sure he had not misheard the question, just as surely as his questioner knew that the Republicans had long since gone into battle wearing whatever was to hand. Open necked shirts and khaki trousers were standard, or overalls when they could get them. With disillusioned Francoists going over to the Republicans, uniform and all, and more than a few equally disillusioned Republicans running in the opposite direction, by now the armies were barely distinguishable from each other.

'The radio! You were found with a radio.' Another blow. Tom thought Dan, wherever he was now, would forgive him the lie:

'It belonged to the boy who died. He was the radio man.'

'Get him out of here.' Federico's voice was at strangulation point. Had he been able, Tom would have smiled at the thought.

It was over. He was thrust into the corridor and hustled bruised and bleeding to his cell while the next man took his place.

Two days later, in the nurses' quarters at the hospital in town, Isabel had finished her duty and gone to her room. An evening dress lay on her narrow bed. Josefa, Federico's wife, who was staying at the castle with her husband and their infant son, had written asking her to join them for dinner. In spite of her antipathy towards Roberto's cousin on the rare occasions she had met him, Isabel had replied that it would give her great pleasure to accept. Deliberating with the nurse who shared her room over which of her two gowns to wear had been a rare distraction from their work. Neither of them had been aware, when they left their well-appointed homes, that they were also about to forego their entire social lives. The cotton uniforms and sensible shoes provided on their arrival would, they had imagined, hold some magic glamour of their own as they went about their tasks as angels of mercy. Each had packed no more than four elegant outfits along with their dainty underclothing: two suitable for luncheon parties, two evening gowns to be worn at soirées given by local members of society. How blissfully unaware they had been: the clothes had rarely seen the light of day in almost a year, and then taken from their travelling chests only to be checked for moths.

Isabel's companion helped her dress and fussed with her hair, envious and pleased for her, and extracted the promise of a full account of the occasion. If, as was rumoured, General Franco had arrived in Burgos, he might well be at the gathering. A young novice came to tell Isabel that a car was waiting for her at the door.

Tom's torturer sent for him again. This time, his pain erupted into screams. He heard himself sobbing, and hated himself for it. There was nothing he could tell the fascist bastard. There was nothing to tell. It was common knowledge by now that the Brigades had been disbanded. And he was certainly not privy to any plans the Republicans might still have up their sleeves. If they had any – which seemed less likely each time more Spanish prisoners were brought in with tales of defeat.

'I understand you have been – how shall I put it – friendly with one of our nurses?' The commandant's tone was warm. 'An attractive girl. You have good taste, my friend.'

'I have no idea what you are talking about.'

Federico rose to his feet. His hand slammed, palm down, on the desk which was, Tom noted inconsequentially, a thing of beauty. Its elaborately carved rim depicted cherubs entwined with flowers; the surface gleamed.

'Then what is this?' Federico removed his hand as if the polished sheen disgusted him. Tom's bloodshot eyes made out a piece of white card lying where the hand had been. Federico lifted it by a corner, turned it over and held it up long enough for Tom's eyes to focus then replaced it, face up, on the desk. The clock on the wall ticked steadily. A minute passed. Perhaps two.

'Now!'

A guard stepped forward to pin Tom's arms. Another tied rope round his ankles. Federico came from his desk to check the knots. Satisfied, he sat again, chin resting on prayerful hands, staring at his victim. A smile bloomed. His eyes, Tom judged, were the cruellest he had ever seen.

A fist crashed into his stomach, winding him. A booted foot on his buttocks sent him face downward to the floor. The boot slammed again, this time against his ribs. Greedy hands hauled him to his feet. More blows struck against his skull until the flashing lights gave way to blackness. He thought of the nun's habit and wondered if she was there, too, in the darkness.

He had no idea how much time had passed when his swollen eyelids flickered with some thought of life. His eyes were sore, his vision blurred almost to blindness: the stone walls and hessian curtain separating him from Franco's soldiers looked like dark-stained wood. He was surprised to find his pain much worse. He thought of the care he had been given, and being told that he would soon be back in Scotland. Other memories lurked behind the beckoning darkness. He would have gladly followed it were it not for a voice inside his head insisting that something or someone needed help. It was hard, so hard to forgo the promise of peace and comfort in the blackness, so hard to keep his eyelids open. Familiar obsidian eyes stared down at him. He sighed. Everything was all right, everything was the same as before. He tried to speak her name. The blurred face moved away. Tilting lances from a lamp hanging from the ceiling pierced his head with more agony.

'He is awake? Good! Come here.' He recognised the voice; remembered its owner's name. The tone was amiable and could not be trusted. He moved his head awkwardly in the direction of the sound. Federico was addressing a figure dressed in blue. Isabel? He dismissed the idea as ridiculous. He had been mistaken about the woman's eyes. The swirling mesh of pain cleared enough for him to see that she was dressed in an evening gown of pale blue silky stuff entirely unlike the serviceable uniform of a nurse. The high-heeled shoes were wrong too. Not Isabel then. He was disappointed, but pleased at the way the silky stuff of her dress clung to her small, slim, rigid body much like armour.

Federico was still speaking.

'A pity. He looked quite agreeable earlier. Unfortunately, I had to teach him a lesson. It is not seemly for a rojo, especially a foreign rojo' – he spat the word a third time: 'for a rojo to touch our loyal Spanish women. But you are not loyal are you, señorita. You are like your uncle perhaps.'

'My uncle?' she whispered.

'Your uncle Eduardo was also disloyal to Spain and to our beloved Caudillo.'

'I don't know what you mean.'

'I advise you not to play games.' Federico's tone returned to terrifying softness. 'You will of course be punished. You must be cleansed of your sin. You may atone for those of your uncle at the same time.' He lifted himself from his chair. Tom was reminded of a snake he had seen in the mountains, unfurling with apparent leisure from its nest as it sensed some small, soft animal nearby. The woman backed away as the Commandant approached her.

'Where do you think you are going? My men are outside. You don't believe me?' His voice rose again to a high-pitched shout. 'Get in here!' The door opened. A guard strode into the room.

'Get out!' Federico screeched again. The man halted unsurprised, saluted and left. The door closed silently behind him.

'You see,' Federico said, 'I don't lie. I never lie. So you must believe what I say about your uncle. You will receive your punishment gladly and so re-establish your family's loyalty, honour and love for the Caudillo. Without it, I doubt he will bless your marriage to my cousin.'

Tom could no longer delude himself. The woman was Isabel, terrified and needing him. He struggled to his feet cursing the hindering rope, and fell, defeated, to his knees.

Federico reached for the heavy knot of hair at the nape of Isabel's neck and twisted it, turning her face to his. He thrust his fingers into her mouth.

'No screaming,' he instructed. 'It upsets me.'

He walked her backwards as if dancing with a puppet and pinned her against the exquisite desk, one hand still exploring her lips and tongue, the other reaching for her skirt. He sighed a gentle remonstration. 'This would be less unpleasant if you were willing, but then it would not be a punishment would it and we are neither of us here to enjoy this. Don't move,' he ordered as she tried to turn her head away. 'Do you want me to call back the guards?'

Tom closed his eyes wishing he might at the same time close his ears to the sound of softly rustling silk, to Federico's gathering excitement. Tears ran salt and bloody down his cheeks. He heard Isabel cry out just once in the ugly stream of busy grunts and wheezing. He willed her ordeal over but the clock ticked on uncaring and the seconds counted many minutes before Federico's shout of triumph came.

'Now, salute me as you would our Caudillo.'

Tom opened his eyes. Isabel was still pinned against the desk. Federico tweaked her chin.

'Be grateful for what I have done on his behalf.' He stood her upright, kissed her on each cheek, pushed her towards Tom and buttoned up his fly.

'I think we have all reached an understanding.' His smile, Tom saw, was at the same time chiding and benign. With no change in tone, he added, 'Say farewell to this piece of shit before you go.'

She stood there not understanding it was over. Federico repeated the order firmly, kindly. 'Go, my dear.'

Then, as she turned towards the door, 'Wait!'

He took up the photograph from where it still lay on the desk, tore it in half and offered her the pieces. 'Give him this. It will remind him of what he cannot have. Give it to him.' But

Isabel stood dully unaware and it was Federico who crossed the room, held out the pieces and dropped them on the floor in front of Tom.

He was still kneeling, neck bowed as if begging her forgiveness. He looked up into her eyes and knew that what he read there would burn in his memory forever. He watched, helpless and silent, as Federico took Isabel's arm and led her to the door.

The guard stood in the aperture, her coat folded on his arm. She stood submissive while he held it open and helped her slip her arms into its sleeves as if he were a well-trained butler and she an honoured guest. He crossed to the chair by Federico's desk, took up her evening bag and returned it to her with a small, respectful bow then turned to Federico, saluted, took Isabel's elbow and ushered her through the door.

She felt the draught as it closed behind her, saw her attendant's arm raised, pointing the way she must take to the lower floor. She moved, dazed, through the dark emptiness of the castle passageways, thought herself lost and began to run. The panic-stricken clatter of her shoes echoed round corners, running with her like the ghostly footsteps of a score of fleeing women. She reached the staircase and looked down to the hall below. The guard who had admitted her was seated at the desk beside the outer door, half-hidden by a newspaper. She took hold of the banister and began her descent, eyes fixed on the curl of cigarette smoke rising from behind a turning page. Her footsteps, dull against the wooden stairs, repeating their tapping, echoed chorus as she crossed the flagstoned hall. The man, seemingly unaware, continued reading as she edged past his desk, no more visible to him than her ghostly companions. She raised her hand to the latch, begging it to lift silently. The newspaper rustled, a small sound but enough to make her freeze. The guard ordered her to wait. She dropped the latch and cowered back against the door, watching the slow folding of the newspaper, the eyes narrow behind wispy smoke. Yellowed fingers stubbed the butt in a dirty ashtray and reached for the telephone. He spoke into it, listened, laughed a reply and told her the car that had brought her here was waiting at the gate.

Other guards on duty in the moonlit courtyard regarded her incuriously as she passed. She understood then that she was not the first woman to have been invited to dine with the Commandant, to leave in frightened, shameful disarray. Her driver, eloquent on the journey to the castle prison, was silent as he returned her to the hospital. Had he spoken, she would not have answered. The self that contained her consciousness floated elsewhere and her numb body had no wish to reclaim it. Dark miles passed outside the window. As they neared the town she recalled Josefa's letter and her own innocent reply. But there had been no guests, no wife to greet her, no child to admire. Only a guard to meet her at the door and lead her to Federico's quarters on the upper floor.

The driver broke his silence, saying they would soon be at the hospital. Isabel raised her hands as if to smooth her hair, then dropped them to fumble in her bag for her pass. The car halted. The driver appeared outside her door and opened it. She stepped down, avoiding his eyes, holding her torn skirt in such a way as to disguise its state. She hurried up the steps, rang the bell, handed her pass to the porter and ran to her room, not caring that she had missed her deadline and that her dishevelled appearance would be reported. She stopped outside her bedroom door, her hand on the latch: her companion would be awake, anxious for the promised account of her evening. She would notice the torn dress, see where blood had seeped through the pale blue silk and left it stained. She pushed the door ajar: there was nowhere else for her to go. No sounds of sleeping or of wakefulness came from the nearest bed; a shaft of light from the passageway fell across an empty pillow. She whimpered her relief and would have locked the door behind her had it been possible, not caring that the girl may have been called to work a double shift in her absence and would return tired and overworked, in no mood for stories. She huddled on her bed, wrapped in her own arms, aware of nothing now except the pain where he had thrust himself inside her.

Much later, she stripped off her torn clothes, poured ice-cold water from a ewer into the washstand basin and wiped every hated trace of blood and maleness from her. She crept into her bed and found nightmares waiting to travel with her through the remaining hours of darkness.

The next day brought no reprimand for her late return. Christmas came, its celebration irrelevant and bringing her no joy. She stood in willingly for nurses living close enough to spend at least some hours of the festival with their families. Her physical wounds began to heal but she dared not contemplate the fact that her blood had not come in its due time, other than to suppose the lack a result of her injuries. Each day's exhaustion brought some respite from the nightly images of her ordeal: the terrible bleeding thing that had been Tom's face, the terrifying memory of Federico's smile. She attended Mass but would not go to confession in spite of Sister Magdalena's urgings that there she might find solace for what so clearly troubled her. She argued that there would be ample time to see to her soul when she was less busy. The nun noted the bitter brightness in her eyes, the darkening circles emphasising hollowed cheeks. At last she understood and feared for the girl. She had heard rumours of the Commandant's cruelty but had not supposed him evil enough to harm one of his own. She ordered Isabel to rest.

'I must work! I am needed!'

'Your dedication is admirable, child, but to work yourself to exhaustion is foolish.'

'Forgive me, Sister, but I am merely following your own very good example. You have often reminded me that hard work will benefit my soul.'

'You will not argue with me, Isabel!'

New terrors filled the quiet spaces of the room to which she was immediately confined. For two days, thoughts and feelings she had thought to stave off with rigorous work invaded through the walls and ceiling. As she slept and dreamed, those same walls moved to crush her. She woke, screaming, to find a novice sitting with her; sometimes Sister Magdalena prayed at her side. Such vigilance surely proved the magnitude of her sin. Dared she die? Had God's wrath been sated or did he require her presence in another hell?

On the third day, stillness came. Not peace, just emptiness. A little death, but with no bright angels standing by to guard her.

Chapter Six

When, two days later, Isabel was allowed from her bed, she made no attempt to leave the room. Nor did she respond to the unquestioning kindness she was given. Even the prayers offered by nuns and lay-nurses in the hospital chapel failed to thaw her ice-cold serenity. Sister Magdalena, while trusting in God's ultimate wisdom, elected to add a worldly remedy to the mix. She wrote to Roberto, telling him that Isabel was unwell and would be returned to her grandmother's home as soon as arrangements could be made. She did not mention the nature of her illness, or her suspicions as to its cause.

He came as soon as he received her letter. The nun, although surprised at the speed of his arrival, accepted that friends in high places might, on God's instruction, expedite His wishes. In light of Roberto's probing as to the onset of the sickness, she mentioned Isabel's distress following her visit to the castle. His face darkened in such a way as to leave her in no doubt of his repugnance for his cousin. She did not tell him of her gentle examination of the girl, what it had revealed. That was a matter between Isabel and herself and, in time, the confessional. Roberto was a man and a doctor and would discover something, if not all of the truth, on his wedding night. By which time it would be too late to do anything about it. Isabel and her reputation would be safe. Magdalena's task meanwhile was to pray that Roberto was as good a man as she believed him to be. She went herself to Isabel and found her sitting in her room, an unread book discarded on the floor. She did not look up as the nun entered, and made no response to the news of Roberto's arrival.

'I believe he has come to ask you formally to become his wife,' Magdalena said. 'He is a good man, child. It would be a wise solution.' She waited a moment more for some sign that Isabel had understood. 'I will see you in my office in half an hour.'

Isabel heard the door close. Her fingernails jabbed deep into her palms. She had not once thought of Roberto since her encounter with Federico. She had thought of Tom, of his eyes telling her that he shared her pain, that he loved her and always would; that he would rather die than lose her. In that moment she had been sure that she would never see him again.

She entered Magdalena's office exactly thirty minutes later. Outwardly composed, she had anticipated the nun's presence and was disconcerted to find Roberto there alone. She stepped back as he moved towards to her, her body stiffening as he cupped her face in his hands, tipping it to kiss each cheek. She drew away and asked him why he had come.

His appraisal of her was of professional concern as well as love. The nun had not exaggerated. Isabel's uncharacteristic demeanour, as well as her pallor, was proof enough.

'Sister Magdalena wrote to me that you have been ill. And so I am here.'

'It is nothing, Roberto. I am perfectly well. I need to rest a little, that's all. Then I will continue with my work.'

'I have come to take you back to Andalucía.'

'I am needed here!'

'This isn't the front, querida. There are many strong, young women in Burgos to take your place.'

'Then I will ask to be sent to Catalonia.'

'The Republicans are running for their lives, Isabel. God willing, it will soon be over. Besides, your grandmother is anxious to see you.' As he reached to take her hands she steeled herself not to pull away.

'I had intended to wait until it was ended before asking you formally,' he said. 'Now I see that by marrying you sooner I could have kept you out of harm's way and too busy to run off to war. May I ask you now to be my wife? I want nothing more than for you to be safe and happy.'

She wondered if he could feel her panic and forced herself to breathe calmly. Perhaps he would think her behaviour normal in a girl receiving her first proposal, however long anticipated. She looked up at the kind, familiar face. In a long-ago, innocent life-time he had been her dearest companion. He had protected her like a brother, taught her to be daring and fearless, had dried her eyes and teased her back to laughter when she fell from her pony. He had declared his love for her when he was twenty-three and she barely twelve years old. A long-forgotten warmth flowed through her. She could not love him in the way he wanted but she understood that in cherishing his love for her she might, with God's forgiveness, find peace.

Roberto moved to embrace her. But the nightmare would not be dispelled so easily. Tom's face, swollen and bloody, appeared like a mask between them. The ugliness of Federico hovered over them all. She could not, in all honour, marry him.

'I'm sorry. So very sorry.'

'Hush. There's no need to punish yourself this way. It's over now.'

She stepped back, her cheeks burning as if he had struck her. How could he know? She searched his eyes, and found nothing more than care and love. Whatever he had alluded to, it was not that. He could not have looked at her so steadily and known. He loved her and had offered her a way out of her earthly hell. What came after would be between herself and God. When the baby came, she would pray to the Virgin that her secret be kept.

She breathed deeply, calming herself to speak the words she must say now, or perhaps never.

'I would be honoured to be your wife.'

His eyes spoke his pleasure and relief.

'How soon can we be married?' she added, trusting he would not query her seemingly abrupt change of heart.

'As soon as you are completely well. Meanwhile, I insist on placing you in my mother's care. You will of course be married from the Casa del Rosal.'

'I should like that. But I must see my grandmother first.'

'Of course.' He laughed. 'She will enjoy giving you the scolding you deserve!'

'I'm surprised she let me go,' she said, wretched that her grandmother's mostly incontestable wishes had not prevailed that day too. 'She said it had to do with Uncle Eduardo – a debt repaid.' Federico, she remembered, had said something similar. She shuddered, glad now of Roberto's closeness.

'It happened a long time ago,' he said. 'It has nothing at all to do with you. I'm surprised Doña Mercedes thought it might.'

'The wedding,' prompted Isabel. 'How soon?'

'I shall to return to Catalonia as soon as you are settled in Puente Nuevo. My orders are to remain there until Barcelona is in our hands. After that we can be married as soon as you like. Three months at most.'

Fear again... 'Three months?' ... and quickly hidden with a teasing laugh. It was not so hard, already, to pretend.

'Why not immediately?'

Roberto laughed with her. 'Such impatience is unseemly, woman, albeit flattering. What do you suppose your grand-mother would say?'

'That I'm impetuous of course. And that it would take a hundred years to turn me into a lady. But why wait, Roberto? We've always known we would marry some day. There's no need for a formal engagement.'

He smiled wryly. 'I doubt my mother would approve.'

'I'll persuade her,' Isabel insisted and laughed again. 'If she won't agree, I shall run off with the Army again.'

He doubted that also but was relieved to note this much return of her spirit.

There was no question of their travelling the more direct route through Madrid: in spite of Franco's expectation of its speedy fall, in spite of the long siege and the deaths of a third of the Internacionales alongside their Spanish comrades, the capital was still in the hands of the Republicans. Arrangements were made instead to spend the first night of their journey in Salamanca then travel south through the safety of Extremadura. The roads would be bad in either case. Much of the territory had been fiercely fought over and there were no resources for repairing the war-ravaged and neglected highways, let alone the lesser roads. Roberto was allocated an official car which he would drive himself. Army commissions along the way allowed for sufficient petrol for the journey. With them they would take two nuns making their way to their mother convent in Salamanca. They would be company for Isabel while Roberto was engaged in Army matters, and act as her chaperones. Engaged or not, it was inappropriate for her to travel with him so far alone.

The official pennant, ensuring unimpeded progress on the road to Valladolid, fluttered on the bonnet of the black sedan. They were, Isabel thought, cocooned in an unreal existence, safe from the passing world outside, at least for the time being, with neither world having the least significance to herself. The nuns in the back seat required no entertainment other than their own silent thoughts. She stared through the windscreen at the harsh landscape of rocks and winter fields, at villages ruined by the passage of the war. From time to time they passed black-clad women stooped over barren furrows. She supposed they were picking up stones in unlikely optimism of spring planting, or searching perhaps for some overlooked morsel to sustain themselves and their children. Some stood as the car went by, watching like gaunt scarecrows before bending again to the unforgiving soil. Compassion gnawed at the edges of Isabel's own raw misery. She had not shared their hunger but supposed that when the Republicans destroyed their villages, the women had experienced another fate not dissimilar to her own. She dropped her head. The older of the nuns leaned forward to touch her shoulder.

'Save your tears, daughter. Those women are Communists or worse.'

It had not been the Republicans and their allies, then, who had caused this village's devastation: a village, Isabel saw, which like so many others they had passed, seemed not to own one man nor have a single house undamaged.

'How is it possible to feel for them?' the nun continued, sensing Isabel's distress. 'Surely you have heard of the churches they have burned, the clergy they have murdered? Believe me, they don't deserve your pity. Or your mercy. They showed us none. Child, I was there.'

'Our Sisters were hacked to pieces before our eyes.' The second nun spoke so softly that Isabel thought she had misunderstood. But the voice went on behind her, sad and hollow, telling how soldiers had come to their convent and to others, of the murders, rapes and burnings. They had not escaped unscathed themselves. The first nun hushed her. Isabel's eyes welled with more tears. She had heard the rumours, whispered among the nurses, but none had believed that even communists would stoop to such desecration. It was small consolation knowing they would burn in hell for their wickedness.

They stopped in Valladolid for a meal and brief respite from the confines of the car, and came late that afternoon to yet another impoverished hamlet. Others they had passed had shown at least some sign of life; this one seemed utterly abandoned. Roberto slowed to avoid the many potholes and fallen masonry in the otherwise empty, unpaved street. The pennant hung limp against the car. Isabel shielded her eyes against the low, red sun and pointed to a shadow sliding from the doorway of a dilapidated hovel. The skirted figure moved to the middle of the street and turned to face them, one hand resting on her hip, the other holding a shawl across her skinny chest. The car crawled forward, devouring her long shadow until they were close enough to see her eyes staring from a face as still and hard as stone. The Sisters murmured their unease as more women seeped from the adjoining houses. Roberto's foot tensed against the brake, bringing the car to a halt.

'Ignore them, Señor Doctor. Drive on.'

'You are probably right, Sister. Even so….' He reached across Isabel to the glove compartment and took out a revolver.

The women crowded close now around the car. One or two had infants in their arms. Blank-eyed, ragged toddlers clung to ragged skirts; wretched faces strained towards the car's closed windows. Its occupants were still, the women and children mute, the only sound a weak mewling from some small unseen creature, a kitten perhaps or starving cat. A bundle of rags was lifted for Isabel to see, and returned to an empty, useless breast. Skinny fingers tapped against the windows. Hands begged, palms open, then dropped away. The child's crying ceased. Silence, complete and awful, seemed to smother and condemn them all. The baby's mother lowered her eyes, and turned away.

Others followed, vanishing back into their broken houses until only the first remained. At last, she too stepped from their path, her eyes still holding Isabel's, the gulf between them described by nothing more than a fragile piece of glass. Spittle splashed against the window and slid down the pane. The car moved on leaving the woman in a veil of dust. Ahead, the glorious city of Salamanca waited, its fabulous sandstone gold against the setting sun.

They came to the outskirts an hour later and arrived soon after at the convent. The nuns who lived there and who had heard something of the sufferings of their convents in the east, received their sisters with relief and tears. Isabel was shown to the small and sparsely furnished cell where she would spend the night and, later, joined the nuns for prayers. Afterwards, alone in her room, she knelt again, but her disordered mind refused communion with the crucifix above her bed or with the gentle, painted image of the Virgin opposite the small window. She woke early, surprised to find she had slept well. She found matches by the candle on the bedside chest, struck one and watched its flame catch the wick and dance against the shadows. She poured water from a jug into a small stone basin and began to wash, invigorated by the icy coldness. Her clothes, taken while she slept, lay clean and pressed on a chair by the door. She dressed and knelt again. Above her, a shaft of light penetrated the small, high window, lighting the Virgin's eyes.

Roberto came before the sun was fully up, bringing with him a plump, well-dressed woman. Doña Felicia, he explained, was to travel with them as far as Cáceres. She greeted Isabel and resettled herself in the back seat of the car among those of her belongings that could not be fitted in the trunk, her ample knees wrapped in a travelling rug to keep out the chill.

The nuns who had shared their journey yesterday stood waving from the door and were still visible through the rear window when Doña Felicia began a lengthy discourse on her recent visit to Burgos and the kindness shown her there by the Commandant. She prattled on, unaware of Isabel's suddenly rigid back or that the girl's neck had turned red and then white under her loosely folded chignon. Nor was she disconcerted by Roberto's lack of comment when she spoke of her pleasure in discovering the Commandant to be no less a person than his cousin. She had found Don Federico utterly charming, she said, and a credit to his more illustrious relatives. She had met him at a soiree given by Generalísimo Franco's wife, Doña Carmen, in support of the society women who ran the local orphanage – where, incredible as it seemed, they cared not only for Catholics but also for children of dead communists. Astonishing! She herself doubted the wisdom of the arrangement, but it was not, of course, her place to comment. A more pressing matter had been her difficulty in obtaining transport for her journey home, her husband being delayed in Salamanca. The Caudillo relied on him absolutely for advice, yet he had been unable to procure a car and driver for her. She had mentioned her difficulty to her hostess who had mentioned it to the Commandant – who had instantly assured her that he would arrange everything. As indeed he had, since she was now travelling to her home with his cousin, Don Roberto Álvarez and his delightful fiancée.

'He mentioned how pretty you are, my dear. Such a pity I didn't know you were in Burgos. I would have arranged an invitation for you. It would have been such a pleasure to introduce you to Doña Carmen.'

Isabel's nails bit more deeply into her palms when she heard that Federico's wife had been in attendance.

'I'm sorry to say Doña Josefa added very little to the occasion. Such a mouse of a woman.'

Their chattering companion could not know, any more than Isabel herself, that an invitation had indeed been sent, and intercepted by Sister Magdalena. The nun had replied that Isabel was indispensable that evening and could not be given leave to attend.

Doña Felicia's soliloquy required few responses. The wearying, distressing monologue continued for an hour or more, covering such confidences as to why Don Roberto, an aristocrat with no need of employment – she trusted he would take no offence at her kindly meant observation – had felt called to the study of medicine and then to arms when his dear mother must surely wish him safely at home, especially since his elder brother, God rest his dear soul, had died in the defence of Puente Nuevo so early in the war. She paused just long enough to cross herself in silence before giving loud thanks for her most excellent husband who was, at this very moment, attempting to persuade the Caudillo of the importance of an immediate thrust upon Madrid.

Roberto responded courteously, if infrequently, to the unceasing stream, silently deeming her last comment the only one of intelligence, albeit her husband's and not her own. Isabel remained mute, wretched at the woman's chatter, appalled that the hand clasping her own so warmly this morning had so recently touched Federico's. She leaned forward, reached into the glove-box and felt her fingers curl around the barrel of Roberto's pistol. The peroration behind her ceased as she cradled it in her hand. She ran a finger over the silver chasing.

'Have you ever used it?' she asked Roberto. 'It's very handsome.'

'It was given to me by my grandfather,' he said. 'Be careful. It's loaded.'

'What happened to the other one?'

He paused. 'It was given to Federico.'

'What a pity,' she said, 'to divide such a handsome set.' She reached forward and replaced the gun.

Her supply of gossip exhausted, and unaware that for a little more than a minute her life may have been in some doubt, Doña Felicia had fallen asleep, sprawled across the boxes on the seat beside her. Thus she remained as they passed through the endless dry and rocky landscape of Extremadura where only dust-covered trees, sparse olive groves and occasional bull herds showed any sign of life.

They came at last to Cáceres, its roofs weighted with huge nests overflowing the chimney tops, habitats of storks that for centuries had made the town their home. Sensing the close proximity of her own good bed and board, Doña Felicia stirred, grunted, sat upright and directed Roberto to a large white house on the outskirts of the town. A footman and an elderly maid appeared through a high wrought iron gateway. Soon Doña Felicia was standing among a growing, then diminishing, pile of packages, giving orders and inviting her companions to take refreshment in her commodious home; to stay the night rather than complete their long journey in one day. Roberto thanked her and declined: his dispatches were due in Seville that evening. Doña Felicia chattered on, offering felicitations to his mother, Doña Elvira, and to Isabel's grandmother. Finally, unbearably, she drew Isabel to her, offering good wishes for her wedding and an unmissable hint that an invitation would be accepted with pleasure.

In spite of the pain and anger that had consumed her throughout the day, Isabel's mood eased as the car crossed at last into Andalucía. She knew that Roberto felt it too, this sense of gladness, of coming home. Night was falling and they were already skirting Seville when she reminded him of his dispatches. There were none, he said. And she too was able to laugh at their escape from the good señora.

An hour later, high enough and cold enough for snow to be lightly falling, they came to the hill on which the little town of

Arcos stood. The road, winding even higher through a clustering of white houses, ended at the entrance to a wide, paved square with the Town Hall flanking one side. The red and yellow flag of Franco's Spain hung from its balcony.

Word of their arrival had preceded them. The car had been seen approaching from the north. As Isabel alighted, a small, black-clad figure, following a child with a bobbing lantern, hurried down the steps and across the square. Her head was uncovered in spite of the cold, her hair wound in a tight grey bun against her neck. This was Mercedes, the adored grandmother whom Isabel had charmed and vexed in even measure since the day she was born.

'Abuela!' Isabel cried, running to her.

Mercedes reached to take the girl's face in her hands. 'I'm not sure if I should scold you or be happy to see you.'

The small boy stood by the car, not quite daring to touch it, his black eyes round as saucers.

'Be happy, Doña Mercedes, for both of us. Isabel has agreed to marry me.'

Mercedes turned to embrace Roberto.

'The Virgin be thanked. It's time she came to her senses!'

A figure emerged from the Town Hall, wrestling his arms into his coat sleeves.

'Don Jaime will be filled with envy,' Mercedes said, looking first in the direction of the approaching Mayor and then at Roberto's car. 'The one he has is so far gone it can't be repaired. Ah, Don Jaime, good evening. Be sure to give Don Roberto a good supper while you talk. And a comfortable bed afterwards. Pablo will see us safely home. We'll see you in the morning, Roberto.'

The two women, child and bobbing lantern moved away across the square and up the dozen, time-worn steps to the street above. Iron-grilled windows peered from small white houses as they passed. The lane widened in front of the church and led them to a smaller square flanked by leafless trees. Come summer they would give shade to the patrons of the small café on the corner. A large house stood opposite, its stout door studded with iron nails and dark with age.

The door flew open. Expira, Mercedes' maid and companion of more years than Isabel's memory could count, ran out to meet them uttering cries of pleasure mingled with thanks to the Virgin for the girl's safe arrival. She planted loud kisses on her cheeks, hugged her fiercely, said she looked as if she hadn't eaten in months, found a peseta in her pocket for the boy and drove Isabel and her mistress into the house. The boy tucked the coin into his palm along with one Roberto had slipped into his hand earlier, and vanished into the darkness to make his bed in some barn or stable where he might be warm.

When Mercedes came, as was her habit, to Isabel's bedroom to say goodnight, she found her finishing a cup of camomile tea. Her granddaughter's bright smile did not fool her any more than when she had laughingly pushed away her supper saying that the journey had taken away her appetite.

'Sleep now,' Mercedes said. 'Tomorrow, before Roberto comes, you will tell me what is troubling you.' She took the cup and went from the room, leaving the door ajar just as she had when Isabel had come to live with her as a child and said she was frightened of the dark.

Next morning, Isabel dallied in her room before going down to breakfast. Then, as Expira came and went with food and coffee, she chatted to them both of her wedding plans, giving Mercedes no opportunity to talk with her alone before Roberto came.

Chapter Seven

The Casa del Rosal, Roberto's home, had stood for almost three centuries in three-storied grandeur around its central patio, cherishing its family through good times and bad. Older palaces and houses stood on the far side of the bridge, built by Moors who had ruled the town for seven hundred years before being ousted by the Catholic Kings. In its own, less extensive, lifetime the Casa del Rosal had seen countless Álvarez babies born, watched over people dying and comforted those who mourned.

Isabel had arrived with Roberto in the early afternoon, glad that in the flurry of their departure from Arcos there had been no time for her grandmother to probe. Roberto had left soon after to call on the superintendent of Puente Nuevo's hospital. A report was due on the state of the wounded there. How many men would be fit to return to the front? How soon? She changed into a long skirt and lace-cuffed blouse and went downstairs to find Doña Elvira sitting by the fire in her sumptuous drawing-room. She wandered over to the tall, lead-paned windows to stand looking out at the garden.

'Sit down, child. Why so restless?'

'I've been sitting all day.' The late-afternoon light was fading, orange trees and formal hedges turning gloomy. The rose bush that climbed the high, white garden wall – that in summer spilled its flowers into the street and whose predecessors had given the house its name – mocked her with its leafless shadow.

Behind her, reflected in the glass, a maid came with a tray holding a decanter and glasses. She put it on the small table at Doña Elvira's side then knelt by the fireplace to add more wood. Logs sputtered in protest. Her footsteps, silent on the rugs, padded against the marble-tiled floor as she crossed the room to close the wooden shutters. Isabel turned from the window. Unable to ignore Doña Elvira's invitation any longer, she went to sit beside her. Chandeliers glittered into life, casting phantom jewels on high white walls. Mirrors gleamed in ornate frames, flanked by portraits of Roberto's ancestors.

'A glass of manzanilla, child?'

'Thank you, no, Doña Elvira.'

'Soon you will call me Mama.' A smile eased sadness from the older woman's eyes. 'I have always thought of you as the daughter I never had.' The softness faded. 'My own daughter, however, would not have disobeyed me. Loyalty to the Caudillo is not only admirable, it is expected. Even so, your conduct was grossly improper.'

'Forgive me, Doña Elvira, but others did the same.'

'Can you imagine the pain you would have caused Roberto – to say nothing of your grandmother and myself – if you had come to harm?'

Isabel stared at her lap. Was it true, as the nurses had whispered, that an experienced women could read innocence or otherwise in the eyes of another? How clearly had her own eyes spoken yesterday to her grandmother? She had no illusions. If Roberto's mother guessed the truth there would be no marriage.

'I'm so very sorry to have caused you such displeasure,' she said, not daring to look up. 'It was wrong of me to go.' She bit her lip and prayed the bitterness behind her words had not betrayed her.

'We must thank the Virgin for returning you in one piece.' Elvira took up her glass, sipped, approved and returned it to its silver coaster. 'Why so pensive, child?'

'I was thinking of the wedding,' Isabel lied.

Elvira nodded. 'You will of course go to the cortijo for your honeymoon. It will be pleasant there in the spring.'

'I should like to be married immediately.'

Elvira's eyes widened in astonishment.

'What nonsense. Three months is concession enough. A year would have been more suitable.'

And long enough, Isabel thought, to cause her downfall. As would the three-month engagement already proposed by Roberto.

'Your wedding must do credit to this house and this family,' Elvira said, 'and that cannot be done at a moment's notice.'

Her future mother-in-law's resources were bound to be taxed in any case, Isabel supposed. It was much harder now to acquire things once taken for granted, things once easily obtained by those of means. Even so, persuasion that an elaborate ceremony would be neither appreciated nor appropriate, let alone that it was vital to proceed with haste, would be impossible. Tears pricked her eyes.

'Forgive me, Doña Elvira. I know I'm being foolish....'

'Whatever is it, child?'

'It has been my wish to become Roberto's wife, to belong truly to this family, for as long as I can remember. If Roberto came to harm in Catalonia it would break my heart, as I know it would yours. And if I were not to have had the joy of being his wife, then God forgive me, I wouldn't wish to live.'

Her trembling body, at least, was behaving with honesty. If the card she had played was to be rejected, she would be committed to a life of shame; shame that would embrace not only herself but everyone she cared for.

Doña Elvira gazed at the burning logs in the hearth, thinking, perhaps, of her first-born son, Manolo. The town, sympathetic to Franco's Movimiento, had been attacked by the Republicans in the first months of the war. The invaders had shown no mercy. Manolo and many other citizens had been murdered, their bodies tossed from the buttress above the gorge. Roberto would almost certainly have met a similar fate had he not been with Franco's armies in the north. With Manolo dead and the town re-taken by the Nationalists, Isabel knew how much it had been hoped, expected of her that, young as she was, she would agree then to a formal engagement. Had she done so she might by now have produced the family's longed for heir and, in doing so, given Doña Elvira some solace.

'I do not have your strength of character, Doña Elvira,' she murmured. Please don't think me foolish.'

'We will talk of this again tomorrow, Isabel.'

Elvira was alarmed. Roberto had spoken of Isabel's illness and unusually sombre mood, but she had not anticipated this. She wondered briefly if the girl might be pregnant and dismissed the notion instantly as unthinkable. Roberto's sense of honour would never allow it, and she believed she knew Isabel well enough to be sure no other man would dare approach her. She was, Elvira decided, behaving as impetuously as she always had. Yet her argument gave reason for reflection and concern. What if indeed the unthinkable happened: if Roberto did not return from Catalonia?

The following morning, and in the days that followed, a flurry of activity disturbed the usually unhurried household. Dispensa-tion was sought and granted to expedite the marriage. Roberto's leave was extended, the priest visited, the date agreed. With her mind made up, nothing was permitted to thwart Elvira's expect-ations. Problems were surmounted, solved, bypassed or ignored.

Isabel's request that the occasion be celebrated with simplicity was brushed aside. Seamstresses were hired to assist Elvira's dressmaker, and fabrics ordered from Seville. When told that a particularly fine satin could no longer be had and that there was none of such quality in the whole of Spain, Elvira contacted friends in Paris. Her dressmaker could not fault the lovely fabric duly sent from France. No one asked what bribes had been necessary, what favours requested or repaid to procure its swift delivery. Scissors sliced and snipped in the small interior chamber allocated for the work. Feet rocked treadles, the machines atop them chattering along with women's voices. Snatches of flamenco accompanied fittings of the exquisite wedding gown. Items of a hastily but perfectly stitched trousseau appeared as if by magic. The mantilla, Mercedes insisted when consulted with some difficulty via the unreliable telephone line to Arcos, would be from her own family. Worn first by herself and then by Isabel's mother, it had lain undisturbed in layers of tissue paper for almost a quarter of a century. Not to be outdone, Elvira produced a tall, intricately detailed ivory comb to support it: a family heirloom worn by Álvarez brides for generations.

With the wheels of Elvira's organisational skills in motion there was little need for Isabel to concern herself with the turmoil around her, and if she hid, apparently untouched, in the eye of the storm she had called into being, her future mother-in-law was far too preoccupied to notice.

When news came of Tarragona's fall, Doña Elvira paused long enough to hold a small dinner party in celebration and to wonder, since war's end was apparently at hand, if she had been unnecessarily sensitive to Isabel's fears.

The pall that suffocated Isabel's soul loosened. Day after day, the unquestioning warmth of Roberto's love sustained her. She began to think it not impossible that one day she might love him in return. At the very least she would be a good wife to him.

Ten days had passed since their arrival in Puente Nuevo. The January day was unusually mild and they had gone together to sit on a blue-tiled bench in the garden. The air was scented with winter jasmine, Isabel's mood benign. She talked happily of Roberto's return from Catalonia and the life they would make together when the war had ended.

Perhaps it was that reminder, that the war would soon be over, that caused her to think of Tom and remember his promise to return for her. Resigned now to the course her life must take, she hoped he would forgive her betrayal. She supposed, in any case, that he would not want her now. She asked Roberto if he knew what had become of the man who had spared his life on the battlefield. He glanced at her, his expression enigmatic.

'As it happens I did look into it. The survivors of the International Brigades were to be repatriated, as you know.' He paused as if reluctant to go on. 'Many will have reached their homes by now. Others have not been so fortunate. The railway line outside Barcelona was mined by the Republicans. A futile effort to prevent our advance. The train carrying the Scotsman was derailed. I believe he was among those who died.'

Isabel rose, turning from him so that he would not read the shock in her eyes, the pity for the man she had loved, still loved, and who was now dead thanks to the stupidity of the very people he had fought for so unwisely. She murmured an excuse and would have walked back to the house had not Doña Elvira hurried down the path towards them waving a letter.

'From General Franco himself,' she called. 'Federico has told him of your engagement. The Caudillo has written personally to send his blessings for your marriage.'

She sat beside Roberto to read the letter aloud, telling them of the Generalísimo's desire to take this happy opportunity for recognising the debt owed by Spain to Roberto's elder brother,

Manolo, and to inform them that Commandant Federico Martos Estepa would attend the wedding, not only as a member of the family but also as the Caudillo's emissary.

Elvira had long since forgiven Franco his humble origins, believing him to have been sent by God for Spain's salvation. She was deeply honoured by his letter.

'Have you nothing to say for yourself, child?' she cried, clearly puzzled by Isabel's silence. 'The Caudillo is doing you a great kindness. Federico is one of his closest confidants. Permitting him to attend your wedding when the army is so busy winning this terrible war bodes very well for Roberto's future.'

She left them then, hurrying back into the house and calling back to them that there was still a great deal to be done. Isabel had no doubt that her next hour would be spent discreetly informing friends and acquaintances of the Caudillo's personal interest in her family. Waves of panic overwhelmed her. She sat on the bench, afraid that her trembling legs would betray her, and caught hold of Roberto's arm.

'I don't care if he is one of Franco's favourites. Federico is evil. I don't want him to come!' And then, as if to explain her outburst, she added, 'You must have heard how he treats his prisoners.' Roberto's eyes flashed with rare anger, whether at her words or because of Federico's imminent arrival she did not know or care. He took hold of her shoulders and shook her. For a moment she wondered if he knew. Tears welled in her eyes.

'It would be wise not to offend either man,' he told her. 'We cannot refuse this gesture.'

She had no reason to doubt his words. There was nothing more to say.

Mercedes arrived from Arcos two days before the wedding. Isabel was glad to see her but avoided any chance for private talk. Later, as she passed Elvira's sitting room, she heard the two agreeing that such distraction was natural in a bride. She breathed more easily and thought her secret safe. On the wedding morning, Mercedes came to her room and dismissed the maid, saying she would dress her granddaughter herself. Isabel, standing in her white satin petticoat, had no option but to acquiesce.

'I had begun to think I would never have a moment alone with you, child! So much fuss!'

'You know how Doña Elvira is.'

'Indeed I do!'

Mercedes lifted the wedding gown from the bed. Isabel raised her arms and shivered as the folds slithered, snake-like, down her body.

'Naturally a celebration is expected when a man of Roberto's status marries,' Mercedes conceded. 'Although with things the way they are it does seem just a little inappropriate.'

She turned her round to fasten dozens of seed-pearl buttons into their loops. The devil laughed, sending tell-tale shivers up Isabel's spine. She wondered again if her grandmother had guessed the truth. The words had been lightly spoken, yet perhaps held a more ominous significance than reference to the restraints of war. She moved away to sit at her dressing table and concentrated on the reflection of Mercedes' gnarled hand in the mirror as it lifted her ivory-backed hairbrush. Bristles eased their way through long, dark hair, tugging from time to time as if to rouse her from her apathy. A deep red winter rose lay reflected in the glass. She toyed with it, oblivious of its beauty and the speck of blood that rose on her finger. Mercedes' hand put down the brush, took the rose and pinched off its thorn. Lips kissed the finger to take away the hurt. The hands returned to sweep the glossy mass of hair into a heavy knot, securing in it the long tines of Elvira's exquisite comb.

The mantilla lay spread across a chair, ivory with age.

Mercedes took it up and held it against her cheek, conjuring a memory of her long-dead daughter. She brought it to her silent grandchild and draped it over the comb, tweaking it a little this way and that, securing it with hidden pins and fastening the rose in its folds like a pool of blood in a bed of ivory lace. She touched her granddaughter's chin with her finger and turned her face towards her.

'Why won't you tell me what is troubling you, child?'

'It's nothing, abuela. Really, it's nothing. I'm a little tired that's all.'

Mercedes patted her shoulder. That Isabel was pregnant she had no doubt. She had seen it, together with dark sorrow, in her eyes and in the barely perceptible rounding of her hips and breasts. She wondered if Elvira knew; if the marriage had been hastened in order not to shame her son. But if Roberto was the father, as must surely be the case, why was Isabel so apprehensive?

Barely six weeks had passed since her encounter with Federico when Isabel knelt to speak her marriage vows. Among those gathered in the church was the man who had defiled her. A small, dark, unsmiling woman stood at his side: his wife Josefa, mother of his son. Wisps of incense floated from a swinging censer. As a child, Isabel had believed it made from flowers by angels. Now, it smelled of bitter ashes.

The congregation fell to its knees, rose and fell again, an obedient tide ordered by habit and the incantations of the priest. The Virgin, blue-clad and silver-crowned, gazed down on the kneeling woman, wax tears reflecting light from candles at her feet. When, at last, the invocation of divine blessing drifted through the cavernous space and the ensuing silence could be born no longer, a guitar sounded from a shadowed recess, its single strident chord echoed by a human cry so plaintive it must surely have been torn from the singer's soul. A second guitar rippled from the darkness, then a third. Palms added an intricate tattoo. The voices of the coro surged in exaltation. Isabel turned with Roberto towards the mass of smiling faces. It is fitting, she thought, this music that tears the Andalucían soul, that tells of the greatest joy, the most profound of sorrows.

She placed her hand on Roberto's arm and began to walk with him down the long aisle. Federico inclined his head as they passed. She tasted bile: she had cheated the man at her side and might have run from him even then had Roberto's hand not reached to cover hers and steady her. She was his wife now, daughter-in-law of the noble Álvarez family and in that she would find strength. She stepped out into the winter sunshine to receive the people's acknowledgement and applause, her eyes glittering with what they took to be happiness and rightful pride.

That night, lying in the matrimonial bed where her husband had been conceived and born, Isabel willed herself to accept what must come. But when Roberto took her in his arms and moved to lie above her, she flinched and watched his eyes dull to acceptance.

'You're tired,' he murmured, moving to lie at her side. 'I won't force you against your wishes.'

She lay wakeful and afraid long after he had succumbed to his own weariness and when sleep did come at last, it came with terrible, familiar dreams.

Chapter Eight

Left to themselves the following day, the newly-wed couple occupied themselves apart. Isabel spent time in the garden, secateurs in hand, wandering from shrub to shrub and finally settling her attention on the rose bush where her efforts at pruning tended to brutish rather than benign. Later, finding Roberto on the patio engrossed in a book, she went into the house and asked a maid to bring her any garments that might need repair. If the woman considered such work an unlikely pastime for a bride, she hid it well, expressing her gratitude and admitting that the past weeks had offered little time for such matters. Isabel worked diligently until dinnertime then said the detailed work had given her a headache and retired to her room. When Roberto looked in on her, he told her he would sleep in his dressing room rather than disturb her.

Next morning, at breakfast, Elvira commented on Isabel's quiet demeanour then added, sotto voce to Mercedes but loud enough for her daughter-in-law to hear, that it was natural in the circumstances. Roberto's own contribution to the conversation was, as ever, kind, if reserved, much of his attention given, quite properly, to his mother. Elvira's smiles in return spoke volumes, as did her light-hearted comments betraying hope that a grand-son, if not already conceived, would be so without delay.

Isabel ate little and escaped to her room as soon as the meal was over, excusing herself with last minute preparations. All too soon a maid came saying that Roberto was waiting in the court-yard with the horses. She went downstairs to find him mounted on his favourite Spanish Grey. A groom stood nearby, holding the black Arabian designated for her use on visits to Puente Nuevo. Doña Elvira and her grandmother were already at the door. She embraced them then crossed the yard and allowed the groom to help her into the saddle. Roberto called his goodbyes to Doña Mercedes and his mother and turned his horse towards the street. Isabel followed, remembering to look back and wave as they rode out under the archway.

They came to the curved white outer wall of the bullring and then the marketplace, acknowledging greetings along the way and coming eventually to the bridge that linked the ancient part of the town with the new. It had been built two centuries before and Puente Nuevo had been named for it, reasonably enough at the time, replacing as it did a much older, narrower span lower down the gorge. The river surged below, thrusting between im-mense buttresses and plunging into the deep cleft of the tajo on its eager journey to the plain.

Their horses' hooves, clattering at a brisk trot across the bridge, sounded a slow and careful thudding on the steep path that zigzagged down the side of the ravine. The serranía stretched into the distance like patches on a pastel coloured cloth. At their backs, dwarfing them, showering them with spume, the falling river thundered onto the wheels of mill-houses clinging to the rock like precarious toys. It was ironic, Isabel thought, that this soaring crag should have stood for centuries against Puente Nuevo's assailants: Roman, Moor and Christian, while not in the least obstructing her own oppressor.

She paused with Roberto at the foot of the incline. The great rock's morning shadow reached ahead. Sunshine lit distant hills.

She dug in her spurs. Her mount lunged, skittering pebbles, found its stride and raced towards the bright places where she had ridden day after happy childhood day, galloping across the angel-painted hills with Roberto, racing through ochre valleys and sauntering beneath the trees: a freedom not permitted nearer town where gossiping tongues would have deemed such behaviour in a young girl of her class unseemly, unsuitable and downright dangerous. Dangerous! What did they know of danger! She raised her whip and spurred her horse again. The wind lashed her face and tugged at the knot of her hair, loosening it. She and the mare sped on, black manes streaming. The cliff face of Puente Nuevo may not have withheld Federico, but out here, in the wild enormity of the serranía, the devils that pursued her could not reach her. By the time she met them again she would have found the strength to deal with them.

Roberto too spurred his horse, matching Isabel's pace for pace. He saw that the clean, cold wind had stung her eyes and recalled a day, long ago, when she had fallen and tried to hide her tears. He had helped her remount and offered to lead her pony. Indignant, dishevelled, her hair escaped from its snood and tumbled about her shoulders as it was now, she had challenged him to complete their race. Later she had displayed her bruises proudly. That day, he had known he loved her and had sworn to protect her always. He wondered if she would tell him of the pain she carried now, but thought she would not. She had been a child then, angry and fearless. Now, for reasons he had not yet fathomed, she was angry and afraid.

Their wild ride eased to a walk. A little after midday they dismounted by the now tranquil river to rest their horses and themselves. They treated each other kindly, unpacked their picnic lunch from Roberto's saddle-bag, and commented on the expertise of Elvira's cook. They talked of how pleasant it was to ride across the serranía on a sunny winter's day. Replete, content in each other's company, they remounted and resumed their journey.

They came to the cortijo with the sun low in the sky. Dogs barked a welcome as they rode in under the wide, white archway. Barefoot children and servants in rope sandals ran to greet them. Their horses were led away to the stables. The old peasant woman who cared for the house in the family's absence kissed Isabel, accepted a similar salutation from Roberto and ushered them inside. A meal awaited them and Isabel ate well before pleading tiredness. The woman pinched Roberto's cheek as if he were still the child who had pestered her for sweet things in her kitchen, and followed her new mistress upstairs. She laid out her nightdress and brushed her hair then returned to the kitchen to complete her duties. Later, with a rising, silver moon lighting her way, she crossed the yard to join her husband in their small, lime-washed cottage and when her own tasks were done, urged him to pray with her that Don Roberto's efforts that night would prove fruitful. She lowered herself to her knees and pulled him down beside her. He nudged her ribs.

'How could he fail?' he said. 'I heard you chanting spells when I passed the kitchen.'

'The same spells I used for Doña Elvira more than thirty years ago,' she agreed. 'And look what happened? An heir. Nine months to the day.'

'They worked for us too,' he said, climbing into bed and pulling her after him.

'Too well,' she replied. 'Our first came eight months after our wedding.' She thought of her sons, of her grandsons. Two dead, two more still fighting somewhere in the north. Don Roberto had told them that Barcelona had fallen. Madrid would be next and then it would be over. She offered up more prayers, turned on her side and slept.

Upstairs, in the house across the yard, Isabel lay awake, waiting for Roberto, knowing that if she was to save herself, it must be now. When he came to her, she lifted the warm quilt as if in invitation, careful not to seem too eager, afraid he might question her earlier reluctance. She stiffened as he took her in his arms, then forced her reluctant body to move against his as if her own desire was at last, albeit shyly, awakening. He touched her with exquisite gentleness, his stroking fingers bringing calm. No one, she realised, had ever touched her breasts before, except the maid at bath time, and she herself as she grew into womanhood. She recalled her pride in the small, firm globes, her wonder at their slow, voluptuous swelling. Tentative pleasure coursed through her as he kissed first one purple tip and then the other. When finally he entered her, and in so doing erased all evidence of violation, she sighed with wonder at his gentleness. It was done.

Sleep came to her slowly, softly, the dark beams of the ceiling shrouding her in shadows. Drifting, she came to where the Virgin stood in the church, candle-lit, tranquil, a faint blush painting her ivory cheeks. The image smiled, raised its hand and said that she had no need to fear: her husband, by God's grace, was now the father of the child she carried. The words slid away, leaving a dreaming peace Isabel had not thought to know again. This was not the first time an angel had interceded by way of a dream and spoken to a fearful woman of a miracle wrought by God. Tomorrow she would go to the cortijo's tiny chapel and kneel there in humility and gratitude. She fell more deeply asleep, secure in her belief in the Virgin's goodness, unaware that Roberto lay wakeful at her side or that in the act of love he had discovered, if not all her secret, then at least some part of it.

Sensing that she slept, Roberto got up, threw on his clothes and left the room, thinking to ride hard across the hills to quell his anger. Instead, he paused at the foot of the stairs: his departure would likely wake the servants. He turned towards the kitchen and found it still warm from the ashes of the wood stove and smelling, as kitchens should, of kindly things and comfort. He pulled out a chair and sat staring into the hearth, recalling the day at the monastery when the nun, Magdalena, had told him of Isabel's interest in the enemy soldier: a man he had trusted with his life. He thought he had learned then what it meant to suffer heartache. He laughed, softly, bitterly. Days before his interview with the well-intentioned Sister, he had delayed the order to send the Scotsman to the prison barn because he had believed him still too sick to work alongside the other men in the fields; too sick for physical effort of any kind.

He rose from his chair, impatient to confront Isabel, then paused. Not now. Perhaps in the morning. He would be calmer then. He drew the chair closer to the stove and sat again, thinking of the marriage vows he had made two days earlier, the marriage he had consummated an hour ago, the visit he must make to the church, this time to request annulment. As the slow night wore on, he thought too of the silent vow he had made to Isabel when she was twelve.

He did not touch her again, nor did he tell her of his intention to end their marriage. They spent their days riding, each keeping up a pretence that all was as it should be, their exertion leading to no more than a desire to spend their nights in sleep. They returned to Puente Nuevo and Roberto left for the front next morning.

In mid-February news came that the President of the Republic had gone into exile. General Franco declared the Republic itself to have been illegitimate. Membership of left-wing parties and Masonic lodges was now a criminal offence. In March, as the war moved inexorably towards Madrid, Isabel told her mother-in-law that she was expecting a child. Elvira beamed her delight and immediately called in the elderly and utterly reliable Don Alfonso, doctor to the family since before her own marriage. He examined Isabel and informed Elvira that her daughter-in-law was in excellent health and that all was proceeding as it should. Privately, he felt – since Doña Elvira was so besotted with the idea of the coming child and heir, and unlikely to reprehend either Roberto or the young mother should the baby arrive inconveniently early – that there was no reason to advise her that the pregnancy was rather more advanced than she supposed.

At the Casa del Rosal, each peaceful spring day followed another. Elsewhere, the remains of the Republican army and its disjunct allies clung to the last frail straws of obduracy. On the twenty-seventh of March, the Nationalist Army walked into the silence of Madrid. The following days saw smaller cities fall without resistance. The war was over. Isabel walked with Doña Elvira to the church to light candles and thank God for General Franco and their deliverance. That afternoon, she took her sewing basket to the garden and took out the delicate, lace-edged garments she was stitching for the coming child. She worked for several minutes before letting her hands fall to her lap, her attention caught by pink rosebuds already thrusting from their green shelter against the high, white wall. A breeze had set the bush to shadow dancing in the sunlight, rocking the small, precocious buds. An answering quiver came from the child. She smiled, glad that her attempt at pruning the bush had not harmed it, glad that Roberto would soon come home.

She was immersed in her work, forming perfect stitches on a small white dress, when a maid came from the house with a letter. She took it, dismissed the girl and prised it open. A small cry escaped her as she scanned the single, parchment-coloured page. Federico, hearing of her pregnancy, had written offering congratulations. He told her that had also written to Roberto, suggesting that, should the child be a boy, he might be named as godfather. He would, he said, consider the child as dear to him as if it were his own.

A cloud passed across the sun, darkening the roses. The letter drifted like a dead leaf from her hand. The Virgin had cheated her. Lied to her. She could no longer delude herself. God had not forgiven her: Roberto was not the father of the child she had begun to love.

She refused to leave the house and no longer invited friends to visit. Word began to filter through the community that she had become a little strange. Concerned at the change in her daughter-in-law, who now avoided her whenever possible, rarely appeared for meals and refused to attend Mass, Elvira called Don Alfonso. He told his patient that her desire to spend her pregnancy in solitude, although unusual, would likely do little harm, but that she must eat regularly and well, if not for her own sake then for that of her child.

She turned away, her mind filled with images of the women she had seen in the fields and villages on her journey from Burgos with Roberto, women who had looked like scarecrows. She thought of the baby who had been too weak to cry, who had perhaps died in its mother's arms in the broken street while she watched from inside the car. Perhaps the woman had been happy to see her child die, for its own sake as well as hers.

The next day, Doña Elvira wrote to her son insisting that he must, by any means, be spared from his duties to attend his wife. She asked why he had not already returned home since the war had been over for at least three weeks.

He arrived late one evening. Isabel was in her sitting room, an unread book on her lap. She ignored his greeting, turning to him only when he spoke her name again and drawing away when he came towards her.

When she had written to him of the coming child, Roberto's first, unthinking reaction had been pleasure quickly followed by the memory that she had not been a virgin on her wedding night. There had been no time to set in motion the annulment of his marriage, nor time to deal with his own devils as he followed Franco's victorious army towards Madrid. Isabel's letter had expressed happiness in her pregnancy; the sad, withdrawn woman before him now was soon to be the mother of a child that might, or might not, be his. He had loved her since childhood as sister, sweetheart and then wife. He still loved her. It was not in him to cast her aside.

She stood as he reached to touch her, moving away from him and gathering her loose garment about her as if she had no wish to share with him the burgeoning evidence of pregnancy. He steeled himself to ask when the child would be born, but the only words he found were to express dismay at her lethargy.

'It's nothing,' she lied, her voice heavy as if her few words caused too great an effort. 'It was wrong of Mama to worry you.'

When Don Alfonso called, as he did each morning now, he could do no more than express increasing concern. Isabel must eat or she would lose the baby. Roberto took him to one side.

'May God forgive me, but I don't care if the child lives or not. What's wrong with her?'

'May God forgive you indeed!' the doctor retorted. 'As for your wife, I have done my best, Roberto. I have known you all your life and cared for your family as if it were my own. I would have no harm come to any of you.' He sighed, raising his shoulders in an eloquent shrug; his long-fingered hands, palms uplifted, gestured helplessness. 'There is nothing more I can do. I believe the problem lies in her mind. She appears not to care if she lives or dies, and that is God's jurisdiction, not mine. Now, Doña Elvira is waiting to see me. This strain is too much for her, Roberto. She is suffering badly. I beg you to see if you can talk sense to your wife.' With a final glance at his patient, the doctor turned and left the room.

Roberto knelt at Isabel's side. 'Is it true you want to die? Why, Isabel? In God's name speak to me! Let me understand so that I can help you.'

'I should like to go to Arcos.'

He stayed with her a moment more, then left the room. He found his mother and the doctor in the salon and told them of Isabel's request.

'That's ridiculous, Roberto. She's far too sick to travel.'

'Mama, I will agree to anything she wants.'

'What do you think, Alfonso?'

The doctor studied his gold-monogrammed coffee cup. 'In a week or two she will be too ill to make the journey. I believe a change of scene might do her good. It would also be good for you, Elvira. You too have suffered a great deal. Yes,' he continued more briskly, 'Yes, Roberto, it can certainly do no harm. If your mother will allow you the use of her car and you can scrounge enough petrol for the journey, I see no problem. And you, Elvira, I shall escort myself to your cortijo where you must promise to rest for at least a month.'

It was a relief, Elvira thought, to have the decision made for her. And for Isabel. It was true that she was tired, true that her own health was suffering. She had done all she could. Perhaps Mercedes would have more success with the girl.

'Of course Roberto may have the car. As for petrol, I shall write to Federico. He seems to have taken an interest in Isabel's welfare. No doubt he will pull the necessary strings. For myself, since it is not yet summer, I shall not take up your suggestion of a visit to the cortijo. I should die of cold and boredom. But I will rest, I promise you. I will stay here and you will visit me three times a week. You will teach me to play chess and tell me if my new shipment of Rioja wine is as good as the last.'

Alfonso laughed. He put down his cup and rose to take her hand in his. 'A tempting offer, Elvira. I shall take you up on it.

As for Isabel, I do believe Doña Mercedes may be the one to change her ways.'

Elvira smiled at her old friend, grateful for his good sense. With God's grace, Mercedes might indeed bring them all through this crisis and to the safe delivery of the child.

Chapter Nine

A new war was already rumbling into existence, one in which Spain would take no part: there were no resources, and none to cope with Spain's own ongoing toll of death and hunger. Mercedes' cook had gone to her village to nurse her brother. His leg had been badly damaged in the war and gangrene had set in. There was nothing to be done now but care for him as well as maybe and watch him die. Expira had taken over the kitchen and was occupied there when Roberto came. Mercedes opened the door herself, exclaimed at the sight of the wan, exhausted girl in his arms and called to Expira to bring warm broth to Isabel in her room.

She led Roberto to the bedroom her granddaughter had used since childhood. Roberto laid her down, covered her with a quilt and reiterated what he had told Mercedes on the phone: that Don Alfonso had been unable to ascertain the cause of Isabel's illness.

'You are a doctor, Roberto. What do you think?'

'She would not let me examine her.'

Something in his eyes told her that more questions would remain unanswered. She let it go at that and told him to fetch Isabel's luggage. By the time he returned, Expira was standing at one side of the bed, clucking her concern, while Mercedes sat at the other, feeding broth to the girl as if she were still a child. Isabel swallowed several mouthfuls, too feeble to refuse.

'Tonight you will stay here, Roberto. Tomorrow you may return to your duties and leave Isabel in my care.' Mercedes handed the still half-full bowl to Expira. 'She will be safe, I promise you.' She took Roberto's hand and patted it, unhappy that her granddaughter's sadness had not, as she had hoped and expected, been mended by her marriage. What she had not realised then, but was sure of now, was that Isabel's condition had nothing whatever to do with her husband.

In the week that followed, Isabel ignored Expira's daily scoldings, pushing away food prepared with care and love. She seemed not to mind where she was, or why. Mercedes' gentle encouragement gave way to exasperation. There was nothing to be won, she told Expira, by treating her granddaughter as if she were a much-loved, obstinate, ailing child. Isabel was an adult, soon to be a mother and such foolishness could not be allowed to continue.

'Leave us, Expira. I wish to speak to Isabel alone.' The maid took up the tray of untouched food, deeming it unwise to argue. She smiled encouragement at Isabel, caught her mistress's frowning glance and left the room. Mercedes remained at the foot of the bed, raising herself to the fullness of her short stature and glowered her displeasure.

'You will stop this foolish nonsense immediately, Isabel. You have allowed Expira to wait on you hand and foot without offering a word of thanks or kindness. She has gone without sleep thinking of things to tempt your appetite. I did not bring you up to treat others with such little regard and I am offended that you think you may do so in my house.' A satisfying spasm flitted across the girl's face.

'Since you will not tell me what ails you, then I must tell you.

Roberto is not the father of your child and the sooner both you and I face that fact the better.'

Isabel's cheeks turned red then whiter than the almonds Expira had blanched and put by her bed. She inhaled sharply and might have spoken had not Mercedes interrupted her denial. There would be no lies, no more deception.

'It is the truth, Isabel. You know it and now I know it. If you wish it to be our secret then so be it, but what you have done is no fault of the child. You have no right to deny it life, nor take your own. Unless, of course, you wish to follow the Devil's path.'

Isabel's eyes returned Mercedes' barbs.

'What would you know of hell, Abuela?'

'What I know, Isabel, is that I sat with your mother while she died. She died because she was unable to give birth to a child that wanted to be born, just as I believe yours wishes to be born whoever its father may be. I am not asking you to tell me who he is. I am asking you to be brave and strong, for yourself and for me, but most of all for the innocent child you carry.'

Isabel's eyes brightened suddenly with tears. Her voice came in a dull whisper. 'What shall I do, abuela?'

Mercedes sighed her relief, moved to sit at her side and took her in her arms. They would come through this together, she, her granddaughter and the child.

'The baby is due towards the end of September, am I right?' Isabel nodded. 'Well Roberto is going to think his child has come a little early, that's all. Women have been practising such subterfuge since the beginning of time. You are not the first.' She patted Isabel's hand. 'And now you will eat. Yes?'

'Yes.' Isabel smiled through her tears. 'Oh, abuelita, you can't imagine how hungry I've been!'

Mercedes went to the door and called to Expira to bring back the tray.

When, some weeks later, Roberto came to visit her again, he was relieved to find Isabel much improved. He suggested she might return with him to Puente Nuevo. Mercedes demurred.

'She has only just begun to recover, Roberto. It would be foolish for her to travel again so soon. She will be well enough to go home long before the child comes.' Which was not in any way a lie, except that the baby would arrive safely in Arcos and Roberto would be advised to hurry to his wife's side, his son having decided to greet the world several weeks before his due time.

The first letter came while Isabel was at church with Expira, a loose gown hiding the true state of her pregnancy. The first time they had gone, Mercedes had remarked drily that there were some things a woman should confess to her priest, others she should not. That, too, was the natural way of things. Expira had added that if God was good then he forgave such omissions; if he wasn't they would find out about it all in good time. Meanwhile, there was cooking and cleaning to be done.

Mercedes turned the envelope over in her hand, wondering at the stamp that showed the head of the English king. She felt no guilt as she prised it open, careful not to tear the flap. She cared only for her granddaughter's well-being and the safe delivery of the child. If the letter's contents were harmless she would reseal it and give it to her, if not…

There were two sheets of paper. The second ended with a name unfamiliar to Mercedes, an abbreviation of Tomás perhaps. A man then, and possibly the father of Isabel's child. The letter was penned in excellent Spanish and told how the writer had attempted to return to Spain after the fall of Madrid. Entry had been denied him at the border. It was likely, he wrote, that he would soon be called up to serve in the war against Hitler. He had not forgotten his promise to her, although keeping it would now take longer than he had expected. But he would come for her as soon as he was able. Meanwhile, would she write to him? He was desperate for news of her. Even if she no longer felt for him as he believed she once had, he would not rest easily until he knew that she was safe and well.

Mercedes ripped the letter into pieces and dropped it with its envelope onto the hot coals of the kitchen stove.

Chapter Ten

Tom stared out through the porthole of the flying boat. Trusting less to the vagaries of the Spanish postal system than in Isabel's angels, he had written to her soon after his arrival in England: an arrival not marked by a hero's welcome, but by official reprimand. The British government, while thinking Franco little better than an upstart and a rogue, and knowing communists to be worse, was far from pleased with those of His Majesty's citizens who had joined the International Brigades. Tom's interview had been brief, his experience with radio noted. He was drafted into the Air Force, trained in radio direction finding and sent off to another war. He thought it likely his first letter had not been delivered and he had written to Isabel again. The passing months had become three years and she had not replied. Nor had his letters been returned. He would write to her from New Zealand as he had from all his other postings, and then no more. He thought of the promise he had made to her and not kept, a promise annulled perhaps by her silence if not by time and circumstance. He wondered if the great distance that separated them now would make it easier to forget her. By his reckoning Arcos was at a point on the globe more or less opposite his own. He stared out at the sea below, imagining he might conjure her from the waves, then scoffed at such absurdity. Twelve hours away in Isabel's world it was past midnight. He had no mind, even if it were possible, to disturb her dreams with foolish thoughts.

Ahead, against a sweep of unbelievably blue sky, an equally unlikely accumulation of pristine, billowing whiteness floated on the sea.

The pilot glanced over his shoulder, a grin splitting his broad face. 'Aotearoa!' he yelled. 'Land of the Long White Cloud!'

The Sunderland's winged shadow skimmed through the turquoise water: an enormous mythical fish racing with them to a land slowly emerging from a cotton-wool cocoon. The Maori name, Tom thought, was apt. What navigators they had been, those men and women who had long ago advanced on this isolated place in their great canoes with only the sun and the night sky to guide them and their stories to tell them what they might find there. What hope and exhilaration they must have felt, knowing the land they were searching for must surely be hidden inside that great white cloud. The last ten hours of bumping through air-pockets above the Tasman Sea hardly compared with the gruelling voyages of those long-ago adventurers, but Tom's sigh of relief at the thought of the Sunderland's impending arrival was eloquent. As was the pilot's roar above the racket of the shuddering fuselage: 'Look at her! Home Sweet Bloody Home!'

Tom grinned and turned his attention to the map spread on his knees. It showed two main islands with a third, much smaller, to the south. 'That's Stewart Island, otherwise known as Maui's anchor,' the pilot had advised him earlier. According to Maori lore, the long middle island was a canoe in which a demi-god called Maui had gone out fishing and caught himself a whopper.

And indeed, Tom thought, the most northern of the three islands – labelled by the English inhabitants with prosaic simplicity: The North Island – did look extraordinarily like a huge fish, though how the Maori had ascertained its shape he had no idea. The pilot added that with the fish being almost as big as the canoe (the equally prosaic South Island) it was lucky Maui had never got around to hauling it in, or the whole country would have sunk without trace years ago. And, come to think of it, it was just as well the bloke had kept his anchor out because he didn't see the point of flying all this way just to find the bloody thing had drifted off course!

Scatterings of dots on the map were lesser islands, some no more than large rocks hugged in against the long and lonely coastline. Tom's index finger navigated rivers, rested on hilltops and lingered over unpronounceable names.

He thought of the many New Zealanders he had met since the onset of the war. The small country's contribution had been swift and generous. Her people, like others in the Empire, called Britain 'Home' even if they had never set foot in the place. They had rushed off to Europe and Africa in the motherland's defence without a second's thought that German Raiders might sail this far to lay their mines and terrify the far-flung subjects of King George.

The country, far from the rest of the world, surrounded by vast and empty seas, was still vulnerable. With the Japanese keen to join the fray that vulnerability had increased a thousand-fold. The Radar Committee in London had recommended that a communication system be set up throughout the Dominion. The technology was new and secret. Tom's task was to oversee the installation of the units and assist in the training of their operators: men and women who would plot the course of enemy ships and planes and do their best to keep the southern Pacific Ocean safe.

They were flying now above the Rangitoto Channel, named for the island volcano standing sentinel at the harbour entrance.

Lazy white caps curled at its base. The seaplane banked. To the right was a small naval base. Opposite, a town grew from green volcanic hills, their lush sides sprinkled with white sheep that looked, from this distance, like small and improbable snowdrifts – or slowly ambling puffballs. Fiery Nature, Tom surmised, was slumbering. An expansive white building, a memorial to the dead of earlier wars, stood on one such hill, its graceful columns mindful of a far distant time and place.

He folded the map, smoothing a crease that by chance followed a river's course through farms and flaxlands and ended where it debouched through sand dunes into the Tasman Sea. He fastened his seat-belt in time for the pilot's roar of 'Hang on to your hats,' and the seaplane's bone-shaking contact with the water, thus informing them that they had indeed arrived and, by a seeming miracle, in one piece.

Part Two

Chapter Eleven

The farmhands of Fenton had long since heard Europe's clarion call to war, exchanged their pitchforks for bayonets and gone off to defend the British Empire. Adventurous single women had left towns and cities to take their places on the land. Most took to the work like ducks to muddy puddles. Others, remembering childhood stories of Bo Peep and fields of daisies, discovered an aversion to cows.

The most recent incumbent at The Oaks had been of the latter persuasion, causing Margaret to suppose that her younger daughter's current escape-or-die crisis had been brought on by the land girl's abrupt departure. Her husband, Jim, reckoned they were well rid, that Eve would soon settle down again and that the cows were a whole lot happier without a homesick townie carrying on about bright lights and shop windows in the milking shed.

Regular weekend visits to the farm by their elder daughter,

Lizzie, were now not only welcome for their own sake but essential to the smooth running of the place. Not that Lizzie could imagine staying in town over the weekends anyway. She was a farmer's daughter born and bred, lured from the land by her love of children, her weekdays spent running the township's one-classroom school. She imagined she would settle down one day with a farmer husband and raise her own noisy brood; meanwhile, she was well content with her life, and proud, as was everyone in the district, of the local boys who had gladly donned uniforms and gone off to war.

The small town where she boarded with her mother's friend, Polly Jenkins, served as a hub for the surrounding farms. The general store sold everything from cans of corned beef to cattle feed and farm implements, with the post office located in a corner at the back. A two-storied, wooden-verandah'd hotel, its grey weatherboards in need of a new coat of paint, stood next door. Thirsty farmers on forays into town were in the habit of enjoying the amenities of its public bar while their wives shopped or gossiped in the chintz-curtained tea-rooms by the railway station. There was a bank and a police station, a chapel and a church. The church hall was used for Sunday School and whist drives, occasional dances and films shown once a week. Beyond it stood a row of neat wooden bungalows, Polly's among them, and finally the school. Beyond that, nothing but the river and farmland in all directions.

That Sunday, with the afternoon milking done, and the cattle ambling their placid way back across the paddock, Lizzie shut the gate and turned to follow Eve along the squelching, muddy track to the homestead, hungrily anticipating the rewards of their mother's labours in the kitchen. Eve's long-legged, slouching stride, her oilskin hat pulled low to keep off the rain, indicated, if more proof were needed, that her mind was on other things. This afternoon's catastrophe in the cowshed, Lizzie guessed, did not augur well. Her sister's dreams of freedom and a glamorous life in the city had begun, she reckoned, around the age of twelve. Ten years on, Eve had yet to understand that falling from her horse, wading through flooded paddocks because the stop-bank had failed, being yelled at by her father and kicked by a fractious cow, all on the same day, was simply part of God's great rural plan.

Eve trudged ahead along a path bordered by raised beds of vegetables, and stamped up the wooden steps to the house. She began working her mud-laden boots against the metal scraper by the kitchen door as if her life depended on it. It possibly did, Lizzie conceded, as she too reached the shelter of the wide back porch.

Eve flopped on to a wooden bench under the kitchen window, laid one leg across the other and pulled at a reluctant boot. Two tugs later the boot dropped to the decking, her foot still captive.

'Drat the thing!' She glared at her mud-caked hands, leaned back against the green-painted weatherboards, closed her eyes and let out an enormous sigh, aimed, Lizzie imagined, at the hopelessness and never-ending annoyances of her life. Long eyelashes fluttered, parting to reveal wide, blue-grey tragic eyes. Eve raised a languid hand and gestured muddily towards the rain-screened hills to the north.

'There's a whole world out there. The war will probably go on forever and I'll be stuck here with every halfway presentable bachelor volunteered and gone. I told Dad if that damned paddock flooded again I'd be off, and this time I mean it.' She reassessed her boots, kicked ineffectively at one heel with the toe of the other and turned to Lizzie with a wry, disgruntled grin.

'Funny isn't it, considering the pair of us, that you're the one who went off to see the world.'

'Hardly that!' retorted Lizzie, who had by this time removed her own boots, placed them by the laundry door, gone inside to hang up her raincoat and come out again. Training as a teacher in Wellington and returning with her certificate to teach at a school less than twenty miles from home was not exactly 'seeing the world' in anyone's language. But she had never had Eve's restless spirit, much less the pioneering enterprise of their immigrant great-grandfather. The first James Oakes had sailed the world before falling in love with the wild, wide plains of the Manawatu, taking up land some miles inland from the river estuary and naming it 'The Oaks' in spite of there not being a single such tree on the property. Their mother called it her 'paradise found', and Lizzie loved it too with all her heart.

'Here,' she said, taking hold of one of Eve's boots and apply-ing an efficient and productive tug. Eve wriggled her freed toes then turned her foot to contemplate the darned heel of a hand-knitted sock. It was unlikely, Lizzie thought, dealing with the second boot, that in this lost corner of the world her sister would stumble across the sort of life she craved. Eve was prone to announce with clichéd regularity that she hadn't an ounce of hayseed in her blood despite having been reared alongside their father's cows. She had revelled, she said, in the freedom of the fields right up to the day when she had taken proper notice of all the fences and discovered claustrophobia. At fifteen she had declared it lucky she hadn't been born a cow, since so few of them had the good sense to either knock down the fences or jump over them.

'Do you remember that photographer at the A&P Show just before the war saying that with my looks I ought to be in Auckland?'

Lizzie nodded. 'A lot's changed since then.'

'Not here it hasn't.' Eve stood up, looked vaguely for her boots and discovered them already placed neatly alongside Lizzie's. 'Except that I'm nearly three years older. Time's running out, Liz.' She sat again, this time on the top step of the porch, hugging her knees and staring out across the damp paddocks. An equally dejected and damp strand of hair curled against her forehead. Lizzie leaned on a veranda post, grinning down at her sister, thinking how incredibly lovely she was in spite of the mud and her bad humour, and how utterly impossible it was to get mad at her. No one had been at all surprised when Eve had won the Manawatu Queen beauty contest hands down at the last big A&P show before the war. A reporter had taken pictures of her for the local paper and said that with a personality and looks like hers she should head up to Auckland and get herself a job as a mannequin in a city store. It had gone to her head a bit at the time, but with the men of the district straining even harder at the leash to escort her to country dances, picnics and the pictures, she had soon forgotten all about it. Or so it had seemed until the war started and boys of an age to interest her had been called up. Many a farmer's son, too, on hearing a call to arms other than Eve's, had volunteered, reserved occupation notwithstanding. As her social life disintegrated around her, she had begun to talk more seriously of leaving home. Their father told her to stop dreaming. The boys would be back. With luck she'd fall for one with a bit of land of his own. She'd settle down soon enough all right. Just like her mother. Took to country life like a duck to water. And look at Lizzie. She'd come running back to Fenton as soon as her teacher-training was over. Couldn't get back quick enough. He'd be obliged if Eve would take a leaf out of her sister's book and stop all her nonsense.

'You'll get over it, girl. City life isn't all it's cracked up to be, you know,' had been his parting shot as he strode off down the paddock that afternoon. Not that he'd have the slightest idea about that, Eve had muttered to Lizzie and to her father's receding back, since he'd never travelled more than fifty miles from the farm in his whole life.

'You'll end up an old maid if you stay here, Liz,' she said. 'Why don't you take the plunge and come with me.'

'And how do you suppose I could do that, even if I wanted to, which I don't. I love my job and the children. I'd hate Auckland. Wellington was bad enough. What makes you think you'll find a spare man up there these days anyway? At least there are a few farmers left.'

'God, Lizzie. They're all over forty!'

Lizzie leaned down to pat her shoulder. 'Cheer up, Sis. Things'll look better in the morning.' And it was true that if events followed their usual course, Eve would have forgotten her city dreams by breakfast time, just as she had forgotten all the other hare-brained ideas that had come hurtling into her life, been declared vital and discarded a couple of days later.

'I'm going, Liz. I'm going to get myself a decent job and a wardrobe full of nice clothes. I'll wear high heels every day, and walk down proper streets with proper pavements. And I'll find myself a husband.' A wide grin lit Eve's face, accompanied by a spluttering chortle. Eve's Impending Hysterics, their father called it. 'It'll be such enormous fun, Lizzie. You'll be really sorry if you don't come too.'

The kitchen window opened behind them.

'Get yourselves washed up, you two,' their mother called. 'Your dad's already in. Tea will be on the table in five minutes.' Her head vanished back inside. The window closed.

'Mother will be worried sick if you go now,' Lizzie said.

'If the Japs invade they're just as likely to land on the coast right here. Besides, what's to worry about? Think of all the American servicemen on R and R in Auckland.'

'I am,' said Lizzie.

On weekdays they ate in the kitchen but Margaret insisted that

Sunday tea was Sunday tea, and so, on Sundays, they ate their evening meal in the cream wall-papered dining room with their feet resting on an elderly floral carpet and the green velvet curtains drawn against the paddocks and rolling hills beyond the flatlands. Margaret's best silver, cut glass water jug and glasses sparkled on the damask cloth. A venerable grandfather clock ticked in the corner.

By the time Eve came downstairs her father was already setting to, working the carving knife against the steel, bringing its blade to satisfying sharpness. She took her usual place opposite Lizzie, flashed a bright smile round the table, picked up her initialled silver napkin ring – a christening present from Cousin Freda – pulled out the well-washed, faded damask square and placed it across her knees. She ignored a warning glance from Lizzie and announced that she had made up her mind to go to Auckland and that this time there was no point in trying to dissuade her. Without pausing for the protest she knew would come, she added that she would be leaving almost immediately.

'You're not going, my girl and that's all there is to it.' Jim, gave the knife edge a final check against his thumb and began slicing the meat. Margaret paused, vegetable spoon in hand, hoping that this time there wouldn't be a row.

'Pass, Lizzie's plate would you, dear?'

Eve obliged, her wide and guileless smile a portent of things to come. Her mother added vegetables from the kitchen garden to the roast lamb and kumara laden plate and handed it to Lizzie.

'Get that in to you, dear. Set you up for the week.'

'I'm going. I've decided.' Eve seemed undismayed by gathering clouds at Jim's end of the table. 'I'm not a child for heaven's sake. I'm nearly twenty two. No potatoes for me thanks, Mother. I'm not going to hang around here forever. I've already written to Cousin Freda. She says I can stay with her any time I like.'

'In a pig's eye you can!' Jim exploded. 'I'm not having you living with that woman. Bloody Commie!'

Margaret sighed. 'I had hoped this would be a pleasant family dinner.'

'There's no reason why it *shouldn't* be pleasant. I'm not the one making it *un*pleasant.' Eve tone was pure sweet reason. She smiled at her father and handed his plate down to her mother for a generous helping of home-grown carrots and cabbage and mashed potato. 'Pass the gravy, Liz.' She ladled the rich brown liquid first onto her father's plate and then her own, placed her hands in her lap, winked at Lizzie and lowered her eyes for Grace.

Jim scowled and cleared his throat. 'Guard our lads out there at the front, Lord, and grant them tucker as good as we are about to enjoy right here in the safety of our home and country. For what we are about to receive may the Lord make us truly thankful. Now, Eve, I don't want to hear another word about it.'

'Amen,' said Margaret. 'How's the Faraday boy, Lizzie? Over the chicken pox yet?'

'Should be better in time for the school concert. And Ellie hasn't caught it, thank heaven.'

'Can't have Cinderella with spots all over her face,' Eve said. 'Or she might have to stay home and marry a farmer.'

Margaret crossed her fingers beneath the ample folds of the tablecloth and swiftly steered the conversation to safer ground. 'That reminds me. I want you to take some eggs and butter to Mrs. Faraday for me, Lizzie. And there are some seed potatoes for Polly out the back.'

Whether due to the crossing of fingers or to a running out of steam, the conversation remained with township topics, comfortably dissecting people, their occupations and idiosyncrasies before moving once more to farming matters, the war and shortages of this and that. They were, after all, a close-knit, loving family, despite Eve's and Jim's occasional fiery, short-lived squabbles. Good country food and satisfied country stomachs no doubt helped. Silver cutlery clinked pleasantly against good china in counterpoint to the mellow ticking of the grandfather clock. It wheezed into importance and chimed the half hour. Margaret glanced round the table well pleased with her brood.

With the washing up done, and the best china put away in the cabinet for another week, Eve carried a tray of tea through to the sitting room. Her father was fiddling as usual with the radio, her mother busy with a basketful of mending. Lizzie crossed to the well-stocked bookcase, chose a small volume of poems and settled in a capacious armchair. Eve poured the tea, put the striped cosy back on the pot and handed round the bluebell-patterned cups and saucers. She took her own cup over to the settee, sat with her legs tucked under her and reached for the magazine Lizzie had brought from town. She flicked through letters to the editor, household hints and recipes. The pages turned more slowly when she reached the fashion section.

Later, in the gabled, rose-wall-papered bedroom the two still shared when Lizzie was at home, she said, 'I can't stand it any more. I'm going. I really am going.'

'Oh, shut up and go to sleep.' Lizzie buried her head in her pillow. She was weary from her day's work and soon slept soundly, not stirring until her father clumped along the passage-way to the bathroom next morning. Sounds of pans and crockery came from the kitchen. She yawned and stretched, glancing across the still dark room. The bundle that was Eve lay curled and probably grumpy under the bedclothes.

'Might as well stay put if you want. I'll give Dad a hand.' Eve's mood, first thing, was often unreliable. If sleep had not erased her plan to leave, she would likely upset the rearranged family apple-cart all over again – a matter, Lizzie thought, best left till after breakfast. She reached for her shirt and dungarees, dressed in the dark and hurried down to the warm, bright kitchen where her father was already sitting down to a cup of tea.

'That sister of yours got her bags all packed then?'

'Still fast asleep.'

Jim raised an eyebrow as if Eve's absence from the kitchen at this hour was in some way unusual. 'Well I'll be blowed! Whoever heard of a farmer's daughter sleeping in?' He drained his cup and pushed back his chair, scraping the linoleum. 'Best leave Lady Muck to her feather bed, then.'

'Jim!' scolded Margaret, referring equally to the lino and his language.

'Righto, where's me gumboots?'

'Right where they always are,' said Margaret.

Lizzie walked with her father down the track then left him to go on to the milking shed while she cut across the paddock. The herd's shadowy bulk waited by the five-barred gate. She thought of Eve still curled up in bed, or perhaps stumbling sleepily downstairs to the kitchen, unaware that yesterday's rain had gone and that the flood-bank was secure. The crisp morning air promised a fine, sunny day. She pushed through the mêlée of warm bodies and unlatched the gate. The undulating river of black, white and brown moved through, its closest parts receiving a friendly slap in passing.

'Heard from the boys lately, Ben?' she called as the first of the cows wandered into their accustomed stalls. Ben Hohepa had been coming to help out with the milking and odd jobs around the place for as long as Lizzie could remember.

'Got a letter last week. Both doing all right, I reckon.' The Maori Battalion was somewhere in Africa, involved in heavy fighting. That much they knew, but little else. Letters home were heavily censored.

Jim, passing with a bucket, paused to give Ben a slap on the back: man talk for 'I understand how you're feeling,' or in more local parlance, 'She'll be right.'

Lizzie moved along the rows, washing udders. 'Tell them I was asking after them when you write, will you, Ben?' It was strange, she thought, that even here where they spent so many companionable hours together, they never really spoke of the fear that was in their hearts – that one day Ben would receive a telegram saying one of the boys had been wounded, or worse. Best not to dwell on it of course, but even so…. She ran her hand over the cow's flank, glad she had no brother out there in the mayhem.

When, two hours later, the last animal had backed out from its stall and made its way through the shed and out into the yard, Lizzie was working in the separator room.

'Righto, girl,' Jim shouted through to her. 'Time for breakfast. Then I'll get you into town. Get that lot back in the paddock would you, Ben?'

Father and daughter were halfway to the house when they spotted Margaret hurrying down the track towards them, her anxious voice audible long before they could make out the words.

'She's gone, Jim!'

'What's she on about?' He increased his stride. Lizzie broke into a run.

'Eve's gone!' her mother called again as the gap between them narrowed.

'Don't be daft,' Jim said. 'She can't have.'

'Jim, she left a note! It was tucked into the milk book. She knew I'd be doing the accounts this morning.'

'Good grief, I never thought she'd really do it,' he muttered, torn, it seemed, between despair at the apparent loss of his daughter and admiration for her spunk. He reached for his wife's shoulder and gave it an awkward pat, his large hand unaccustomed to such gestures, especially in broad daylight. 'Don't worry, love. She won't have got far. Lizzie and me will pick her up on the way to town.'

Back at the house, Lizzie took the stairs two at a time. Eve's bedclothes were in a tumbled heap, just as they had been when, in the near dark, she had thought her still in bed. She stripped off her dungarees, took up the skirt and blouse folded over the rail at the foot of her bed, dressed, snatched up her bag and ran downstairs. There was no point in suggesting Eve was unlikely to come to any harm: the appetising smell of sausages, eggs and bacon emanating from the kitchen hadn't penetrated her father's consciousness enough to suggest breakfast might be in order before setting off in search of his unruly younger daughter. Outside, the engine of the truck roared into life. Lizzie hugged her mother and told her not to worry. She would ring from Polly's house as soon as they got to town. She ran down the steps, hoisted herself into the cab beside her father and was hardly in her seat before they were bumping down the long farm track.

'She can't have got anyone to pick her up, I'd have heard them.'

'She could have hitched a lift on the road,' Lizzie reasoned, thinking Eve must have been long gone by the time she had offered her the luxury of a lie-in. She had probably reached town hours ago. From there she would have had little difficulty hitching more rides all the way to Auckland.

The truck lurched from the track, slewed and sped off down the tree-lined, metalled road. Charlie Cartwright's red Royal Mail van was parked a mile further down. Jim jammed his foot on the brake, bringing the truck alongside and sending mud and gravel skittering from its wheels. The postman, busy sorting a handful of letters in his van, glanced out of the window to see what all the fuss was about. Lizzie looked at her father. He was enjoying himself. She was sure of it.

'Not seen Eve by any chance have you, Charlie?' Jim shouted.

'Should I have?' the postman replied. 'Bit early for your Eve I'd say. Nothing wrong is there?'

'Just run away to Auckland, that's all. Not your problem, Charlie. Daughters! Who'd have 'em, eh?'

'Too right, Jim.' Charlie emerged from his van, letters in hand, and winked at Lizzie. 'Hope you find her all right.'

'So do I, Charlie,' Jim muttered darkly. 'So do I.' Not that there was much he could do when it came down to it. Eve was of age. She had every right to a life of her own. But he didn't want her messing about in a city with all that coming and going of soldiers and sailors and all the rest, and him not there to warn them off. Neither did he want Margaret's cousin Freda filling his younger daughter's head with all sorts of pacifist rubbish. Especially not in the middle of a bloody war. No wonder the woman had never married. No man in his right mind would take her on. The suffragettes had a lot to answer for in his opinion. He slammed the truck into gear and sent it in a forward leap.

Charlie bent to check his elderly van for damage done by pebbles spat up by Jim's equally venerable truck, then watched them go, shaking his head. It was common knowledge that Eve Oakes had more on her agenda than ending up a farmer's wife in the Manawatu, or anywhere else for that matter. You could hardly blame the girl for that. Not with her looks.

'What time did yesterday's overnighter go through?' Jim asked, swerving suddenly to avoid a fallen branch in the road. The truck heeled over like a tacking yacht. Lizzie clutched the dashboard.

'Nine o'clock.' In different circumstances and in a different mood her father would have stopped and got out to heave the branch out of harm's way. 'We'd only just gone to bed. She might've caught the milk train though.'

'Or she could have hitched a lift all the way. We're on a wild goose chase, Liz.'

Which is what Lizzie had realised all along. She was grateful her father had at last come to the same conclusion. There was little point in trekking through the whole province with their quarry already halfway to Auckland.

'She'll be back, Dad.' Lizzie patted her father's arm, thinking he looked a bit like their old farm dog, Jake, when Ben was late with his tucker.

'Why couldn't I have had two daughters like you, Liz? Sensible, like your mother. Would've made life a lot more straightforward.'

'She'll be all right, Dad. Eve's a survivor.'

'God knows how your mother's going to take this.'

'She'll take it very well once she gets used to the idea. Eve was always going to fly the coop one of these days. She wants more than country life has to offer, that's all. Mother has always known that.'

'Well I guess she would at that. Your mother was a bit of a rebel too in her time, y'know. Could've knocked me down with a feather when she agreed to leave Wellington and settle down to life on the farm'

'Well there you go then. Chip off the old block, distaff side. She'll be all right, Dad.'

'So you've said. Several times. C'mon. Let's get you to Polly's and I'll take me and this old jalopy home.' He turned the truck into Fenton's main street, took a hand from the wheel and clapped it to his forehead. 'Damn, I forgot Polly's spuds. Yer Mother'll lynch me.'

He'd miss Eve's high spirits all right even if she was bloody useless around the farm most of the time. He'd have to get on the blower to Ben. See if the old bloke could find time to give him a bit more of a hand, though he was already putting in a couple of days a week at the Sanderson place since their boy joined up. He brought the truck to a shuddering halt alongside Polly Jenkins's picket fence. Lizzie pecked his cheek, promised to come over next weekend, jumped down to the road and stood watching as he sped off the way they had come. As the dust settled behind him on the road, she opened the gate and walked up the newly swept path between flowerbeds and neatly clipped box hedging to her landlady's white-painted, weatherboard bungalow. Polly wouldn't be expecting her to turn up for breakfast. Just as well she kept her larder well stocked. Lizzie was starving.

There was no phone connection at Freda's, so there was nothing for it but to wait, more or less patiently, for a letter from Eve and hope she wouldn't take too long about it. In a second burst of parental outrage Jim threatened to get the police on to it. Margaret told him not to be ridiculous. Eve had a head on her shoulders as well as her dreams. She wasn't likely to come to any harm. They should have let her go last year when she first broached the subject of staying with Freda. There was nothing wrong with a girl her age wanting to see what the world had to offer beyond Fenton. She was sure Auckland wasn't the den of iniquity Jim imagined it to be, nor was Freda the devil incarnate. Their daughter would be perfectly all right and would he please stop going on about it or he'd give her a headache.

'Politics!' Jim muttered darkly. 'Women and politics! Bloody lethal combination.'

'Don't swear, Jim! Freda's all right. Just calls a spade a spade that's all. Some of her ideas are a bit odd maybe, but she's good at heart.'

'Good?' Jim exploded. 'Have you forgotten that summer she

turned up here just after we got married? Said she was writing an article called 'Women in the Field' or some such rubbish. Pestered every woman in the bloody district, then took it into her head to go to that Young Farmers' meeting at the church hall, remember? Nearly caused a bloody riot. Kept sticking up her hand, demanding to know about workers' rights. What would a woman like her know about work? Never set foot in a paddock in her life. Bloody cheek! Nearly got herself lynched.' He sank into the battered brown leather armchair by the kitchen stove. 'She'll be filling up Eve's head with all that commie rubbish. A daughter of mine a bloody Red!'

'Jim, will you please stop swearing! I expect Freda votes for the National Party like the rest of us, whatever she says.'

'Once a Red, always a Red,' said Jim.

A letter duly arrived from Eve telling them she had hitch-hiked to Auckland and was safely ensconced at Freda's. The excitement of her departure, the nearest Fenton had come to a scandal in years, died down. The community settled back into its quiet routine. Then Lizzie wrote to Eve saying that the whole district was abuzz: the Army had set up a training camp just outside the town. If she was still looking for a boyfriend she might as well come home since a field full of potential suitors awaited her. Eve replied that not even two fields of soldiers would persuade her to exchange her high heels for the gumboots and dungarees of Fenton. She was enjoying her job on the beauty counter of Smith and Caughey in Queen Street and fully expected to be moved upstairs to Gowns in the very near future. Besides, she already had a boyfriend. Several in fact. She hoped Lizzie would hurry up and take advantage of the army camp and find one for herself before it was too late.

Trust Eve to find work selling lipstick and face powder, Lizzie thought, when other young women were doing their bit in factories, training as nurses or joining the forces. Land girls were meanwhile still flowing the other way, their patriotic zeal directed towards farms and milking sheds. Those who hadn't scuttled back to their mothers at the first sight of a cow pat agreed with the local girls that providing solace for the newly arrived recruits was a matter of duty as well as pleasure.

The Country Women's Institute did their best to keep an eye on things. Dances were organised in the church hall. With Polly newly elected as President, Eve would have been pleased to know that non-attendance by Lizzie was not an option. She was as much in demand as any of the girls. Not that she let it go to her head like some. Her popularity, she was sure, had rather more to do with the extreme shortage of females than with suddenly acquired good looks. On the rare occasions when she thought about it, she supposed herself rather plain. Since going through the normal insecurities of adolescence, and having to wear spectacles at school because she couldn't decipher the teacher's writing on the blackboard, she had ceased to worry much about her appearance. The angels had been just, she decided, when they handed the family good looks to Eve. A girl with a heart set on winning beauty contests was unlikely, after all, to get far without a pretty face and figure. As it was, she had more dancing partners than she could manage. There were dozens of young men left over after the more confident among them had made their choices among the prettiest girls. Lizzie took the shyest of them under her wing. She was puzzled as to why one – a boy clearly terrified of the young and not-so-young women he was expected to lead around the floor – came so often. When she tried to talk to him, he blushed and turned away. One night, as soon as Charlie Cartwright, who had been inveigled into the job of MC, announced the 'Ladies-Excuse-Me', she tapped him on the shoulder. He turned, his eyes wide as a startled colt. Lizzie put her left hand on his right shoulder, took hold of his left hand with her right, and nudged him backwards towards the dance floor. They had gone twice round the room before he plucked up enough courage to speak. Then he blurted out that he had seen her outside the school with the children weeks ago. He had come to the hall in the hope of meeting her but had been too scared to ask her to dance and wouldn't be dancing with her now if she hadn't asked him first. She held on to him when the music ended, steered him in the direction of the supper room and found a quiet corner where they could sit and talk. She asked him about his home. He came from a small town further north, he said, and had never been away before. What scared him most was thinking about what would happen to his mother and sisters if the Japs landed. Lizzie suspected he was just as scared thinking of what might happen to him when he went off to join the fighting. He looked, she thought, as if the whole weight of the war rested on his thin, young shoulders. Latent confidence blossomed in Lizzie's kindness. They danced again, Paul's arm tight now around her waist. As the music ended in a rippling drum roll, he leaned his cheek for a moment against hers and whispered in her ear that he thought perhaps he loved her. His own ears, she noticed with a surge of tenderness, had turned bright red.

They stood among the crowd of dancers, applauding the quartet: a young saxophonist from the camp, the vicar's wife at the piano and a couple of local boys, too young to go to war, on the drums and double-bass. Paul, seeming two inches taller now, offered Lizzie his arm and led her from the floor. He asked if she would come with him to see the Laurel and Hardy showing on Friday week. She said she would.

The Pathé News screened first. Pictures of tanks in the African desert flickered on the screen. Paul reached for Lizzie's hand. The war that was so very far away loomed closer. There were cheers when the commentator spoke with understated British zeal of 'our brave boys at the front'. Lizzie's throat was suddenly too dry to join in. She was glad when the cartoon started. Soon everyone was chuckling at the one-eyed, spinach-loving sailor and his girlfriend, Olive Oyl, and raising the roof with a vigorous, out-of-tune rendition of 'I'm Popeye The Sailorman'. The Laurel and Hardy film was scratchy, the audience's laughter loud, helping them to forget for a little longer that many in the hall that night would soon be overseas. Afterwards, they walked together back to Polly's gate. Paul kissed Lizzie's cheek, hesitated for a moment then kissed her mouth as well. She hugged him, said she would see him soon and turned away up the front path to the door.

In spite of Eve's chiding, Lizzie wasn't entirely inexperienced in matters of the heart and knew that falling in love didn't necessarily lead to happy-ever-after. The first time she was kissed had been under the mistletoe when she was six years old and her suitor almost seven. They had promised to marry each other when they grew up but by the time he was eight he had decided he didn't want to play with girls any more. Five years on, a farmhand's son had caught her in a fumbling embrace, then told her he was practising for when he was old enough to invite Eve out to the pictures. She had expected things to improve when she arrived in Wellington to be trained as a teacher. Instead, she found that coming home late to the hostel from romantic assignations caused such repercussions with the matron as to have been hardly worthwhile. She was not in love with Paul, but she liked him and would be sad when the time came for him to go.

Three weeks, another dance and two films later, she took him home to meet her parents. The next week, he told her he was being shipped out. He didn't know where. He promised to write. A month went by. It was Polly, seeing her so worried, who telephoned the camp. When Lizzie came in from school, she sat her down with a cup of tea and told her that Paul was dead. He had been killed in a motor accident while on pre-embarkation leave with his family.

Chapter Twelve

As the months went by, The Country Women's Institute pondered on more ways to extend their war effort. Polly suggested a Queen Carnival: they were popular up and down the country and a good way of raising funds. Fenton, she said, might go one better and combine the carnival with a horticultural competition. Not wanting to be left out of things, the farmers put their heads together and decided to put on an agricultural and pastoral show. Committees were formed and after much to-ing and fro-ing between chairmen, a consensus was reached: both events would be combined in one grand occasion. It wouldn't be on the scale of the pre-war A&P shows, of course – entries to the farming section could well prove thin what with so many men in reserved occupations volunteering for the forces – but everyone agreed it was a wonderful idea. Just what was needed to raise funds along with flagging spirits.

The whole district set to in a flurry of busyness. Farmers' wives found jams and preserves tucked away for special occasions in their larders. They kept back enough milk to make more butter, baked bread and biscuits, scones and cakes, and gave up taking sugar in their tea. Farmers and the hands who had stayed at home, or were fortuitously home on leave, fussed over prize stock and spruced up ploughs and carts and harnesses. Girls permed each other's hair and agonised over whether they dared risk the vast extravagance of spending good money and precious clothing coupons on a new ball gown. Those entered in the beauty pageant suffered even greater agonies on the subject of bathing costumes for the swimwear section. With Eve Oakes away in Auckland it was anyone's guess who might win.

Lizzie thought so much talk of hairstyles and all the rest a big fuss about nothing. Her old ball dress would do well enough. Polly thought otherwise and insisted on making her a new one. She had some taffeta, she said, that she had put aside before the war. She had thought of turning it into a bedspread but had never got around to it. She draped the fabric over Lizzie's shoulder, pronounced the colour perfect, set to cutting out the pattern and spent whatever spare time she could find measuring, pinning and sewing. When, at last, Lizzie tried on the finished dress, she had to admit to being pleased.

Cheery strings of bunting had been hung between the telegraph poles along Fenton's main street. Rays of early morning sunshine crept up Polly Jenkins's neat front path, edged round Lizzie's bedroom blind, streamed across improbably bright yellow roses on the blue linoleum and climbed onto the bed. A lusty cockerel crowed in the yard next door and – as if all that were not enough to wake her – Polly rapped loudly on her door, calling that breakfast was already on the table.

Lizzie pushed back the bedclothes and pattered barefoot to the window. She raised the blind and pushed up the sash, disturbing a tui busy in the flax bush outside. It had rained in the night; the garden smelt of grass, damp earth and the flowers in Polly's herbaceous border. The sky had cleared, the already bright canopy broken by a few white fluffs of cloud. She could hear Old Sam clopping down the street with the milk cart. Lizzie leaned out as he stopped by Polly's gate.

'Could you leave an extra pint please, Mr. Edwards?'

'Got it right here. Thought you might need extra. Your dad entering that bull of his this year?'

'Yes he is. You wouldn't believe how pleased he is with him.'

'Red rosette is it?'

'Probably!'

'See you later then. Don't forget you've promised to help out in the big tent this afternoon.'

'I won't.'

Old Sam walked on. A high-sided International grumbled down the other side of the road, heading for the showground. A large bull swayed in the back. The young woman at the wheel slowed as she neared the house. She saw Lizzie at the window and tooted the horn.

'Hi, Lazybones! Town life making you soft?'

Lizzie laughed. 'I suppose you're hoping to get a rosette for that animal of yours again. No chance!'

'We'll see about that.' Gears grated. The truck rattled on down the road.

With breakfast eaten and the dishes washed and put way, Lizzie helped Polly load trays of flowers and vegetables into the back of her elderly Morris Eight.

'Looks like you're entering every single class in the gardening section.'

'Just about.' Polly eased her ample figure into the driver's seat. 'I'll eat my hat if I don't win 'Best in Show' for my kumaras this year.'

More vehicles from outlying farms were making their way through the town. Polly manoeuvred the laden van backwards down the drive. A horn blared as a truck pulled up on the wrong side of the street, blocking her way.

'What the...... .' She stepped smartly on the brake, craning her head to see what was happening.

'I thought the Japs had landed,' she shouted, recognising the occupants and waving at the truck.

Jim wound down his window, grinning. Margaret leaned across from the passenger seat.

'Looks like you've got a load on there, Polly. Got enough room for Lizzie, or shall we take her in the back?'

'Plenty of room. You go on down. We'll follow.'

The showground, a large paddock half a mile out of town, was already in a state of lively chaos when Polly drove in through the open gate and parked alongside Jim's truck. Large posts for the wood-chopping competition had been put ready in their holes the day before. Trucks arrived in a steady stream, disgorging sheep and cattle into pens. Women and teenage boys were setting up trestle tables under canvas awnings, loading them with fresh farm produce and flowers for sale. Farmers and their daughters towed farm implements into place beside the ring where stock would be judged, egg and spoon and sack races run, and members of the pony club would show off their skills. Groups of children ran and shouted, sometimes helping but mostly in the way. The Union Jack and New Zealand Flag, set side by side on the high-poled roof of the big marquee, flapped in the early summer breeze.

Polly went off to deposit her collection of entries in the judging tent, leaving Lizzie and her mother to arrange jams, cakes, vegetables, flowers and pickles in readiness for their customers. Folk from further afield, mindful of the shortage of petrol coupons, arrived in overflowing cars. Soldiers, lucky enough to have hitched a ride, strolled from stall to stall, some on the arms of local girls who had promised to wangle them an invitation to the dance that evening.

When Polly returned from checking out her horticultural

competition to give Margaret a hand, they sent Lizzie off to enjoy herself elsewhere. She found her father under a striped awning with a group of like-minded farmers discussing the merits or otherwise of a new type of electric milking plant. The agent had just finished his demonstration. Jim explained its workings to Lizzie and asked her what she thought. Not that her opinion would make any difference, she realised. Her father was clearly sold on the idea. To humour him, and for her own satisfaction, she gave the matter serious consideration before agreeing with him: it made sense to give it a fair go, she said, new-fangled or not, what with the shortage of farm labour and the constant pleas from the government for farmers to increase their yields. The one good thing about the war, Jim reckoned, careful not to raise his voice in the hearing of men whose sons were away fighting, was that it seemed set on bringing prosperity to the farming community. He reckoned he was about to make a smart investment. The Old Country needed everything they could send.

The sun was high when they wandered over to Margaret's and Polly's stall, stopping along the way for a passing banter with one or two of Jim's drinking friends from town and hailing folk from outlying farms. Margaret, well satisfied with the morning's sales, had set out a picnic lunch on a large white table-cloth spread between tartan rugs. Lizzie and Jim said they were starving. They tucked into egg sandwiches, a lamb pie cooked by Polly and mugs of tea from the thermos until Jim swore he couldn't manage another bite. He belched, begged their pardon and lay back on the grass, his battered, second-best trilby covering his face.

'Right, I'm off, Mother,' Lizzie said, remembering her promise to take a turn at the bar in the refreshment tent. Jim shifted his hat, stirred himself enough to remind her that he would be parading Red Gauntlet in the ring in a couple of hours, closed his eyes and began to snore.

Lizzie pushed her way through the throng of farmers and townsfolk standing at the entrance. It was hot inside the tent, and no less crowded. Jack Edwards and his wife, Elsie, were working flat out behind long trestle tables.

'Am I glad to see you!' Elsie called, spotting Lizzie and throwing her a large, white apron. 'Pop that on, love, and give us a hand. Flight Lieutenant Johnston!' she shouted above the babble to a ginger-haired man in Air Force blue at the far end of the bar. 'This is Lizzie Oakes come to help us out. She's a dab hand with the school milk, I hear, so let's see how well she can handle the beer, eh?'

The airman flashed her a smile, and was reclaimed by jostling, thirsty customers.

For two hours Lizzie filled beer jugs, served hot pies and bags of crisps, enjoyed the banter of the noisy crowd and remained acutely aware of the man in RAF uniform not far along the makeshift bar. She wondered how it could be that a British officer should be in New Zealand when so many of her own countrymen had gone the other way into danger. She grumbled as much to Elsie who said she thought he was connected in some way with the recently erected and heavily camouflaged building out at the coast and would she be a dear and pass him some clean glasses. Lizzie obliged, received a grin for her trouble and wondered if the rumours were true about a top secret system that could warn of impending invasion. The town had taken on a renewed air of importance as the story spread. If the arrival of the army camp had made the war seem less remote, the thought of a concealed installation to spy on an advancing enemy made it even more so. But as the days and weeks passed with no untoward happenings or warnings, gossip over fences had returned to the more pressing matter of decorations for the marquee. The goings-on at the coast had largely been forgotten by everyone, including Lizzie, until now.

She noticed that he used his left arm a little awkwardly. A flying accident perhaps. He was about thirty, maybe a bit younger. And attractive. He met her eye, smiled again with one eyebrow cocked as if trying to guess her thoughts. She turned away, embarrassed at being caught out.

Tom had noticed that Lizzie's finger lacked a ring. Her response to his mute messages had been cool. Perhaps there was a boyfriend somewhere. She was less sophisticated than many of the girls he had known, but pretty in a fresh-faced, country way. He liked the way her blue-grey eyes sparkled behind her serious-looking spectacles and the easy way she joked with the men at the bar. His uniform was usually enough to attract any girl he fancied but not, it seemed, in the case of Lizzie Oakes.

By two thirty the tent had begun to empty as even the most determined drinkers moved back outside to catch the afternoon's judging. Lizzie busied herself among the tables, collecting glasses and carrying them over to where Elsie was working up to her elbows in an enormous suds-filled bowl. She deposited the final load on the table and picked up a tea towel.

'Leave them, dear,' Elsie said. 'Your father'll skin us if you're not there to watch him walk that blessed bull round the ring. Isn't that right, Jack?'

'Isn't what right?'

'Lizzie's off now.'

'Righto.'

Tom was wiping pools of spilled beer from the bar. 'You too, my boy,' Elsie called. 'Jack can cope with the stragglers.'

'Too right, lad. Get Lizzie to show you a thing or two while you're here.'

Lizzie was struggling with an apron tie that had turned into a knot.

'May I?' said Tom coming up behind her.

'Of course,' she answered, turning round to face him and meaning that, yes he might come with her, but not that she needed any assistance. She was aware that her voice had sounded sharp, and was annoyed with herself for being ungracious. This man, a Scot judging by his accent, had done nothing that might cause her offence except to make her wish, just for once, that she had been blessed with Eve's looks and why oh why, if she had to wear spectacles, hadn't she chosen the prettier, more expensive frames from the optician's meagre collection? At the time, she had thought the plainer pair better suited to her position as a serious teacher of small children. She kept her flushed cheeks turned from the cause of her embarrassment and told herself she was being childish. The knot came loose. She pulled the apron over her head and folded it on the bar.

'Come on, then,' she said, attempting normality and not succeeding. 'See you later, Mrs. Edwards, Mr. Edwards.'

She led the way across the lumpy field to the judging ring, pointed out the last of the rosetted heifers leaving with their proud owners and wondered what else to say. She hoped the Flight Lieutenant would think of something, since she could not. That he thought her worse than rude was obvious. She could not know that he was feeling completely nonplussed by her, and equally unsure how to proceed in the matter of getting further acquainted. Various possible questions came to Lizzie's mind; comments about the day to Tom's. All were discarded as intrusive or mundane and left unuttered, then Lizzie came up with the obvious and asked where he was from.

'Scotland,' said Tom. 'I'm a city lad. All this is very new to me.'

And the conversation might have ended there, or started up again only to go down another equally short track, had not help been at hand in the guise of two children hurtling across the field towards them, one seemingly disguised as a sputtering Spitfire, the other holding a ribbon with a curly fleeced lamb gambolling on the other end.

'Miss Oakes! Miss Oakes! Benjie came second!'

Lizzie greeted them with obvious pleasure.

'Well good for Benjie. Flight Lieutenant Johnston, may I introduce two of my pupils. This is Ellie Faraday and this young man is her brother Eddie.'

'I'm going to be a pilot when I grow up,' said Eddie. 'Spitfires. I'm going to shoot down hundreds and hundreds of Japs. Where's your wings?'

'I don't fly,' said Tom, 'No wings.'

The small boy was scornful. 'How come you're in the Air Force then?'

'We don't all fly. There are lots of other exciting things to do.'

'Nothing's as exciting as flying! What's your job then?'

'Aha,' said Tom, tapping the side of his nose. 'I'm not allowed to tell.'

'A secret agent!' Eddie's eight-year old eyes grew into saucers. 'Did you hear that, Ellie? He's a spy! I'm going to tell Mum!' He ran off making staccato gunfire sounds, arms outstretched as he zoomed and banked. Ellie ran after him with Benjie in pursuit, blue ribbon fluttering.

'Sorry about that,' said Lizzie, laughing. 'They're pretty excited.'

'I'd be excited too if my pet lamb had just won a prize.' He looked at her, one eyebrow raised. 'So, you're a teacher?'

'For my sins. Oh look. Here comes Dad with Red Gauntlet.'

From then on it was easy. Tom seemed genuinely interested. He asked about the different breeds, what the judges were looking for, the value of each coloured rosette, and shared her delight when Red Gauntlet was awarded the much coveted champion of champions.

'I'd like to congratulate your father, if I may.'

Lizzie grinned. 'He'd appreciate that.' She ducked under the rope fence and led him to where the bulls were being penned.

'Dad, this is Flight Lieutenant Johnston.'

'Well done, sir.' Tom extended his hand. 'That's a fine looking animal.'

Jim warmed to the young man immediately. He had a good firm handshake too. Always a good sign that.

'Pleased to meet you, son. Saw you earlier doing sterling work in the beer tent.' He clapped him on the shoulder. 'Join us at our table tonight if you like. If no one has a prior claim on you. Lizzie would be glad of the company.'

Lizzie wished the ground would open up and swallow her. She returned her father's grin with daggers, coolly assured Tom that his company would indeed be a pleasure at the dance that evening, then apologised for having to rush off. Her mother, she said, would soon be packing up her stall and would need a hand. Her father's voice came after her as she ran across the field.

'Don't be daft. She won't be shutting shop for another hour at least.' Drat, he thought, turning again to the airman at his side. How on earth was he going to carry on a conversation without Lizzie there to help? One look at the young man's hands and it was obvious he knew bugger all about farming.

'Hold still, for goodness sake, Lizzie. Whatever's got into you?' Margaret had finished struggling with Jim's bow tie in Polly's spare bedroom and was now in Lizzie's, vainly trying to restrain her daughter's wayward mop of hair with pins and combs.

'Oh leave it, Mother. It's no use.' Lizzie reached to pull out the pins, watching her hair spring back around her mirrored face in its usual mouse-coloured frizz. She snatched her evening bag from the dressing table and took out her spectacles. How ridiculous she had been to suppose she might leave them there all evening, blurring everything for vanity's sake. She pushed them onto her nose and glared at her image. 'What's the point. Sow's ears and all that.'

Margaret knew better than to argue. 'Whatever you think best, dear.'

Although more biddable than Eve, when her elder daughter's mind was made up there was really not so very much to choose between them. She wondered if the young man Jim had mentioned might be the cause of Lizzie's unusual concern about her looks. She missed Eve, but remembering the chaos of her younger daughter's preparations in the past, decided that one glamour puss in the family at a time was quite enough.

There was a tap at the door. Polly's head appeared. 'Ready yet?'

'We're having a bit of a problem with Lizzie's hair.'

'Oh,' said Polly, departing again in a rustle of magenta silk.

'Other girls spend hours perming their hair to give it a bit of a curl, Lizzie.'

'Not like mine, Mother. That's the point.'

Polly swished back into the room. 'I got these from Mrs. Platt on the craft stall. Thought I'd wear them myself but talk about mutton dressed as lamb. Might suit you though, Lizzie. Here.' She tucked six wide silver pins studded with turquoise stars into Lizzie's curls. Three delighted faces stared back from the mirror.

'They match my frock perfectly.'

'Must have been meant for you, then. Lucky I spotted them.' Polly whisked Lizzie's spectacles from her nose, popped them into their case and tucked it back in the evening bag she had made to go with the dress. Then Jim barged in wanting to know what all the fuss was about and whether they intended spending the whole night on their titivating.

If the day had been a brilliant success, the dance that followed was a triumph. The ladies of the CWI had transformed the inside of the marquee into a large and magic grotto. Cream-feathered sheaves of toetoe tied with fat multi-coloured paper bows stood round the canvas walls and stage; bunches of balloons, blown up earlier in the day by red-cheeked grandmothers, dangled from paper streamers strung across the roof. Painted light-bulbs glowed red, white and blue above couples dancing to an eight-piece band. Silver cups and coloured rosettes, their winners' names printed on neat white cards, took pride of place on a table garlanded with ferns.

Master of Ceremonies, Charlie Cartwright, called for a drum roll and ten pretty girls walked onto the stage for the evening dress section of the beauty pageant. It was no small satisfaction to Lizzie to see Tom's attention only momentarily diverted as they paraded back and forth and took turns posing in the middle of the stage. The judges conferred. Five semi-finalists were chosen and paraded once again. It was clearly a tight contest but at last a winner was declared and crowned, and Tom was able to resume his interrupted discussion with Jim on farm practice and milking machines.

'Don't get him on to cattle, Tom, or he'll never stop.' Margaret pleaded. 'I don't want to hear the word cow until tomorrow morning's milking. Which reminds me, Jim, go easy on the beer, or you'll have a sore head.'

'Take your partners,' Charlie roared as the new Manawatu Queen left the stage to applause and stamping feet. 'I reckon a slow foxtrot would be in order after all that excitement.'

Tom led Lizzie out onto the floor. They had danced every single dance together, except for two. Those he had dedicated to her mother and Polly. It would have been three if Elsie Edwards hadn't turned him down on account of her aching feet. Lizzie had taken her spectacles from her bag an hour ago, deciding that vanity wasn't worth the annoyance of not knowing if people on the other side of the dance floor were waving to her or someone else. Tom said they suited her. He thought her hair was pretty too and wished she could see for herself the way the little stars caught the coloured lights as he twirled her round the floor.

Lizzie, like every girl who has fallen in love while dancing in a young man's harms, hoped the fairy tale would last forever.

Chapter Thirteen

In the weeks that followed, Lizzie knew that what she felt for Tom was entirely different from Eve's romantic notions, or her own for that matter. It wasn't much like the love affairs in the novels on her mother's bookshelves either, where exotic riders lifted lovely heroines into the saddles of white Arabian steeds and galloped off to secret rendezvous in the desert – or wherever the authors' wild flights of fancy took them. But if what she was experiencing now was true love, and Lizzie was quite sure it was, then it was exactly the way she wanted it to be. Eve, and girls like her, might find the notion odd, but what Lizzie felt was powerful and earthbound, and made her think of fields of mown hay and harvest time. She asked Tom if he thought that seemed silly.

'Absolutely,' he said, and kissed her. 'Anyone with the least bit of sense should feel absolutely silly from time to time.'

'Idiot!' she said, and kissed him back.

Polly took to him in a big way. Her own mother had come from Scotland, she said. Hearing his brogue was music to her ears.

'There's to be no nonsense, mind. It makes no difference that Lizzie's a grown woman. I promised her mother I'd keep an eye on her, and as long as she's under my roof, I intend doing just that. Besides, I don't want either of you doing anything you might regret later.'

Lizzie blushed. Tom looked Polly straight in the eye and said he would allow nothing, absolutely nothing, to harm Lizzie. Startled by the vehemence of his declaration and then clearly pleased, Polly said she was off to the kitchen to make some tea. While she was gone, Tom seemed distracted, calling Lizzie 'Isabel' – not once but twice – and seeming not to notice. Some past girlfriend, Lizzie supposed, though she would rather think it a slip of the tongue, or a pet name. She wondered if she should mention it, and decided not. After tea she asked him – teasing Polly by asking for her approval – if he would like to spend his next weekend leave at the farm. He said he would like nothing better.

'I know Polly approves but I hope it's not getting too serious,' Margaret said to Jim as she put down the phone. 'He could be sent off goodness knows where at any time, like that other boy she liked so much.'

'Jumping the gun a bit aren't you?'

'Well she wouldn't be inviting him home if she wasn't fond of him, would she? Polly thinks she is. And Lizzie's not exactly a here-today-gone-tomorrow type.'

'Like her sister, you mean?' Catching Margaret's reproachful glance, Jim retreated to safer ground. 'I don't think you need worry too much about Lizzie's bloke. Seems to have got himself a nice little number of a job out there at the coast. Only action he's likely to see is what the seagulls drop on him.'

Margaret was at the kitchen window when she saw them coming up the track from the road. She set the kettle on the hob, whisked a batch of warm scones onto one of her best willow-pattern china plates, smoothed her hair and went out onto the porch to welcome them. Lizzie, she thought, looked radiant. Perhaps a trick of the early morning sun though she doubted it.

'Hello, Mother. Hope we're not too early. We got a lift with Charlie. You remember Tom, don't you?'

'Of course I do. How are you Tom?'

'Very well, Mrs. Oakes. It's very kind of you to invite me to stay.'

'Call me Margaret, dear. We don't stand on ceremony here. Come on in. Show Tom up to the spare room will you, Lizzie, then we'll have a cup of tea. You can unpack later.'

'Dad still milking?'

Margaret shook her head. 'He's down at the east paddock. Melody's broken through the fence and got herself into the swamp.'

Lizzie groaned. 'Not again! Is she all right?'

Her mother nodded. 'Ben seems to think so. Found her there this morning. Your dad's taken the tractor down to get her out. She'll be spooked of course.' She glanced at the kitchen clock. 'And now they're behind with the milking.'

'Right,' said Lizzie. 'As soon as we've had a cuppa and you've sampled one of Mother's scones, we'll get to it, eh Tom?'

'Give the poor man time to breathe. He's hardly walked in the door!'

Tom was eager to lend a hand. He'd been born and raised in a dark, northern city and not seen a decent blade of grass, let alone a whole field of it, until he was seven. The school outing that summer had been to a farm. He'd been astonished to discover that the milk in the bottle standing each morning on his mother's doorstep had come from a cow. He'd wanted to milk one ever since. Lizzie grinned. She said she'd show him how it was done and that he'd get more than his fill of grass and cows this weekend if that's what he wanted. She crossed her fingers and hoped it was. It was raining again: soft, silvery mist unlike last night's downpour, the sort of rain Ben described as Rangi's tears. That meant good luck, didn't it? She'd have to ask him. Her father would say it was a load of nonsense, of course, and point out that whatever type of water was falling from the sky, Melody's escapade into the rain-soaked lower paddock was anything but good fortune.

Dressed in some old working clothes of Jim's, with his own belt taking up the slack, and an old oilskin and a spare pair of gumboots, Lizzie reckoned Tom looked the perfect picture of a farmer. He grinned at Margaret and said he hoped he would live up to his appearance. As she watched them go, and in spite of the fears she had expressed to Jim, Margaret felt sure that her daughter had found herself a very suitable young man indeed.

They found Ben up to his waist in the swamp, trying to get a halter round the neck of a very large, very uncooperative and terrified Clydesdale. Jim had the tractor running, ready to haul her out. Melody had worked herself knee-deep into the mud and Ben was having trouble finding a firm enough footing. When Tom offered his assistance Jim gave him a dubious look.

'Not really your sort of thing, I reckon.'

Tom replied if there was one thing he knew about, it was mud. He didn't mention the pack horse that had fallen into a hole in a muddy tributary north of the Ebro and broken its leg; how there had been no question of putting the creature out of its agony until the precious cargo of ammunition had been removed from its back; how he had stood by its head to calm it while the work was done. He remembered the animal quieting, watching him with trusting brown eyes as he spoke soft Spanish words, trusting him still as he pulled out his pistol and fired the coup de grace.

Melody's eyes rolled wickedly as he waded over to her, calling strange words in what Lizzie could only describe as a singsong sort of voice. Beside her on the bank, her father shook his head and muttered, 'Bloody fool.' She crossed her fingers for the second time that morning. Tom reached the Clydesdale, still uttering soft, indecipherable words. Melody ceased struggling almost at once. Lizzie was astonished, and even more so when Tom stood, head bent, listening to the animal's nervous snorting, then nodding as if he understood its meaning. The horse did no more than twitch her ears when he reached for Ben's halter, and stood quietly while he slipped it on. Jim tipped his hat to the back of his head, said, 'Well, I'll be blowed,' and started up the tractor. Lizzie, unaware that she had been holding her breath, exhaled loudly and uncrossed her fingers.

Jim backed steadily away from the bank. The rope took up the slack. Ben gave Melody's huge bulk a hefty shove from the rear and the mud gave up its victim with a reluctant and profitless slurping. Lizzie grinned broadly as Tom continued his quiet discourse with the horse who, finding the mud firmer now beneath her, waded beside him to the bank as if the whole thing had been a fuss about nothing. Jim, speechless for once, climbed down from the tractor, clapped Tom on the shoulder, found his voice and told Ben to take him up to the farmhouse and get Margaret to hunt out some dry clothes for the pair of them. He and Lizzie would check for damage and catch them at the milking shed. And they'd better get a move on. The bloody cows were bellowing fit to bust their udders.

When Tom arrived at the shed with Ben, each now dressed in over-large shirts and trousers, he seemed surprised at all the paraphernalia required for milking. He'd expected milking stools and buckets. Jim and Ben stared at him in amazement.

'Dark Ages, lad,' said Jim. 'Dark Ages.'

'Take no notice of them,' Lizzie said. 'Dad only bought into dairy farming a few years back. Before that it was flax and a house cow or two. He can hand-milk with the best of them. Keep Annabel outside will you, Ben? When I've finished here, I'll give Tom a go at the real thing.'

A numbered tag pierced each cow's ear. Tom asked why, and was told it was so they could tell the animals apart and keep a record of their yield. He said he'd supposed they would have names, not numbers, and received another of Jim's sardonic looks. Then Lizzie was ready for him, a bucket in each hand. He followed her outside, wondering aloud why Annabel had the privilege of a name when all the others didn't.

'Hand reared,' she explained. 'Knows she's special. Don't you, pet?' She placed one strategic bucket beneath the cow's udders, upturned the other for a seat, leaned her head against Annabel's flank and began to milk. It looked easy enough, Tom thought, itching to have a go. Lizzie milked steadily for a while then moved aside to let Tom take over.

'Damp your fingers first. And make sure you keep the bucket wedged between your legs or she'll have it over. Rest your head against her flank. That's right. Now, take hold of her teats, pull down firmly and don't forget to squeeze.'

He did. Nothing happened. He tried again. Annabel turned her head to stare at the novice with an expression best described as astonishment, then turned away, raised her head and bellowed as if he had done her some mortal harm. A well-aimed hoof clanged against the bucket and sent it flying. Milk spilled around Tom's feet. Jim and Ben, observing from the shed door, roared with laughter. Lizzie tried not to smile, and said it would get easier with practice. But Annabel was having none of it. After several more attempts Tom gave in, leaving Lizzie to finish the job.

'Here, lad!' called Jim. 'Come and give me a hand with these.'

Learning how to flush milk from the pipes and what Jim referred to as the releasor proved unproblematic, but when he went to rinse Annabel's milk pail, Jim was at his side in a flash.

'Warm water first, lad, not hot, or you'll have the milk coagulating and sticking to the bloody bucket.'

Later, after a hearty, albeit belated breakfast and time well-earned lingering over a second pot of tea, Jim took Tom off to check a couple of fences. That Tom was enjoying himself was clear. He seemed to fit in easily, not minding Jim's friendly jibes and advice to set him right. He was pronounced a dab hand with the fencing and later in the day elected to stay on the job, preferring the vagaries of number eight wire rather than confront Annabel and her like twice in one day.

At half past six, well content with the day's work and their visitor's willingness to lend a hand, the family tucked into lamb chops and mint sauce, and regaled Margaret yet again with Tom's misadventures in the milking shed.

'Don't worry, lad. You'll soon get the hang of it.' Jim eyed him speculatively. 'Farming interest you then, does it?'

'Very much.' Tom felt at ease with these people and their way of life. He could do worse, he thought, than come back here after the war and take up land of his own. He grinned at Jim. 'Could I make it, do you think? As a farmer?'

'Well you've got a way with horses, that's for sure.' Jim glanced at Lizzie and added, as if it might have some relevance, 'Hate city life, don't you, girl?' She blushed. Margaret quickly changed the subject.

'There's a letter from Eve, Lizzie. On the mantelpiece. You might like to have a look at it later on.'

'How is she?' Lizzie gathered up used plates and cutlery, hoping Tom hadn't noticed her scarlet cheeks. 'It's ages since she wrote.'

'Got her mind on higher things,' said Jim.

'Now, Jim, don't start!' warned Margaret. 'She's doing all

right for herself. They've offered her a job as assistant buyer as well as doing the fashion parades. Your father pretends not to approve, but he's actually quite proud of her.'

'How's Freda's paper going?' asked Lizzie, keen to get back at her father. She turned to Tom. 'Cousin Freda edits some sort of local rag. She tried to inveigle Eve into helping her but I don't think she's had much luck!'

Tom was interested. 'How local?'

'Mostly Auckland. It's called The Workers' Diary. Freda and some of her friends started it up years ago. Very left wing. Dad doesn't approve.'

'Sounds interesting.'

'Oh, now don't go telling me you're a bloody Leftie too,' Jim exclaimed. 'Not a pacifist by any chance are you?'

'Jim, please!' Margaret remonstrated. 'Tom's in the Air Force. Of course he's not a pacifist. Now that's an end to it. You know the rules. No politics at the table.'

The hint was taken and dessert brought in, a rich treacle pudding and custard the like of which Tom said he hadn't tasted in years.

'Time for the news,' said Jim, when they had eaten their fill and more. 'Then an early night. We've a full day tomorrow. You up to it, lad?'

'Indeed I am, sir.'

'Good on you. We'll make a farmer of you all right.'

Chapter Fourteen

As news from the Pacific filtered past the censors' blue pencils, Tom's 'mucking about at the coast,' as Jim had called it, took on a more ominous significance. He wanted Eve home. Margaret wrote to their daughter, tactfully suggesting she might perhaps consider the matter. Jim added a vehement postscript. Neither approach brought the hoped for response. Eve replied that she would come home for Christmas, as she had promised, and not before. In a note enclosed for Lizzie she added that she hoped Tom would be staying around long enough for her to meet him.

But by Christmas, Tom, who had found an ease of heart in Fenton and was sad to leave, was travelling the length of the country inspecting other coastal units. He had known he would be posted elsewhere sooner or later and had not planned to form relationships that would prove hard to break. He wondered if he was in love with Lizzie. Best not enquire too deeply – just accept that their friendship, the affection between them, had meant a lot to him. Knowing her had been very different from the casual affairs and equally casual farewells he had experienced with other women. Even the memory of Maria, a girl he had loved enough to want to marry and who had died with her family in the bombing of Guernica, brought no more now than sadness for her youthful death. He remembered only her long, dark hair caught up in a bandana, her passion for the Republican cause.

Only one face remained sharp and clear in his mind. Passing years had dulled the pain, but not erased it. How could he possibly love Lizzie when it was so terrible to love too deeply, to care so much?

He wrote to Lizzie and tried to tell her how he felt. He ripped up the letter. He thought it probable that the two women would have liked each other, and was surprised by that. They lived on opposite sides of the world in entirely different cultures, yet he was certain that in other circumstances they would have been friends. He began a new letter telling Lizzie how much he missed her. He did not ask her to wait for him.

It was autumn when he arrived in Wellington. The team of scientists and technicians working there under Sir Ernest Marsden had been making important advances. Die-hard generals and captains, battle skills honed in the First World War, were slowly coming to the realization that radar was not a toy devised by youthful technologists for their own amusement, but a likely deciding factor in the outcome of this second war. The Americans had installed a primitive system at Pearl Harbour. The incoming Japanese planes had been spotted. The tragedy was that no one had understood the data well enough to be able to make use of it. Now, with the Americans unable to fulfil their own needs, Admiral Halsey had requested more sets be sent up to the Solomons from New Zealand.

Tom finished his report on the need, or otherwise, for the continued manning of New Zealand's coastal radar units and was granted two days leave. He had kept up a regular and affectionate correspondence with Lizzie and could no longer deny the depth of his feelings for her. He wrote saying he planned to spend his short leave in Fenton. He did not tell her that on his return he was to report directly to Sir Ernest, that he was to be instructed in all there was to know about the improved radar sets and then be posted to the Solomon Islands to assist the Americans.

In spite of the five months since she had seen him, Lizzie's feelings hadn't changed, and Tom's letters reassured her always of his fondness for her. She dared believe he loved her. The thing was, she admitted to Polly, she just couldn't imagine loving anyone else in quite the same way. Polly said it must be Tom's natural Scottish reticence holding him back from telling her the same thing. And, by the way, if they were really set on having a picnic lunch at the coast, she'd found a spare petrol coupon, so they might as well take the van.

Which was just as well, Lizzie thought, as she drove to the station. It was almost winter and the forecast indicated an unpleasant change in the weather.

An unexpected and unkind awkwardness hung between them in the early morning quiet of their reunion at the station. It was as if, Lizzie thought, their expectations had been too high, that they had become strangers with no sign of the ease they had found in their letters. As they drove towards the coast, their conversation was polite, even stilted, encompassing nothing more treacherous than enquiries on Tom's part as to the welfare of her family and on Lizzie's to generalities regarding her work at school.

She parked the van at the end of the road and suggested they climb the dunes and work up an appetite for their picnic. Her unvoiced hope was that the effort of scrambling to the top might also ease the awkwardness between them. If not, it would at least preclude the need for conversation. 'Go easy,' her mother would have said. 'It'll come right in the end.' There's not enough time, Lizzie argued in her head. The day after tomorrow Tom would be gone again.

They stopped on a rise of shifting sand and orange-green pingao to catch their breath. In front of them, the surging Tasman reached seemingly forever, merging with the grey horizon. Twigs and other debris skittered on the beach. Waves crashed, clutched at seaweed cast up by an earlier tide, and retreated, hissing. A lone seagull wheeled above them, its doubting cries echoing the thoughts of the woman on the sand below.

'I'm glad you're not out there,' she said. 'I mean, I know you're doing your bit and that it's selfish of me when there are so many boys away fighting, but......'

'Cold?' he asked. He took a hand from his pocket and put his arm round her shoulder.

'Not really.' She leaned into him anyway, glad of this small contact, hoping it might break the chill between them. She thought how little she really knew him. He never spoke about his work, had told her hardly anything about his life, except for occasional stories of his childhood in Scotland. He had brushed away her questions as to how he had hurt his arm.

'Did you fight in Europe before you came here?' she asked, unable to think of anything else to say and doubting he would tell her anyway.

He stared past her, his gaze reaching far beyond the white-caps.

'Yes, I fought in Europe.' His voice held the same guarded tone he always used when she probed. 'Not this war.'

He didn't explain and Lizzie understood that she had ventured once more into a part of his life that was not hers to share. Which war did he mean, for heaven's sake? The silence she had hoped to break fell again, as wide as a world between them.

'They'll be shipping me out soon.'

She turned to him, stunned.

'Where?'

He shook his head. 'I can't tell you that.'

She looked up at him, searching his eyes for something that would tell her not to be afraid. Instead she found again that dark something in his soul that she could not, was not allowed to reach. His voice was distant, almost formal when he spoke again.

'I nearly didn't come, Lizzie. I thought it would be easier that way. For both of us. But I wanted to say goodbye. To see you again before I left.'

Please, God, no! she thought. Don't let him mean he's never coming back. Please don't let him say that. And then she understood how stupid she had been, how stupid to have thought he meant it when he had spoken of his plans to settle in New Zealand after the war. He was going away, probably to England, and he wasn't coming back. She turned away, not wanting him to see how much it mattered, angry with him for not making it easier for her, for both of them, by writing to her and telling her that he had changed his mind.

'I've a wee present for you,' he said. 'So you won't forget me.'

As if she ever could, or would.

'I hope you'll like it.' He reached into his pocket, uncurled her clenched, cold fingers with his other hand and placed a tiny box in her palm. Lizzie looked at it, at the unreadable expression on his face, and then at the box again. He took it from her and opened it. A diamond ring, tucked in ruby velvet, caught a glimpse of sun that dared intrude between the clouds.

'It should fit,' he said. 'I got Polly to send me that wee gold thing your mother gave you so I'd get the size right.'

She remembered how worried she had been, how Polly had said she wasn't to fret, that the ring was sure to turn up soon. Now she was terrified this even more precious thing would fall and vanish into the sand, never to be found again.

'I could kill you!' she whispered. 'And Polly. I've been so worried.' But not about her mother's ring which she had found tucked in the same corner of her jewellery box where she had left it. 'Just wait till I get my hands on her.'

'I wouldn't do away with her too soon, lassie. She's laid on some supper. Dundee cake and half a bottle of her best sweet sherry. She told me you'd say yes. Else I'd never have plucked up the courage.'

'Of course I'll say yes.' She turned her hand so that he could ease the ring onto her finger, and it seemed that they both sighed with relief. She hugged him, her cheek pressed against his over-coat. The wind was rising, whipping the white-capped waves to a frenzy, closing the clouds again, reminding her of how scared she had been when she first knew she loved him, as scared then as she was now that the war would take him from her.

He stood her from him, gripping her arms, hurting her through her coat. 'They'll give me embarkation leave before I go. If I get permission, would you marry me straight away?'

Lizzie stepped back, startled at what she sensed to be a declaration of desperation as well as love. Of course she wanted to marry him, had longed for him to ask her, so why was she hesitating now?

His hands eased their grip. 'I'm sorry. It's wrong of me to rush you. It's just that I've been thinking all morning Polly must have got it wrong about how you felt, and now I'm terrified some lumping great farmer's lad will spirit you away while I'm gone.'

She laughed and shook her head. 'It's all right, Tom. It is, really. You took me by surprise that's all.'

What was she afraid of? The demons she thought she had seen lurking behind his eyes? She wondered at her excessive imagination. And if she hadn't imagined them, she would marry him anyway and deal with them later. She owed Tom, and herself, as much happiness as they could grasp in this mad, uncertain world at war.

'We'll go out to the farm tomorrow to tell Mother and Dad. Polly will be so pleased.'

'I should hope so,' he said. 'Much as I detest sweet sherry, it'll take more than one glass to calm my nerves.'

The next day was a Sunday so there was no chance of a ride in Charlie Cartwright's mail van. Instead, they hitched a lift in a lorry heading out of town, took a short cut across a couple of fields and arrived at The Oaks just as Margaret and Jim were finishing a mid-morning cup of tea. Tom wasted no time in asking Jim if he might marry his daughter. Not that it would making any difference either way, Lizzie said, bringing her hand from behind her back and showing off her ring: they had spent too much time apart already and had agreed to marry as soon as it could be arranged. Neither of them mentioned Tom's imminent departure.

Her parents were delighted at the news. Jim shook Tom's hand and said he would be proud to have him for his son-in-law. Margaret kissed them both, protested that they had given her no time to organise the wedding, and said she would make more tea. Jim snorted and went off to find a couple of bottles of home brew. Margaret put the kettle on the hob then telephoned Polly. Lizzie must be measured for her wedding dress and a shopping expedition arranged right away. Jim came back with the bottles and four glasses and said he couldn't see what all the fuss was about. With a war on they couldn't afford a fancy wedding anyway.

He drove Tom and Lizzie back to town the following after-noon, dropped them at the station to say their goodbyes and headed for the pub. Considering Margaret's urgent call to Polly on the party line the previous day, and the messages back and forth ever since, it was hardly surprising that word had got out. When he walked in the door several of his cobbers were already at the bar anticipating a celebration. He shouted drinks all round and said he'd known from the start the lad was a good'un. Turn him into a bloody good farmer in no time. As for the wedding. It was going to be a bloody corker!

'Mind you,' he said to Ben in the milking shed next morning. 'I'm still not sure about that chap's politics.' Ben nodded sagely, and pointed out that once the war was over and Tom got himself settled on his own bit of land, he'd see sense. A bloke usually did.

Eve rang to ask what she should wear for her role as bridesmaid.

'Nothing too fancy,' Lizzie said. 'I don't want any fuss.'

Eve chuckled. 'Trust me, kid. I have exquisite taste.'

Her sister was becoming more American by the minute, Lizzie thought, and wasn't at all surprised when the conversation came round to her latest beau. She'd lost count of the number of boyfriends wending their way in and out of her sister's life since she'd left home. This time it was serious, Eve insisted. Lance was a naval officer, American. They would be announcing their engagement quite soon. Lizzie thought it best not to ask what had become of her previous fiancé and was unable to recall for the moment whether this was the second or third time Eve had pronounced herself the almost-proud-owner of an engagement ring.

'Just our secret for the moment, okay, Liz? Mother and Dad have such limited horizons. They might not take too kindly to the thought of an American for a son-in-law.'

'Well, Tom's from Scotland and they seem to have survived that all right.'

'It's not quite the same thing, is it? The States not being part of the Empire and all that. I thought I might invite him down for your wedding, if that's all right with you. They're sure to adore him when they meet him. I did wonder if we might have had a double wedding but Lance says he'd rather get married back home because he's from such a big family. I'm going over there the minute the war ends. Lance says there'll be a surrender any day now. You and Tom must come over as soon as we're settled, Liz. And Mother and Dad, if they can tear themselves away.'

'What does Cousin Freda think of him?'

'Don't ask! Can't stand him. The feeling is mutual. I had a lot of trouble persuading him she's not a communist.'

'Dad thinks she is.'

'I know, but I couldn't have him thinking we have a Red in the family, now could I? I only told a couple of little white lies. Well, I had to. He comes from a very good family. True blue American. I'm dying to meet them. Oh, by the way, she's coming down.'

'Who?'

'Freda. She's not really such a bad old stick. Says to tell you she promises not to stir things up with Dad, though it'll probably take a miracle to stop her having a go at him. She was absolutely wild when the government banned her newspaper. Not conducive to the war effort or something. Must go. This is costing a fortune.'

With that the line went dead. Lizzie stood with the receiver in her hand feeling giddy – a normal state of affairs after a call from Eve – and wondered how she was to tell her parents, without her father flying off the handle, that Cousin Freda was coming down to Fenton. She rang Tom to pass on Eve's news and was surprised when he reacted with some vehemence to the closing of Freda's paper. She told him she wasn't much interested in politics herself but was pleased to hear that he was looking forward to meeting her elderly and somewhat eccentric relative.

Chapter Fifteen

Jim drove into Fenton to meet Eve and Lance from the train and found that his daughter had come alone. He remarked on the impracticality of her high heeled shoes, told her he was glad to see her anyway and where was her latest boyfriend then?

'Lance,' she said coolly, 'has been unexpectedly recalled to duty. How are things at home?'

'Lizzie's running round in circles and your mother's clucking like a broody hen. Weddings! Pity your bloke didn't turn up. Could do with another man about the place at a time like this.'

'Yes, well don't worry. I'll have everything sorted in no time.'

'Strikes me near misses are more your line.'

'I mean,' said Eve, 'that I've helped several of my friends with their last minute wedding hitches and seen them safely up the aisle.'

'Like I said. Always the bridesmaid.'

'Shut up, Dad. Or you can put me on the next train back to Auckland.'

'Truce?' he offered.

'Truce,' she agreed, and turned away to stare at the passing fields.

Things were a little flurried at The Oaks but there was no sign of the chaos implied by Jim. Margaret had prepared a supper tray for Eve who, she remarked, looked pale. Privately she put it down to her daughter's concern for her absent, and probably temporary, American boyfriend. Eve said she wasn't hungry, that 'pale' was the fashion. Jim snorted and would probably have made what, to him, would seem an entirely appropriate remark had Margaret's elbow not been at a convenient distance from his ribs. Fashion or not, Margaret hoped a few days of good, country air would put a bloom on her daughter's complexion. A good square meal wouldn't hurt either. Mannequin parades notwithstanding, the girl needed feeding up.

'I've put you in the guest room,' she said. 'I don't want you keeping Lizzie up all night talking.'

'Come up now,' said Lizzie, reaching for Eve's hand and pulling her to her feet. 'I want to show you my dress.'

Of equal importance was her need to know why her sister hadn't told them anything about Lance beyond giving his apologies to their mother and repeating what she had told their father about his recall to service. Such behaviour in a girl so recently engaged, however secretly – let alone Eve's usual candour regarding her conquests – was extraordinary. It was also necessary to find out exactly when she intended informing their parents of her plans to emigrate.

'I'm hoping you'll leave it until after the reception,' Lizzie said. After she'd left with Tom was what she really meant. Tears were perfectly acceptable at weddings, especially from the mother of the bride, but she had no intention of staying around to witness her father's reaction to the news. Eve, lost in her appraisal of the wedding dress, made no comment.

'I'm a bit of a coward, I suppose,' Lizzie persisted. 'But it is my special day and I don't want any ructions. Freda's being here will ruffle things quite enough, I expect.'

Eve laid the dress across a chair, burst into tears and sat

down on the bed.

'Oh, Eve, I'm so sorry.' Lizzie went to her and wrapped her in her arms. 'I'm being dreadfully selfish. You must be so worried about him.'

Eve pushed her away, fumbled for a handkerchief and said she wouldn't upset Lizzie for the world but it was just awful how badly she had wanted their father to approve of Lance and how much their mother would have adored him. They had planned, she said through more sobs, to announce their engagement at the reception.

'Well, why don't you announce it anyway? I'm sure Lance would want you to. Honestly, Eve, I don't mind. Really I don't. And that way I'll be there to back you up if Dad gets difficult.'

'You don't understand,' Eve said. Lizzie found a clean handkerchief and helped mop up more tears. 'He told me he had lots more leave yet and there'd be no problem getting permission to leave Auckland for a few days. So I said I'd like to write to his mother before we announced it officially and he said his family had just moved and he couldn't remember the new address offhand and he'd have to give it to me later. We were at a dinner dance, sharing a table with some of his friends. He was a bit drunk and when I asked him what he had told his family about me, he gave me this funny look and said he hadn't told them anything. Everyone heard. It went terribly quiet, then they started talking all at once and laughing as if nothing had happened, and the band started up again and he asked me to dance. So I did, because I didn't believe he'd meant it and if I hadn't, I'd have rushed off in tears and made an even bigger fool of myself. He told me he was sorry for what he'd said and that he really did love me. And I thought everything was going to be all right. Then he said I'd been just great but I must have misunderstood about the engagement because he was already married to a girl in Connecticut and he was rejoining his ship in two days. Oh, Lizzie, I could have killed him!'

And so could I, thought Lizzie. No wonder there are wars. She insisted Eve stay right where she was, went to the guest-room for her pyjamas, helped her undress and tucked her up in her old bed.

'What will Mother say?'

'Nothing,' said Lizzie.

'Remember to leave the curtains open so you can wish on the nearest star,' said Eve. Two minutes later she was fast asleep.

Lizzie woke to find Eve's pillow empty and the covers tossed. A rainbow arced across the sky between the open curtains, one end reaching down to the roof of the milking shed. When she was a child, Ben had told Lizzie that rainbows were a sign from Rongo, the god of peace, good harvests and good fortune. She smiled, thinking she would take this one as an omen indicating Tom's making good his promise to Annabel. Given time, he had assured them both, he'd get the hang of all things bovine. She reached for the carved box lying on her bedside table, lifted the lid and unwrapped the folds of soft cloth. Inside was a pounamu pendant, a wedding gift from Ben and further token of good fortune. He had carved the box himself and polished the pounamu to shining hardness. Yesterday, when he gave it to her, he had murmured a Maori blessing and told her that its twisting design symbolised eternity and the bonding of lives.

The bedroom door opened. Eve came in with a breakfast tray. It was time, she said, for Lizzie to get up, unless she had plans for leaving her man alone at the altar.

'How come,' she asked, resting the tray across her sister's knees and sitting beside her on the bed, 'that you've got this husband thing worked out so well and I keep getting it all wrong?'

Lizzie reached for her hand and squeezed it. 'You'll find the right man one day, Sis. I promise.'

Eve forced a smile. 'Better make sure I catch the bouquet, then. Chief bridesmaid's prerogative. Eat up. Got to keep up your strength.'

Lizzie emerged from the bathroom smelling from top to toe of Eve's rose-scented bath salts. Eve then ushered her to the dressing table. Whatever it took, she said, she would tame Lizzie's hair into absolutely the latest style. With her wayward curls brushed, combed and pinned to her sister's satisfaction, Lizzie declared herself delighted with the result while silently doubting it would stay that way long enough to matter. Margaret put her head round the door, saw that her elder daughter had everything under control and went to check on Jim. Eve applied subtle touches of powder, lipstick and mascara then took up the tiny wedding hat and secured it with a pearl-topped hatpin. She arranged its wisp of veiling over Lizzie's eyes and grinned at her in the mirror.

'You,' she said, 'are sensational.' She turned away to take the bridal dress from its hanger and held it open while Lizzie stepped into the slim, calf-length skirt, careful not to crush its pale-cream linen. A warmly-lined, navy-blue coat would be added later, making a going away outfit: a practical and necessary solution to the shortage of clothing coupons. Eve was impressed. She had forgotten how adept Polly Jenkins could be with her needle when she put her heart to it.

'She should show some of her creations in Auckland,' she said. 'I might be able to interest our head buyer.'

Lizzie laughed. 'She'd hate that. She'd have no time for her vegetable garden. She told me she'd never have learned to sew in the first place if her mother hadn't made her choose between that or piano lessons. All she ever wanted was to dig in the garden and make mud pies.'

146

'Talking of mud,' said Eve, glancing at the pair of high-heeled linen shoes by the bed. 'You'd better wear your gumboots to the car.'

Ben had been up since dawn, decking out one of the farm carts and setting off to town with Melody around the time Lizzie noticed the rainbow outside her window. When the family arrived in Fenton in Jim's car, the big Clydesdale was standing by the gate, enjoying the contents of her nosebag while Ben and Polly shared a pot of tea and Anzac biscuits indoors.

After a last minute titivation in Lizzie's bedroom, pinning on corsages and collecting the bridal bouquet from the hall table, the party was pronounced ready to set out for the church. Jim lifted Lizzie into the cart, careful of both his daughter and her dress. Margaret and Polly arranged her on a chair draped with an old blue velvet curtain, then sat themselves on cushions on the bench seat behind her. They looked, Eve said, handing Lizzie her bouquet and taking her seat in front beside her father, just like the Queen of Sheba and her ladies on their way to her coronation. Jim took up the whip and gave it a hearty crack. Melody moved amiably forward with Ben walking at her side.

The church smelled of beeswax and fern. Polly, in spite of the mid-winter season, had worked her usual miracles. Brightly coloured posies from her collection of dried flowers were tucked into white ribbons at the end of each pew. The altar was garlanded with ponga and sweet-scented winter jasmine. The little church was packed. People had come from miles around to wish Lizzie well.

Melody was waiting outside when the bridal couple reappeared. Her only misdemeanour had been to sample a garland or two from the cart. She stood steady under a shower of confetti when Tom and Lizzie climbed aboard and when Ben gave the word, set off at a spanking pace for the hotel, harness bells jingling.

As soon as the guests were mingling, drinks in hand, Jim made a beeline for Freda. He had spotted her across the room, talking her head off to a local town councillor. The man was clearly in dire need of rescue. Jim took his wife's cousin to one side.

'Just wanted to thank you for keeping an eye on Eve.'

'Great girl you've got there. Lizzie too of course,' said Freda. 'I wouldn't worry your head about Eve. She's a survivor.'

'Just like you, eh?'

'Hardly!' Freda guffawed and struck an unlikely approximation of a mannequin's pose in her sensible shoes, well-worn jacket and best tweed skirt. 'But give her time.' She clapped him on the shoulder and sailed off across the room like a small brown frigate, her felt hat, crammed squarely onto iron-grey hair that morning, listing at a jaunty angle. Jim watched her barge through the guests surrounding the bride and groom, take Tom to one side and raise her beer glass. It was probably just as well he wasn't close enough to hear her salute to the man who, if the rumours she had heard were correct, had fought in Spain against Franco.

The bedroom door gave a genteel click as the elderly porter drew it closed behind him. Lizzie was sure he knew. The receptionist downstairs had guessed too. She took off her pretty, ridiculous hat, and found a piece of confetti caught in the veil. She felt, she told Tom later, like a child about to thieve apples from an orchard, excited and just a little bit scared. He busied himself with his own undressing while she changed into her nightgown, another of Polly's masterpieces: a lovely thing of satin edged with white lace and a wide ribbon tied in a bow at the neck. He turned to her and took her in his arms. With no more than the thin stuff of her gown and his cotton robe between them, the last of her shyness sped away into a vastness of overwhelming love. He lifted her onto the bed. She felt his fingers at her throat, loosening the satin bow. Startling, expectant sensations rippled through her. The gown slithered to the floor.

It was still dark when she opened her eyes. She stretched, remembered their love-making, and began to ache for Tom again. She reached to kiss him and felt his lips tighten against hers. His body shuddered, a small movement and then more violently.

'Tom?' she whispered. She shook him gently but he didn't wake. She turned from him to switch on the lamp and as her own eyes grew accustomed to the sudden brightness, saw his pupils moving rapidly beneath his eyelids. He was dreaming, she realised; maybe having a nightmare. She wondered if his mind, free at night to explore things he would not talk about by day, was imagining the enemy he would face all too soon. She thought of Paul, the young soldier from the camp, and remembered how scared he had been. She hadn't thought Tom would be afraid. She touched his cheek. He threw his arm across his face, guarding against some unseen thing, and began mumbling unintelligible words. She caught hold of his arm.

'Tom?' She shook him again. 'What is it?'

His eyes opened, staring, not seeming for a moment to recognise her, or know where he was. Then relief flooded his face. He pulled her to him and began to make love to her, silently, slowly at first and then so urgently that Lizzie's concern for him evaporated in the wonder and sweet pain of it.

When she woke again a chambermaid was at the window pulling back the curtains. Pale strands of sunshine lit the room; footsteps and the clang of trams sounded from the street below. The maid wished her a good-morning, said that breakfast would be served in the dining-room, and left. Tom opened his eyes and smiled up at her. She kissed him and asked if he remembered dreaming in the night. He was quiet for a moment then said that, no, he didn't remember. She poured the tea the maid had left on the bedside cabinet and handed him his cup. He seemed distant, somehow, reminding her of the day at the beach when he had asked her to marry him, the day she had been sure there were things in his life he didn't want to share with her. She wondered if he ever would, if last night's nightmare was bound up, somehow, with the darkness she had seen in him then.

He said little as they dressed, giving monosyllabic answers while Lizzie chattered – in an attempt to keep her own mood on an even keel – about all the things they planned to do that day. Downstairs, in the busyness of the dining room, Tom's mood began to thaw. He, too, talked enthusiastically about their plans and how much he was looking forward to showing her places he had visited during his short time in the capital, and Lizzie showing him the places she had known while training to be a teacher. Perhaps, Lizzie thought, when he reached across the table to take her hand, she had imagined his earlier moodiness. Later, walking the windy streets of Wellington, riding the cable-car and laughing with him over the smallest things, she thought briefly of his nightmare. Excitement and her own sleepiness, she decided, had made it seem worse than it really was.

Back at the hotel, worn out and happy, she allowed Tom to undress her, then fell with him, laughing, onto the bed. She straddled him, unfastening buttons and braces, finding courage to match her curiosity as, little by little, she uncovered then explored his still unfamiliar body. When Tom rolled with her so that she was again beneath him, she drew him into her, intuitively obeying desire and sweeping with him into a roiling ocean. Exquisite currents pulled her deeper until she rose, gasping, on a cresting wave, surging with it until it released her to float, at peace, in its inexplicable, sweet warmth. She uttered a tiny sigh and opened her eyes. Tom's eyes gazed down at her, filled with love and wonder enough to drown her all over again.

Again, sleep came swiftly, deeply; again Lizzie woke in the middle of the night to find Tom muttering at her side. She strained to make out the odd sounding words. Did he speak other languages? She realised again how little she knew of the man she had given herself to so utterly just hours before. She waited until he was quiet and was again settling back into sleep when he abruptly raised himself from his pillow and sat staring at the opposite wall. He shouted what seemed like a warning of great danger and then a name, 'Isabel' – the name he had called her months ago at Polly's. A moment later, he fell back onto his pillow and into a profound sleep, leaving Lizzie wide awake beside him.

Next morning, when the chambermaid had gone, she steeled herself to ask again if he remembered his dream. He had terrified her, she said, attempting a small, unconvincing laugh. He put his teacup on the bedside cabinet and took her hand. He had had such episodes before, he said. There was no need for her to be concerned. He was sorry he had disturbed her sleep. He would try not to do so again.

Although he made valiant efforts to ensure her enjoyment throughout the day, his own pleasure was clearly little more than pretence. Later, when they made love, he seemed detached from her, distracted. Left unfulfilled, she understood what it was to feel jealousy. Had he not been leaving so soon she might have asked him to explain the words he had shouted; might have teased him, even, about sharing her bed with a rival. But he would soon be gone and she would take no risks with the short time they still had together.

There were no more nightmares. Lizzie pushed the shadowy, imagined visitor from her mind. Six days after their arrival in

Wellington, she was on the quayside hugging Tom, telling him to take care, reaching for him again as he turned away to push through the crowd, losing sight of him in the surge of uniforms as he made his way up the gangway. She searched among the men crowding against the rail, found him and waved, glad that he was too far away to see her tears. The gangway rose, hawsers were cast aside. The ship sounded three mournful notes of fare-well as tugs nudged its grey bulk out into the stream. She could no longer be sure which face was Tom's. The ship grew smaller, vulnerable, its human cargo soon no bigger than toy soldiers. It slid behind the headland, the smoke rising from its funnel merging with the greying sky until it too was gone. Lizzie turned away among the sombre groups of fathers, mothers, wives and sisters, and envious younger brothers.

Back in Fenton, her weekdays filled with teaching, her weekends busy at the farm, she might have believed the last few weeks a dream were it not for the aching emptiness inside her, and Tom's letters. He couldn't tell her much, he wrote, except to say he was well and that he loved her. Boredom and mosquitoes were more of a problem than the enemy just now. Some of the chaps had come down with malaria but he had managed to avoid it. He loved her and missed her more than he could say.

Lizzie wrote daily of the farm, the children at school, the smallest happenings in the town. She waited until she was sure, then wrote to tell him she was expecting a baby.

'You look a bit peaky, dear,' the postmistress said when she went to post the letter. 'Missing that husband of yours, I expect.'

Lizzie nodded.

'Ah well, by all accounts it'll be over soon and you'll have him safely home again.' She didn't add that she had received a telegraph that very morning reporting a local boy missing in action somewhere up in the Pacific.

Spring gave way to an early summer. Lizzie left her job and moved back to the farm. As the weeks went by, she reduced her more onerous tasks and occupied herself instead with forays into the vegetable garden and helping her mother in the house. She was eight months pregnant when Charlie Cartwright brought the letter saying Tom had been recalled to London.

Margaret took her weeping daughter in her arms.

'Heavens, Lizzie, don't carry on so. Women have been having babies for centuries while their men are away playing soldiers.'

When the time came and the effort of giving birth exhausted and hurt her so, and Polly and the midwife had come, it was her mother Lizzie wanted most of all. Margaret wiped the sweat from her daughter's face, held her hand through the worst of the pain and, when it was all over, placed her grandchild in Lizzie's arms: a perfect boy-child with wisps of red-gold hair.

Half the world away in Puente Nuevo, the woman Lizzie had briefly imagined to be her ghostly rival – and then forgotten – shared her pain. Doña Elvira had ordered her son from the birthing room an hour ago. Doctor or not, a father had no business there. Roberto paced the hallway, pausing from time to time at the foot of the staircase before joining Don Alfonso in the drawing-room.

'Relax, man!' The doctor handed him a glass of cognac. 'They will call me if I'm needed. This is women's business. Ours, at the moment, is to enjoy this excellent brandy.'

In the high-ceilinged bedroom above, Isabel cried out again. A baby boy slid into the midwife's hands, red faced and bawling. Elvira, satisfied that all was well, kissed her daughter-in-law and went to inform Roberto of his son's safe arrival. A small girl hurtled along the gallery from the nursery, a maid in pursuit.

'It's all right Inés, I'll see to her.' Elvira took the child's hand. 'Come with me, Rosario. You can help me give your Papa the good news.'

'Has my sister come?'

'You have a brother.'

'I want a sister! Tell Mama to send him back!'

'And what would God have to say about that, I wonder? He has sent you a little brother and you will have to make the best of it.' The girl loosed her hand and raced ahead, treading more carefully when she reached the stairs, running again when her feet were safe on the tiles below. She shouted to her father.

'Papa, God has sent the baby!'

He met her in the doorway. The child, arms akimbo, looked up at him and added glumly, 'But it's only a boy.' Roberto smothered his shout of laughter, took Rosario's hand and led her back across the hall. He kissed his mother at the foot of the stairs, told her Don Alfonso was waiting for her in the drawing-room, and went with his small daughter to see his wife and son.

'So all is well, Elvira.'

'Yes, Alfonso. All is well.' Her friend and doctor heard the relief in Doña Elvira's voice, and understood. He had observed Isabel carefully for signs of her former madness, but she had remained strong and healthy in mind and body throughout her second pregnancy; he had kept close watch over Rosario also and found nothing of her mother's former weakness in the child. All was indeed well.

Part Three

Chapter Sixteen

The day was mild for August. The kitchen door stood open, letting in clean smells of hot soapy water and wet linen from the laundry off the porch. Margaret was at the scrubbed wooden table, making shortcrust for an apple pie. Her small red-headed grandson sat in a high-chair nearby, his chubby hands busy with a lump of dough while Vera Lynn sang 'The White Cliffs of Dover' on the wireless. Margaret hummed along, with Hamish adding an occasional offbeat timpani, thumping his dough to dun-coloured flatness with the child-sized rolling pin Jim had carved for him. From the yard outside came the sound of an axe slotting into wood. They were almost at the bit about the valley blooming again when the song stopped mid-note, overcome by static. Margaret's off-key accompaniment trailed into a resigned sigh. She put down her wooden pin, dusted her flour-white hands on her apron and was about to go over to the white-painted dresser and give the wireless a quick, restorative thump when it surged back into life. The clearly enunciated tones of the announcer apologised for the break in the programme and said that an important broadcast was about to be made direct from London. More static followed, then the King's voice crackled over twelve thousand miles of airwaves all the way from England. Margaret clapped her hands to her mouth, then turned and ran to the door.

'Jim, Lizzie, get in here quick!' she shouted. 'The war's over!'

Hamish looked up to see what all the fuss was about. His mother's quick footsteps sounded on the boards outside. Lizzie appeared at the door, wiping her wet hands on her apron. Laundry suds speckled her forearms. Margaret pointed to the wireless as the halting speech continued.

'….to all of them and to the women who shared with them the hardships and dangers of war, I send my proud and grateful thanks. The war is over. You know, I think, that those four words have for the Queen and myself the same significance, simple yet immense, that they have for you….'

'Jim!' Margaret shouted again, this time through the window overlooking the yard. 'Didn't you hear me? The war's over!' The sound of chopping ceased, the abrupt silence shattered by a jubilant oath.

Margaret took her daughter in her arms. Hamish, sensing his own importance diminishing, beat the high chair with his rolling pin and yelled. Lizzie scooped him up, swung him in the air then sat down rather suddenly in her father's big leather armchair by the stove, her face buried in the child's mop of marmalade curls. Jim stomping in, forgot for the first time ever to remove his boots. He lifted Margaret from her feet, received a good-natured scolding for his trouble, kissed her and set her down again. Hamish looked up at his mother, frowning at the fuss.

'Daddy's coming home, Hamish. Daddy's coming home.'

He recognised the name. It belonged to the man in a picture by his bed, a picture that had to do with 'God Bless Daddy' at bedtime and sometimes made Mummy sad. He scrambled to the floor, his attention caught by a bright pink, evidently much-loved, knitted rabbit with impossibly long, floppy ears. Jim put an arm round Margaret while the King finished his speech, then pulled Lizzie up from the armchair and waltzed them both round the room as the radio blasted forth with 'God Save The King' followed by 'God Defend New Zealand.' Lizzie's near sobs of happiness turned to hiccups. Margaret, close to tears herself, reached for her handkerchief, said that was quite enough of Jim's nonsense and that she'd better put the kettle on.

'Tea?' Jim roared. 'How about a couple of bottles of my best home brew!'

But tying up the loose ends of war was more time-consuming and complicated than the too-simple business of starting one. The grey ships that had lost no time in transporting naïve, enthusiastic men and boys far from the tedium of muddy paddocks and wire fences seemed less hurried in the matter of bringing home the survivors of the sand and quagmires, the foxholes and barbed wire of Africa and Europe.

Ben's youngest was one of the first to come. Warm spring days stepped casually aside as others exchanged their tommy guns and tanks for ploughs and tractors, their uniforms for gumboots and corduroy trousers. They yarned with their mates over pints in local pubs, recalling good times and comradeship, vying with each other over tales of heroism. Often drunk and sometimes sober, that summer they drank many toasts to absent friends.

❧ ❖ ❧

A light snow was falling on the small Spanish town of Arcos. Mercedes sat by her window, well wrapped in rugs against the chill, her feet warmed by the hot coals of the calentador. She peered out through the shutters, observing with still sharp eyes the comings and goings in the square below. A handful of men, seeking warmth and company, had gathered round the castañero's brazier on the corner while the more affluent breakfasted on churros dipped in bowls of hot, sweet chocolate in the café. The shoe-black came, ill-clad and shivering, to ply his trade. A stranger appeared from the direction of the main plaza, glanced round the square and went into the café. He reappeared almost immediately. Mercedes watched him walk over to the castañero. He bought a paper cone of chestnuts and stood eating them beside the brazier, glancing from time to time towards the house. Chills that had little to do with the cold outside riffled against Mercedes' skin. The stranger tossed the empty cone into the fire and strolled across the square towards her, disappearing from view as he moved beneath her window. She supposed she would soon hear the doorbell jangle, and Expira's heavy footsteps moving along the passage to answer it. The man's head reappeared, then his dark muffler and coat. He looked up, scanning the house, readjusting his hat and smoothing back the forelock of red hair that had escaped from under its brim. For the briefest moment, Mercedes' eyes met his. She felt her mind tighten like a guitar string too finely tuned, likely to break the moment it is struck. He turned and walked away. The bell had not sounded.

She had recognised him at once in spite of his red hair. She had not expected that. But she had known his eyes. She remembered how they had smiled up at her, burning her mind while the heat of the kitchen stove curled the edges of his photograph. The envelope bringing his second letter had arrived the day before Rosario's birth. It had been bulkier than the first and she had pulled the pages from it, thinking to separate and crumple them, rather than risk the whole not burning quickly. The photograph had fallen to the floor. She had picked it up and seen the man she believed to be the father of Isabel's child, a man whose features spoke of no Spanish ancestry, whose hair and skin and eyes were pale and whose child might well take after him. But Rosario had greeted the world next day with skin the colour of good olive oil, her eyes as dark as that tree's ripened fruit. Tufts of black hair had similarly proclaimed her southern heritage.

As a further blessing, the Virgin had granted the baby a tiny mole beneath her left eyebrow. Mercedes' relief had been profound: Elvira had one just like it, as had several of her forebears. She would be delighted – if she had any doubt about the matter and Mercedes was sure she had not – at this imagined proof of her grandchild's lineage. Had she not known otherwise, Mercedes too might have been fooled. Isabel's secret was secure.

A third letter came after Roberto had taken Isabel and the child to Puente Nuevo. Enclosed was a photograph of the man in military uniform. There were times, Mercedes thought, when it might be deemed fortunate for young men to die in battle, and for young women to tire of waiting for their absent lovers. She had thrown the letter and photograph onto the coals, just as she had before, and watched while first his uniform then his face and smiling eyes had been consumed. She prayed it would be an end of the matter, but more letters had come. Those too she had burned. The last had been sent from a country on the far side of the world. There had been no more.

She struck her cane sharply on the floor. She would tell Expira what she had seen. Dear Expira, always so sensible, so loyal. Footsteps ran up the stairs and along the passageway. A tap sounded on her door. A girl, no more than fourteen, entered.

'Where is Expira?'

'She died, señora. Two months ago. My mother and I care for you now. Do you not remember?'

I am getting old, Mercedes thought. Old and stupid and forgetful. She turned back to the window. The man had gone, a flurry of white flakes obliterating all sign of his coming.

In Puente Nuevo, Isabel was at breakfast with Roberto and his mother. Elvira was immersed in correspondence from friends in Paris, Isabel in a shorter missive from the Mother Superior in Arcos, written at the request of her grandmother's housekeeper. Aware of her increasing frailty, Roberto had invited Doña Mercedes to live with them the previous year but the old lady had refused. Persuading her to leave the house where she had spent her entire life had been impossible then and would prove no easy matter now. Isabel sighed. This time there must be no refusing. Elvira was fond of her and would make her welcome. The children adored her. She put the letter to one side and took up her coffee, thinking to leave the matter until her husband emerged from behind his newspaper.

'My God, it's not possible!'

Elvira looked up from her letter. 'What is it?'

Roberto passed the page to his mother. With a murmured comment that he had matters to attend to, he excused himself and left the room. As Elvira turned her attention to the article, Isabel heard her gasp. Blood had drained from her mother-in-law's face.

The newspaper fell to the table. Federico Martos Estepa, dressed in full military regalia, stared up at her. He had been murdered, his obituary said. His killer, Pedro Valera, a Republican sympathiser, had been incarcerated.

Chapter Seventeen

What must it be like, Lizzie wondered, as the train swayed and rattled along the narrow gauge to Wellington, to father a child and never to have held that child in your arms nor smelt its sweetness. Her excitement at the thought of seeing Tom was accompanied by an awareness that he might have changed. An older woman sitting opposite, her hair newly permed in tight brown waves, told Lizzie that she too was on her way to meet the troopship. Her husband, she confided, was a good man, unassuming and a little shy. Before the war they had worked together in their small-town grocery store, never spending more than a few hours apart. She was afraid he might be different now, that he would think the shop tedious after so much excitement and that he would find her dull. A younger woman, overhearing, turned from the seat in front and told them she had met her husband just a year ago. He had been due for call-up and they had decided to get married right away. They hadn't had time or money for a honeymoon.

'He writes, of course,' she said. 'But it's not the same is it?'

No, it isn't, Lizzie thought, remembering the day, almost three years ago, when Tom had sailed off to only God knew where and she had felt she was losing some vital, newly found part of herself. The crowd had been sombre, and she had felt utterly alone.

Next morning, walking along the wharf with her new friends, jostled by excited men and women, boys and girls, chatting and joking with complete strangers, it felt as if all of their lives were about to begin again. Cargo ships were tied up at the neighbouring wharves, others waited to come in. A warship stood out in the stream, its task done.

A shout went up. Someone had spotted smoke rising from behind the headland. The ship seemed to grow from the sea, a toy at first and then the real thing, steaming across the harbour towards them. Like a film running backwards, Lizzie thought. Except that this time it was the bow of the ship she could see and there would be a happy ending.

Cheery blasts from the funnel drowned out cries of welcome as the ship came alongside and loomed above them. Ropes were thrown and secured. Lizzie looked up at the shouting, waving men crowding against the ship's rail. Tears welled in frustration. She couldn't see him. What if Tom hadn't boarded the ship in London? What if…?

The gangway came down. Men streamed ashore and were swept into a net of grateful, reaching arms. Others seemed hesitant, as if things were not quite as they remembered.

The last of them came down the gangway. She pushed her way through the crowd, looking, looking… Strong hands took hold of her shoulders and spun her round. He pulled her to him, crushing her then releasing her, staring down at her as if he could not believe his eyes. Her own eyes searched his and found behind the reflection of her own chaotic hopes and doubt, a calm, deep pool of sureness. Sighing, she leaned against him, wondering how she could have believed, even for one moment, that he would not come back to her.

'Swing,' Hamish ordered. His grandparents obliged, each taking a small hand and swinging him between them along the platform towards the train approaching from Wellington.

Margaret caught sight of Lizzie at a window as it puffed into the station. Hamish, as excited as any small boy could be all morning, was suddenly shy when a stranger helped his mother down to the platform. This, he supposed, was the mysterious Daddy everyone kept talking about. The Daddy who had come on a ship and was to live with them all at The Oaks. He hid himself among the patterned flowers of his grandmother's Sunday best cotton frock.

'Give him time,' she said as Lizzie bent to hug her son. 'He's been so excited.'

His grandfather had hold of the stranger's hand and was slapping him on the shoulder. The man winked at Hamish and knelt down on the platform, not too close. The small round face topped with marmalade curls appeared from Margaret's skirts and grinned.

'Home,' said Jim, picking up the suitcases and leading the way to the car.

To everyone's pleased surprise, Hamish elected to sit on Tom's lap for the journey home, telling him, in childish syllables translated by Lizzie, how he had helped turn the handle to make ice-cream for tea and that there were some new puppies in the stables.

Tom's face, Lizzie noticed, as they pulled up at The Oaks, was utterly unreadable. Jim said to go on in, he'd bring the bags. With one hand fast over Hamish's and his other arm round Lizzie's waist, Tom followed Margaret up the steps to the front verandah.

'Home,' said Lizzie, smiling up at him as they entered the wide and welcoming hallway.

'Yes,' said Tom. 'Home.'

After a visit to the puppies followed by a hearty meal ending with the promised ice-cream, Hamish's excitement turned to tiredness and grizzles, then louder wails when Lizzie said it was time for bed. She wondered how Tom was taking to this less attractive side of fatherhood. As if on cue, he turned to Hamish saying he had a story to tell him about a very large and friendly bear he had met on the platform at Wellington Railway Station. The wailing reverted to grizzles and a badly hidden glance of interest in Tom's direction. Encouraged, Tom said the bear had given him specific instructions: any stories told about him must be told in bed. The bear would probably be along to listen to them too. He hoisted his intrigued son onto his shoulders and set off upstairs with Lizzie following behind.

Later, with the child fast asleep and cuddled against the big brown teddy bear Tom had tucked earlier into his bed, Lizzie said: 'You're very good at this.'

'Natural reflex,' said Tom. 'Like being good with horses.'

She might have told him then about the farm Jim had his eye on had Margaret not called up the stairs to say the kettle had just boiled and she was making another pot of tea.

'There's a farm coming up for sale a couple of miles from here,' Jim said as soon as they had made themselves comfortable in the sitting room. 'Lizzie mentioned it yet?'

'I was saving it for tomorrow. I thought maybe we'd had enough excitement for one day.'

Jim waved an arm as if casting all possible protests aside. 'Needs a fair amount doing. I wouldn't put you wrong there. You'll have to start small. Make improvements as you go along. Place is going for a song. Old chap wants out. Wife died, son-in-law bought it somewhere in the Pacific. Off to live with his daughter in Levin. Throwing their assets and sorrows into the one pot. We've talked this over, Lizzie's mum and me, and we've decided to help with the down-payment. No, don't interrupt me, lad. We've made up our minds so there's no point arguing. Lizzie has had a look over the house. Reckons it'll do the three of you. Plenty of room for expansion later on. All you have to do is pop along to see Frank Castleton at the bank and Bob's yer uncle.'

'For goodness sake, Jim,' Margaret said, handing him his cup and managing, at last, to get a word in. 'There'll be time for all that tomorrow. Let the boy settle in before you start organising his life.' And noting Tom's non-committal, polite response, it crossed Lizzie's mind that her husband might well be feeling his entire future had been mapped out in his absence. He had not said much about it in his most recent letters but she had taken it for granted that he still wanted to settle in New Zealand. She would follow him to the ends of the earth if she must but it would break her parents' hearts, and possibly her own, if it was in his mind to take his small family back to Scotland.

She told herself she was being ridiculous. Hadn't he agreed, as soon as he entered the house, that this was home?

However important the occasion, the rhythm of country life dictated an early end to the day. Back upstairs, Tom went again with Lizzie to Hamish's room and stood by his bed, watching their sleeping child.

'Don't mind Dad,' Lizzie whispered. 'He's just so pleased to have you back.'

'I'm grateful for your father's interest.' Tom bent to stroke his son's soft, flushed cheek, his face speaking wonderment at his part in the creation of this child. 'And for the way he and your mother have cared for you both while I've been gone.' He straightened, patted Lizzie's shoulder, and promised to speak to Jim in the morning.

'Give it time, Lizzie. This is a very different world to the one Tom's been used to. It'll take him a while to settle down but it'll all work out. It usually does.' Margaret was as wise and pragmatic as ever, her next words surprising: 'You know what I think? I think he's jealous of your Dad. It's a male thing. Deep down where he doesn't even know it himself, he's jealous that another man has been caring for his wife and child. Once he's got a lair of his own he'll be fine, you'll see.' In her mother's opinion, the modern male had made little progress since they all lived in caves. Lizzie elected to leave it at that, at least for the time being and in spite of her certainty that Tom's mood was due to something other than the rate of evolution.

They went to look over the nearby farm the following day. Tom made no comment as they went through the house and Lizzie didn't tell him she had already set her heart on it. As they walked over to the run-down milking shed, she dared ask him if he had changed his mind about becoming a farmer. He stared at her, amazed.

'But this is what I've dreamed of, Lizzie. It's what kept me going all the time I was away, knowing I was coming back to you and Hamish, that we'd start our lives together properly in a place like this.'

Lizzie hugged him with relief, quelling a last insistent doubt and deciding that her mother had been right.

In spite of the generally run down state of the house and farm, the bank manager agreed with Jim: there was nothing a healthy young couple couldn't fix with a bit of time and effort. With Jim on hand to help them get started, they would be making a sensible investment. The previous owner was moving out in a couple of days and had no objection to them getting started on the place right away while the paperwork went through.

Tom set to work next morning, scything tall, neglected grass then borrowing the big mower from The Oaks to finish the job. By the following week Jim was showing him how to fix loose weatherboards and Ben had come over to help repair the roof.

Shiny, corrugated sheets soon replaced old and dubious iron. The bright red roof pointed out by Hamish in one of his picture books would have to wait. The aftermath of the war dictated, among other deprivations in this part of the world and possibly elsewhere, that paint was available only in white or dark forest green. Lizzie stood on the newly weeded front path watching Tom perched on the gable above the porch fixing the broken finial. Her mother was right. He was whistling as cheerfully as a bird building its nest.

With the outside of the house weatherproof and secure, it was time to start indoors. New wallpaper would have to wait, along with red paint, until supplies were again available. Meantime, there were floors and doors and skirtings and broad windowsills to be stripped back to pearl-gold kauri and revarnished. There were bedspreads to be made and new covers for a sofa and a pair of armchairs no longer needed at The Oaks. Polly sent Charlie Cartwright over with a rug for the sitting room.

By April, Lizzie was certain she was pregnant. She worried that it was too soon: the list of things still needing to be done by spring was daunting, and they were planning to buy stock for their first herd next month. A couple of paddocks were in good order but a second child, although much wanted, was well down on their list of priorities.

Tom had no such doubts. He was thrilled, he said, and Hamish would be thrilled too. He'd been going on about babies ever since Christmas when a small boy on a neighbouring farm had said his baby sister had been found under the tree.

'Whatever happened to gooseberry bushes?' said Lizzie.

Hamish appeared at the bedroom door dragging his teddy bear by an arm. Bruno, he said, scrambling up onto the bed, had fallen down and needed a bandage. Tom checked the bear for wounds, assured him no bones were broken and asked if he thought having a baby brother or sister in a few months time might be a good idea.

'Of my very own?' Hamish asked. Satisfied that it would indeed be so he and Tom played polar bears under the big white sheets until it was time to get dressed. They were so very lucky, Lizzie thought, remembering the women whose husbands hadn't come home, or whose marriages had suffered from the long estrangement. And Eve who had still not found the husband she wanted so badly, whose boyfriends still came and went and never stayed for long. The months since Tom's homecoming hadn't always been easy and had brought many readjustments, but Lizzie felt her days blessed. They had rediscovered their love for each other and, in mutual delight, seen it flow around their child.

Sarah was born in November. Then Eve came home for Christmas in a flurry of smart clothes and perfume, bringing presents and her latest boyfriend. According to a letter sent earlier to Lizzie, Derek was a brilliant fashion photographer set on lifting Eve's modelling career to new heights. He was also madly in love with her and would soon be walking her up the aisle.

In spite of Margaret's efforts at peacemaking between Jim and the flamboyant young man, the visit was not a success. Six months later the relationship was over, the row that preceded its ending so public that editors of fashion pages – part-suppliers of Eve's bread and butter – wanted nothing more to do with her. Designers who had clamoured for her to wear their creations on the catwalk ran for cover. She moved back in with Freda, learned shorthand and typing, and began earning her keep by copying articles for the left-wing newspaper – which against all odds was up and running again.

Well, thought Lizzie, one could never accuse Eve of being short of a surprise or two.

Chapter Eighteen

In Puente Nuevo, Rosario had long forgiven the Holy Mother and Her Son for sending her a brother. She had been attending a small, select class of similarly well-born girls for almost a year and nowadays had sisters in abundance – not only among her fellow students but nuns who ruled the convent classroom and seemed impossible to please. On Saturdays, with no requirement to attend either school or Mass, she put aside such tiring things as learning psalms and her catechism. With their maid, Inés, following close behind with her shopping baskets, she walked instead with her small brother to the market by the bridge. Sometimes there were beggars hunched by the bullring's curved white wall hoping for a few centimos. Juan asked why their outstretched hands were so thin. Rosario said God had given them claws instead of fingers. Today, mindful of a lecture on charity from the nuns, she stopped to consider the matter more fully.

'May I give that woman a centimo?' she asked the maid.

'No you may not.'

'The Sisters say that that giving charity is good for the soul.'

'That's different.'

'Why?'

'Because the Caudillo says it is wrong to give money to beggars. He's forbidden it.'

'Why?'

'Because it makes a bad impression and encourages them to be lazy.'

Juan, given an unexpected opportunity to stop and look, stared at a man standing on one leg like a stork in his picture book – except that the stork didn't lean on a stick the way the man did. The boy balanced on one leg to show that he didn't need a stick. The man grinned, showing blackened teeth.

'But they're wearing rags, Inés,' Rosario insisted, determined to win favour from the Holy Mother and so avoid more chastisement from the Sisters. 'And winter's coming. They'll be so cold.'

'They're Reds, child. They don't feel the cold. They're used to it. Anyone would think you'd never seen beggars before.'

Her charity seemingly misplaced and the Holy Mother left unappeased, Rosario began to walk away. Juan caught her hand and pulled her back. He pointed to a man in a threadbare jacket, its sleeve folded and tied with a piece of string where his elbow ought to be.

'Why is his sleeve like that?'

'Because he's had his arm cut off.'

'Why?'

Rosario shrugged. 'Because he's a Red, I expect.'

'Don't be silly,' said Inés. 'Now come along.'

They passed another man propped against the wall, both trouser legs folded much like the other man's sleeve. Juan wanted to ask what had happened to his legs. He glanced up at Inés and decided not to. He thought of Don Ignacio, his father's friend. Don Ignacio wore a jacket with an empty sleeve. So Don Ignacio must be a Red too. He hadn't known his father had friends who were Reds. Reds were Communists and Freemasons. Not that he really understood the words, but he knew such men were bad because Inés and Grandmother Elvira had said so. Don Ignacio wore a black suit like his father, and black shiny shoes, and he had a gold tooth and a clean white shirt, and he had told Juan that the best thing he had ever done in his life was to fight for General Franco. He would have to ask Inés about Reds again when she was in a better mood. Or great-grandmama Mercedes who got a bit muddled sometimes but didn't mind his questions.

Some stalls outside the market hall were festooned with blue and white ceramic pots and plates, others with iron pans and implements. Others still had saddles and bridles for sale. The lottery seller stood with his white stick by the entrance, calling for people to try their luck. The first time Juan had seen him, he had been frightened by the man's strange, white eyes and Inés had explained that he had been made blind in the war. She stopped now to exchange a handful of centimos for a ticket pinned beside the medals on the man's jacket, crossed herself to enhance her luck and ushered the children into the dimmer world of noise and interesting smells indoors. An old woman sat hunched on a stool inside the wide entrance, her knees swathed in rusty skirts to her ankles. Extracting a promise from them to be good, Inés stopped to buy sugared almonds for the children. The crone scooped the nuts into paper cones, twisted the tops and put them into their outstretched hands. She told Inés that gypsies had been seen nearby and warned the children to turn their backs should one appear. Rosario asked why. The old woman leaned closer. A hair protruding from a mole on her chin levelled with Juan's ear.

'They have the Evil Eye. If they see you looking they will turn you into goblins.'

'Be quiet,' Inés said. She nudged the children away, telling them not to be frightened by the woman's nonsense.

'I'm not frightened,' Rosario said. 'I'm never frightened.'

The maid selected bread from a stall and moved on to the next aisle to poke her finger into the glassy eyes of fish and check their freshness. Knowing that the filling of the baskets would take some time, Rosario looked about her, searching for more interesting distractions. She spotted a convent school-friend shopping with her mother.

'May I talk to Francisca?'

The maid looked to where Señora Jimenez stood with her daughter by a vegetable stall, caught her glance and nodded.

'Five minutes,' she said. 'And take Juan with you.'

Rosario led her brother towards the piles of cabbages and carrots. Concealed briefly by a high stack of crates from both Inés and the Jimenez's, she turned towards the door, pulling Juan after her. The almond seller was busy with a customer and did not see them as they slipped outside.

'Where are we going?' Juan asked.

'To find the gypsies. I want to get close enough to see their eyes.'

Several old men were sitting on stone benches in the market courtyard, smoking black tobacco. They were poorly dressed but not so shabbily as the beggars they had seen earlier, and Inés had greeted one or two of them on their way into the market. A better prospect were half a dozen scruffy boys kicking at a stone on the other side of the square. They were thin and dirty enough to be gypsies, Rosario supposed. But it was difficult to tell. She led Juan closer. None seemed the likely possessor of an evil eye, except perhaps the tallest, a boy not much older than herself. Eyes as dark as her own glanced their way, catching Rosario's stare. He stopped the stone with his foot, picked it up and walked towards them, tossing it from hand to hand.

'Guapa,' he murmured, when he was close enough for her to hear.

Rosario was astonished at his cheek. She didn't doubt herself attractive, but it was the first time any boy had dared tell her so. She raised her chin, closed her eyes and sighed, hoping to make clear her annoyance at being addressed in such a way by some-one so inferior. The boy snatched her bag of almonds and ran off, laughing. She would have chased after him into the maze of lanes beside the market had she not seen Inés approaching, almost dropping her baskets in her haste. Francisca Jimenez and her mother trailed behind. People had turned to see what the fuss was about.

'I can't take my eyes off you for a moment!' the maid said coming up to them. 'I credited you with more sense, Rosario. I'll have to tell your Mama how bad you've been.' She wouldn't, of course, since she herself would be the recipient of the reprimand to follow.

'I saw him staring at you,' Francisca whispered as they walked away. 'Were you frightened?'

'I'm not frightened of anyone,' Rosario said. 'Especially gypsies with evil eyes.'

'He stared very hard,' said Juan. 'But I don't think he was a gypsy. I think he was a Red.'

'He's a boy,' Inés said. 'Which is reason enough for your sister not to talk to him.'

'He's a brat,' a woman standing by the lottery seller offered. 'Probably a bastard left behind by the Republicans. May they rot in hell.'

Anxious for their charges' ears, Señora Jimenez and Inés hurried the children on.

Francisca nudged her friend. 'What's a bastard?'

Rosario shrugged.

As usual, while the weather was still fine, the children spent the siesta hour in the garden with their mother. Rosario bent with seeming diligence over an embroidery sampler, her mind on the morning's encounter.

'Mama, if someone is a bastard, what does that mean?'

She picked at a knotted thread, unaware of the shock that replaced her mother's previously calm expression. Isabel rose from the tiled bench without answering and went into the house.

Inés did not put the children to bed that night. The maid who undertook the task would not, or could not, tell them why, so they asked their Grandmother Elvira when they went to her sitting room to say goodnight.

'Inés,' she said, 'had to leave this afternoon to visit her mother.'

'Why?' asked Juan.

'Because she is sick.'

'She wasn't sick this morning,' Rosario said.

'The message came while you were out. Now go to bed.'

'I want to say goodnight to Mother.'

'Not tonight.'

'Is she sick too?'

'She has a headache.'

'I want to say goodnight to Father.'

'Well he's not here, is he, so you can't.'

'Where is he?'

'With your Mother. Now kiss me and go.' She beckoned to the hovering maid.

Rosario had forgotten her newly-discovered word by the time a new maid was found, and could not have imagined, anyway, its significance to her mother regarding her own birth. Nor could she understand why she was confined to the house except for morning attendance at school and going to Mass. Her father, whose only task in Rosario's eyes was to love her and submit to her every whim, remained as unmovable as her mother in the matter of excursions to the market. Her annoyance was confounded when he not only gave Juan permission to join the boys there in their games of football, but gave him a leather ball as well.

'Next time you see him, you can kick that boy instead,' she told him, remembering her stolen almonds.

'If you mean Diego, I expect he could be a professional football player if he wanted to, but he says he's going to be a bullfighter.'

'Then I hope he gets gored,' Rosario said.

When Diego boasted that when he was a matador he would be as rich as Juan's father, Juan, knowing he would never be permitted to follow such an enviable path himself, was generous enough say that his friend would probably be as famous as Manolete.

'I'll have you in my cuadrilla,' Diego said. 'You're light enough on your feet to make a good banderillero. When the time comes, I'll take you with me to Seville.' He looked across the square to where Juan's maid sat gossiping with friends and added with a touch of scorn and to Juan's chagrin: 'When you're old enough not to be babied by a maid, that is. I might even take you to my farm.'

'You haven't got a farm.'

'Not yet. But my mother is seeing Martín Ramirez.'

'The matador?'

'Of course the matador. When he's not travelling with the corrida, he comes into town from his cortijo every week to do that thing to her that makes a woman's belly swell. I've watched them.'

Juan stared at the older boy.

'Is your mother's belly very big?'

'Of course not,' Diego scoffed. 'After he's been with her she lights a candle to the Virgin and tells her not to send a baby.'

Chapter Nineteen

As late spring drifted through Puente Nuevo, on the other side of the world the summer was already over. A small boy, the same age as Juan, ran down a farm track, kicking autumn leaves. He came to the gate and stood waiting for Mr. Cartwright and his bright red Royal Mail van. He hoped Mr. Cartwright would bring his grandson, Simon, with him. Simon was a year older and Hamish's best friend. They had met on Hamish's first day at school. Simon had taken him under his wing, helped him tie his shoelaces and shown him which peg was to be his very own. He had even let Hamish sit with him at his desk. Simon, Hamish told his mother, was very clever.

But at the farm, it was Hamish who knew the way of things, telling Simon how to reach into warm nests to collect eggs from the chickens, and describing in considerable and surprisingly accurate detail where calves and piglets came from. On rainy school holidays, they helped Lizzie in the kitchen, making pastry and inventing new shapes for jam tarts. The hardest part was waiting for them to cook and waiting again until they were cool. They blew on them, put their fingers in the jam, said ouch and blew some more, then crammed them into their giggling, sticky mouths.

This morning there was no Simon, only letters. Three of them.

Two, Hamish thought, looked like the sort to make his mother frown.

'Simon's got a cold. And Mr. Cartwright's got a new van. And there are three letters.'

Lizzie lifted Sarah down from her high chair. The toddler set off towards some coloured wooden blocks left scattered on the hand-knotted rug beside the desk. Lizzie turned her attention to her son. The frown he guessed would come spread over his mother's face when she saw the two brown envelopes.

'More bills?' he asked, shaking his head in such fair imitation of his father that Lizzie laughed.

'More bills,' she confirmed. She sat down at the desk, opened the two envelopes, sighed and put them to one side. The third was blue, from the bank, and informed them that the manager would like them to call in on him next time they were in town to discuss their mortgage.

'Mummy, look at Sarah!'

The little girl had succeeded in solving the oft-explored intricacies of the desk cupboard and was tugging at a box filled with papers of the 'might be needed one day, but not immediately' kind. Lizzie put down the letter just as child and box tumbled to the floor with a double thud and accompanying howl. She lifted her daughter from the scattered pamphlets, clippings and photographs, ascertained she had come to no harm and dumped her, still yelling, on the far side of the rug.

'Keep an eye on her while I fix this would you, Hamish?'

She knelt to gather up the contents of the box, her mind on the mounting bills. A recent outbreak of mastitis had come at a particularly bad time. The badly drained lower paddock by the river was to blame. Or rather, they were to blame themselves for not anticipating the early rains and shifting the herd to higher ground. A new tractor, high on their list of wishes, would have fixed the problem. Instead the field had turned to untimely mud.

'What I wouldn't give,' Lizzie muttered, 'for a sympathetic bank manager.'

Frank Castleton, her father's friend for years and whole-hearted supporter of their decision to buy the farm, had recently retired. The bank's new incumbent, city born and bred, was an entirely different kettle of fish. His power – perceived and actual – wielded over long-time residents of the district, was far from appreciated by most. Several had gone so far as to mutter about taking their business elsewhere and what did he know about farming anyway? A handful admired his business acumen, insisting he was a man for the times. And to be fair, Lizzie thought, more than one local businessman or farmer had reason to be grateful, in the end, for his seeming tight-fistedness.

She picked up a brochure sporting a bright blue tractor. Her father would have been glad to help them out with its purchase but Tom was too proud to ask. It would be hard, she thought, to make a choice between father, husband and bank manager when it came to prizes for obstinacy.

Sarah had stopped howling. Lizzie turned from the scattered papers to see her children engrossed in building a brightly coloured castle. Sarah stood up and placed a yellow wooden block on top.

'Isn't she clever, Mummy!'

Sarah clapped her hands, reached her chubby arms to push the castle over and tumbled, chortling, onto the rug.

'Indeed she is.' Still on her knees, Lizzie held out her arms and gathered them to her. 'What's a new tractor when I have such amazing children?' The discarded brochure lay beside her. She picked it up. 'Here, Sarah, you have it.' Sarah said 'Bwew Twactor' and set about tearing it into pieces. She was, Lizzie suspected, a girl after the bank manager's heart.

She turned back to her task, sorting papers to be thrown out or kept. A long-forgotten cigar box had opened in the tumble.

Tom had put his service papers in it, years ago, for safe-keeping, along with photographs of wartime friends. His demob papers were on top, under them remembered snapshots and small mementoes, and a photograph of Tom she hadn't seen before. He was smiling, unshaven, loading up a donkey and dressed, Lizzie thought, like a French peasant. She would tell him what she had found when he came in for lunch. He'd probably forgotten about the cigar box and would enjoy a nostalgic look through its contents – perhaps remember his adventure with the donkey and tell her about it. She shuffled the papers and photographs into a pile and was about to return them to the box when she saw a stained white card caught in the side. She eased it out. It had been torn and the pieces taped together. She turned it over. Dark eyes stared at her from one of the loveliest faces she had ever seen. A nurse, judging from the white coif covering much of her smooth, dark hair. Lizzie sat back on her heels. An old girlfriend, she supposed. But Tom had kept no other mementoes of past loves. Why this one? It was possibly no more than a draught from the open door that caused goose bumps to rise on her arms. It was an unlikely thought but might this be the woman who had haunted Tom's nightmares in the first days of their marriage? The woman whose name and existence Lizzie had chosen to forget long ago.

Sarah had fallen asleep on the rug, clutching the twice-loved and battered teddy bear brought by Tom from England after the war. Hamish had gone outside to play. Lizzie sorted through the last of the papers from the larger box, put the smaller one on top and returned it to the cupboard. She looked in the desk drawers for the small key to secure the door, and was still searching for it when Hamish came to tell her that the goat was in the vegetable garden. Lizzie closed the drawer, her thoughts distracted by threatened carrot tops and lettuces.

The morning's chores were done, the goat's wooden stake

hammered back into the ground and the animal busy with its task of keeping down the grass when Tom came striding across the yard with Hamish on his shoulders. He ducked him under the lintel with an inch to spare.

'Hey, mind my head!'

'Heavens, laddie, if you grow any taller I'll have to build a new door.' Tom lowered him into his chair, ruffled Sarah's amber curls and turned to give Lizzie a quick hug.

'Mind the spuds,' she scolded, lifting the bowl above her head out of harm's way. It was good to see Tom back to his cheerful self after months of worrying about the farm. The last thing she wanted was to tell him that the bank manager was on their tails again. She chatted cheerfully enough throughout the meal but, later, when Sarah had settled for her nap and Hamish had gone outside again, she poured two mugs of tea and handed Tom the letter. His mood darkened as she had known it would.

'What the hell does he want this time?'

'We are a bit behind with the payments.'

'I told him about the mastitis. He said he'd give us more time.' His chair scraped against the floor. For once Lizzie didn't tell him to mind the lino. 'I'll have it out with him right away.'

'The bank will be closed by the time you get there,' Lizzie said as he reached for the phone. 'Finish your tea.'

Tom's hand stopped above the photographs she had left lying on the desk. His face changed from anger to something else. Lizzie's fingers, cradling her mug of tea, felt cold.

'Who is she?'

'No one.' He picked up the phone. 'Her name's Isabel. A nurse. I was wounded.' He asked the operator to put him through to the bank, made an appointment for the following morning and went outside without another word.

Lizzie went to the desk, took up the photographs and put them in the drawer.

'There's no need for you to come,' Tom said when Lizzie came into the kitchen next morning after breakfast wearing her town coat.

'I need a few things from the store,' she answered. 'No point making a special trip. I've told the children they'll be spending the day with Mum and Dad.'

Hamish came in from the hall, his arms half in and half out of his coat. 'Grandma probably needs a hand with a few things,' he said in a tone that brooked no argument and referred, no doubt, to the ice-cream churn.

Tom was silent on the drive to The Oaks, except once when he spoke sharply to Hamish for teasing Sarah. The image of the woman in her nurse's cap seemed etched on the windscreen in front of Lizzie. How much, she wondered, feeling a surge of long-forgotten jealousy, had Tom's mood to do with their problems at the farm and how much with the torn picture?

Their arrival at the bank was entirely different from visits to old Mr. Castleton. Rather than being welcomed like friends and ushered immediately into his comfortable office, they were kept waiting for almost half an hour in a small and starkly modern reception area. When, at last, they were shown into the larger but now equally unfriendly office, the unsmiling secretary put their files on the desk as if the contents might be suspect and left the room. The manager checked his watch, offered a cursory good morning, opened a file, perused it, closed it and opened another. He was taking his time, Lizzie thought, in coming to the point. The secretary returned with a tray of tea and biscuits. Chocolate biscuits! Might the impending bombshell be even more serious than they had imagined? The manager looked up, took a sip of tea and returned his attention to the files. The silence overlaying the quiet rustling of paper was unbearable.

'I understand poor drainage had a lot to do with that mastitis business,' he said at last. Lizzie was about to retort that if they'd had a new tractor, they wouldn't have poor drainage, then thought better of it. There was no point in antagonising the man.

'From these figures it would seem you've pulled through rather well,' he said. 'I see no reason why the bank shouldn't advance you the loan. A new tractor would see those paddocks fixed up pretty smartly, I should imagine. Yes. Good idea. Best get on to it right away.'

He could have knocked Lizzie down with the proverbial feather.

'You must, of course, continue to be diligent. Make cutbacks where you can. Can't have you falling behind with your mortgage.'

'Pompous ass!' Tom muttered as they drove off. 'What would he know about cutbacks.'

'We've got the loan,' said Lizzie. 'That's all that matters. In a couple of years we'll wonder what we were worrying about.'

Dawn was still a long way off when Lizzie opened her eyes. One of the children must have woken her: it wouldn't be the first time Hamish had taken it into his head to get up to play in the middle of the night. She got out of bed. Tom stirred and grunted. She told him to go back to sleep. She was at the door when he began to mutter.

'What's that, dear?'

Instead of answering, he continued with his mumbling, making sounds that reminded her of the odd language he had used years ago in his nightmares. Lizzie stroked his shoulder.

'Hush, dear.'

Instead of quieting, the mumbling became an agitated, incomprehensible babbling and then a shout of warning followed by a woman's name. The name of the woman in the photograph. He was quiet again by the time Hamish hurtled into the room and into his mother's arms, screaming that a monster was coming after him. She held him tight.

'There's no monster, Hamish'

'Yes there is, there is, there is! I heard it.'

'It was just Daddy having a bad dream.'

Her son clung to her, his screams subsiding into hiccups.

'Promise?'

'Yes, I promise.'

The screams had penetrated Tom's nightmare. He felt a cool hand touch his forehead. Lizzie's hand. He opened his eyes. Hamish was leaning against the bed, staring at him. He struggled to sit up.

'Whassamatter?'

'Stay where you are,' said Lizzie. 'I'll get you something to help you get back to sleep.'

'I'm fine,' he insisted. 'Hamish, laddie, what's wrong?'

'He thought you were a monster.'

'Why did you make that noise, Daddy?'

'Did I make a noise? I'm sorry, laddie. I don't remember.'

'I'm going to put Hamish to bed,' Lizzie said. 'Then I'm going to make a cup of tea. I don't know about you but I could do with one.'

'Sounds like a good idea.'

'Mummy, I can't possibly go back to bed. There might be another monster in my room. A real one. Or a ghost.'

'Well how about I come with you to make sure they've gone,' said Tom, 'while Mummy makes me a cup of tea.'

'He went out like a light,' he said when he joined Lizzie not long after in the kitchen. 'After I'd checked for lions under the bed and bears in the wardrobe. Sarah seems to have missed all the excitement. She's sleeping like a log.'

Lizzie poured a mug of tea and passed it across the scrubbed wood of the kitchen table.

'Tom, we have to talk. Really talk.'

'I know.'

'Is it the photograph?'

He pushed the mug away and dropped his head into his hands.

'Tell me, love, please. Whatever it is, it won't change the way I feel about you. It couldn't.'

'I know. That's not why I didn't tell you before. It's just that I've tried so hard not to remember.'

Slowly, painfully as if lifting a dressing from a still-raw wound, he told her: told how he had served in Spain, his passion for the Republican cause, the fight for democracy; how Franco's rebel forces had opened the dams of the Pyrenean tributaries to the River Ebro leaving them trapped with little cover and short of supplies. He told of the order not to retreat, of the sweltering heat, the relentless bombardment; of Franco's dream of total annihilation. Ten years on, the sounds and sights of the battle-field were no less clear. He heard planes roar overhead intent on obliterating the ill-equipped, near starving and desperate, disparate groups moving forward, falling back, going forward again and again. He saw bombed towns and bridges, comrades lying dead and wounded, saw an enemy officer coming towards his hiding place just feet from where Dan lay sprawled across his victim. He felt the excruciating pain as he raised his gun, remembered Roberto's eyes meeting his for one brief moment as the doctor knelt to tighten Danny's tourniquet. He told Lizzie he must have lost consciousness because the next thing he knew he was in a hospital bed staring up into a pair of obsidian, hostile eyes. Isabel's eyes. He told her how she had nursed him in the poorly equipped monastery-turned-hospital, that she was lovely and brave and that they had come to love each other. Finally, he told her of the journey to Burgos, and of the rape he could do do nothing to prevent.

'Do you still love her?'

'I don't know,' he said. 'I don't even know if she's still alive. But it seems I can't forget her. I'm sorry.'

He tried to tell her that what he felt for her was different, that life without her wouldn't be worth living. The words wouldn't come. Did he still love Isabel? Perhaps. Even after his marriage he had cared for her enough to revenge her pain.

He couldn't bring himself to tell Lizzie about that.

Chapter Twenty

Doña Mercedes had been living at the Casa del Rosal with Isabel and her family for almost three years when Doña Elvira, apparently in good health, surprised them all by dying shortly after the demise of her old friend and doctor, Don Alfonso. On The Day of the Virgin the family was in mourning.

Isabel was in her room. Her maid, Carmela, had helped her dress and gone downstairs. She turned to her mirror, tweaking her black lace mantilla so that it fell just so. Her dress was not new. It would have been an unnecessary expense, even for a festival such as this, and thoughtless to blatantly express her privileged situation while so many of her countrymen still lived lives of appalling hardship. Many still went from one period of mourning to the next without pause. Franco's war, waged to set the people free from the scourge of the Republic, to bring them back to God's beneficence, had ended more than ten years ago. Yet the poor still numbered in their millions. The people of Spain were starving. Bread rationing had ended only after the fortunately excellent wheat harvest the previous year. It was ironic, then, that few could afford the loaves now available while those who had the means to do so made unashamed use of the black market. She had heard talk of such poverty among the Andalucían people, and doubtless elsewhere, that families had nothing better to eat than cabbage leaves supplemented with weeds and thistles. They were dying, as a consequence, of slow starvation as well as sickness and disease. Tuberculosis had been rife for years in the surrounding villages. She had asked Roberto many times to explain to her the true state of things, but he had merely patted her hand and said that things would improve in time. When she suggested that perhaps Franco and his advisers no longer knew what they were doing, he told her that to meddle in men's affairs was unwise. For her children's sake, and his, she had pushed her wider concerns to one side, grateful that her countrymen still counted the bullfight among their blessings and that the demand for Álvarez bulls was as high as ever. She touched her fingers to the crucifix at her throat and turned to leave the room, her black skirts rustling.

She paused downstairs in the doorway of the still sumptuous drawing-room. Proud Álvarez ancestors looked out from their portraits as they always had, unaware that the furnishings were a little faded now. Roberto stood by the window. Rosario performed pirouettes nearby, lit by spotlights of sun. Pools of it shimmered on the black silk of her swirling skirt. Mercedes, frail now, sat in a high-backed armchair by the open doors leading out onto the patio, her black lace fan stirring lethargic, rose-scented air. Juan, in a scaled-down captain's uniform with a black arm-band on its sleeve, stood quiet and attentive at her side.

Rosario dropped into a curtsey. 'I shall be the prettiest girl in the whole parade, don't you think, Papa?' She smiled up at him, her head tipped to one side,

'Indeed you will.' He took her hand, raised her from her curtsey and turned with her to where Isabel stood framed in the doorway. 'And your mother will be the most beautiful woman.'

Rosario twirled away towards Mercedes' chair. 'I wish you were coming with us, abuelita. Then you would see how everyone will look at me.'

The fan snapped shut. Mercedes reached to tap her sharply on the wrist. 'Where did you learn such vanity, child?'

Isabel looked at them, smiling. 'From her father, I imagine. You pay her too many compliments, Roberto.'

'She reminds me of you when you were her age,' he said. 'Do you remember, Doña Mercedes? She tried to flirt with me.'

Isabel smiled again, remembering a long ago Day of the Virgin when she had thought herself entirely grown up. She had wanted Roberto to think so too.

'I'm touched that you remember.'

'How could I forget you in that dress! It had so many lace frills, I thought you were a meringue!'

'Go,' Mercedes said. 'Or you will make me laugh and then I shall cough.'

She watched them go, glad of their happiness, grateful for her part in it. The rose-bush stirred outside, lulling her with its perfume. Her fan fell to her lap as she closed her eyes.

Francisca, Rosario's best friend, was waiting with her mother at the corner of the street. The girls greeted one another as if they hadn't met in weeks, admired each other's dresses and linked hands to walk together to the church. Juan hung back, disinterested in their girlish talk. Their parents came a little way behind, delighted by the enchanting picture made by their daughters. Circlets of pink rosebuds, cut from the Casa del Rosal's garden that morning, crowned white veils covering long, dark hair. Two brides, Isabel thought. One dressed in black. She pushed away a memory that came, unbidden, to her mind. There would be no mourning for her daughter, no secrets when the time came for her to marry.

Thoughts of her own wedding no longer brought her pain. The evil done to her by Federico had, in a sense, been mitigated by the manner of his death and her certainty that he had been sent straight to hell to be consumed forever by its agonies. Pedro Valera, whoever he may be and whatever his reasons for murdering Federico, had done her a service. She thanked him silently and squeezed Roberto's arm, feeling, as always, gratitude for his goodness. Closing her mind to any lingering dark thoughts, she turned to Francisca's mother, saying how pretty her daughter looked in her frilled, white satin dress. Roberto whispered 'meringue' in her other ear. She pinched him hard, then pinched her own arm to stop herself from laughing.

A poster of the matador, Martín Ramírez, caught Juan's eye. This morning, the citizens of Puente Nuevo were honouring the Virgin; this afternoon, they would go to the bullring for the corrida. Ramírez had chosen to fight Álvarez bulls and the aficionados had been laying bets all week. Juan hoped Diego would be there. The boys at the market had proved poor company without him. His schoolfriends, much as he enjoyed their games, were no match either.

Roberto, too, was thinking of the corrida, of his bulls, and of Martín Ramírez. It was almost a year since the matador had last appeared in Puente Nuevo. Roberto, in his role of President of the Bullfight, had met with him briefly the previous morning and seen him later in the street. The woman on Ramírez's arm had caught Roberto's eye and turned away. He thought, for an instant, that he recognised her, then changed his mind. There was really very little similarity. He had not seen her for a dozen years and Josefa would have changed. Besides, it was scarcely likely, impossible even, that his cousin's widow would consort with a bull-fighter, however wealthy or famous and no matter her own circumstances.

Roberto had had as little as possible to do with Federico after the Civil War ended. He had heard, of course, that Josefa had left her husband and taken their child with her. It would have been a simple matter for Federico to have had them returned to him, but he had not done so. Gossip had it that he thought himself well rid of them, even that the child had been fathered by another man. Roberto had met Josefa only briefly at his own wedding, but had formed enough of an opinion of her to preclude any such possibility. The silent woman had clearly been terrified of her husband. He felt no pity for Federico, either for the loss of his wife and son or for the manner of his death. He had attended the funeral, Josefa had not. He had made no enquiries as to her well-being and supposed she had long since returned to her own family. Troubled by memories evoked by Ramirez's companion, Roberto wondered if perhaps he should make enquiries as to the welfare of Federico's son.

They were at the bridge now, mingling with others who had joined their progress to the church. People called greetings and paused to ask after the well-being of this one or that. Some dropped alms into the hands of beggars; others, believing the Caudillo right in declaring such encouragement bad, if not for the stomachs of the beggars, then assuredly for their souls, gave glances of disapproval. Finely attired young men clattered by on horse-back, raising wide-brimmed Cordoban hats to perambulating acquaintances and calling to less affluent citizens to clear the way. A phalanx of them trotted towards a teenage boy standing in the middle of the bridge, its leader seeming not to have made up his mind whether to ride round or over him. The boy leapt on to the parapet at the last moment and stood there, his hands on his hips, fearless of the chasm beneath him. As the riders passed, he doffed his cap then dropped in a graceful movement to sit, legs dangling.

'Sister Catarina says I may have a vocation,' Francisca said to Rosario as they, too, set off across the bridge. 'I shall become a nun.'

'I thought you wanted to marry Luis.'

'I've changed my mind.'

Rosario moved an arm's length away to study her. Yes, she thought, her friend would look well in a habit.

'I shall marry,' she said, moving close again. 'Sister Catarina says I have absolutely no vocation at all.'

'Who will you marry, do you think?'

'Someone handsome and very rich. It's important to have good connections.'

Francisca nudged her. 'That boy is staring at us.'

Rosario had already seen him on the parapet and recognised him. Juan had pointed him out to her in the street some months ago. Diego Montero, he said, was his closest friend and destined to become a famous matador. She had replied that she was not impressed by his choice of playmates, and wasn't Diego the name of the boy who had stolen her almonds and caused her so much trouble? Juan, she remembered, had been devastated when the boy had moved away from the town.

They were almost level with him now, then close enough to hear his murmured 'guapa' as they passed.

'He meant you, Rosario. He was looking at you!' Francisca was shocked that someone dressed like a farmhand, however handsome, should have the temerity to speak to either of them, let alone utter a piropo in the guise of a compliment to her friend.

'I hope he falls into the gorge.' Rosario said. She tugged Francisca's hand, quickening their steps to the other side of the bridge.

At the Casa del Rosal, Carmela had filled a small jug of freshly squeezed orange juice and taken it to Doña Mercedes. The old lady was drowsing in her chair. The maid tiptoed out again, leaving the door ajar so that she would hear her call when she woke. But Mercedes was not sleeping. She was remembering how her daughter had loved the scent of roses, how the sight and smell of them had given her comfort throughout the travail of Isabel's birth so many years before. The Angel of Death had shared her watch for two days and nights, but with God's grace, her daughter and the baby had survived.

'You loved your husband too well,' Mercedes murmured. 'And he you. A shame he did not love you well enough to stay out of your bed.'

Three more pregnancies had followed, all ending in blood and sorrow, the fourth in her daughter's death. From sorrow, joy; from joy, sorrow, Mercedes reasoned. That is the way God wills it. But he is a cruel God. The roses nodded. Such beauty, such wicked thorns. Her fan slipped unnoticed to the floor

A figure appeared beside the rose bush. The maid perhaps? The shadow moved and became a man. Eduardo then. Her son come to visit her at last.

Too many years had passed since her youngest child had left her. She remembered the pain of his going, how he had said that, although a monarchist, he would rather give his life for the Republican cause, declare himself a communist even, than accept Francisco Franco Bahamonde as his country's leader. Like his king, he would go into exile. She had cried, pleaded with him and told him that he shamed her. When he fled to Mexico rather than endanger his family, she had let it be supposed that he had died in Franco's service. She suspected that Roberto had learned the truth and used his influence – as had his cousin Federico – to prevent reprisals, ostracism at the very least, from being visited on Isabel and herself. For her granddaughter's sake she had chosen to forget him.

'Ay, my son,' she muttered to the silent figure in the garden, 'Who am I to speak of your shame? A mother's heart suffers a greater dishonour when it denies her child a place to rest.'

Sunlight brushed the shadowed face and she saw it was not

Eduardo after all, but the image of him. He leaned towards her, hand outstretched, offering a single, perfect rose. She took it, smiling, and reached to touch his face. 'Your son was good,' she said. 'He understood what I could not, but I have seen things. Such evil things!'

He held out his hand, raised her from her chair, and led her out into the sun-filled garden.

On the other side of town, the Mass had ended. A silver litter stood by the Virgin waiting to convey her through the streets. Early that morning, women had come to dress her in a deep blue velvet cloak, heavy with jewels and silver thread. On her head they had placed a crown, an exotic, fragile thing of silver filigree.

The people made their obeisance and drifted out into the sunlit courtyard. The children came first. Miniature brides were ushered to the front of a slowly forming column. Taller bride-sisters stood behind; then came brothers: small captains and generals in scaled-down uniforms. Nuns hovered, ensuring good behaviour.

The priest had remained inside the church to oversee the Virgin's safe transfer to her litter. Her bearers arranged themselves three on each side then stooped as one, muscles bulging, as they lifted the unwieldy conveyance and their Lady to their shoulders. The priest crossed to the portal to check his waiting flock. Satisfied that all was as it should be both inside and out, he walked down the wide steps and crossed the courtyard to stand between two black-garbed acolytes at the head of the procession.

A sigh rippled through the crowd. Their Virgin was coming. She appeared in the doorway and began moving towards them. A cortège of widows, well-born women of the Order, their faces hidden behind black mantillas, stepped into place behind her. The priest raised his staff and the people set off like a slow tide carrying its brilliant queen.

Rich and poor had crowded into the narrow streets to watch, not minding when they were pushed back against hard, high stone walls as the families of the confraternity passed by with their Virgin. Today was her festival and those who prayed to her sisters in other churches had come to honour her in their name. Grown men cried 'Madre!' and fell to their knees. The woman they called Mother stared ahead, as impervious to their adoration as she was to the widows not of her entourage. Dressed in shabby black with rough cloth shawls covering their heads, they gazed up at her in the simple, unshakeable belief that she and her equally adored likenesses would intervene to ease their suffering, eventually.

The procession circled the town before returning the image to her church. Diego had climbed back onto the bridge parapet for a better view. Rosario felt her heart skip at the sight of him, and then again when she pictured his fate should he fall. He caught her eye and grinned.

With the Virgin safely back in her niche, the children were free to break ranks. The nuns smiled. The Virgin was happy. Today there would be no call for undue discipline or punishment. Juan, finding Rosario among a group of schoolfriends, took her hand and pulled her to one side. He had seen Diego, he told her. She feigned indifference, then said she supposed he was referring to the gitano on the bridge. Juan grinned. His friend's sleight of hand, did his sister but know it, equalled that of any gypsy. How else had he filled his ever-hungry stomach before he went to live with Ramón Ramirez? Fruit, Juan had discovered, was all the tastier for having been snatched from a market stall or plucked from the other side of a high garden wall. There were knives, too, and coins and purloined silver buttons. Best of all had been the pistol Diego had unwrapped from a piece of cloth while swearing him to secrecy. Juan's first thought was that it had been stolen it from his father. Later, he had found its twin in its usual place in his father's desk. Diego said it was a sign: from then on they would be brothers as well as friends.

'He says he is to start training for the bullring next year,' Juan said to Rosario. 'We talked once,' he added wistfully, 'of going together to the Maestranza in Seville.'

His sister was scornful. 'Imagine that! Juan Álvarez a bull-fighter! That would give Papa cause for concern!'

'Diego thinks you are very pretty,' Juan retorted. 'And that would concern Papa even more!'

With no nuns close enough to see, Rosario gave him a sharp kick on the ankle. Juan responded with a satisfying yelp.

'Think yourself lucky Sister Catarina didn't catch you,' he said from between clenched teeth. 'Or you'd have to say a thousand Hail Marys. Two thousand even.'

They ran across the square to join their parents. Families were already leaving in anticipation of luncheon prepared by their cooks and maids. Most would return for the afternoon corrida to see the matador, Ramón Ramírez, despatch his bulls.

The iron-studded outer door swung open as they neared the house. Carmela ran out into the street, stumbling in her grief.

'I heard her cry out, señora. I went to her immediately, but it was too late. I have sent for the priest, señores.'

Comprehension took seconds that seemed much longer. The bright, happy day dulled. Smiling faces folded into disbelief. Carmela had misunderstood, or they had not understood her. They ran through the half-tiled entryway, across the front patio and the wide, tiled hallway to the drawing-room beyond. They found Mercedes still sitting in her chair, apparently asleep. Isabel dropped to her knees. Her beloved abuela was ivory-still. Her black lace fan lay closed beside her on the floor, a scrap of per-fumed velvet caught in its folds.

The family, already in mourning for Roberto's mother,

mourned again. The shutters that looked out across the street remained closed. Saints Days and birthdays came and went, quiet celebrations lacking an integral part. Eyes would glance, unthinking, towards the chair by the window as if to share a merry thought with its occupant. The listless shadow of the rose bush moved and they would sigh and look away.

Chapter Twenty-one

Rosario leaned on her windowsill. The shutters were open again, the long days of mourning over. Geraniums tumbled in sunlit tangles of red and white from the wrought iron balconies opposite. It seemed to her that the old house sighed with relief, just as she had sighed when told she need no longer wear her sombre mourning dresses. Her sigh had become a shout of joy when her father said they were to spend the long, hot summer months at their cortijo in the hills. She missed abuelita Mercedes most dreadfully but she was sure her great-grandmother would appreciate her gladness at dispensing with her hot black clothing, and would understand her longing for the freedom of the countryside and the uncritical companionship of her pony.

She moved from the window to flop down on her bed, then turned to lie on her back. Sun-painted geranium shadows danced on the ceiling. Soon she would be lying in the dusty grass of the serranía. Instead of daily reminders to behave with dignity as became her station, there would be months of freedom from her studies, and from the nuns who still rapped her knuckles for the least of reasons.

The household bustled with a busyness not seen in months. Closets were opened, boxes and trunks packed and repacked, decisions made and unmade. Then, three days before their departure, Rosario woke to find her nightdress specked with blood. She was alarmed then proud when Carmela told her its meaning. The maid called her mother who came to congratulate and kiss her, and spoiled the moment by saying she could not now ride on horseback to the cortijo. She must travel instead in the cart with Carmela and the cook. Pride gave way to childish petulance but no amount of foot-stamping or wheedling would change her mother's mind. For the first time in her life, Rosario was too shy to approach the father she adored and who, in almost everything, could be counted on to take her part.

A donkey stood waiting between the shafts of the cart in the courtyard. Nothing in the world, Rosario thought, could be more humiliating. She scowled a refusal when a groom came to help her and scrambled up herself to sit beside Carmela. Juan and her mother were already in the saddle, their horses' harnesses jingling as the animals tossed their heads in anticipation of the long day's journey across the serranía. The cook bustled from the house clutching last-minute items from her kitchen and declaring that without them neither she nor her culinary expertise could survive life at the cortijo. The man who was to drive the cart retorted that if she added one thing more, neither he nor the donkey would survive the journey.

With his small retinue at last complete, Roberto mounted his Spanish Grey and led them out under the courtyard archway and along the cobbled streets. When they reached the cliff top, the cart's occupants got down to walk the steep descent rather than risk being tipped into the rushing fall of water. When the pathway levelled they climbed in again. Horses and riders set off at a gallop. The cart was left to trail behind. Rosario's stomach ached. Becoming a woman was, she decided, the worst thing that had ever happened to her in all her life.

It was evening when they came to the fields where the

Álvarez fighting bulls were raised. The white walls of the farm buildings came into view in the distance. Rosario was tired and dusty. Every bone in her body ached. The riders, resting their horses some way ahead, waited for the cart to catch up. When, at last, she trundled with Carmela and the cook under the wide, white cortijo archway, flanked by Juan, her parents and two grooms, she barely acknowledged the dogs and children who ran out to greet her. Grooms from the cortijo stables led the horses away. The housekeeper took Rosario's hand and led her into the house.

That night she slept deeply, as children do and even newly arrived women may. She woke next morning to find her bleeding finished and laughed with relief. Today she would ride in the hills with Juan, just as they had planned.

They had weeks of exploring ahead of them and had not been many days at the cortijo before finding a previously undiscovered path no more than an hour's ride from the house. It was already well into the afternoon and too late to explore it further that day. Next morning, they arrived in the kitchen with the dawn, interrupting the cook's prodigious yawns with a request for supplies to last a full day's adventuring.

A groom brought their ponies and hung full water-skins from their saddles. The cook's packages went into their saddlebags.

It was still early morning when they reached the narrow path that led first through a sparse copse and then among close-gathered leafy trees. The ponies picked their way over gnarled roots and fallen leaves. Twigs snapped. The riders ducked, avoiding low-hanging branches. A rivulet, the cause of so much lushness, trickled over a rocky bed, flowing from a wider stream. Stones skittered from the ponies' hooves and splashed into its dancing path. Wavelets collided with small rocks, their flying droplets turned to jewels by filtered sunlight. The wide bank narrowed and became steep, then disappeared under tangled grass and rocks. The children nudged their ponies into the shallow water, walking them along its narrowing course until it, too, vanished underground. Lightly trampled vegetation showed the way to a steeply rising track. They followed it until the trees gave way to scrubby bushes opening, at last, onto a wider path. A massive rock loomed opposite.

'La Centinela!' Rosario exclaimed. 'This must be the road to El Rocío.'

The rock almost blocked the centuries-old pass. It was a wonder the high-wheeled wagons could pass it on their yearly romería to the Virgin of The Marshes. She let her reins rest loose against her pony's neck, gazing up and then along the winding road. A hard day's ride to the east would take them to Puente Nuevo. To the west, six days journeying away, lay the Guadalquivir and El Rocío. She sighed, wishing away time, longing to be old enough to make her first pilgrimage to the shrine of the Blanca Paloma.

Her musings on that still far-off happening were interrupted by Juan's prosaic, more immediate suggestion that they find somewhere to eat their lunch, perhaps on the far side of the rock. They dismounted and began searching for a way round it. At the eastern end they found a well-hidden cleft wide enough for their ponies to enter. Juan said it looked as if it might lead to a cave and had probably been a hiding place for bandits.

Instead of a cave, the cleft led out onto another path not much wider than a goat-track. The landscape ahead seemed harsh after the lushness left behind on the other side of the road. In spite of Juan's complaints that if they didn't stop immediately to eat their lunch he would probably die of starvation, they remounted and rode on. Eventually, Rosario pointed with her crop to a patch of spindly bushes that would give them some, if not much, shelter from the sun.

They had almost reached it when hoof beats sounded on the path ahead. A rider broke from the trees and was almost on them when he suddenly reined in. Rosario cried out and nudged her pony closer to Juan.

'Juan, my friend! I heard you had arrived at your cortijo. I was on my way to see you.' The boy doffed a battered Cordoban hat and bowed to Rosario. 'Señorita Rosario. I'm glad to make your acquaintance again.'

'Diego!' Juan laughed in astonishment. 'We thought you were a bandit!'

'An honourable profession! Unfortunately I am merely a slave to Don Ramón who is in Seville for the corrida and where, with any luck, he will meet his maker.'

Rosario was too amazed to speak. She had recognised him at once. This was the boy who had balanced, uncaring, on the bridge, Juan's friend, the boy who, years before, had stolen her almonds. She lifted her chin in what she hoped was casual disdain. Diego chuckled as if he found her both pretentious and amusing. She dropped her eyes and plucked at the leafy debris caught in her pony's mane.

Recovered from his surprise and delighted to have his friend's company, Juan invited him to share their meal.

'I have wine,' said Diego. 'My step-father keeps a good cellar. Let me assist you, Señorita Rosario.' He dismounted, and stood, arms raised to lift her down. She was well used to the touch of her father's, or Juan's, hands on her waist when they helped her dismount, even those of the grooms. But she had never before slid into a stranger's arms. She wondered if Diego felt her shiver, detectable surely even through her riding jacket. He held her for perhaps a moment longer than he need and then released her. With her customary aplomb returned, she challenged his quizzical smile with a steady appraisal of her own.

Later, sprawled under the trees with their horses grazing

nearby and their own stomachs satisfied, Diego told them of his life at Ramón Ramirez's cortijo and how, with the priest's insistence as to the probable discomfort of his soul if he did not do so, the matador had, at last, married Diego's mother. Hearing that Juan's family had arrived at the Álvarez estate for the summer, he had been travelling there that very day in the hope of meeting his friend.

'And his beautiful sister,' he added, turning his head to smile at her. Perhaps because she had drunk more wine than she was normally permitted, Rosario felt her stomach turn. The sensation was unusual but not entirely unpleasant.

'Do you remember, Juan,' Diego asked, 'how we talked of becoming bullfighters?'

'Of course I remember. We were going to run away to Seville together!' Juan laughed at the impossibility of such a dream.

'I'm to join Ramón's cuadrilla next season. I'll be a matador – and a far better one than Ramón – before you can even think it.' Diego poured the last of the wine into his mouth. 'What will you do with your life, Juan?'

'My father wants me to become a doctor but I'd much rather be a bullfighter. You're so lucky, Diego.'

Lulled by her share of wine, Rosario closed her eyes while her companions' voices coursed back and forth with talk of future dreams and past adventures. Half asleep, she imagined a blare of trumpets, the sun flashing on his suit of lights as Diego entered the arena between two lesser matadors. When the President gave the signal, she conjured the bravest, biggest bull she could conceive and watched it run from the tunnel at the far end of the arena, swinging its head from side to side, confused and angry at finding itself in such a place. She heard Diego call out to it, his voice gentle as if encouraging a shy friend, flicking his yellow-lined pink fighting cape to catch its eye. The bull turned, head low, snorting its disdain for so small a creature. It pawed the sand with a contemptuous hoof and charged. Diego's cape swirled. A horn passed close by his thigh, and then again and again as the matador turned, light as a moth, drawing the animal closer still. The crowd roared its delight and the picador came on his horse to bring the first tercio to an end. When a banderillero stepped forward to begin the second, Diego waved him aside. He would place the darts himself. He sped across the sand, made a half turn, his slippered heels raised, his body arching like a bow as the bull passed beneath his arms. The crowd shouted olés for his exquisite placing of the darts. He turned to where Rosario sat and smiled. It was time for the final tercio, the faena and the death. He doffed his montera to the President, called for permission to kill the bull, turned to her again and threw the cap. She stood as it whirled, small and black towards her, caught it, and sat with it held against her breast. He had dedicated his first bull to her! The matador exchanged his capote for the red muleta, a cloth no more extravagant than a piece of red flannel on a stick. Murmured olés echoed through sun and shade at each pass of the faena. The exhausted bull swayed in the heat. Diego called for the sword, concealed it beneath the muleta and fell to his knees. He begged the bull to come at him one more time. They eyed each other, small man, great beast, one of them about to die. A matador will say that the look passing between the two at that moment is one of purest love. The die had been cast, loaded perhaps, but the game still dangerous to both. The bull waited, gathering its strength – and charged. Diego was still on his knees, his hand on his sword. He rose from the sand like liquid, his body lifting to its fullest height as if in slow motion and yet so swiftly no one could have sworn they saw it happen. His sword flashed high, then down, bringing death with one perfect thrust between the shoulder blades to the bull's aorta. Rosario, sighing in her sleep, heard the crowd roar again. The President, her father, was signalling that Diego Montero, the greatest bullfighter in the whole of Spain, was to be honoured not only with both ears but the bull's tail also.

Juan nudged her with his foot. Rosario sat up, rubbing her eyes. The sun had moved at least an hour to the west and Diego had gone. She stumbled to her feet, brushing twigs from her riding habit, annoyed that her dream had turned out to be just that and its subject ill-mannered enough to have gone without taking leave of her. Her temper was not improved by the thought of the long ride home and that they would be admonished for their tardiness. On no account, she said, must Juan mention their meeting with Diego. Even had he been suitable company for her, which he most certainly was not, her brother was neither fit nor old enough to chaperone her in the company of young men. She put one foot in her stirrup, still grumbling. She hoped, she said, that he wouldn't make a habit of bumping into his stupid friend.

When they arrived back at the cortijo, they found their parents entertaining visitors. Carmela hustled them to their bedrooms to change their clothes. She had made excuses for them, she said, and they had not been missed.

A day or two later, Rosario found Juan in the stable-yard, about to leave without her. When pressed, he told her he had arranged to meet Diego. He had not thought she would want to join them, considering her opinion of his friend. Hadn't she reminded him herself that it was improper for her to spend time in the company of a young man without a suitable chaperone? She shrugged and said that if he chose not to mention it, neither would she, and that she might as well go with him since she had nothing else to occupy her time. Juan said he would rather go alone. He had things to discuss with Diego.

'What things?' she asked.

'The sort of things men discuss when women aren't around.'

Rosario said she knew as much about the raising of bulls as

he did, if that's what he meant. He said it wasn't. She said she would tell their parents he was consorting with ruffians.

'He's not a ruffian! He might have been once but he isn't now. Father won't mind, but if you tell him, I'll say you spent a whole afternoon with Diego.'

'What was I supposed to do? Ride home alone?' Rosario flounced off, sulking.

A pattern of sorts was set. Some days Juan asked her to ride with him, some days he went off alone. Sometimes she agreed to go, sometimes she refused. There were days when Diego's work kept him busy at the Ramirez cortijo, other times when he met them by the brook bordering the Álvarez estate, or in the shade beside la Centinela on the road to El Rocío. He showed them a hidden pathway leading from the cleft to a shallow bowl-like space at the summit. Few people knew of it. He thought perhaps it had been used by the Republicans as a hiding place before the Caudillo wiped them from the face of the earth. It made a good lookout.

'They'd have been trapped up here,' said Juan.

Diego shook his head. 'There's another way down. Another track about a kilometre long. It comes out onto the Rocío road further west, where the path is wider. I'll show you.'

One night, after a day deemed too hot for riding, Rosario woke to the sound of gravel against glass. She got out of bed and went to her window. Juan was in the courtyard with Diego, one arm round the older boy's shoulder, the other raised in a signal summoning her to let him in. She went downstairs, careful to avoid treads that creaked, and across the flagstones to the door. She opened it and found Diego on the other side, supporting her lolling, smiling brother.

'Too much wine,' he whispered. 'I'll take him to his room.'

'It's lucky for you both that my father is in Puente Nuevo,' Rosario hissed. She beckoned to him to follow, thinking it fortunate that Juan had retained sufficient wits to quiet the dogs. Antique firearms and ancient sword-crossed shields lined the staircase walls; stags' heads and horned bulls stared balefully as they passed. She tiptoed along the upstairs passageway wishing Diego might be as silent with his burden, and thanked the Virgin that the iron hinges had recently been oiled. Juan's door opened to her touch with hardly a creak.

Diego carried him to the bed and dropped him there much as he might heave a sack into a barn. In different circumstances Rosario would have berated him loudly for his trouble. She glared at him instead: too bad if he expected her to escort him down the stairs again. He could find his own way out and it would be his own bad luck if he were caught.

'I wanted to say goodbye,' he said. 'My stepfather returns tomorrow. I won't be seeing you again.'

Her anger melted into disappointment. 'Don't tease me, Diego. We'd planned to meet again at la Centinela. I want to climb to the top again.'

He shrugged. 'I've neglected my tasks, and now I'll have to pay for it.' He leaned towards her, took her chin in his cupped hand and kissed her mouth. An unfamiliar sweetness surged through her. She closed her eyes. When she opened them he was gone.

Isabel got up from her bed, sure that a sound alien to the sleeping house had woken her. The passage outside her room was empty, her children's doors closed. She went to the top of the staircase and looked down. A movement caught her eye. A face stared up at her through a shaft of dying moonlight and then vanished. She gripped the handrail, too shocked and frightened to call out. Footsteps crossed the hall below; a door closed. She was about to call out to wake the servants but turned instead towards her room: what she had seen had been nothing more than a trick of the light and her over-active imagination, the sounds she had heard no more than the night-time creaking of a very old house. There had been many times when she had jumped at the slightest noise in the night, or risen from her bed, still sleeping, and hurried from room to room as if searching for a place to hide. Each time, Roberto had come after her to lead her back to bed and she had woken to find him holding her, telling her that she had had a bad dream and that no harm would come to her. Thinking of him eased her mind. Tomorrow he would return to the cortijo and she would feel safe again.

She crossed to the washstand. The copper jug glinted as she lifted it to pour its contents into her washing bowl. As she bent to splash her cheeks and forehead, a memory of Tom came unbidden to her mind. She smiled, remembering how she had told him that his red hair had brought to mind her grandmother's copper pans; remembering his laughter. She dried her face and lay down on the bed, allowing other elusive, comforting memories to invade her mind and hold at bay the phantom on the stairs: the imagined boy-ghost with Federico's eyes. When she woke, Carmela was at the window opening the shutters. The newly-filled ewer gleamed in the sunlight.

Juan, Carmela said, was unwell and had kept to his bed. She did not tell her mistress that she had found him still clothed, his shirt reeking of stale wine, and that she had undressed him, sponged him, put on his nightclothes and flung the window wide.

Isabel went immediately to see what ailed her son. She found him, as Carmela had said, pale and complaining of a headache. His forehead was clammy but she doubted he had a fever. At lunchtime, if he was no better, she would send for the curandera. Roberto would not approve but with the nearest doctor in

Puente Nuevo, people in the surrounding villages had little option but to rely on prayer and wise women's herbs. The mere thought of a bitter dose from one of the curandera's bottles or small cloth sachets had been known to invoke a cure.

As she went downstairs, sunlight caught the glass eyes of a mounted stag. Isabel laughed at her foolishness in thinking they had stared at her, last night, from a human face.

She found Rosario already in the dining room, toying with her breakfast.

'Juan is unwell,' Isabel told her, and was surprised to see a small, grim smile flit across her daughter's face. 'If you want to ride today, you will have to take one of the grooms.'

'I don't want to ride.'

'At least eat some breakfast.'

'I'm not hungry.'

Isabel's own appetite was lacking. A headache threatened. She told a maid to bring coffee to her in Roberto's study.

A half-finished letter lay in front of her on the desk. The window beside her looked out onto a sandy courtyard where a groom was setting up a series of jumps. Rosario passed the window leading her pony. The exercise would do her good, Isabel surmised, perhaps blow away whatever cobwebs were causing her ill humour. She watched her set the pony at a bar, heard her shout to the groom to clear her way, and shout again when she misjudged the stride. Isabel sighed. She had not brought up her children to be rude to servants. She would have to reprimand Rosario later. She was about to continue with her letter when a maid came to tell her that the overseer wished to see her.

The man came in and stood in front of the desk, grinding his cap in his hands. He had suspected for some weeks, he said, that someone had been caping the young bulls. This morning he was sure of it. He had discovered also that Don Roberto's wine cellar had been broached, and that his master's favourite mare was missing. He had supposed señorito Juan had taken the animal for an early morning ride. He had only just learned that the señorito was unwell and had not left the house that morning.

The man hung his head. Isabel felt her headache returning and anger with it.

'Your laxity is unforgivable. Didn't you hear the dogs barking?'

'No, Doña Isabel. They didn't bark. I would have heard them.'

'Then one of the servants must be responsible. And for the missing wine also, I imagine.' So the shadow on the stairs had been human after all: a servant with an imagined grudge almost caught in the act and then escaping on Roberto's best broodmare.

'The servants are all accounted for, señora.'

'Then how do you explain the dogs not barking? How do you account for that?'

'I can't, Doña Isabel.'

'Were they poisoned?'

'No, Doña Isabel.'

'Are you certain the house was locked last night?'

'Yes, Doña Isabel.'

'I trust you are not about to tell me that we have been visited by a phantom?'

'No, Doña Isabel.'

She drummed her fingers on the arms of the chair. Phantom! How ridiculous to say it. The man, superstitious peasant though he might be, would think her mad. The intruder had been flesh and blood and known to the cortijo. Why else had the dogs remained silent? No wonder she had thought his eyes familiar. In her sleep-filled state she had confused a servant with someone who had once terrified her. How stupid she had been. The figure on the stairs had been young, not a grown man. A man who, in any case was dead.

She told the overseer to send a message to the nearest Guardia and to report to Roberto as soon as he arrived from Puente Nuevo. The matter, she said – in such a way as to include the man's own future – would then be dealt with more fully.

Juan appeared at lunchtime declaring a hearty appetite. Rosario's usually high spirits had miraculously returned. Isabel wondered at the resilience of children. It was a shame to have to upset them over the thefts but she would rather they learned it from her than from gossiping servants. Rosario's face whitened with what her mother took to be anger at the news. Juan excused himself from the table, saying he was not hungry after all.

When Roberto returned some hours later he called the overseer to his office and chastised the man but did not dismiss him. When Isabel questioned his wisdom, he said that even the loss of so good an animal did not warrant ruining the man's life. As to the thief, the Guardia were already looking into it. She asked if the overseer had mentioned that some of the bulls had been caped. Roberto's face darkened. He called Juan to his study. His son, red-faced and stammering, admitted his guilt. No one else had been involved, he said. He alone was responsible.

'Anyone with the least understanding of the lidia,' Roberto said, his voice lifting in rare anger, 'knows that when a young bull is shown the cape it quickly learns it has nothing to fear other than a harmless piece of cloth. Were I to allow those you have tampered with into the ring, they would refuse to fight or, worse still, perform with such cunning as to put the most skilled torero in great danger.'

It was usual for a degree of glumness to accompany the days before their return to town. This year, Isabel felt nothing but relief. In Puente Nuevo the family, indeed life in general, might regain its equilibrium. Told that he was to be confined to the cortijo in punishment, Juan shut himself in his room. Rosario, no less dismal, spent her last days of freedom wafting around like a distraught heroine in a medieval tragedy. Even Carmela lost patience, loudly declaring her hope that, on her return to school, the nuns would bring the girl to her senses.

Mention of the good sisters caused Rosario to realise that the summer was indeed almost over. She went to her father. She would like to take her pony on one last ride. If he would allow it, she would like Juan to accompany her. Assuming his son had learned his lesson, and thinking to ease a little of the cortijo's gloom and end the holiday on a lighter note, Roberto agreed.

By mutual consent they chose to go again to la Centinela. They found the concealed entrance and scrambled to the summit and the broad, curving space where Diego had once built them a fire and cooked a rabbit for their lunch. The view was vast: a never-ending land of browns and yellows with patches of dark green trees. The great cliff face of Puente Nuevo rose like a far-off fortress to the east. The sea they had never seen lay many miles to the south. To the west, hidden by distant hills, was the village of El Rocío.

'It's hard to believe the world is a round like a ball,' said Juan. 'It looks more like a giant's dinner plate.'

'In that case,' Rosario said. 'The trees must be cabbages.'

They agreed that the rocks were strange meats and fish, the sand-coloured soil a bowl of saffron-flavoured rice. Rosario turned onto her stomach and stared down through a cavity in the rock. 'I can't see where it ends,' she said.

Juan lay beside her, peering into the darkness. 'Perhaps it goes right through to the other side of the world.'

'If it does, I should like to climb down there and come out where I'd never have to see Mother Angelica or the Sisters ever again.' Rosario turned over to lie with the sun warm on her face. 'Sister Catarina says she knew a nun who sailed in a ship all the way round the world to a country on the other side. It had green hills and mountains. And rivers bigger than the Guadalquivir.'

'What was it called?'

'I don't remember.'

'I expect she meant Australia. That's on the other side, I think.'

Rosario considered for a moment. 'No it wasn't that. She said the grass is very green, much greener than in Andalucía, and that shafts of light shine through the forests and turn the plants to silver.'

'Brother Ignacio says children on the other side of the world have brown skins,' said Juan.

'Like gypsies?'

'Darker than that. More like Africans, I should think.'

An eagle flew in the high, blue dome of the sky. Rosario thought of the stolen mare. The blaze on its forehead was the same shape as the eagle's wing.

'Do you think Diego stole the mare?' she asked.

'I thought he was my friend,' said Juan.

'Did you really cape the bulls?'

'We both did.'

Rosario squinted her eyes against the sun and watched the creature soar. She flung her arms wide, her face to the sky. 'It must be the most wonderful feeling in the world,' she said. 'To fly.'

Chapter Twenty-two

In Tom and Lizzie's farmhouse beyond Fenton, Sarah was playing 'school' in the kitchen with her dolls. The phone rang one short peel, then two long. She got up from the rug and reached for the receiver.

'Johnston's,' she said. 'Sarah speaking.'

'Hullo, dear. Is Mummy there?'

'Mu-u-mmy, it's Gran.' Lizzie was in the bathroom washing mud and blood from Hamish's knees for the second time that morning. 'Hamish fell out of the tree again, Gran. And Henry trod on two cabbages and Mummy's new parsley seeds. Daddy's going to mend the gate tomorrow. And Mrs. Jenkins has made me a new dress for Simon's birthday party. I'm going to be a pink fairy and Simon and Hamish are going to be pirates.'

Lizzie appeared beside her and took the receiver.

'Hello, Mother.'

'I've just rung Freda.' Margaret's voice was anxious. 'She said she'd tell Eve I called and that I mustn't worry. But I can't help it, Lizzie. It was on the news again this morning. Mr. Holland was saying the strike is a communist plot and that the watersiders and all the rest of them are trying to overthrow the government.'

'I know. We heard it too.'

'All those carcasses rotting on the wharves! It's too awful. I said I'd like to go up to Auckland to see if Eve's all right and your father went up the wall. Look, dear, I've picked a bad time to call. He'll be in for lunch any minute. We'll see you on Sunday as usual?'

'Of course, Mother. And try not to worry.'

Lizzie was about to put down the receiver when she heard a whispered conversation on the line. 'Morning, Trevor,' she said. 'Everything good over your way?'

There was a grunt, followed by a click. Some people's lives, Lizzie thought, must be terribly dull: Trevor wasn't the only neighbour to listen in on the party line. What they would do without Eve and her dramas to spice up their lives she couldn't imagine. Her mother's latest concern for her younger daughter's welfare would do nicely to fill an otherwise quiet afternoon and set phone lines buzzing. She put water on to boil for the peas she had shucked earlier and checked the shepherd's pie browning in the oven. Whatever she was up to, it was thoughtless of Eve not to get in touch. She must surely know how worried their mother would be just now.

It must be almost five years, Lizzie thought, since Eve's glamorous life had come to an abrupt end and she had moved back in with Freda. Thanks to the secretarial course she had taken, neatly typed, infrequent letters had duly arrived in Fenton: letters that had undergone a change of tone when Eve began going to political meetings with Freda. She had gone at first, she said, to take shorthand notes for Freda's paper in part-payment for her board and lodging. She had been bored mostly, and amused, until the day came when she realised she had been absorbing – quite without meaning to – the essence of things previously alien to her. 'Indoctrination' their father had called it. It was bad enough having one spinster in the family behaving like a suffragette without dragging his daughter into politics. If it was fulfilment she wanted, it was high time she discovered a more natural way of going about it. And he didn't mean running off with another of her fancy boyfriends either. Margaret concurred with that sentiment at least, and so did Lizzie. Not that either of them had taken Eve's political interests seriously, supposing it just another of her phases. But Tom, reading between his sister-in-law's occasional but still amusing lines, had begun to sense an unease in the country unreported in the local paper. A month or so had passed with next to no contact at all, then Eve had written home to say she had married Archie Evans, a watersider. The news had travelled rapidly over party lines and teacups, shocking the rural community to its conservative core. She hadn't mentioned it sooner, Eve wrote, because she knew how her father would react. True to her divination, Jim went through the roof. Margaret cried because they hadn't been invited to the wedding and Eve's letters home stopped altogether. To hear Jim rant, one might suppose it entirely his daughter's fault that the watersiders were bringing the country to its knees. Freda's paper had been banned again, which wasn't really surprising in the circumstances. Why she didn't call it quits and retire gracefully, Lizzie had no idea.

When Tom came in for lunch, she told him of her mother's call.

'What's your Auntie Eve up to now?' he said, ruffling Sarah's curls.

'Trouble again, probably,' said Hamish.

'That's quite enough of that,' Lizzie said, even if she did agree with him.

'I've an idea,' said Tom. 'I've to go up to Hamilton in a couple of weeks to see about some stock. Why don't I take an extra day and carry on up to Auckland? I can check this Archie fellow out at the same time. I doubt he's the blackguard Jim fancies him to be!'

'That's a marvellous idea!' said Lizzie. 'I'll phone Mother

right after lunch and tell her. She was talking of going up herself but of course Dad's being impossible.'

'How about coming with me?'

'Me too?' said Hamish.

'Not this time, old son.'

'That's not fair!'

'Point is, I mentioned to your Granddad that I'd give him a bit of a hand at The Oaks. D'you think you could stand in for me?'

'Reckon I could. I could help Gran with the ice-cream churn too. She says it's too much trouble with her arthritis.'

'I can do that too,' said Sarah. 'And I can play with the new kittens.'

'That's all fixed then. We could go up next week, Liz. Make a bit of a holiday of it and see about the stock on the way back. I'll get old Ben over to keep an eye on things for a few days. What do you say?'

'I say you're a genius!'

Later that day Margaret recalled a message Freda had asked her to pass on to Tom. It had been a bit vague. Something about having met a recent immigrant from Scotland who thought he might have known Tom in Spain. What with worrying about Eve, she'd forgotten all about it. It was probably just as well she hadn't mentioned it. The neighbours on the party line had plenty to gossip about without speculating about her son-in-law's past political leanings. She reckoned she'd let sleeping dogs lie. She certainly wasn't going to bring it up on Sunday. The watersiders were causing enough trouble without having Tom's brief flirtation with anarchists brought up at the tea table.

'Reckon you two are off on a fool's errand,' said Jim when the family gathered for tea that Sunday at The Oaks. 'Bloody trains are bound to go on strike again.'

A thin, chill mist drifted over the fields and across the track. The train whistled in the distance.

'It's coming,' Hamish shouted.

'We'll be back before you know it,' Lizzie said, giving them both a hug.

At lunchtime, the train stopped at Taumarunui just long enough for the consumption of meat pies and tea served in thick china cups. By early evening they were approaching Auckland. The volcano at the harbour entrance loomed above the darkening waters of the gulf. A long line of ships lay idle in the stream.

'Look at that,' Lizzie exclaimed. 'Dad's right. They *are* holding the country to ransom.'

They had sent no warning of their arrival to either Freda or Eve so stayed that night at a small hotel in the city. Next morning they asked the receptionist where to catch the Three Lamps tram and set off down the hill to Queen Street. As they turned the corner, they saw a crowd gathering outside the Town Hall, its numbers swelling as people converged from all directions.

Lizzie's hand tightened on Tom's arm.

'Is it the watersiders do you think?'

'Looks like it. Some sort of meeting, I expect. They seem peaceful enough. Let's sort out that sister of yours and leave them to it.'

A dozen men came down the street towards them.

'You with us then?' one of the leaders called.

'Shouldn't think so,' said another. 'Dressed far too fancy by half.'

Some smiled. Others touched forefingers to their hats as they passed.

'Aye, I'm with you,' Tom called after them.

'For heaven's sake!' Lizzie tugged his arm.

'Those watersiders are beyond a joke,' a woman at the tram stop said. 'There must be over a thousand of them down there now.' Their tram, wary of the people crossing to and fro across its rails, trundled up the hill and hissed to a stop beside them. The conductor leaned out to tell other would-be passengers that if they wanted Meadowbank or the Zoo, they were out of luck. No more trams were coming through.

The conductor put them off at the Three Lamps stop and pointed out the side street they were looking for. As they made their way between two rows of dilapidated workers' cottages, Lizzie said there must be some mistake. The number they had for Eve brought them to a place as bad as all the others with its peeling paint and cracked windows. Two men were coming from the house carrying a worn settee. Kitchen chairs, a battered arm-chair and a bed lay stacked on the footpath. A woman came out on to the porch and began to remonstrate with the men.

'Repossession agents,' muttered Tom. 'Come on, lass.' He took Lizzie by the arm and propelled her forward. The woman turned towards them. Her tired features shifted from anger to amazement then settled for something in between.

'Lizzie? Tom? My God, what are you doing here?'

Lizzie stopped in her tracks, her own feelings reflecting Eve's, although in different degrees and for different reasons. Not so long ago, her sister would have declared preference for a death shroud rather than exhibit herself in the street wearing an apron, let alone the outdated, faded print dress under it. She wore no make-up, her hair was bound in a turban: the sort that made Lizzie think of hidden curlers. She brushed past the repo men, ran up the broken wooden steps and took Eve by the shoulders.

'What on earth's going on? Why didn't you let us know? Mother has been so worried. We all have.'

Behind her, Tom accosted the men. Lizzie turned to look. The larger of the two glared at her husband, chin jutting, arms folded across his chest. 'Only doing our job.'

Tom took out his wallet and extracted a note. 'Here, take this. It should be enough to keep your boss happy.' A handful of florins appeared on top of the five pound note. 'And a bit extra for the pair of you for your trouble.' The man grinned, pocketed the note and half the coins and handed the rest to his companion. He shook Tom's hand, then turned to Eve.

'No hard feelings, eh? Tough times all round now, I reckon. We'll take this lot back inside then shall we?'

Eve nodded, dazed, and walked down the steps to collect a kitchen chair. Lizzie followed and picked up another.

'We live in the kitchen mostly,' Eve said, leading the way indoors. 'Just like at home.'

Hardly that, Lizzie thought, as they made their way down the dim passageway to the kitchen. There were damp, peeling patches on the once cream walls. The place was musty with mildew. She tucked the rescued chair under the kitchen table. An old and splendid oak dresser stood against one wall.

'A hand-me-down wedding present from Freda,' said Eve. 'I told those men I'd kill them if they touched it.'

Family photographs on its shelves, and pretty china cups and saucers offered some relief from the sad state of the room. As soon as she had learned of her sister's marriage, Lizzie had arranged for the tea-set to be sent by mail order from an Auckland store. There were patterned dinner plates too, recognised from her childhood. A gift from her mother, Lizzie guessed. She'd bet a pound to a penny their father didn't know.

'Why didn't you tell us things were so bad? Mother and Dad would hate to think of you living like this. They'd have come round given time.'

'Oh come on, Liz! Dad's ideas are cast in iron. You know that. He'd never forgive me for marrying a union man, not in a thousand years.' Eve crossed the patched, brown lino to the sink and turned on the tap. Water drummed into the kettle. Drops trickled down its sides and hissed as she placed it on the hob.

'He made his feelings clear years ago. I wasn't going to let him spoil my wedding day.' She laughed, an echo of the old Eve. 'Imagine it! An Oakes turned socialist and married to a water-sider! He'd rather die! Archie said to tell him to come up so he could deal with him.' She took cups and saucers from the dresser and set them on the table. 'Remember how I wanted to run off and live in America after the war? Well, my knight in shining armour was here all the time! He declared himself a conscientious objector. Never left the country!'

Lizzie was appalled. 'He did what? Oh no, Eve. He can't be. Tell me you're joking.' There was no way their father would ever forgive her sister now. A 'conshie' was lower than the lowest form of life in Jim's book, and not much better in Lizzie's either. Tom would probably agree. Well of course he would. He had fought in the war. Just because he leaned a little more to the left than Lizzie would have liked, that didn't make him a communist. Not that they ever talked about it, of course. In that, as in most things, Lizzie was in agreement with her mother. Politics was not a suitable topic for family conversation, especially at the dinner table. Her father's opinions were unavoidable but, by and large, based on sound thinking. In spite of his ranting, none of them had seriously believed Freda would have much influence on Eve.

'Better not mention it to Dad,' said Eve.

'No,' agreed Lizzie, delving into her bag and producing a fruit cake she had brought with her from the farm.

'My God!' said Eve.

'It's just a cake,' said Lizzie.

'Marie Antoinette!'

'Who?'

'Let them eat cake,' Eve quoted, taking a plate from the

dresser and handing it to her sister.

Tom came into the kitchen with the second pair of kitchen chairs.

'I don't know how to thank you,' Eve said.

'A cup of tea would do nicely.'

Lizzie closed the door against the draft coming down the passageway, glad Eve hadn't suggested she take off her coat.

'What's this?' she bent to pick up a sheet from a pile of news-print.

Tom glanced over her shoulder to read the bold, headlined query: 'Democratic New Zealand or Fascist Spain?'

Lizzie turned to Eve, her face incredulous. 'I thought Freda wasn't allowed to publish this rubbish any more. Heavens, Eve, you're not still involved, are you?'

Eve shrugged, but her face had paled. 'It was banned months ago. Doesn't mean we stopped publishing.'

'What if those men saw them and reported you to the police?'

'Oh come on, Lizzie,' Tom remonstrated. 'They probably read this stuff themselves.'

'She's right,' Eve said. 'It was stupid of me to leave them there. I don't think I could bear it if they sent Archie to prison again.'

Tom shot a warning glance at Lizzie. 'We're on your side, Eve. Isn't that right, Liz?'

But Lizzie's opinion was otherwise. Oh lord, she thought, pulling out a chair from the table and sitting down. Not only did my sister's husband spend most of the war in prison, he's a potential peacetime jailbird as well. And a communist. She rather wished Eve hadn't mentioned Archie's transgressions; give her a month or two more of this and she'd have hot-footed it back to Fenton with no one any the wiser.

'We're family,' she said. 'That's enough isn't it? I don't like this talk of taking sides. That's what causes all the trouble. I don't understand why sane people want to get involved in politics in the first place.' She contemplated her sister across the table. Eve had changed, and not only in the manner of her dress. She was no longer an irresponsible butterfly. She had buckled, but only temporarily, and would continue on her chosen path, ill-found or otherwise. She felt the stirrings of respect and some regret and wondered if, beneath the awful turban, Eve's hair, too, had lost its careless frivolity. She reached for her sister's hand.

'Of course I'm on your side. Always have been and always will be.'

With shrewd and kindly prodding from Tom, Eve began to talk of her work with Freda. She told how meeting others of the small group dedicated to the survival of The Workers' Diary had caused her view of the world to change. It was as if she had looked over her shoulder, she said, and seen the slow un-ravelling of her unlikely journey; seen that her parents' beliefs, although sincerely held, did not admit the entire truth and that her own carefree life had had little to do with the world as it really was. Freda's fury at governmental high-handed tactics had begun to affect her own thinking. When the watersiders were offered four-and-sevenpence-halfpenny an hour – and rejected it as an insult and because no family could live on so little – she had become fully involved with their cause, and with Archie. Then had come the partial lockout with men sacked for two days at a time for refusing to work overtime for such a pittance. The lockout, which the press insisted on calling a strike, had been made absolute. Eve's voice was angry now. How could the gov-ernment allow the children to go hungry? Hadn't the workers and their families been punished enough?

Lizzie's conservative foundations were rocking. She saw her own children, plates piled high with plentiful fresh food. In front of her The Worker's Diary accused: 'Elderly folk are beginning to die of neglect. Our children are at risk of pneumonia and other diseases.' She stood up to rescue the forgotten kettle.

'I'll make the tea, shall I?'

'Thanks, Liz.' Eve grinned ruefully at Tom. 'Well there you have it. I doubt when you left Fenton you expected to turn up a couple of Reds in the family!'

'I've known a few in my time,' he said. 'Good people mostly. I've been called one myself you know.'

'Tom fought in Spain,' Lizzie explained. 'Not that he's really a communist, of course.'

'Of course not,' said Tom, and winked at Eve.

'Seems I'm not the only one to keep secrets in this family then,' she said. 'My God. Me married to a socialist and Lizzie to an anarchist! Poor old Dad.'

Lizzie filled the teapot and carried it to the table. Heavy foot-steps sounded in the hall. Eve pulled the turban from her head. Familiar, blond waves fell to her shoulders. She grinned at Lizzie.

'Hardly practical, but Archie likes it.'

The door opened. A large man stood in the aperture, his face registering surprise at the sight of strangers in his kitchen. An elderly woman in tweeds, with last night's paper tucked beneath her arm, pushed past him to take stock.

'Well, well, well,' said Cousin Freda. 'Lizzie and Tom! And about time too!'

Archie gave a grunt of what Lizzie took to be pleasure. So this was Eve's knight! In spite of his size he seemed shy, not at all what she had expected. A suit would be entirely inappropriate, especially made of shining armour. He would look very much at home, she thought, with an axe in his hand. A real asset, in fact, when it came to chopping down a tree. Or at hay-making. It wasn't hard to imagine him tossing bales up on to a rising stack. If this was the sort of man to take Eve's fancy, she need have looked no further afield than Fenton! But unlike most of the farmers she knew, Archie was soon involved in a lively political discussion with Tom and Freda, a discussion way beyond Jim's occasional and dismissive ranting.

Eve concocted lunch for them all from the supplies Archie had brought with him from the effective, and illegal, Relief Committee. Thanks to Lizzie's cake, she wouldn't have to suffer the embarrassment of there not being enough to go round.

Whether she liked it or not, the conversation, Lizzie realised, was likely to run a political course all afternoon. Everyone, it seemed, was taking sides. Other unionists, as well as the locked-out watersiders, were declaring strikes up and down the country. More relief organisations were being set up as more and more families found themselves with little or no money to buy food. What was left of Lizzie's quiet resignation was shattered when Freda, helping herself to a second slice of cake, asked if she realised she had committed an illegal act by bringing food to her sister's house.

'It's only a cake for heaven's sake!' Lizzie retorted for the second time that day. 'If I want to bring Eve a present – food or anything else – who's to stop me?'

'It's illegal to give help of any kind to a watersider or his family,' Archie offered mildly. 'The young couple next door have a baby. Their family try to help out when they can, but they've been warned they'll be arrested if they're caught.'

Lizzie was appalled. 'Well, bugger the law then,' she said, eyes blazing.

Freda glanced with approval at her cousin's normally placid elder daughter. 'Amen to that!' she said.

Lizzie truly believed that nothing more could surprise or shock her that day, and so was unprepared for the fear she felt when Archie reached for Freda's copy of the Auckland Star and started to read the editorial aloud.

'Time for Action. The government must act rather than talk. It should announce that crowds on the waterfront will be dispersed without hesitation and that The Police Will Be Armed. Should individuals or groups defy the ban The Police Will Shoot.'

Tom brought his fist down on the table. Startled knives and forks clattered on their plates.

'This is exactly what we feared when we lost the fight against Franco! Oh, I know most people thought that irrelevant by '45. Everyone believed the war for democracy had been won. But we always knew the fascists would rise again without due vigilance. What's happening here, right under our noses proves that to be correct.' Not once, in all the years she had known him, had Lizzie seen him so angry.

'Reds under the bed?' Freda snorted. 'More like fascists at the bottom of the garden! Now, about Friday's march. We're not expecting any trouble. The authorities have given permission no matter what the paper says. Oh, by the way, Tom, did Margaret pass on my message about Jock? Thinks he knows you.'

'No,' said Tom, wondering which of his many like-named countrymen this particular Jock might be. 'I don't believe she did.'

What surprised Lizzie, as much as anything else that day, was that her husband's left wing proclivities were evidently a life-long conviction and not the fleeting passions of his youth as she had supposed. He and Freda seemed to have an astonishing amount in common, with Freda knowing as much and more of the events of the Spanish Civil War and its aftermath as did Tom himself. Her protests, when he promised Freda that he would help distribute copies of the latest edition of The Diary, were brushed aside. He was unknown in Auckland, not likely to be suspected of involvement. There was nothing at all for Lizzie to be concerned about.

She remained unconvinced but said little on the tram back to the hotel. Tom offered a penny for her thoughts. She replied merely that she was tired. Next morning, she telephoned The Oaks to assure her mother that Eve was well. She would give her all the details, she said, when she and Tom arrived home on Friday. Well, not all the details, she thought. And certainly not in her father's hearing. Yes, she replied in response to an anxious query, Archie was a kindly man. No, he hadn't shown the slightest tendency to violence and yes she quite understood why her mother would think he might, considering what was being said in the papers. Eve was quite safe, she insisted, and crossed her fingers. The phone began to crackle just as Margaret asked how Archie was managing to provide for them both. Lizzie shouted down the rapidly fragmenting line that she would be seeing Eve again that morning. Her mother was not to worry. She replaced the receiver, thinking the interference opportune and wondering what on earth she was going to tell her parents when she got home.

Her pleas to Tom not to get further involved fell on deaf ears.

'I'm going down to the waterfront before we go to Eve's. I might pick up something Freda can use in the next edition of The Diary.'

'You're not serious, Tom! You saw what it said in the paper!'

'Which is precisely why I want to be there.'

'Well then, I'm coming too. If I have a husband stupid enough to want to get himself shot, I want to be there.'

'No, Lizzie. You go on to Eve's.'

'I said I'm coming with you! You're a bloody fool just like Dad says, but I'm coming with you.'

As they approached the wharves at the foot of Queen Street, Lizzie could hardly believe her eyes. There were soldiers every-where, and sailors and airmen, all in battle kit. Hundreds of them. Tom was no less astonished.

'It looks like a war-time command post!'

Although the ranks of naval ratings seemed to be holding

only batons, the gathering soldiers had bayoneted rifles. Tin hats and fighting gear offered a strange contrast to the trilby hats and suits of businessmen hurrying from trams and ferries to their offices, and to the gloved and hatted secretaries and shop girls in head scarves. They were accosted at the intersection with Customs Street and told to be on their way. Lizzie explained that they were visitors from the country. They had planned a pleasant early morning walk along the waterfront, presuming, wrongly it seemed, that the troublemakers had been persuaded to stay at home. She smiled at the constable, thanked him for his sensible advice, gripped Tom's arm and steered him out of harm's way.

'He's right. It's got nothing to do with us. And I don't mind admitting I'm terrified. I think we've quite enough information for Freda, don't you?'

'Indeed we have, lassie.'

A convoy of covered lorries drove past.

'Must be the strike-breakers Archie was on about,' said Tom. 'The men who've joined the new union.'

They counted twenty-one lorries.

'Perhaps the government is right, after all,' said Lizzie. 'I mean if so many men have joined the new union, perhaps the ones who haven't, like Archie, have got it all wrong.'

'We don't know how many men are under those tarpaulins,' Tom said. 'Archie has it on good authority that only a handful of men have signed on, so you can be sure most of this will be for show.'

Even had Archie been wrong and the lorries carrying full loads of 'new unionists' through the picket, one thing was certain, each man had the protection of at least five armed servicemen. Black police patrol cars wove back and forth. A voice shouted that more cars, constables aboard and engines running, had arrived at the central police station.

Seeing those she guessed to be watersiders standing quietly beyond the lines of uniformed men that morning, Lizzie knew that what she was witnessing was not the violent, irresponsible political action reported by the press. She remembered how Archie had spoken of his concerns, his quiet, protective love for Eve. She was confused and upset. Past beliefs dictated that those elected to govern would do so with wisdom and for the benefit of all. What she had experienced these past two days did not add up to anything that made any sense to her.

They separated some distance from the wharves, Lizzie to go straight to Eve's, Tom to an address given to him by Freda. He was to pick up copies of The Diary and take them around the pubs where locked out workers were still welcome whether or not they had the price of a pint to spend.

A few trams were still running on Queen Street but how regularly and where they were going, Lizzie had no idea. Yesterday, Archie had described the route he had walked prior to the lockout. Lizzie set off up the steep hill, pondering the upheavals and insights of the past two days. It seemed she had inadvertently joined a game of see-saw, one end loaded with people who had a very different agenda to her own. She was alone at the other, suspended and unsure how to get off.

Eve's door was open. Lizzie found her sister in the kitchen on her knees, surrounded by sheets of cardboard.

'Placards,' she said, waving a welcome with her paintbrush. 'For the march.'

'Oh,' Lizzie said 'Yes, of course.'

Large blank squares of card lay in an untidy pile. Others, already filled in with their painted slogan, were spread across the floor to dry. Palings lay in another pile waiting to be attached to the finished placards. Lizzie hoped Eve wasn't planning to carry one and make herself conspicuous. She almost spoke the thought aloud, then bit her tongue. Freda had said it would be all right. The march had been carefully planned. There would be no trouble. Which was hard to believe considering the scene she had just witnessed at the waterfront.

'Need a hand?' she asked.

Eve grinned and pointed to some charcoal on the table.

'You do the lettering,' she said. 'And I'll fill in the paint.'

Lizzie settled beside her on the floor. 'Just like art class in the Infants,' she said.

'You used to draw sheep,' said Eve. 'I particularly remember you bringing home a picture of a lamb with pink eyes and two tails.'

'That reminds me. We have to head back to Fenton tomorrow. Tom has arranged to look at some stock on the way home.'

'You'll miss the march.'

'I'm missing the children,' said Lizzie. She didn't add how pleased she would be to have Tom away from Auckland before Friday. She reached for another blank sheet and began to outline: Hear the Other Side of the Story, Domain, Sunday, in clear and carefully spaced letters.

'Not bad,' said Eve.

They worked steadily for the best part of another hour, singing childhood songs and remembering adventures in the hay barn and school picnics at the beach and how, in those far off days, the sun was always shining.

Eve added a flourish to the last placard. 'There,' she said. 'Democracy at work. Let's have a cuppa.'

When Tom arrived, he told them he'd decided to stay on until Monday.

'But I've already told the children we'll be home on Saturday at the latest,' said Lizzie.

'They've asked me to speak in the Domain. Let folks know there's at least one farmer on their side.'

Lizzie retorted that he'd probably get lynched and added that she'd had enough. He could stay on if he wanted but she was going home.

Next morning a banner headline in the paper informed her that the railway workers were on strike again. She telephoned The Oaks. Margaret said Jim would send one of his men over to Tom and Lizzie's place in case Ben needed a hand. There was nothing at all to worry about. They might as well take advantage of a few days' extra holiday while they could. The children were having a great time and not missing them at all.

Now whose doing the reassuring, Lizzie wondered as she replaced the receiver. She thanked heaven her mother hadn't probed too deeply about Eve. The mention of placards and marching would create an uproar in Fenton. Tom could do his bit for democracy on Sunday and then, trains willing, they could both go home. He had offered her one small consolation, that he wouldn't march on Friday. He would stand on the pavement and cheer on the unionists from there. He said he hoped Lizzie would be there with him.

The unionists, their wives and supporters gathered in Queen Street, voices blending in a low roar as their numbers grew. Tom and Lizzie stood watching from further up the hill. The crowd of bystanders was swelling too and seemed, for the most part, not unsympathetic. Hands waved from a passing tram. Unionist hands waved back. The authorities had given permission for the march. There would be no trouble. The route was to be uphill, away from the wharves where the presence of the locked out workers might seem antagonistic. There would be no violence and no reason to provoke it. The march would bring Aucklanders flocking to the Domain on Sunday, their curiosity whetted, anxious to hear facts straight from the mouths of those who were experiencing hardship first hand. The union side of the story would be told and justice would be done.

An arm was raised, followed by loud cheering. The scene looked almost festive as the unionists moved off four and five abreast behind a slowly moving tram. Lizzie wondered which of the waving placards was held by Eve, and whether she would spot Freda in the crowd.

The marchers had covered almost half the distance to where Tom and Lizzie stood when the leaders seemed to hesitate. Lizzie craned her head to see what had caught their attention. A line of black police cars had turned into the street and was coming down the hill. The leading car swerved in front of the tram and brought it to a halt. The vehicles behind it swept to either side and stopped, blocking the entire street. Helmeted constables erupted from the cars to form a line in front of their barricading vehicles. Reinforcements poured in on foot from side streets, batons at the ready. Marchers attempting to turn back were blocked by others pressing forward to see what was happening. The constables raised their batons and charged into the crowd. Men and women fell to the ground. Others clutched their heads and arms, stumbling as they tried to get away. Eve and Freda were somewhere in that mêlée. Archie too. The pavements were clearing as the onlookers fled. Tom took Lizzie by the hand and began to run with her down the street.

The constables evaporated as quickly as they had come. People were milling around, bemused and angry. Others lay bleeding on the ground. Tom led a woman to the kerbside, saw her safely claimed by a friend and turned back to find Lizzie on her knees in the gutter, ripping strips from her petticoat. Blood seeped through the fingers of a large man sitting by her on the kerb, his head in his hands. Tom knelt to help tie the makeshift bandage. The man smiled his thanks, looked a second time at Tom and grinned.

'Freda mentioned you were in town.'

'Jock? Jock McPherson? My God! What are you doing here?'

'Much the same as you, laddie. I was to give them a wee spiel in the park come Sunday. About the fascists and their evil plans for humanity, the bloody bastards. Begging your pardon missus.'

Eve arrived, limping and bruised. Archie was with her, his usually placid face a study of bafflement and disgust.

'Have you seen Freda?' Lizzie asked.

'Someone's taken her home,' Eve said. 'She's hurt. Not too badly. She'll be all right.'

Archie leaned down to inspect Lizzie's handiwork.

'He'll need stitches,' she said.

Archie nodded. 'We'll get you up to the hospital. This is Lizzie Johnston, by the way. Eve's sister. And her husband, Tom. He fought the fascists in Spain.'

'Aye, I know,' said Jock as Tom held out his hand and hauled him to his feet.

It was decided that Eve and Lizzie would go to Freda's to see if she was indeed all right. It had been awful, Eve said, to see the fight dying in her eyes and how, suddenly, she had seemed old. They found her tired but recovered enough to swear her fighting spirit far from dead. She'd been fed and watered like a good war-horse, she said, and would feel even better after a good night's sleep. They left her tucked up in bed and caught a tram to Eve's. At the hospital, on the other side of town, Tom was telling Jock about being sent out to New Zealand during the war and how he had met Lizzie.

'Ye're a lucky devil on both counts,' Jock said and added that much of his war had been spent fighting alongside New Zealanders in Africa. Perhaps it was so much desert that had made him hungry for a sight of their green and pleasant land.

'Great lads,' he said. 'So long as ye slept with one eye open or next morning ye'd find half yer gear missing. Ye'd not meet a more innocent-looking, wide-eyed bunch either! What me, Jock? Stole yer wee hankie, Jock? Never! But I'd choose none other beside me in a scrap. I thought maybe I'd emigrate here right after the war, then I got myself elected onto a union committee and a few more years rolled by, as they do. When I read that the workers here were having a rough time of it I thought maybe I'd come over after all. See what I could do. Bloody fascists!' A passing nurse glared and asked him to kindly keep his opinions to himself. A patient muttered, 'Bloody Pommies, more like' then seeing the look in Archie's eye, moved to a chair at the other end of the room and disappeared behind a magazine.

Later, with Jock patched up, Tom and Archie took him with them to the cottage at Three Lamps. Lizzie had laid on a plentiful supper for them all, bought from the surprised owner of the corner shop. Before long, the conversation turned to Jock's first meeting with Tom at the Ebro. It was almost, Lizzie thought, as if a flood gate had been opened. For the first time in years, Tom could speak of his experiences with someone who had known the horror of it all, someone who had not only fought for the same cause but had known the despair and terror of a Spanish prison.

'Ye'll have no trouble in remembering Commandant Federico then?'

Silence. There were no words, Lizzie thought, to describe the look on Tom's face at that moment. She wondered if Jock knew of Tom's interrogation, whether he too had suffered such brutal questioning; if he knew about the girl in the photograph and the terrible thing that had been done to her.

'Ye had even more cause to hate him than the rest of us.'

Still Tom said nothing, then in a tone that sent a chill up Lizzie's spine, he said, 'He's dead.'

'So it's true then,' Jock murmured. 'Well, that's one bastard less in the world.'

The odd, unfocussed expression lingered in Tom's eyes. It's as if the rest of us are merely onlookers, thought Lizzie, from another place, another time. As if we don't belong here.

Archie glanced at the clock.

'I'm for my bed. It's been a long day. You'll stay the night, won't you, Jock?'

'Of course he will,' said Eve. 'Tom and Lizzie are in the spare room. Jock can have the settee.'

'That's good of you, Eve. I'm thinking we've a few more miles to travel before Tom and I turn in. You won't mind, will you lass?'

'No. No, of course not.' Lizzie rested her hand on Tom's shoulder. 'Don't stay up too late.'

The day had left her exhausted but it was impossible to sleep. Her mind was churning. The lumpy mattress on the single bed and Tom's coat for warmth on top of a thin blanket didn't help much either. Nor did the light seeping through the curtain from the street lamp outside. She reached for her watch, and squinted. One thirty. She would fetch a glass of water, remind Tom that it was already Saturday and that she was anxious to make an early start – so long as the trains were running again. She pulled on the dressing gown Eve had lent her – one from her more flamboyant days by the look of it – and made her way back along the passage to the kitchen. A strip of light spilled round the unlatched door. She reached to push it wide, then hesitated, unwilling to break the silence on the other side.

Jock's voice came, then, soft and concerned. 'Will ye no tell me what happened, laddie?'

'I went back.'

Lizzie's hand dropped from the door. Back where? To Spain? When? She remembered the long wait for Tom to come home after the war. Had he....? No. She was being ridiculous. The secret nature of his work had delayed him, nothing more.

'Is that so?' Jock again, speculative, admiring. 'And ye got out again in one piece? The men of the Brigades are still marked, ye ken.'

'I was working for Intelligence by then. I had contacts. One of them was sympathetic enough to get me some papers. I thought the game was up when I ran into Pedro Valera, one of the guards at the prison. He could have earned himself a hefty reward for turning me in to the military police.'

'Valera? I remember him. One of the few decent human beings in that place. Said he hated all the killing. I think he pitied us. I remember the day a boy from his village was brought in and shot. I didn't see him around after that.'

'He told me he was tortured. They said he was keeping information from them. He denied it, so Federico let his thugs have their way with him until they broke him. Pedro told them the boy's family had been hiding Republican sympathisers. There may have been some truth in that but he had no way of knowing it at the time. They shot the boy's entire family and then Pedro's too. Then they sent him back to his village. It was a pile of rubble.'

'Where did ye meet him?'

'In Seville.'

'Seville?'

'On my way to Arcos. There was someone I had to find.'

Lizzie's mouth formed the woman's name. Isabel! He had gone back to find Isabel!

'Valera was working as a shoe black, barely scratching a living. I didn't recognise him at first. He knelt down in front of me, got out his brushes and set to work without a word. Then he started talking. Just the usual pleasantries at first. Eventually he said he'd recognised me and that I must pretend not to know him. He said that all the walls in all of Spain listen with Franco's ears, that the sky sucks up secrets and the clouds take them straight to the Generalísimo. I offered to buy him a meal but he said he didn't want food. He was used to hunger. All he wanted was revenge. He asked if I would help him.

'He'd heard that Federico had been stationed in Seville early in the Civil War and had gone back there afterwards with his wife and son. Pedro decided to hang around till he found a way to kill him. Then he thought murdering the child would be easier and might be revenge enough. By the time he'd worked it all out, the woman and the boy had disappeared into thin air. I'd realised by then that Pedro was at least a little mad. And I suppose I caught his madness. Anyway, I agreed to help him.'

'For the wee nurse you were sweet on?'

'Yes, for Isabel.'

'And did you succeed?'

'We did.' He was silent for a moment. 'I escaped by the skin of my teeth. When I got over here I had my London contacts find out what had happened to Pedro. He'd been caught and taken to Madrid. It doesn't take much imagination to guess what his fate would have been.'

'No, indeed,' Jock murmured.

'The thing is, at the last moment Pedro lost his nerve. However much he hated the man, he wasn't a killer. Couldn't go through with it. I murdered Federico and I was glad to do it. Pedro took the punishment for what I did.'

Lizzie turned away. She walked back along the passageway, one hand pressed against her stomach, the other to her mouth as if to hold in the pain. Her husband had killed a man. Perhaps that wasn't so strange. People killed people. That's what wars were about. He could have killed many, yet she knew he had not. But he had killed for Isabel. She got into bed and turned her face to the wall so that when Tom came he would think her sleeping.

Part Four

Chapter Twenty-three

Six years had passed since Rosario had first seen the rock they called la Centinela on the Rocío road and dreamed of making her first pilgrimage. Since then, she had twice before made the week-long journey across the serranía with the Brotherhood of Puente Nuevo.

A pair of unyoked, impassive oxen waited outside the church. Silver bells attached to their purple trappings jingled as the animals lowered their heads to feed from a small mound of hay. Two men leaned against the high stone wall, drawing in pungent black tobacco, exhaling wisps of smoke into the hot, dry air. When the butts were short enough to burn their yellowed fingers, they stubbed them on the cobbles with their boot heels, eased their bodies from the wall and stooped to lift the heavy yoke from the dust. They laid it on the beasts' broad shoulders and attached it to the shaft of a white, flower-decked, silver-canopied cart. Behind them, the church doors opened, releasing the Rocieros from its dim interior like a chattering flock of brightly plumaged birds.

Like the other women, Rosario wore a long, low-waisted, deep-flounced dress. The one she had chosen for today was a dusky pink, scattered with white dots, its frills edged with lace. A gold crucifix hung at her neck framed by a white fringed shawl. The stout boots on her feet might have seemed incongruous but for the traditional staff of the Rociera in her hand and the pilgrim's medallion dangling from a green ribbon reaching almost to her waist. She had felt a moment of ecstasy inside the church. On the steps outside, watching the noisy bustling preparation, her euphoria lingered, together with a fleeting moment of pity for those not sharing her good fortune.

High-wheeled, horse-drawn wagons, their arched canvas roofs garlanded with flowers, wheeled into place around the tree-lined square. Shouts and laughter echoed against the high walls of the church. The strumming of guitars mingled with snatches of song. Young men on horseback, some with frilled beauties perched like exotic flowers behind them, trotted back and forth. Sunlight caught rich embroidery as the Simpecado was brought from the church, carried down the steps and placed in the silver and white cart. The Virgin, as was customary, would remain in Puente Nuevo while her standard led the Rocieros westward across the serranía.

A horse clattered to a halt in front of her, barring Rosario's way. Its rider doffed his wide-brimmed, grey hat.

'Señorita Rosario!' She recognised him at once, although there was little to identify him now with the roughly dressed farm boy she had known when she was a child. Nor did he look much like the banderillero she had seen three years ago walking with Ramón Ramirez and his cuadrilla through the streets of Puente Nuevo. He had seen her watching from her balcony and raised his montera in salute. At the corrida that afternoon he had crossed the sand like quicksilver, his banderillos held aloft, just as she had dreamed him years before, the bull's horns sweeping so close that she had cried out and clutched her brother's arm. If Diego had been killed, she told Carmela later, she was sure she too would die. She was in love, she said. Quite hopelessly. Hopelessly indeed, Carmela had agreed, brushing tangles from her long, black hair. She had patted Rosario's hand and told her she would get over it in time.

She hadn't, of course, although Ramón Ramirez had not come again to Puente Nuevo with his cuadrilla. Fate, she decided, had kept Diego from her until he acquired sufficient status to satisfy her father. That he was a gentleman now she had no doubt. He was dressed in the tight grey trousers, cropped jacket and silver-spurred, high-heeled riding boots of a caballero. He, too, wore a gold medallion on a wide, green ribbon; he, too, would be be travelling to El Rocío! Warmth burned beneath the knot of hair lying against her neck. She turned away before it could rise to her cheeks and pushed her way through the crowd to join her parents.

The oxen lumbered across the square pulling the Simpecado to the head of the cavalcade. Roberto, standing by the leading wagon, lifted Rosario to sit beside her mother. He put his foot on the high wheel and leapt up after her, caught up the reins and flicked them on the horse's rump. As they moved off at a slow walk, Rosario leaned out to look back at the trail of carts and riders following behind. She was hoping to catch sight of Diego, hoping he hadn't invited some flounce-dressed girl to ride behind him, a flower in her hair and an arm clasped round his waist.

They were well clear of the town when the height of the sun announced the hour to eat and the siesta to follow. Wagons and riders pulled into a small clearing at the roadside. Tables were set up and food hampers opened. Jugs of wine were handed round. Passing tourists, thinking they had chanced on a gypsy camp, pulled up in their cars, took photographs and drove off again, unaware of the abundance of food and absence of rib-thin dogs. When the midday heat had cooled, the travellers, too, resumed their journey, the Virgin's Simpecado at their head like an embroidered sail on a small white ship, its sea the rugged hills and troughed valleys of the serranía.

As evening fell, they came to a wide, flat strip of wasteland. Shadows drew enigmatic shapes as the wagons moved across the barren, rock-strewn space. A pyramid of twigs and branches stood at its centre, built by people from the nearby village. A match was struck as they approached, its tiny flame drawn into the kindling, forming blue and orange ribbons writhing through the dry and crackling wood.

When the camp had been made ready for the night, pots of food were brought from the wagons and set in place to cook. More villagers, summoned by the firelight, came with fruit and wine. Some were Rocieros, like their visitors, and would come again next morning to travel with them to the west. A hubbub filled the air as friends greeted old acquaintances. Groups formed and broke, formed again and settled at last around the campfire. Prayers were said and appetites appeased, wine skins shared, guitars taken up and tuned. A villager stood to sing an impromptu welcome. A traveller replied with a verse of gratitude for having come safely to this place; another sang of the joy awaiting them in El Rocío. Cupped palms clapped the muted rhythm of the Sevillanas, others beat a sharp, taut-fingered counterpoint. Their feet stamped against the dusty ground as couples swirled beside the campfire, shoulders not quite touching in the weaving pattern of the dance.

Rosario's mind was on Diego rather than her partners' flirting as she danced with first one and then another of the young caballeros. An hour passed before he stepped from the shadows. He gave her besotted escort a brief bow of apology and led her back to the patch of flat, dry earth where the dancers were waiting for the music to begin again. Firelight gleamed on his face. He looks, Rosario thought, like a pagan god. Their arms rose in unison to a single strident chord, spines arching, chins and shoulders aloof and deceiving: mirror images about to be swept by the Sevillanas into a single intricate being.

Roberto, sitting with Isabel among a group of friends, had seen his daughter claimed by a new partner. He recognised him as Diego Montero, protégé of the matador Ramón Ramirez and Juan's childhood playmate. He had met him briefly and seen him working as a banderillero in Ramirez's cuadrilla some years before, and had been impressed enough to think the boy might become successful in his own right. Two years later, Ramirez's career had ended abruptly and in disgrace, and Montero's with it, when the two bulls they were about to fight had been found with their horns shaved to bluntness. Ramirez, Roberto recalled, had pleaded ignorance; a rumour had circled among the aficionados that Diego Montero was to blame. Whatever the truth, the matador had retired from the bullfight in disgrace. Two years later news had come of his death. If Montero's horse and expensive clothing were anything to go by, it would seem he had inherited Ramirez's fortune – which, in spite of any hopes he might be harbouring, did not make him Rosario's equal. Roberto took no pleasure in seeing such a man in his daughter's company, despite the freedom from social mores offered by the pilgrimage. He would have been glad of her brother's watchful eye, but Juan had chosen to remain in Puente Nuevo studying for his entrance to university in Madrid the following year.

Next morning, as they approached the rock they called la Centinela, Rosario's mind was on the long-ago summer when she had climbed it with Juan and Diego. Isabel, misinterpreting her daughter's shiver of remembered pleasure, told her to fetch her shawl from the wagon.

She pushed her way past the swaying rack of brightly coloured dresses and her father's suits and peered out through a slit in the canvas wall. Diego was sure to be riding nearby. Perhaps he would see her and give a signal that he too remembered the place. But the path had narrowed already: there was nothing to see but the beast pulling the following wagon, its head low against the rising dust.

On the third night of their journey, long after the revellers had retired to their wagons, or to sleep under the stars, Rosario lay awake. Diego, not showing any preference, had danced with several girls before approaching her. Later, he had sought her out and pointed to a nearby copse. He asked if she would meet him there. She had laughed but was now unable to sleep for thinking about him. Her parents were sleeping soundly; there would be no harm. She crept from her mattress and threw a long woollen shawl over her nightgown. The wagon creaked as she jumped to the ground. She stood beside its shadowy bulk listening for any sound of wakefulness inside. Cigarette and wood smoke lingered in the air. The dying campfire crackled, sending sparks sputtering red, blue and silver to join their sisters briefly in the sky. Young men smoked and talked, dark shapes wrapped in blankets against the chill night. She peered into the darkness. What if Diego had changed his mind? For all she knew he was sitting with the shadowed figures by the fire. Perhaps he was already rolled in his blanket fast asleep. A match flared by the copse. She hesitated a moment longer then ran towards the trees. The tiny signal flared again and died. As she neared the place, a shadow moved beside her. An arm circled her waist. A tobacco scented hand silenced her before she could cry out. For a split second she wondered what she would do if the hand were not Diego's. In spite of the Caudillo's efforts, there were still bandits in the mountains, and gypsies. Worse still, her father might have heard her go and wondered why she had not yet returned. Indulgent as he was, he would not forgive her an adventure such as this. She twisted round to face her captor. His silencing hand slipped from her mouth to her chin and tipped it. She closed her eyes. He had kissed her the night he had brought Juan home drunk to the cortijo. They had been children then, but she had not forgotten the way his mouth had felt against hers, nor her regret when he released her so quickly. This time his lips lingered, demanding more. She would have cried out with the surprise of it had his tongue not found hers, astonishing and silencing her. His hands reached under the fringes of her shawl, cupping her buttocks through the thinness of her nightgown, kneading them like pliant dough. Flickering, fiery shocks pulsed through her as Diego drew her closer to him, his hardness pressing against her soft belly. Like a lodestone, she thought, a lodestone that would hold them together forever. He kissed her again, then held her from him.

'Go to bed, querida. We have a long day's travelling tomorrow.'

She opened her mouth to protest.

'Go,' he said again.

Considering what has passed between them in the night, Rosario was astonished, next morning, to see Lucía Romero, a girl who had joined them at their first campsite, riding behind Diego. Rather than put up with her mother's enquiries as to what was upsetting her, she said she had a headache and would ride inside the wagon. Separated from the sight of the girl's lithe brown arms round Diego's waist, and by the rack of clothing from her mother's anxious glance, she gave way to a rage of tears. A mirror attached to a pole supporting the canvas roof reflected a tragic but satisfying image. Even with eyes pink from crying she was more than a match for her rival. When Diego asked her to dance with him that evening, she would demand an explanation.

But he did not ask her to dance. The remnants of the meal had long been cleared away. Flagons of wine were passing hand to hand and Diego had not so much as looked her way. She circled the campfire, careful to make her progress seem utterly casual. Diego caught her eye and turned away. She bit her lip, barely holding back tears and an exclamation of anger, wondering what she had done to offend him. That evening, her many willing partners were surprised to find the usually exuberant Rosario Álvarez subdued and entirely uninterested in their attentions. She told her mother her morning's headache had returned and retired to bed long before the dancing ended.

When enough hours had passed for her to be sure that even the watchers by the campfire would be sleeping, she climbed down from the wagon. She had seen Diego tether his horse, Negrito, apart from the others and knew it was his habit to sleep close by. The black horse whinnied softly as she approached. Saddlebags were stacked nearby but there was no sign of its owner. An animal snuffled and grunted in the undergrowth. If it sensed her presence, a hungry wild boar might well attack her. Perhaps a starving gypsy dog had wandered from its camp. She was about to retrace her steps when she heard rustling and smothered laughter, and then a moan that froze her to the spot. She pressed up against Negrito, petrified. The sounds died away to a long silence followed by more laughter and soft words. There were two voices, one a woman's.

A flash of coloured shawl passed close by her in the moonlight. A hand caught her shoulder.

'It's late,' Diego said. 'Good girls should be fast asleep in their wagons with their fathers on guard beside them.'

She whirled to face him.

'Diego!' Fear flooded away into relief, then anger. 'Was that the Romero girl?'

'Girl? What girl?'

'Why did Lucía ride with you today?'

'She twisted her ankle. What was I to do? The poor girl was hobbling.'

Rosario doubted that. The girl who had crossed her path a moment earlier had shown no sign of any such affliction.

'I'll ride with you tomorrow, shall I?'

'I think not, querida.'

'Why not?' She stamped her foot and regretted the childish impulse when he laughed. He pulled her to him.

'Your father would not approve.'

She reached up, linking her fingers behind his neck. 'I love you, Diego. Don't tease me.'

'What do you know of love, querida?'

She was surprised that he understood her so little. Last night he had held her so close he must surely have felt her heart beating against his ribs in rhythm with his own.

'Love,' she said 'is the freedom an eagle feels when it flies above the serranía.'

'Your father will never allow you that freedom with me.'

'I'll go away with you.'

His laugh was a breath against her cheek. 'And shall I be the one to open your cage, little eagle? Go now.' He patted her lightly on the rump as he might a foal. 'We will talk again in El Rocío.'

'Promise?'

'I promise. Now go.'

She ran towards her father's wagon. Once she turned back, her face shining like a waxen virgin in the moonlight.

'Love,' Diego murmured. Yes, it would be all too easy to love her.

Chapter Twenty-four

The Brotherhood of Puente Nuevo came to El Rocío on the Saturday of Pentecost, weary from the long journey and the travail of bringing animals and wagons safely through fast-flowing rivers; weary too from nights spent dancing under Andalucía's sky. Members of Brotherhoods from far-flung towns and hamlets streamed in their thousands to the isolated sand island in the marshes, their bright clothing dulled by the dust of the often arduous, sometimes dangerous journey. As each community arrived, however large or small, however tired, they went first to present their embroidered banner to the Virgin in her shrine, then carry it to the great altar beneath the eucalyptus trees and set it there among its sisters.

Wagons filled the sandy streets, hundreds more circled the village. Friends not seen in twelve months greeted each other. Wine skins and gossip passed among them. As the sun began to set, the people moved through the streets, coming from all quarters of the little town, laughing and singing, flowing into the great square beneath the trees like leaves drawn into a whirlpool.

The Simpecados shone on the altar in the dying sun. Three thousand burnished horses and their riders stood in four ranks at the perimeter of the crowd. At a signal, they set off in an undulating, dappled tide of black, brown and grey towards the

Virgin's shine, the tangling mass of people unravelling to walk behind them. Three hours went by before the tail of the vast procession passed by the sanctuary.

Drums and the music of a thousand guitars filled the village all that night. Exhaustion was shrugged aside. Horsemen raced across the sand, girls whirled with their partners like uncaged exotic birds drunk with unaccustomed freedom and a little wine.

The church bells rang at dawn. The yawning sun rose and rested for a moment on the horizon, seeming to listen to the last weary voices still drifting out across the marshlands.

At ten o'clock, two hundred thousand souls gathered in silence in the square. Riders dismounted to kneel beside their horses on the sand. The Simpecados, standards of the Virgin's other selves, shimmered on the altar. The priest came and as he spoke into that vast, expectant silence each person present believed they heard the voice of God Himself. Like generations before them, His Holy Mother had drawn them here to receive Her blessing. No one knew just how long ago it had occurred, the miracle of the small, carved Virgin found under a tree and named the Blanca Paloma, Queen of the Marshlands, the Virgin of El Rocío.

The fiesta continued all that day and again throughout the night, although with less vigour and in lesser numbers than before. Rosario slept beside her parents, overcome with tiredness. Next morning, she took a bright, clean dress from the rack. She had seen little of Diego since their arrival. Today, she was determined to find him in the crowd outside the church and be with him when the Virgin was brought from her sanctuary.

Men from the nearby village of Almonte had gone early to the shrine. The Queen of the Marshes was their own and they were prepared to fight for the honour of carrying her out to the people. Men from other villages, equally determined, used fists and elbows, fighting as men will to claim the object of their love.

Rosario raised herself on her toes to see over the heads of those in front. It was hopeless. She would never find Diego. She could see the Virgin now, coming towards her, swaying above the people's heads. The crowd pushed her further forward. As the figure passed, the Virgin's painted eyes met hers as if a promise had been made.

Perhaps it was the joy of being so close to her, perhaps because of the bodies pressing so tightly around her, but it seemed that the earth tipped and shifted. The Virgin's view lurched too, trembling as more hands, anxious for their turn, reached out to grasp some part of her conveyance. A strong arm circled Rosario's waist, steadying her.

'Diego!' It would be pleasant, she thought, to die with his eyes on hers, his smile accompanying her to heaven. More pleasurable though to feel so alive and secure in the curve of his arm.

'Meet me inside the shrine before we leave for Puente Nuevo,' he said. She felt his arm slip from her waist as he disappeared back into the mass of people. She turned to go after him and found herself staring instead at Lucía Romero. The girl was laughing.

'Think you're a match for Diego? A man like him needs a woman, not a silly, fainting girl.'

Rosario's hand itched to slap her. 'You,' she said, 'had best watch your tongue!'

Later, with the Virgin returned to her sanctuary and her parents occupied with making ready for the journey home, Rosario asked if she might go one last time to the shrine. It seemed that her mother might protest, but her father nodded, telling her not to be too long about it. They must go soon if they were to reach their first campsite before dark. She ran back across the sandy earth, unnoticed in the bustle. The interior of the small, white sanctuary was empty of people now and dim, the candles flickering at the Virgin's feet almost spent. Rosario knelt, closed her eyes and waited for him to come. She heard the creak of his leather boots, felt him kneel beside her and his breath on her ear as he whispered to her to follow him. In an even darker recess, away from the watchful eyes of the Virgin, he took her in his arms.

'Are you sure you love me, Rosario?' Her body rippled against his in answer. 'Your father will never give us permission to marry. You know that.'

'But he will. In time. When I tell him I'd rather die than live without you. He would do anything to make me happy.'

For a fleeting moment Diego wondered if she might be right. He didn't doubt Roberto Álvarez's desire for his daughter's happiness. He was also sure his plans for that happiness proscribed men like himself. Whichever way it was to go, it was too late now for him to change his mind. He wanted her and loved her. He laid his hands on her shoulders.

'Are you brave?' he asked. Her eyes told him what he already knew. When he said she must not speak to him again she laughed and said words were unimportant. Their bodies would speak all that was between them while they danced their way back to Puente Nuevo. He would not dance with her, he said. If anyone had suspected their feelings, it must be made clear they no longer cared for each other's company. She protested. People would speculate of course. That was the way of things on any pilgrimage to El Rocío. His hands tightened on her shoulders. She must do as he said or it would be over before it had begun.

She shrugged his hands away. 'How can I be in love and not show it?'

'Secrecy,' he assured her, 'makes love sublime.' He kissed her, gently at first, and then in the way she had longed for. When he released her, she told him she would do anything he asked.

'I will leave the road to ride to my cortijo before we reach la

Centinela,' he said. 'That afternoon you must walk behind with the usual laggards. When you arrive at the rock, tell them you are returning to your father's wagon. The way is too narrow there to pass safely. No one will think anything of it if you take the higher path. Do you remember where it comes out on the other side?' She nodded. 'Wait for me there until I come for you.'

All doubts fled and with them all reason. She would follow him to the ends of the earth. She clung to him as he kissed her again.

'Go now,' he said, releasing her. 'Before your father comes looking for you.'

Inside their wagon, making their final preparations for departure, Isabel asked Roberto if he was concerned by their daughter's increasing, even excessive, religiosity.

He reminded her that many tears were shed at the shrine of the Blanca Paloma, and not only by the young and impressionable. It was natural for Rosario to feel overwhelmed at the thought of being parted from the Virgin. At her age a year seemed much longer. He reminded her, too, of her own tears when she had come here with his family. It was in El Rocío that they had first spoken seriously of their love.

'In Rosario's case, it's the Virgin she loves.'

'Which is exactly as it should be,' he reminded her.

'I had hopes for her other than spending her life in a convent. Although,' she added turning from him so that he barely caught the words, 'I have sometimes thought it might be for the best.'

He wondered if, at last, she would speak to him of the thing that had lain so heavily on her all these years. But she did not and he would not press her. He held her close.

'Our daughter will be married soon enough. I guarantee that within a year of that happy event you will find yourself a grand-mother.'

'And will you love me when I'm so old?'

'Always,' he said. 'In this world and the next.'

I owe him so much, she thought. So much more than he can ever know.

By mid-afternoon the last of the travellers had left the small town to wend their way north, south and east across the vastness of Andalucía. In a year's time, when her people returned to worship the Blanca Paloma, El Rocío would wake again in a brilliant explosion of noise and colour.

Chapter Twenty-five

Diego had ignored Rosario, as he said he would, since their departure. The great cliff face of Puente Nuevo appeared, heat-hazed, a day's journey to the east. She wondered if he had changed his mind. There had been times when she had doubted her own courage and then found it restored by her parents exasperation at her changing moods.

She was inside the wagon when she heard him calling his goodbyes to his fellow travellers and then his voice close by, wishing her parents a safe ending to their journey. She looked out through the canvas slit. He caught her eye and raised his whip in salute, then turned onto the path to his cortijo and was gone. She would do as he asked. If he did not come, she supposed she would starve to death waiting for him, like a heroine in a book.

The caravan halted a few miles further on. In months to come the bone-weary travellers would talk with nostalgia of the privations of their journey. Just now their thoughts were more inclined towards the comforts of their homes. Tonight's camp would be their last. They prepared and ate their midday meal, took a brief siesta and set off again. Rosario joined those walking behind the last wagon. Lucía was among them, unable, Rosario supposed, to seduce another young man into inviting her to ride on his horse. The girl had danced with Diego every night of the homeward journey and had ridden with him for at least some part of each day. If there had been gossip about Rosario's friendship with him on the way to El Rocío, it was forgotten now. Lucía was clearly infatuated with Diego. Watching them dance together had been torture, as had the whispered speculation as to the nature of their friendship. She was not pleased when the girl approached and fell into step beside her. When Lucía took her arm, slowing their pace behind the others, she snatched it away.

'Ah, Rosario, don't be unkind. I've come to say goodbye, that's all.'

'You could do that tonight when we reach your village, if it's so important to you.'

Lucía ignored the snub. 'Shall I see you there, then? Or in Puente Nuevo for that matter?'

'It's very unlikely,' Rosario said.

Lucía laughed. 'I guessed as much.'

Rosario's hand tightened on her staff and then relaxed. Lucía was referring to the social mores of the town, nothing more.

La Centinela's bulk loomed close by.

'I'm tired,' she said. 'My parents will be wondering why I've stayed away so long.'

'You'd best hurry, then. You'll have to take the path over the rock. The first wagons will have reached the place where it juts into the road. It's not safe to pass them now.'

Fate, Rosario thought, had taken a hand. Rather than upsetting her plans, Lucía was proving a useful ally. She ran to the base of the rock and began to climb, pausing to look back from the narrow ledge above the trail. Lucía waved. A faint 'good luck' echoed up the side of the rock. Rosario watched her turn away to catch up with the others.

The winding path took her higher still. The next time she looked down, she could see her father's wagon already at the far

end of the defile. She stopped to watch until the rest of the cavalcade had passed below her, then went on again. Her way was
soon halted by a higher outcrop. An even narrower path wound
behind it, leading her to the other side of the rock and widening,
as she remembered it would, at the summit. This was where
Diego had once cooked a rabbit for their lunch and where, at the
end of that summer, she and Juan had talked of the roundness of
the world. Far below, the line of wagons moved on into the
distance like a small and weary serpent. She was alone for the
first time in her life. No, not quite alone. The eagle, or one of its
progeny, was circling high in the sky. She spread her arms wide
and laughed. It was a splendid omen. The bird circled once more
and then was gone. Rosario scrambled down the twisting path
that would take her to Diego.

An hour passed, and then another. He had forgotten his promise.
Perhaps he had never meant to come for her. Leaves rustled with
the scurrying of small animals. The Rocerios would stop soon at
their final campsite. She would be missed and her father would
come back to find her. It would be dangerous in the dark, but an
hour's hard riding would bring him to her. She wondered what
he would say when he came, what excuses she would make for
being lost. Perhaps he had already missed her and turned back.
She must find the cleft in the rock and wait for him on the road.

A twig snapped nearby. She turned to peer into the growing
darkness and saw a black horse emerging from the trees, its rider
hidden by low branches.

'I thought you'd never come.'

'Do you trust me so little? And Negrito?'

She shook her head and took hold of his outstretched hand,
putting a foot on the toe of his boot and swinging up behind him,
moving from one world to another. With her arms around his
waist and her face pressed close against his back, she began to

contemplate the enormity of what she had done.

Night shadows crawled across the path, leading them to his home. Above them, the sky was a black velvet cloak beaded with stars, the full moon an ivory brooch pinned in its folds.

'There,' Diego said. 'Your new home.'

She looked to where he pointed and saw a low white house with out-buildings around its courtyard. An olive grove climbed darkly up the moonlit hill behind. The house door opened and showed the figure of a woman in silhouette against the light. A servant, Rosario supposed. The shadow melted as they came nearer, yet she sensed herself still observed. Diego dismounted and raised his arms as if to lift her down. One hand lingered at the hem of her dress, touched her ankle and crept up to tangle in her petticoats.

'The hunt is all the more exciting when the quarry is so hard to find,' he said, laughing. He pulled her down into his arms and carried her in through the door.

Next morning, Rosario lay among the tangle of rice-starched sheets euphoric as a sated cat, watching Diego dress. Light-beams through half-open shutters played over his taut, lean body. Her own clothing lay in a crumpled puff of lace and pink cotton on the floor – a rose that yesterday had opened its cool petals to the sun and was now no more than a withered reminder that she had brought nothing else to wear. Diego pulled on his boots and bent to kiss her, laughing when she clung to him. He must go, he said, to see to the day-labourers arriving from the village. He would arrange for clothing more suitable than her rociera finery to be brought to her.

She lay back against the pillows when he had gone. A maid, she supposed, would come soon with water for her to wash. She heard raised voices in another part of the house, then footsteps. A woman entered, thrust an armful of clothing at her and left before Rosario could recover from her astonishment enough to admonish her. Never had a servant treated her with such rudeness. She stared, appalled, at the bundle in her arms. She would give better apparel to a kitchen maid. She searched for a bell to ring and found none. With no other choice obvious to her, she got out of bed, donned the faded blouse and rough grey skirt, and went off in search of breakfast and the maid, words of reprimand ready on her tongue.

The house was small, the furniture solid and wax-scented. Photographs of the matador, Ramón Ramirez, covered one wall of the living room. Diego was there, too, looking much the same as on the day he had passed under her balcony on his way to the bullring. She remembered that she had supposed he would become a matador one day, that her would choose her for his novia and dedicate his bulls to her. She smiled at her girlish nonsense. Persuasive as she might be, and as much as he loved her, her father would not have allowed her to marry a bullfighter. Even as a landowner, Diego's lack of good family would present them with some difficulty. She hoped his landholdings were large enough to sway her father. She smiled again. He would have to agree to her marriage now. In one sense at least, she had already become Diego's wife.

She continued her inspection of the house. It was well-suited to the manager of a substantial estate. There would be other dwellings: the largest, she imagined, occupied by Diego's widowed mother. As soon as she was married, Rosario would insist on moving there herself. This one, really no more than a large cottage, was pleasant enough and sufficient for the older woman's needs. She looked into the dining room, expecting to find some evidence of breakfast. The sideboard was empty, the table clear. She continued on down the stone-flagged passageway to the kitchen and found a maid leaning over a table, kneading dough.

'So,' the woman said, not bothering to look up as Rosario entered. 'You are the girl my son went to fetch yesterday.'

Rosario's hand flew to her mouth. Long moments passed as the words sank in. It was his mother who had brought the clothing and found her in Diego's bed. As her wits returned, it struck her that the woman had no idea who she was. Her own embarrassment was nothing to what the good Señora would suffer when told who it was she had spoken to so rudely; who it was her son intended to marry. She would wait until Diego returned and they would tell her together. It was probable that he had, by now, attended to his labourers and was already on his way to Puente Nuevo to speak to her father.

But Diego had gone no further than his olive groves. When he returned later in the day, he told her it would be some days before he could leave the estate: there was a great deal to be done after his absence in el Rocío. Nor would he tell his mother of Rosario's parentage. It was unlikely to go well for them, he said, should his interview with her father be preceded by gossip.

She agreed to continue with the subterfuge for a few more days. She kept to herself her astonishment at the lack of servants, something that must be rectified as soon as possible. The house boasted no help at all, except for a drudge, the wife of one of Diego's occasional workmen. The woman, his mother told her, did the heavier work and attended to the laundry. Rosario, she said, would earn her keep by milking the goats and looking after the kitchen garden. She bit her tongue and managed to hide her annoyance. Diego was right. No one must suspect who she was until her relationship with him was formalised. Meanwhile, she would treat the whole thing as a game. Señora Ramirez's shame would be all the greater when she learned the truth. The work was not arduous. For a day or two she even enjoyed it. By the fourth day, Diego had still not gone to Puente Nuevo.

'I'm tired,' she said, 'of living like a peasant. You must speak to my father immediately.'

He took her in his arms. 'Soon,' he said. 'First I have business to attend to in Seville.'

'Seville?'

'The horse fair. I have to go.'

'Then take me with you.'

'And have the world think you are some floozy? I shall take you to Seville as a married woman and not before. In the meantime you must go on playing the part of a village girl brought here to help my mother. Agreed?'

It wasn't so very hard to keep up the pretence. It was like living in one of the childish fantasies she had played with Juan – except that this time it was Diego and not her brother who had abducted the beautiful princess.

'A princess who cast a spell on me and came with me willingly,' he reminded her.

'Promise me you will see my father as soon as you come back.'

He pulled her to him. 'Rosario, your father will never agree. However much I beg, he will never forgive me for what I have done.'

'What little faith you have in me, Diego. And in my father.'

It was only when he had gone that her usually benign conscience began to trouble her. It had been a simple matter to push her parents from her mind when Diego was with her. Without him, and with no one but his mother and the washerwoman for company by day and a pillow for her bed-fellow, she began to realise how concerned her parents must be, and to miss her home.

When they found their daughter had been lost on the road from El Rocío, Roberto's fear for her had equalled Isabel's. Several members of the Brotherhood remembered seeing Rosario walking with Lucía Romero. Others said they had seen her climb the rock. There was a path, they said, a short-cut across it. The way was steep and the outer ledge narrow. Perhaps she had fallen. Roberto led a search party to la Centinela. They found nothing more than a patch of broken foliage at its base.

A day or two later, Lucía went to Puente Nuevo with chickens and cabbages for the market. One of Isabel's younger maids, a girl raised in the same village and Lucía's friend, went there to meet her. Lucía swore her to secrecy then confided that Rosario had been mad about Diego Montero. She was certain she had run off with him. The maid told Carmela who went immediately to her mistress.

Roberto's eyes narrowed with exhaustion and disbelief. Other, less identifiable, emotions crossed his face. He stared at Isabel as if he could not believe what she had just told him then erupted in anger.

'How dare she bring dishonour to my family!'

She looked away, her eyes sore with tears. Dishonour, she thought. If Rosario is with Diego, then what she has done is no more than an extension of my own shame.

'It may not be true, Roberto. If it is, be glad she is alive. As I am.'

She wanted to tell him that the blood of devils ran in Rosario's soul; that in his goodness, Roberto must save her from her folly, just as he had saved Isabel herself from the consequences of sin. She moved towards him, one hand lifting as if entreating him to listen, perhaps even to forgive. But he had already turned away, unaware of her gesture and her need. Her hand fell, empty of the courage and hope she might have found in touching him. Not for the first time had she been so close to confession only to watch each opportunity snatched away or lost, and herself shrinking back into fearfulness. She turned to the window. Outside, the roses mocked her with their careless brilliance. She put her hands against the leaded panes and stood there as if crucified. God had forsaken her. If the Devil wanted her so badly, and now her daughter also, then so be it. Her life was a lie and would continue to be so. Had Roberto stayed, she would not have spoken. The price of her confession would have been too high.

Chapter Twenty-six

Roberto rode hard, desperate to find his daughter safe for Isabel's sake, and for his own. His mind veered from the hope of finding her at the Ramirez farm to the despair of what he must do if he found her there with Diego. Even had she not been harmed, propriety ordained only one future for her now. The thought saddened him, softening his anger. He remembered how he had marvelled at her as a baby and delighted in her precocious childhood; how he had come to love her and been glad, in spite of his doubts, to accept her as his true daughter.

Ahead of him, the Ramirez cortijo leaned in against the hill. The courtyard was empty, the only sign of life the figure of a servant kneeling in the vegetable garden to one side of the house. As he came nearer, he saw it was a woman, her hair caught up peasant-fashion in a square of grey cloth, her dress covered by a coarse apron. She had heard him coming and turned her head. She lifted her hand to shield her eyes against the sun, then rose and came towards him. The horse shifted under him, sensing his shock.

'Rosario!'

She reached to stroke the animal's neck, smiling up at him with her mother's eyes, her head tipped at the provocative angle he knew so well. She had used it often enough and to good purpose when wanting to extract some favour from him. It was not in her to approach him in submission.

'Tell Don Diego I would like to speak to him.'

'He's not here.'

'Then fetch a horse. You will return with me immediately.'

'My home is here now,' she said. 'With Diego. He is coming to see you in a day or two to ask your permission to marry me.' Her tone was as casual as if asking whether or not he had enjoyed his ride. Her hand lay against the horse's neck, her fingers laced in the tangled mane.

'You will come home with me now,' he repeated. 'We will discuss your future there.'

'You'll give us your blessing?'

He stared down at her, astonished that she had not understood.

'Have you no idea what harm you have done? The pain you have caused your mother; the shame you have brought on my family?'

Rosario's eyes flashed. 'There is no shame in being in love. If you won't give your permission, I shall marry Diego when I am of age in any case. I had hoped you wouldn't make us wait so long.'

'You will marry no one!'

He waited for some sign of remorse, some comprehension of what she had done, a plea even for his understanding. She looked up at him, arms crossed in front of her. A cricket chirped close by, a dog's bark echoed in the hills. Leather creaked as the tired horse shifted again.

'Arrangements will be made for you to enter the convent. You will go willingly. If not, you will be taken there by force and I shall have Montero imprisoned for abduction.'

Fear flickered over her face, and was swiftly hidden.

'Diego did not abduct me. It was my own choice to go with

him.' Her eyes glittered, obsidian, like her mother's. 'If you separate us forever, I will always love him.'

It seemed as if Isabel stood there, taunting him as she had never done. Fatigue conspired with years of suppressed anger. His vision blurred. A cloud seeped across the earth, staining it with the darkness of blood. He saw a man dead at his feet, another badly wounded. Sun shadows formed the image of a soldier prone in the dust, half hidden by an overhanging rock, his rifle propped against his arm and carefully aimed. He remembered reaching for his own pistol, his hand falling, empty, to his side. His life, then as always, was in God's hands. The white walls of the Ramirez farmhouse darkened to the colour and texture of a hessian curtain. He saw himself walk to the end of a long room and lift a flap in the partition. On the other side, Isabel leaned over the man he had brought in from the battlefield. The expression on her face belied the words she had spoken only days earlier: that enemy soldiers should be left to die where they had fallen. The curtain fell from his hand and closed between them.

Years of pent-up jealousy erupted in a boiling lava. His arm rose. Rosario stood fearless, waiting for the biting heat of his whip. The horse reared, hooves flailing inches from her eyes, its hind legs dancing in the dust as the whip flashed past its shoulder to its rump. Agitated dust swirled in clouds as the animal wheeled and sped away.

Rosario watched him go. She was still there when Diego's mother came from the olive grove, calling out to ask who their visitor had been.

'No one,' Rosario called back. 'No one important.'

The older woman, too, stared after the diminishing cloud of dust, then at the girl.

'There have been rumours,' she said, and turned away towards the house.

Horse and rider dissolved into the hills. Rosario had expected chastisement. Had this been no more than one of her childish pranks her father would have enjoyed the game, neither of them doubting that, in the end, she would have had her way. This time it was not a game but she had not expected such rage, or that she would be afraid of him. Loving each other as they did, she had thought he would understand her love for Diego. But Diego had been right. In this there would be no manipulating her father's love.

She went into the house and to her bedroom. She ignored Señora Ramirez's summons to the evening meal and fell into a fitful sleep, waking much later to the sound of hooves in the yard. Two horses. She was not expecting Diego until the following evening. He had missed her and returned early, perhaps met her father and persuaded him to come back. This time she would explain it better. He would listen to them both and understand. If necessary, she would go home with him, perhaps spend a week or two in retreat at the convent to make amends. The separation from Diego would be hard, however long or short, but she was no longer a child and would learn patience.

She was at the window, about to open the shutter, when the bedroom door opened behind her. A hand, rough with riding, touched her bare shoulder. His breath warmed her neck as he bent to kiss her. All thought of her father faded as Diego lifted her and carried her to the bed, her love for him filling her completely, heart, body and soul.

Next morning, he took her by the hand and showed her the sweet young mare he had brought home with him. It was a gift, he said, an acknowledgement of the depth of his love for her. She ran a hand over its flank, thinking how much she had missed the spirited animal stabled in Puente Nuevo and the colt broken for her at the cortijo the previous summer. Diego, she had come to realise, cared nothing for olives, but his knowledge of horseflesh surpassed even her father's. The animal he had brought her was as fine as any she had seen.

Each day, when their work was done, they rode out into the hills, hobbled their horses and with only the sky to see them, fell into each other's arms. How was it possible, Rosario wondered, to feel such hunger, to appease it and still want more? She didn't care that the hard ground marked her skin or that Señora Ramirez's eyes would fill with scorn at the sight of her bruises.

'Don't expect me to feel shame, señora,' she snapped when the woman commented on a tear in her skirt. 'I'm proud that Diego loves me. When we are married you will regret the way you have treated me.'

The energetic kneading of the dough for the next day's bread ceased. 'Has my son said he will marry you?'

'Of course.'

'Then you're a fool to believe it.' The rhythmic blending and turning of the dough began again.

'Forgive me, señora, but you are wrong.'

The older woman's customary frown etched deeper. She gave the dough an angry thump, turned it, and thumped again. 'Are you pregnant?'

Rosario's eyes glittered but she shook her head.

'Nor will you become so if you have any sense.'

The girl lifted her chin in the way she had when she was angry. 'What business is it of yours, old woman?'

Señora Ramirez's eyes answered with a coldness enough to burn her soul.

'Business of mine? Ask your, mother, Rosario – if you are who I think you are. Diego thinks me mad and won't listen to me.' She turned back to her bread-making. 'Let this be your reward then, and his, for the sorrow he and his father have caused me. All of you may spend eternity in purgatory for all I care.'

Her words made no sense. Exasperated, wishing she could push the woman's stupid nose into the dough she seemed so intent on spoiling, Rosario left the kitchen to find solace in her garden. Her small achievements were hard won but she had come to love the place. In time she would see the goodness of her labours in well-formed peppers, onions, artichokes and fruit. Shielding her eyes against the sun, she looked across the serranía towards Puente Nuevo, wondering if her mother, too, was in her garden, tending the rosebush at the Casa del Rosal.

Part Five

Chapter Twenty-seven

'God, not more tortured saints!' Hamish protested as Simon parked their geriatric but mostly faithful Bedford van at the foot of a steeply rising hill. Hamish Johnston's version of The Grand Tour, along with that of his friend Simon Cartwright had, so far, included sailing tourist class to Southampton, exploring London and driving vast distances through Europe. Simon's penchant for history ensured frequent stops along the way for paying homage to castles and cathedrals.

'Righto,' he said, shading his eyes the better to see what might be, and what their map had told them would be, a monastery nestled in the rocky outcrop at the top of the hill. 'Let's give it a go.'

Instead of following the twisting and apparently little used roadway, which seemed likely to thwart the Bedford with its overly large potholes, they opted for a more direct route – one more commonly used by goats than humans, Hamish guessed. An hour of scrambling and puffing their way upwards brought them to a low, broken wall. They climbed over it and found weeds and wildflowers tangled with long grass and headstones on the other side. Close up, the evidently once lovely monastery looked forlorn.

'Creepy,' said Simon. He stepped back, startled, as an elderly, tonsured figure rose from the grass and came towards them.

'Americans?' he asked.

Hamish recovered first. 'We're from New Zealand.'

'Abajo!'

'Pardon?'

The monk laughed and pointed to the ground. 'Abajo. You come from underneath. From the other side of the world, yes?'

'Yes,' Hamish said, surprised that he would know.

'You would like that I show you round? For a small fee perhaps? We are poor and have few visitors. If you had come one month later you would have found nothing here but memories. And men with hammers. The architects came from Madrid yesterday.'

He had been tending the grave, he told them, of a recently departed Brother. He had hoped to die here himself but God had decided otherwise. The Brotherhood was shrinking. Young monks preferred the active gathering of souls in busy towns and cities rather than contemplation and tending fields. In its wisdom, the Church had handed the monastery over to the government. It was to be transformed into a parador, a hotel, where rich foreigners would come to hunt and go on fishing expeditions.

Their guide ushered them along a cloistered walkway to the refectory. True to Hamish's imaginings, several martyred saints hung in various states of agony along one wall. Clerical gentlemen, more generously clad and less wounded, stared from ornate frames opposite.

'These are portraits of all the abbots since the monastery was first built in the eleventh century.' The monk indicated the wall to their right. 'And these...' he waved fondly at the martyrs on the other side, '... are our Brothers in Christ who died upholding the Glory of His Name. Soon they will leave here forever. Although I believe dear Father Joaquim, who now never leaves his cell, that's him up there ...' the monk pointed to a man so gaunt Hamish thought he must surely be hanging on the wrong wall, '... when he was much younger, of course, will hang in the foyer when the restorations are complete.'

He led them outside again and across a small courtyard. A gate took them to a larger yard surrounded by outbuildings. Another hill rose behind, dotted with piles of what they supposed must be rocks and looked like memorials to some ancient cult. Closer at hand, a broken, once formidable door hung open to a large and gloomy barn.

'Stables?' Hamish asked.

'Once we kept cattle here, and hay. It also stored misguided souls, I believe.' The monk's eyes twinkled. 'That was after the good sisters came. Displaced by women! Imagine that!'

Hamish glanced into the darkness. His spine tingled. If he had believed in ghosts, he would thought the place haunted. Even so, a sensation much like desolation swept over him.

Like the New Zealanders, Juan too was taking a break from his studies. Unlike them, he was spending his summer holiday at home, happy to leave Madrid to fry its citizens without him. Riding out from the cortijo with his father, surveying the vast estate that would one day be his, he rejoiced in Andalucía's benign sky above him, the heat of its sun tempered by a lazy breeze, and the dust rising, languid, from their horses' hooves.

The dire poverty of the villages they visited that day had been ordained by God and ordered a natural hierarchy – or so he had believed until not so very long ago. Nothing had changed since he had first come here as a child. He hadn't seen then the small meanness of the houses, the peasants' lot in scratching far less than a living from dry, unforgiving scraps of land. He hadn't recognised Madrid's poverty either. Had he done so, he would not have considered it his business to be concerned. His eyes had been opened by his fellow students, not by the father he idolised, nor by the mother he adored, not here where thin women nursing sickly babes came to their doors to nod respectfully and young men doffed greasy caps and stared at the ground, muttering: 'At your service, señor, forever, at your service.' For the first time in his life he had an inkling of what that 'forever' meant.

In Madrid he had been drawn, reluctantly at first, into the concerns and arguments of his fellow students. He had heard, for the first time, rumours of the twenty-eight thousand executed on Franco's orders after the Civil War. He learned, too, of the thousands more who had perished in the Valley of the Fallen while building the vast monument ordered by the Caudillo. It was to be his mausoleum and dedicated to the glory of those who had died fighting in his armies. The labourers were men who had believed in another Spain and been worked as slaves until they had, quite literally, dropped dead. Numbers more had languished, and perhaps still did, in the prisons and torture chambers of Madrid. He learned of the thousands who had fled to Mexico and Argentina, of the thousands more still fleeing northwards to the hungry hotel kitchens of France and England, ensuring Spain's decimation.

He was angry that his father hadn't told him of these things, and because he hadn't known the truth, he had argued with his fellow students. How he had argued! Hadn't the technocrats of the politico-religious group, Opus Dei, won Franco's favour and prevailed over the reactionary Falange for the betterment of the people? His friends had countered that since neither the Falange nor Opus Dei supported political liberation, the poor were still poor. Didn't his family own one of the vast land tracts of Andalucía: latifundios owned for generations by a handful of wealthy families; land that, however unproductive, the peasants were not allowed to purchase even if they had the wherewithal, which of course they did not, and where absentee landowners flaunted their good breeding to similarly endowed visitors while feasting on the bounty of the hunt and throwing scraps to the peasants?

The instructive tirade had continued. Juan had listened, stunned. Wasn't it true, his interrogators persisted, that his family visited their country estate only when it pleased them, that the cortijo raised fighting bulls when the land might be put to better use in producing food for the starving millions of Spain; that the peasants lived in hovels fit for pigs? He had protested vehemently. The land was not suitable for crops. His father was nothing if not fair-minded. His peasants had sound roofs over their heads, and food for themselves and their children. His father had been a doctor in Franco's army and still ministered as such to his peasants. Nor did he charge them a peseta for his trouble. They were not his father's peasants, his mentors countered. No man could own another. And how could they pay, since they were unlikely to possess centimos, much less pesetas? Were those who lived and worked at the cortijo paid a wage? Juan admitted that he didn't know. And what of the day labourers who had to travel miles on foot to their work, who didn't know from one day to the next if they would be required again and received no more than a pittance anyway?

Inflamed by passions he had not guessed he owned, Juan had joined his student friends. With them, he had taken to the streets in support of workers from the foundries and factories to the north who had begun to make their voices heard and suffered dire consequences for their short-lived victories. The student demonstration had been swiftly crushed. Roberto would have been mortified to hear of his son's near arrest, would never have condoned the clandestine meetings that had continued in the cafés of the student quarter.

They were returning on their horses to the cortijo when Juan found the courage to speak of his concerns to his father.

'Papa, when I was in Madrid, we talked.... That is.... I've been wondering if perhaps the peasants might not be given some sort of ownership of the plots they farm for their own use.'

His father laughed, but not unkindly. 'That sounds to me like Republican talk, or worse.'

Juan hesitated. It was one thing to confront the Civil Guard in the company of impassioned friends, quite another to confront the father he loved and respected and whose word he had never before questioned.

'The Republicans were wrong of course, but perhaps not in everything.'

'The Church would have it otherwise,' Roberto said. 'What other ideas have been buzzing in that head of yours while you've been away?'

Encouraged, but still cautious, Juan went on, 'That's part of it. The Church, I mean. I think the Republicans were right in separating it from the State. When Franco restored the status quo, I believe he put too much power in too few hands.' He might have said 'in his own hands,' but dared not venture quite that far.

'Perhaps,' Roberto concurred. 'But be careful who hears you say so.'

Juan searched for some remark that might elicit further

revelation. Religious observances were kept by the family, but only as a necessary component of the ritual that is life itself. Political discussion had never been encouraged, and dissension was punishable by law.

Roberto unclasped the wineskin at his waist. 'It is my belief, unpopular as it may be to many of my peers, that politics and religion make poor bedfellows.'

'Now *you* sound like a Republican!'

His father smiled. 'Never that. Above all, I should like to see the monarchy restored. I should also like to believe the Generalísimo when he says he will make Prince Juan Carlos his heir. We shall have to wait and see.' He raised the wineskin in salute to past and future kings, then tipped it. A stream of ruby wine poured into his mouth.

'There's something more, Papa. I should like to continue my studies in America.'

Roberto lowered the wineskin. 'If you go you will not come back.'

'The world is changing, Papa. I want to be part of it.'

'Spain is changing too, albeit slowly.' Roberto turned his head to gaze across the dusty, flat plain to the distant hills that marked the perimeter if his lands. 'You have cousins in California,' he said. 'Your mother's uncle was a Republican sympathiser.' He set his horse to a brisk canter in the direction of the cortijo, leaving Juan to stare after him, open-mouthed.

Later, Juan wondered if he might not then have taken advantage of his father's good humour and brought up the matter of his sister. His one attempt, so far, to ask after her welfare had been met with a sharp rebuke. He had known, of course, of the attraction between Rosario and Diego. He thought of the last time he had let his friend into the cortijo's small ring to practice with the young bulls, the night they had drunk too much of his father's wine. He hadn't seen Diego again that summer. The stolen mare had not been found and no suspicion had fallen on his friend. By the time the family next visited their cortijo, Diego had left to train at the maestranza in Seville. From then on, the bullfight had kept them apart until he turned up in Puente Nuevo with Ramón Ramirez's cuadrilla. Aware that his sister's childhood infatuation had been rekindled by the sight of the handsome banderillero in his embroidered suit of lights, Juan had teased her until she cried. He hadn't dreamed that a few years later she would run off with him.

That evening, Roberto took Juan aside and told him that his great-uncle Eduardo, abuela Mercedes' son, had chosen to make a new life in Mexico rather than fight the Republicans. Doña Mercedes, he said, had been shocked and bitterly ashamed. He had taken it upon himself to enlist his cousin Federico's help. Between them they had ensured the truth was never known. When Mercedes died, he had decided to see if he could find out what had happened to Eduardo and, if he was still alive, to inform him of his mother's death. The network of sympathisers in Mexico and elsewhere was not only strong but very efficient. The letter had been delivered to Eduardo in California. He had replied, explaining his long silence. He had written, he said, just one short, necessarily cryptic letter to his mother telling of his safe arrival. He did not know if she had received it. Knowing that those who left Spain, as he had done, had been declared traitors, he feared further contact would jeopardise her safety and his niece Isabel's future. He had not written again. It had seemed best to simply disappear.

An intermittent, carefully worded correspondence had ensued between the two. Eduardo had become a school-teacher. He had married late in life but not too late to acquire two sons and a daughter. Five years ago, he had left Mexico with his family to live in California. In reply to Roberto's assurance that many exiles were now able to return without fear and that he would be welcome should he choose to visit, he wrote that nothing would induce him to set foot on his fatherland's soil while the Caudillo lived. Since they had both reached old age and Franco showed no sign of dying, he had resigned himself to staying where he was.

If Juan was intent on going to America, Roberto said, perhaps it could be arranged for him to visit his great-uncle's family next summer.

Juan did not, after all, mention Rosario to his father. His mother told him she received news from time to time, that his sister was well but that it would be best if he did not mention her name again. He returned to Madrid in September. There had been no opportunity to visit Rosario, nor the man he had once thought of as his friend.

Chapter Twenty-eight

The years, Lizzie thought, were passing all too quickly. Next year, Sarah would be starting at the new university in Palmerston North and living away from home. She had plans, she had told her parents in a tone that made Lizzie think of Eve, for life beyond Fenton. It was good to know that Hamish would be back before she went. Were both their offspring to absent themselves at the same time, the place would seem quiet as a morgue.

'Letter from Hamish,' Lizzie said, when Sarah came into the kitchen after school.

'Fab,' she said. 'Any snaps?'

'Slides,' said Lizzie. 'They're on the table.'

Sarah opened the yellow box, tipped its contents onto the table and held a slide up to the light.

'Look at this castle, or whatever it is. It looks really old.'

'It's a monastery. Somewhere in the north, I think. Read the letter. Hamish mentions it somewhere. And there's a note from Simon.'

'Seville,' said Sarah, studying the postmark. 'That's not north. It's in Andalucía.' There was a map of Europe on her bedroom wall studded with pins approximating Hamish's and Simon's journey. 'It's the most romantic place in the whole world.'

Lizzie supposed it must be, if only because at the time of writing it had contained the living, breathing wonder of no less a being than Simon Cartwright. Wherever Simon happened to be at any particular moment was exactly where her daughter wanted to be.

Sarah cast a cursory eye over her brother's letter. They had spent three weeks, Hamish wrote, travelling south from Barcelona and had seen enough castles along the way to satisfy even Simon. Sarah settled in her chair to devour Simon's note more slowly. The castles, he said, were fantastic and he was keeping a necessarily brotherly eye on Hamish. A postscript from Hamish claimed that he was keeping a far more necessary eye on Simon. His friend had been smitten by the beauties of Seville, and he wasn't talking architecture.

Sarah threw both letters on the table and flounced from the room. Lizzie watched her go. Eve, she remembered, had been much the same at Sarah's age. She had probably had similar tantrums herself. Pity their poor mother, then, with a double dose of daughters. Sarah had been moody ever since the boys had left. Down in the dumps one minute, happy as a lark if the post brought her a card with 'Love, Simon' at the bottom. One, a picture of a gypsy with a rose in her hair, had set her planning to spend her summer holiday with Eve. She had heard of a woman teaching flamenco dancing in Auckland. Two weeks ago, 'Teach Yourself Spanish' had appeared among the romantic novels on her bedroom bookshelf beside a matching copy of 'Teach Yourself French', acquired when the boys were on their way to Paris.

That evening, when their daughter had been cajoled from her room for tea, only to vanish again soon afterwards, Tom took Hamish's letter and the box of slides from the mantelpiece and sat down with them at the kitchen table. He riffled through the slides, reading the minuscule titles written in Hamish's tidy hand, then picked up two of them, took them to the desk and switched on the lamp.

'It looks different,' he said, holding one in front of the light. 'When I left, it was snowing.'

Lizzie came to look over his shoulder, patted it, and bent to open the cupboard. She rummaged for a while, found a battered black and white snapshot and put it on the desk in front of him. He looked at it and then at her.

'I thought you'd thrown that out years ago.'

'Why would I do that?'

'She belongs in the past. Doesn't have anything to do with us.'

'I've thought about her off and on over the years,' Lizzie said. 'I call her my antipoda.'

'Antipoda?'

She took up the other slide and peered at it.

'We really must get one of those viewer things,' she said. According to the inscription, Hamish had taken the picture from the top of the road outside the monastery. The distant view was of a river running through a broad valley.

'I looked it up. It's on the other side of the world – right on the other side. Underneath our feet, more or less. I read a story once about a woman who believed there was another woman just like her on the other side of the world. She wanted to meet her but she couldn't because every time she moved, the woman she called her antipoda moved too. I've sometimes wondered what happened to her. To Isabel I mean. If she came through it all right and was happy.'

Tom reached for her and pulled her onto his lap. 'Did I ever tell you you're an exceptional woman, Mrs. Johnston?'

'Mmm. I think you have – once or twice maybe.'

'I love you, Lizzie.'

'I know you do. Come on. It's getting late. Time for bed.'

'You know,' said Tom. 'When I was looking at Hamish's

photo of the monastery, I wasn't thinking of Isabel. I was remembering the doctor who patched me up.

Roberto was in his study in Puente Nuevo. If he had supposed his name would turn the creaking wheels of Spain's bureaucracy a little faster, he was disappointed. His request for more information concerning Diego Montero had been delayed for months. He took up the package Carmela had just brought in to him and asked her to put a match to the fire. He waited until she had left the room then broke the official seal.

Copies of documents spilled onto his desk. A rapid perusal confirmed much of what he already knew. Diego had been taken into Ramón Ramirez's household as a boy along with his mother, Josefa. He was later employed as a banderillero in the matador's cuadrilla. Josefa Montero, a further document informed him, had been employed as Ramirez's housekeeper and had later married him. Her name worked liked a needle in Roberto's mind, pricking at an elusive thread.

He turned to the documents detailing the current ownership of the Ramirez farm. Here was something unexpected. It had been generally supposed that the matador, with no sons of his own, would name his stepson as his heir. But Diego Montero was no land-owning caballero. At Ramirez's death the land had passed to the matador's nephew with a proviso that Señora Ramirez, known previously as Montero, would remain there until her death. Her son was to manage the farm, thus ensuring an income for her. At his mother's death, he was to vacate the property which would then be sold. A further envelope produced evidence of gambling debts and money owed to horse-dealers in Seville. Diego's creditors, it seemed, had also believed in his substantial landholding. When the time came for the farm to be sold he would almost certainly be imprisoned, with or without Roberto's help. Rosario, married to him or not, faced a life of penury.

Roberto scanned the papers again, thinking of the woman he had seen emerging from the Ramirez olive grove the day he had gone to bring Rosario home. He had caught no more than a glimpse of her, but it had been enough to be sure she was the woman he had seen on the matador's arm in Puente Nuevo. He remembered that she had seemed familiar to him that day and that he had brushed the thought aside. He could do so no longer. The first and only other time he had seen her had been at his own wedding: Josefa Ramirez had been Josefa Martos Montero, Federico's widow.

Diego Montero, then, was almost certainly Federico's son. Long ago, he had thought to find him and then, for Josefa's sake, had chosen to leave well alone. Had things turned out differently and Diego proved himself above reproach, an alliance with Rosario, although not entirely suitable, would not have been impossible.

Roberto thought again of the day he had gone to fetch Rosario home. He shuddered, remembering how his horse's hooves had flashed past her face. He had whipped the animal not so much from anger at her refusal to go with him, but because her words had unwittingly reminded him of Isabel's lover, a man he had at first respected then come to hate. He had supposed the memory sealed forever. That day it had cracked open like an egg, causing him such torment as to deny all reason.

He pulled open a drawer and took out a picture of Rosario taken during her first pilgrimage. He stared at it for some time before putting it aside. He went to the hearth to add more wood then crossed to the safe in the panelled wall opposite his desk. In it were family documents, together with wartime cases he had thought might be of further medical interest. Where the Scotsman was concerned, he had quite simply been unable to discard the few details he possessed.

He found the file and opened it. Tom's details were attached to an official photograph. He recalled again how he had, at first, thought him a man of honour. Honour! He had not needed medical skills on his wedding night to discover that Isabel was not a virgin. He had been insane with grief and jealousy, had hoped she might confess and so release him. But she had not. He had returned to the front, gladly immersing himself in its horrors, glad to think that Federico's renowned pleasure in his work would have ensured the Scotsman's torture. When advised of his wife's pregnancy, he had considered the likelihood of it having resulted from her affair at the monastery. His second thought was that had she been impregnated before she left for Burgos, that, too, should have been obvious on, if not before, the wedding night. The coming child, he had supposed, could well be his own. If not, she had succeeded in trapping him. It was too late to risk the social stigma of an annulment. Filled with indecision and confusion, he had returned home to find her gravely ill. She had tried to hide from him the advancing state of her pregnancy but he had seen enough to realise soon afterwards that the child could not be his. He had also known that whatever she had done, he could not bear to lose her.

Mercedes had surely understood the true state of things as she nursed her granddaughter through her pregnancy and illness. He could have told her that, since he already knew the truth, her lies about the child's premature arrival were unnecessary. The baby had been conveniently small but his practised eye had known it to be full term. Isabel had been in love with the Scotsman, however much she had tried to hide it from him; the prisoners had been sent to Burgos on the same train. It would not have been impossible to bribe the guards, a cigarette would have been enough. Give or take a few days, Rosario had been born nine months later.

All this he had known, and chosen to forget. He had loved Rosario from the moment he first took her in his arms, a miniature replica of Isabel, other than the tiny and extraordinary mole above her eyelid. If his mother had been surprised at her grandchild's arrival so soon after her son's marriage, any doubts would have vanished at the sight of this apparent testament to the baby's ancestry.

As a child, Rosario had delighted and fascinated him. She had grown into a lovely young woman and he had been proud of her. He stared again at her photograph and then at that of the Scotsman, seeking some likeness. There was none, not one similar feature between them.

He went to the safe again and took out a bundle of papers given to him by his mother for safe-keeping. He put to one side a package containing the many letters of condolence sent at the time of his father's early demise. Another held similar messages received after his brother Manolo's murder in the earliest days of the war. That too he put aside. A third package held correspondence from people Elvira had considered 'useful'. This he opened. On top was the letter sent by General Franco congratulating her on her son's forthcoming marriage; a letter, he remembered, that had caused Isabel great distress. Beneath it was a cutting taken from a newspaper. Federico smirked from the photograph above his obituary, one eyebrow slightly raised as if to draw attention to the mole beneath it.

He reached again for the picture of Rosario. How stupid he had been, how grateful for the miraculous impossibility of the tiny mole above her own eyelid. Some part of his mind had worked it out long ago, and obliterated the idea as too heinous to be imagined. He wondered, ashamed, that he had so easily denied the meaning behind Isabel's dislike of Federico. Dislike? The innocuous word had described his own feelings, not hers. He snatched up the clipping, tore it to shreds and crushed the pieces in his fist. What Isabel had known was fear. How stupid he had been, how supremely stupid. Had he allowed himself to see the truth, he would have murdered Federico himself.

The other photograph, the picture of the man who might have become his friend had their circumstances been different, a man he knew now had done him no harm other than to love Isabel, looked up at him from his desk.

He was startled by a knock. Carmela's face appeared at the door. Dinner, she said, was about to be served. Doña Isabel was already in the dining room. He told her he would come shortly. When she had gone, he gathered up every sheet and scrap of paper from his desk and stood, feeding them, handful after handful, into the fire.

Next morning he rose early. He would not be back, he said, until late that night. He had business to attend to some distance from town.

He rode alone. No one but those immediately concerned would ever know the reason why he must now force Rosario to leave Diego. The serranía opened in front of him, his way marked by rocks and occasional trees, and rivulets that ran faster now than in the heat of summer; a journey marked too by the pounding of his heart that must surely burst with the enormity of his rage. He checked the pistol resting snug against his hip. He would have no compunction in using it. If Diego knew of Rosario's true parentage, that Federico Martos Estepa had been her father as well as his own, then he would rot in hell whether he died today or not. If he did not know, then the never-ending purgatory that was Rosario's destiny awaited him also.

He did not remember falling. He knew only that he was cold

and that the pain was bad.

Something was cradling his head. He thought it might be an arm. His mouth was eased open and drops of bitter liquid scorched his tongue. As the pain lifted from him in slow, receding waves, he opened his eyes and was surprised to see the sun already touching the lowest branches of the conifers. He heard voices calling and the creak of cartwheels coming closer. Strong arms lifted him and laid him down again on sacks that smelt of straw and chickens. Boards creaked under him as the cart moved off. He was afraid the pain would come again. Instead, his head was lifted and more drops of pungent liquid trickled onto his tongue. The cart ceased jolting and seemed to rock him gently. He thought he might be on a ship, heading out to sea. Silky darkness billowed, wrapped and held him until they reached the place where Isabel was waiting. He felt her fingers on his face and tried to smile. He sighed and slept again, unaware that she had been at his bedside through two long nights while he drifted in an out of sleep, terrifying her with incoherent tales of oceans and a voyage to a far off land.

'He means heaven, Doña,' the old curandera told her. It was she who had dosed him with her herbs, travelled with him in the cart to the cortijo and sent her son on Roberto's horse to fetch Isabel from Puente Nuevo. 'But he won't go there just yet. I have spoken with Our Lady, Doña.'

She held out her hand in hope of some tangible gratitude for her services and was not disappointed in the quantity or value of the coins Isabel placed in her palm.

At first, Juan could think of little else except that his father needed him. But as the miles passed, first in fitful sleep on the train to Seville and then in equal discomfort in a dilapidated taxi to the cortijo, his mind turned to what had been his plans for his new life in America. His father and then his mother had written to his great-uncle; letters had passed between Juan and his cousins. Arrangements had been made for him to visit them, and for his enrolment at medical school in California. Instead, his mother's call had reached him in Madrid two days ago and he had made immediate arrangements to travel home. She had told him it was likely his father would take many months to recover and he had not hesitated in saying he would stay for as long as he was needed. He wondered if he might find his sister at the cortijo. If his father's accident and subsequent illness were as serious as his mother had implied, she would surely have come to make her peace with him.

She was not there. She had come, his mother said, as soon as she heard the news. She had spent only a few minutes with her father. Roberto had become agitated and the doctor had advised her not to visit him again.

'I had hoped to find her here,' Juan said.

'She returned home immediately. Naturally she was upset but I think it's for the best.'

'You can't mean that?'

'I am concerned only for your father, Juan. The doctor insists he must not be made excited or upset. You will not mention your sister's name in his presence.'

The doctor's prognosis was that it would indeed take many months for Roberto to recover. Any thought of Juan returning to Madrid was out of the question.

As the days and weeks went past, Roberto began to regain something of his wits and strength. In time, he was able to make the short walk across the yard to the stables. On his next visit, the doctor suggested the family might soon return to Puente Nuevo.

'You mean,' Roberto said, 'that you are tired of coming all this way to see me. Don't I pay you enough?'

'You pay me very well, Don Roberto, but it's time for a

change of scene and something to distract you.'

'Distract me?'

'From whatever it is that is worrying you.'

'My illness is worrying me.'

'It might help to discuss it.'

'Your task, doctor, is to care for my body. Not my thoughts.'

'Indeed so, Don Roberto.'

He refused to leave the cortijo and spent much of his time watching his beloved horses through his study window. His occasional ventures to the stables, short as they were, tired and upset him.

Juan felt certain his father's continued melancholy had to do with his estrangement from Rosario. His agitation on seeing her when he was so ill had been natural enough. Now, sitting in his chair, disinterested in books or games of chess, it might well have crossed his mind that he might die without making his peace with her. His father was too proud, Juan thought, to ask her to come again. For all their sakes, the time had come to end the matter. Rosario must be forgiven and allowed to formalise her relationship with Diego. They would marry, anyway, when she turned twenty-five, with or without her father's blessing, so why not now? What his sister had done was wrong but the painful breach must be healed and his father's health with it.

He went to the study that afternoon and found him staring out of the window. His mother sat nearby, working on a piece of embroidery. He pulled up a stool, took his father's hand and explained as reasonably and tactfully as possible what he had decided.

His mother dropped her needlework, gave an exclamation of anger and tried to hush him.

'She is my sister and your daughter,' Juan insisted. 'We can't go on like this forever.'

'She does not exist!' Roberto took hold of the stick at his side.

287

Juan wondered if he would strike him. Instead, he attempted to rise from his chair, pushing Juan aside when he moved to help him. When Isabel came to him, he brushed her away, too, rose unsteadily to his feet and moved heavily across the room. When he reached the door, he turned to face them.

'She does not exist!'

Isabel took a step towards him.

'No!' he said. 'Leave me. I am going to see my horses. They are less bothersome to me than my family.'

The groom told them he had been working alone in the stables when Don Roberto came. Don Roberto had spoken to him then sent him to fetch the overseer. When they returned together they had found him gone and supposed he had returned to the house. The overseer had gone after him and the groom had returned to his work. He had found his master unconscious on the stable floor hidden by a bale of hay, a bridle in his hand.

The curandera appeared at the cortijo as Isabel put down the phone. She was still there when the doctor arrived some hours later in his car. He shooed her with her herbs from the sickroom and sent Isabel away too. He would call her, he said, as soon as he had completed his examination.

Juan was waiting in his father's study, distraught with grief and guilt.

'It's my fault, Mama. You told me not to mention Rosario. He was going to find her, I'm sure of it. I thought after all this time…. If he saw her, I mean. And now….' He faltered. 'Send for her. Please. He must make his peace with her.'

'And have him suffer even more, Juan? No. I don't think so.'

'She's his child,' he said. 'Just as I am. You can't believe it right to leave them unreconciled.'

She took his face in her hands. 'No,' she said. 'It's not right. It never was. But the fault is not his. You must believe that, Juan.'

Early next morning, the curandera came again. She beckoned Juan to a corner of the courtyard where they would not be overheard.

'Heaven will not wait forever, señorito. I will take a message to your sister.' As an afterthought, she added, 'The mother's dying too.'

'What mother, old woman?'

'Don Diego's of course. Who else? Refuses to take my herbs. Says she's used to pain. She told me...,' the old woman glanced about to be sure they were alone, '...that she's had too much misery in her life and doesn't want to wait around for the misery that's coming. Who doesn't have misery, I'd like to know? Misery, blood and death. What else is there, señorito? What else is there? Two peas in a pod. But not the eyes. She has her mother's eyes.'

'What have peas to do with your magic, vieja?' he asked, smiling at her nonsense.

'There is no good magic in it, señorito. Black peas for evil, or green for death. Take your pick. Your sister and Don Diego, señorito. Blind. Completely blind.'

'Who, old woman? Who is blind?'

'All of you. Don Roberto too. He chose his blindness. Until he was forced to see.'

Her words made no sense, but that was often the way with old women and Juan was grateful to her. Rosario must be told. He handed her a few pesetas from his pocket. She grinned, bit the coins and pocketed them deep in the folds of her skirt. 'May Our Lady bless you, señorito.'

The shutters were closed across Roberto's window. The room, lit only by a shawl-draped lamp, was dim. Isabel knelt by the bed and began to pray. She had ceased believing in God's goodness long ago but He must not be allowed to abandon her again – not before she had asked Roberto's forgiveness. She lifted his hand from the coverlet and pressed his thin fingers against her cheek. Her pain seem suddenly to burst into fragments, the way a small world will when it can take no more of the pressure it has built upon itself. She whispered his name, spoke words that stumbled at first then rushed in a too-long pent-up torrent. Perhaps she only imagined hearing him speak, imagined the fragile fingers curling tightly around hers; perhaps the flame of understanding in his eyes was imagined, too, as they opened and met hers, telling her that he had always known at least some of it, that he had felt her pain and done all he could to ease it; that everything he had done, every decision he had ever made had been because of his unshakeable love for her, his desire to lift her burden and carry it himself.

That evening, Rosario told Diego that if he would not go, she would fetch the priest herself. There was no point, he said, since his mother would have none of it. Rosario set a chair by the dying woman's side. There was no love and nothing to be said between them. Even so, she took her hand. Señora Ramirez turned her head to look at her with something akin to pity in her eyes.

'May God forgive me for not telling you,' she whispered. 'And even now I cannot. You must go away, Rosario. There is nothing for you here now. Go to your father. Beg him to take you in, for my sake. And for your mother's. It was not their fault your family caused me so much pain. Now send Diego to me. There are things he must be made to understand.'

For some reason that neither of them understood, except for the need that it be done, Rosario bent to kiss her. She left the room, found Diego in the kitchen and told him his mother had asked to speak to him.

It was past midnight when he returned to her. He took her in his arms and made love to her, silently, without preamble and with a terrifying fury. Afterwards, she slept and woke later to the sound of a horse in the courtyard. The place where Diego had lain was almost cold. He must have decided, after all, to fetch the doctor and perhaps the priest. She pulled the shutter open and called softly to the shadowy figure mounted on the blackness of Negrito. He gave no sign that he had heard. She thought he would ride through the olive grove to the village on the other side. He would find the priest there and, if not a doctor, word could be sent to the curandera. Instead, he turned towards the hills. Neither then nor afterwards did she understand why she went after him. She snatched up a shawl and ran from the house to the stables. With no saddle and only a rope halter round its neck, she set her mare at a gallop down the track.

Isabel stayed on her knees at Roberto's bedside all that night. At dawn she drew her hand across his face and closed his eyes. She called Carmela and asked her to fetch her son. The maid returned soon to say that Juan could not be found.

The curandera had not kept her word. Rosario had not come. Half an hour's hard riding brought Juan to the path. He turned his horse to follow it and rode on as fast as he dared, ducking under branches, blessing the animal for its nimble tread over roots and hidden rocks. The trees thinned as he rode up the incline to the Rocío road. He found the old curandera there, resting at the foot of la Centinela. He realised, then, that she had walked the entire distance, and with only a pair of worn rope sandals to protect her feet. It would have taken her a full day and night to reach Rosario and return to this place. He had not thought to offer her a horse and doubted in any case that her old bones would have endured the jolting. She lifted her wrinkled face as he came, and raised her thin old shoulders in a shrug.

'Gone,' she said. 'Rosario's gone, and her brother with her.'

'No,' Juan said, thinking exhaustion had confused her. 'I'm here, old woman.'

He dismounted and lifted her to sit before him in the saddle. She weighed no more than a tough old bird, all bones and hardly any meat. He wondered that she had survived her journey.

'Rosario would have been at your father's bedside before he died had I reached her in time,' she said. 'That horse Diego gave her flies like the wind. It has the mark of the eagle on its forehead. The mother's dead,' she added, her head lolling against his chest. 'Diego's men have gone for the undertaker. It's too late for the priest.' She muttered on, then fell asleep with Juan's arm supporting her as they made their way back to the cortijo.

Rosario followed Diego's tracks all morning. Sometimes she caught a glimpse of horse and rider in the distance, appearing from an outcrop of rock then swallowed once more into the landscape. But it was true her horse could fly like the wind. She was catching up with him. He looked back, reined in Negrito and called to her.

'Go home, Rosario.'

He leapt to the ground as she approached. Silver flashed as he lifted his arm to hold his pistol at Negrito's head.

'No, Diego.' She slid from her own saddle. 'No!'

'Everything is finished.'

'Is it true that you will lose the farm when your mother dies? Is that why you're upset?'

He stared at her and laughed. She moved a step closer.

'Are you planning to kill yourself when you've done with Negrito? If so, you might as well kill me too. And our child. We've everything to live for, Diego. The farm doesn't matter. I would make my home in a cave if you asked me to.'

He lowered the pistol. 'Child?'

She nodded.

'The devil's child then.'

She was close enough now to see the madness in his eyes. Sunlight glinted as he raised the gun again and aimed it at her belly. She heard the pistol cock and wondered if she would feel much pain. She thought she would not. She closed her eyes. When nothing happened, she opened them again. Diego was smiling at her.

'This pistol,' he said, twirling it around his finger then laying it in the palm of his hand, 'belonged to my father. I took it as a memento of him the day my mother forced me to leave our home. Juan's father has one just like it.' He raised the gun again and fired.

The circling eagle above la Centinela drew them to the place. They found her horse first, trotting alone along the Rocío road towards Puente Nuevo, and then Rosario, her nightdress and woollen shawl stained with her own blood and her child's. It seemed she had ridden to the rock, climbed it and fallen. She was lucky, they said to each other, to be alive. Two of them rode to the Álvarez cortijo to tell her mother of the tragedy. Those who rode to the Ramirez farm were received by the woman who worked about the place. She told them she had arrived early that morning to find her mistress dead and the curandera already laying out the corpse. The old woman had left as soon as the job was done, saying she had matters to attend to with the living. There had been no sign of Diego, nor of Rosario. No, she said, Diego had not returned. When the labourers arrived for work, she had sent her husband back to the village for the priest.

The priest had confessed Ramón Ramirez often enough to know how matters stood with Josefa Montero's son. It was likely, for the mother's sake, that Diego had only recently been apprised of the late matador's intentions for the farm on her demise. Thinking her far enough from death to absent himself for a few days, Diego had doubtless ridden to Seville to plead his case. Rosario, pregnant and unwed and therefore quite likely already unhinged, had followed him, taken the wrong path and suffered her mishap, the result of which was obvious to all. He would use the incident in a sermon. A fallen woman in both fact and metaphor. Others said that Rosario, learning of her own parent's proximity to death, had been on her way to the Álvarez cortijo to ask Don Roberto's forgiveness. Why she had climbed the rock dressed only in her night attire was less easy to explain. The compassionate thought it a great pity her mission had not been accomplished, but were thankful for her soul's sake that she had recognised her sin. The nuns, into whose care she had been placed, doubted she was aware of much at all. For the moment, at least, they were more concerned with the healing of her body. That done, they would attend to her soul. It seemed unlikely that much could be done for her mind. For days they had ignored her babbling of pistols and horses, but when Diego did not return for his mother's funeral and word came that he had not been seen in Seville, the searchers returned to the serranía. They found his body not far from la Centinela. Wild dogs and weather had rendered it almost unrecognisable and they might not have been sure of their find had someone not commented on the fine pistol lying by Diego's hand. He had boasted of it, they said, and claimed it had belonged one of General Franco's greatest friends. They turned him over and found the hole where the bullet had entered his skull and killed him.

Chapter Twenty-nine

'Do you realise,' Tom said as he waltzed with Lizzie under the big marquee, 'that we first did this twenty years ago? You were wearing a blue frock.'

'Twenty-two,' said Lizzie 'and it was Polly Jenkins' bedspread!' She chuckled. 'Wartime contingency. I had some weird contraption in my hair!'

'I was fascinated with it. And with you. You looked almost as lovely as you do now. How about running away with me?'

'Can't wait,' said Lizzie.

The waltz ended. The dancers clapped. The MC crossed the stage to the microphone. 'Another hand for Fred Wills and his boys before we get you rockin'!'

'I think we'll leave that to the young ones, don't you?' said Lizzie as they crossed the floor to join Margaret and Jim at their table. Hamish was helping out at the bar. Sarah was sitting with Simon and some of their friends at the next table. Up on stage, the MC and an assistant shifted the piano to one side while a stage-hand brought on another set of drums. Five young men leapt up onto the stage.

'Let's hear it for The Invaders,' the MC shouted.

'City boys,' said Jim disparagingly. 'Look at them. Couldn't shift a bale of hay between them.'

'Smart though,' said Margaret.

'Look at their boots, woman. Pointy toes and high heels. I ask you! And what do they call that?' he said as the group began to play. 'Music?'

Simon took Sarah's hand and led her onto the floor. Before his trip to Europe with Hamish, he had treated her much like a younger sister; a tomboy younger sister at that. He seemed to have noticed, Lizzie thought, that a transformation had occurred in his absence.

'Good heavens,' exclaimed Margaret, watching young couples work themselves into what she described as demented corkscrews. And then: 'Is that safe?' as the band launched into something called 'She's a Mod' and which seemed to necessitate such a shaking of heads between snatches of repeated lyrics as to cause damage to their necks.

'Aren't they great?' Sarah enthused, collapsing into a chair beside Jim. 'Don't tell Simon, but I think I'm in love.'

'With Simon?'

'With The Invaders.'

'All of them?' Jim asked.

Then it was Tom's turn to go up on stage. As President of The Agricultural and Pastoral Society it was his task to announce prizes won earlier in the day. The winner of the beauty pageant stood waiting for him, ready to hand out silver cups, certificates and kisses to the winners. Lizzie watched him walk across the floor, thinking how handsome he still was, how much she loved him, and how much she was looking forward to having him all to herself. In a few weeks time they would be on a ship to England, leaving for the honeymoon they had never really had more than twenty years ago.

Next morning, long before it was light, Lizzie woke to find Tom already up and pulling on a pair of old corduroy trousers. She shook the fog from her head and asked him what on earth he was doing.

'Stop bank.' He said. 'Could give way with all this rain.'

It was a downpour all right. She could hear it pounding on the iron roof. But Hamish had checked the bank only last week. It was as solid as could be. It hadn't given them any trouble for years.

'Come back to bed, dear. If you're worried, Hamish can have a look at it when he gets up.'

'Time enough for Hamish to take charge when we've gone.'

Lizzie rolled over to check the bedside clock. Three thirty. She might as well get up. What Hamish would have to say she had no idea. He was itching for them to set off on their travels and leave him to it.

'Let me at least make you a cup of tea,' she called. She pulled on her dressing gown and went after him. When she reached the kitchen, Tom was already gone.

Hamish appeared a minute or two later, his mouth open in a yawn.

'Best let him get on with it,' he said when Lizzie told him what Tom was up to. He reckoned his father would likely be gone for an hour or more, get whatever it was out of his system and come in demanding breakfast as if he had just got in from milking.

Lizzie made a pot of tea. Later, when Hamish had dressed and gone to begin his morning chores much earlier than usual, she went to her bedroom. When she came back, she found Sarah by the toaster in her dressing gown.

'About next year, Mum. Simon's going into his uncle's law firm. I think I might go for a diploma as a legal secretary or something, instead of university.'

'I thought you were going to be a vet.'

'Changed my mind.'

'Better get dressed for school then. You won't get into either course if you don't pass your exams.'

'Mum, it's only just gone four o'clock! Anyway, Simon's picking me up.'

'That's kind of him.' Lizzie thought of the nine mile detour he would have to make to the farm. 'It's a bit out of his way.'

'He doesn't mind.'

It's just as well we've arranged for her to stay at The Oaks while we're away, Lizzie thought. Her mother had had plenty of practice keeping would-be suitors at a safe arm's length when Eve was Sarah's age.

'Well lay the table and get yourself a proper breakfast,' she said. 'And I don't mean toast.'

It was going to be very nice, she thought as she set about making the beds, to be waited on hand and foot for a change. She retrieved a selection of odd socks from under Hamish's bed, eased a slight stiffness from her back and sat for a moment, thinking of the fun she would have shopping with Eve in Auckland for new clothes for the trip to England. Her sister wrote articles for a fashion magazine nowadays, and hadn't lost her eye for style. Archie drove one of the new container cranes on the wharves. Between them they brought in a good income and had bought a nice little bungalow on the outskirts of the city. How things had changed, Lizzie thought. Except when you lived on a farm miles from the nearest country town. She glanced at the clock. She hadn't heard Tom come back in. He must have gone on to the milking shed. She straightened the crease she had made from sitting on Hamish's bedspread and went back to the kitchen. Sarah had finished her breakfast and gone to her room. When Simon arrived, she reappeared wearing lipstick. The faintest smear but even so. Lizzie hoped she would remember to wipe it off before she got to school.

They hadn't long gone when Hamish came in. No, his father

hadn't turned up at the milking shed. He'd go and look for him if she was worried. Lizzie insisted he sit down to eat his breakfast while she donned her raincoat and went off herself to find her errant husband. The closer their departure date had come, the more things he seemed to find needing his attention. Hamish said he was driving him round the bend.

The horse must have thrown him, Tom thought. Funny the way he got on so well with horses yet had never really got the hang of riding. Lizzie rode well. So did Isabel. Not that he'd actually seen her on horseback, of course, but it had been easy to imagine her black hair flying loose in the wind. Roberto, she had told him, was an expert. That wasn't hard to imagine either. He hoped they had married and been as happy as he and Lizzie. What was it she had said about having an antipoda? If there was such a thing, then Roberto must be his. Not that they were alike, any more than Lizzie was like Isabel. But he'd never stopped feeling tied to the man in some way. Funny to think the first time they had seen each other had been along the barrel of a rifle. Tom had known he wouldn't shoot and Roberto's pistol had never left his holster. Death had been around though. Lots of it. Hovering around trying to make up its mind whether it was him it wanted, or young Dan. This time there was no Dan, only himself. He looked up at the sky and saw a pair of frightened blue-grey eyes staring down at him.

Lizzie had seen the tractor tipped on its side like some monstrous blue insect. She had run across the paddock with the mud sucking at her boots as if it was trying to hold her back. When she reached him, he had smiled up at her and she had thought he was going to be all right. She didn't know that Hamish had followed her and found her kneeling beside his father in the mud. She remembered that the rain had eased to a drizzle, and that the stop bank must have been all right because the paddock was draining well after the downpour. A heart attack, the doctor said. He had given her a sedative and Hamish had gone to fetch her parents from The Oaks. Then Sarah came and was holding her, crying too, telling her that Eve and Archie were on their way and had passed on the news to Jock in Australia.

The funeral passed in a blur of flowers and kindness, of disbelief and tears. Not Lizzie's because she was too numb to cry. Eve sent Archie home and said she would be staying on for a while.

She was standing by the window when the tears came. It was evening. Eve had sent the children over to The Oaks. Shadows were drifting across the lawn and sliding over the home paddocks towards the river. Further away, the sun was already slipping behind the dunes into the sea. She told Eve of the day, long ago, when she had gone with Tom to the coast, the day he had said he loved her and wanted to marry her. It had been winter, she remembered, and they had climbed the dunes. Tom had seemed sad and wouldn't, couldn't, tell her why. She talked of his nightmares and how, much later, he had told her about Isabel and said he hadn't been able to forget her.

'I wasn't jealous,' Lizzie said. 'I was at the beginning but not later. I wanted Tom to find out what happened to her. I even hoped I might meet her one day. Does that seem strange? I sometimes wondered what he would have done if I'd been the one to die first. I must have gone to sleep thinking about it, because when I woke up this morning I was certain he would have gone to find her. Oh, I don't mind,' she said. 'Tom loved me and it's not as if he was unhappy with his life or anything like that. Anyway, I've decided I'm going over there.'

Eve wanted to say that Lizzie was distraught, that it was too soon to see things clearly and there was no point in digging up the past, especially when it wasn't even Lizzie's past they were talking about. Discovering the whereabouts of a husband's past love was the last thing most women would think of doing and could only end in hurt. But her sister wasn't 'most women'. She would never feel antagonism towards anyone who loved someone she loved herself. There would be more than enough room in her heart for the mysterious Isabel. Eve took her sister's hand.

'She might not be alive of course,' Lizzie said. 'I realise that. And I don't even know her surname. Even if I did, I don't know how I could go about finding her.' She patted Eve's hand. 'It was just a silly idea. I'll make a pot of tea, shall I?'

In Auckland, Eve told Archie that she couldn't get what Lizzie had said out of her mind.

'Best leave well alone,' he said. 'Sleeping dogs and all that. Anyway, wasn't this woman on the other side? One of Franco's lot? She might not want to be reminded that she once fraternised with the enemy.'

'It's odd, I know, but Lizzie seems really fond of her.'

'And unlike some people I know, she'll have enough sense by now to have thought it through and realised there's no way of finding her.'

'Didn't Jock mention her?' Eve said. 'When he was telling us about his time in Spain?'

'He said something about a photograph,' Archie conceded. 'He never actually met the girl. Said something about Tom having gone through hell because of her. Which is hardly a good reason for Lizzie wanting to meet her, is it?' He pulled her down onto his lap. 'I thought you'd agreed to stay out of trouble.'

'I've been out of trouble for years,' Eve retorted. 'Anyway it's not my trouble, it's Lizzie's. She showed me a picture of her. Of Isabel. She was wearing a nurse's uniform. The photo had been torn. It was patched all over the back with tape. I bet it was the photo Jock mentioned. I think something awful happened to her,

Archie. Something really awful. I think Lizzie knows, but she wouldn't say.'

'If it'll make you feel better, Jock told me she'd probably married some doctor or other and ended up happily ever after.' Archie, kissed her on her nose, thinking that was the end of the matter.

Eve kissed him back. 'I wonder if Jock knew his name? Didn't he say a doctor used to come and talk to Tom at that prison in the monastery?'

Archie sighed. 'It's a long time ago, Eve.'

'He's still got contacts in Spain. Or he did before he went to Australia. I remember him saying so.'

'Jock,' Archie said, 'would turn up his toes if he couldn't find some left wing cause needing his attention. Leave it, woman. It's got nothing whatever to do with you. Lizzie's just feeling upset and confused. Give her a bit of time and all this will blow over.'

Eve settled herself more comfortably in his lap. 'If Jock does remember the doctor's name, perhaps he could get in touch with someone and…'

'You're daft, woman. Completely daft.'

'Which is why you love me. Couldn't we …?'

'All right. All right. I give in. I'll drop him a line if that's what it's going to take to get some peace.'

Jock was surprised to hear from Archie again so soon. He was even more surprised by the contents of his letter. His initial reaction, he replied, was that Eve's plan to help further Lizzie's enterprise, even if Lizzie had been as serious about it as Eve thought she was, was a dubious idea at best. Then he'd remembered how Tom had felt about the girl. If it was that important to Lizzie to lay this particular ghost for him, then perhaps he owed it to Tom's memory to see what he could do.

Chapter Thirty

Isabel looked round the drawing-room wondering what she might take with her. She would not stay on at the Casa del Rosal: it was far too big for her now. She would return to her childhood home in Arcos – the house Mercedes had intended for Rosario's dowry. Plans were already under way for the much larger Casa del Rosal to be leased. The Church would pay a peppercorn rent and use it as an annexe to the convent. Rosario would live there, cared for by the nuns who gladly humoured her belief in her imaginary world: a place, she told them, that was filled with strange brown children with red hair, and unicorns and eagles. Arcos was not too far away for Isabel to visit often. Arrangements were also in hand for the sale of the cortijo. Juan had been firm in saying he had no interest in the land, and she herself would never go there again. He sat with her now, a glass of fino in his hand. How like Roberto he looks, she thought. How like him in so many ways. She would miss him.

The maid came with two letters. Isabel took them from her. The first was from her American cousins saying how much they were looking forward to meeting Juan at last. They hoped she, too, would visit soon. They would just love it if she could be present at her uncle Eduardo's sixty-fifth birthday. She handed the letter to Juan. It had never occurred to her that she might travel beyond Spain. It was something she and Roberto had never discussed. Perhaps she would go. The thought of meeting her wider family appealed to her.

She picked up the second envelope. The postmark was unfamiliar, as was the stamp. Neither did she recognise the handwriting. She prized open the flap and unfolded the several pages. Their contents proved indecipherable. She handed the letter to Juan.

'English, I think,' she said. 'I hope they taught you well at school.'

He smiled and bent to his task, his forehead creased in concentration.

'It doesn't make any sense.'

'Read it to me.'

'It's from a woman,' he said. 'And it's very … personal.'

'I have no secrets, Juan. Not any more.'

He went back to the beginning of the letter and began to read aloud.

At first Isabel didn't understand, in spite of his careful translation. Then came disbelief, and astonishment, hope even, and finally understanding. Juan reached the end of the missive and looked up.

'Is it true?'

'Yes,' she said.

'Will you go?'

'Yes.'

'I can stay on a little longer, if you like. For a week or two. I could go with you.'

'I should like that.'

The road leading up the steeply winding hill is sealed now. Two matching plaques – set into a pair of exquisite iron gates wrought in the flourishing foundries of the north – announce arrival at the Parador del Ebro. Nowadays, the graveyard is neatly kept; gardens spread around the monastery in a wide, bright shawl. There are wrought iron tables and chairs on the patio. Water flowing from the hillside to the fountain is no longer managed by a tap and removed in bucketsful by nurses. It plays as it did when the monks walked and sat in quiet contemplation, its overflow spilling into a trough and chuckling through the tiled gutter that traverses the patio. When Isabel walked there earlier, she noticed the brightness of the place and was glad it had forgotten its sadness.

The stout wooden door to the refectory leads now into an elegant dining room. Chandeliers hang above damask-clothed tables set with sparkling silverware. At the far end, set into the stone wall, a large window looks out over the valley. The room, busy earlier, is empty now except for two women lingering over coffee. Neither speaks the other's language but there is no barrier between them. There are many things that need no saying. For those that do, Juan has proved an excellent interpreter. He has taken Sarah to the jutting parapet outside the parador to admire the view. In the distance, far below, the river wends its way towards the sea.

'Did you know what this place meant to my mother when you suggested coming here?' he asks.

'Mum told me what it meant to my father. Perhaps that's the same thing in a kind of off beat way. She and Dad had planned to come here on their trip. Something about Dad burying his ghosts. She's quite fallen in love with Spain, you know. Keeps on about it being our antipodes and the attraction of opposites and all that.'

Juan laughs. 'I think I understand what she means.' He

reaches to touch the twisting pounamu at her throat.

'Preciosa,' he says.

'Wear it when you give your heart away,' her mother had said when she gave Sarah the greenstone pendant on her birthday. 'That way you'll both be safe.' Which was about as cryptic as Juan's compliment, Sarah thinks, if that's what it had been. She thinks of Simon. She had promised to send him a postcard and has forgotten all about it. She smiles, remembering her schoolgirl crush. Fenton, she thinks, might as well be on another planet.

'Why are you going to California?' she asks.

'To continue my studies. I am to be a doctor.'

'I've been thinking I might train in medicine,' she says. 'And I'd like to travel some more.' She touches the pounamu for luck. 'Maybe to America. I'll write to you, shall I?'

'I should like that,' he says. 'Very much.'

Her hair is as wild as Lizzie's, Isabel thinks as Sarah comes through the door with Juan. But the colour is Tom's. She puts down her coffee cup and reaches for Lizzie's hand.

Hannah Bain is the pen name of Maggie Maxwell, actor, teacher and director. She is also the author of *Fragments from a Figment*, published in 2006.

Isabel was a finalist in the Richard Webster Award unpublished novel competition, 2004.

Praise for *Fragments from a Figment*:

Delicious. I was engaged from the start. Engaged and intrigued and increasingly delighted. The concept is original, imaginative and flamboyantly contemporary; Miranda's arch narrative voice is entertaining and sustained; the writing is clever, stylish, layered, and – best of all – genuinely funny.

Sue McCauley

www.ingramcontent.com/pod-product-compliance
Lightning Source LLC
Chambersburg PA
CBHW021501240626
47154CB00002B/464